D0891754

The Labor Day Challenge

Center Point
Large Print

Also by Susan Page Davis and available from Center Point Large Print:

The Maine Justice Series
The Priority Unit
Fort Point
Found Art
Heartbreaker Hero: Eddie's Story
The House Next Door

This Large Print Book carries the Seal of Approval of N.A.V.H.

The Labor Day Challenge

Maine Justice Series
Book 6

Susan Page Davis

CENTER POINT LARGE PRINT
THORNDIKE, MAINE

This Center Point Large Print edition
is published in the year 2019 by arrangement with
the author.

The text of this Large Print edition is unabridged.
In other aspects, this book may vary
from the original edition.
Printed in the United States of America
on permanent paper.
Set in 16-point Times New Roman type.

ISBN: 978-1-64358-091-3

Library of Congress Cataloging-in-Publication Data

Names: Davis, Susan Page, author.
Title: The Labor Day challenge / by Susan Page Davis.
Description: Center Point Large Print edition. | Thorndike, Maine :
    Center Point Large Print, 2019. | Series: Maine Justice Series ; book 6
Identifiers: LCCN 2018052575 | ISBN 9781643580913
    (hardcover : alk. paper)
Subjects: LCSH: Murder—Investigation—Fiction. | Maine—Fiction. |
    Large type books.
Classification: LCC PS3604.A976 L325 2019 | DDC 813/.6—dc23
LC record available at https://lccn.loc.gov/2018052575

The Labor Day Challenge

Chapter 1

Captain Harvey Larson sat down across from Police Chief Mike Browning in the chief's office. "I'm sending Winfield and Cook to the Academy next month for some detailed homicide training. They're ready."

"Good." Mike poured himself a second cup of coffee. "Things are settling down in your unit."

"Yes, I've got the men I want, finally, and things have been quiet for a couple of weeks. We had that drug case we've been working on with New Hampshire and S.P., but our part's done. Eddie's heading up the investigation on the Stockford murder, and Nate's chasing a cyber perp."

"You've been loaning him out a lot for public speaking."

Harvey nodded. "He did three high school graduations and seven assemblies this spring. Now he's getting calls from civic groups."

"Great. It's good P.R. for us."

"Nate's steady, and he's doing a lot of good with the talks about cyber safety. I let him take Jackie along on the last one."

"Really?" Mike's eyebrows arched in surprise.

"Relax. She took her car and met him in Camden. They spent the weekend up there, got away from the kids."

Mike's phone burbled quietly, and he lifted the receiver. "Browning. Sure." He replaced the phone, rising to his feet. "The mayor's here. Look sharp."

Harvey stood and faced the door with him as Mike's secretary, Judith, a relic from the administrations of the last four police chiefs, opened it and ushered Jill Weymouth into the fourth-floor office.

"Mrs. Weymouth!" Mike stepped forward extending his hand, with genuine pleasure in his voice.

"Chief Browning, good to see you." The mayor turned toward Harvey. "Captain Larson! How's that baby?"

Harvey smiled and shook her hand. "He's terrific, thank you."

"I'd love to see him again. I'll bet he's all grown up."

"Only three months, ma'am, but he is growing fast."

Mrs. Weymouth turned back to Mike as he pulled a comfortably upholstered chair over near the desk for her.

"I'd have called about this, but I had an idea you'd need face-to-face persuasion."

"Oh-oh," Mike said, smiling. He and the mayor sat down.

Harvey felt a prickle of apprehension on the back of his neck. Jill Weymouth was hard to say no to. She was in her second term as mayor of Portland, and she got things done. He liked her. She was good for the city. But her schemes often involved a lot of time and sweat from the other city employees.

"Should I, uh—" He glanced toward the door.

"No, no, Captain. Sit down. I'd like you to hear this, since it involves you."

Harvey sat down, keeping the half-smile on his lips with effort and hoping Jill's latest plan for the good of Maine's largest city wouldn't interfere with his jealously-guarded personal time. As long as he had his evenings and weekends at home with Jennifer and little Connor, he would jump through hoops for her.

Jill smoothed back her short, dark hair and looked first Mike, then Harvey, evenly in the eyes.

"Now, I know this may sound a little frivolous at first, but hear me out. The city of Bangor has issued a challenge to the city of Portland. They want us to compete against them in various areas of public service."

Mike looked blankly at her. "Keep score on who solves the most murders?"

"No, no, it would be a week-long festival Labor

9

Day week. First we'd send teams to Bangor to compete in a firemen's muster and some sort of Parks and Recreation competition. Building a playground and running games for kids, that sort of thing. Good publicity, and the city gets a job done. See which team can finish their part of the new playground first. The kids would score the Parks and Rec people on their games, too. Then they'd send teams down here to compete with the Police Department and Public Works. We're replacing the water lines downtown, you know. We'd save the last section for the two teams to work on and see whose men could complete their section first. Sort of like the golden spike on the Transcontinental Railroad, you know?"

Mike looked over at Harvey. "What are you thinking, Harv? You don't look too happy."

Harvey shrugged. "Don't you think traffic downtown is snarled up enough with the streets torn up all summer, without making a circus of it?"

"Oh, we'll have it all done and working by then, just save a little section for the ceremonial finish of the project."

"Hm," was all Mike said. He leaned one elbow on his desk, chin in hand, frowning.

"You don't think it would work?" Jill asked.

"Maybe, if you don't delay letting people have their water. What would our guys at the P.D. do?"

Jill smiled. She was an attractive woman, and that smile had gone a long way for her.

"That would be the crowning touch. Portland's finest versus Bangor's . . . whatever. We'd set up some sort of crime-busting simulation for the two police department teams."

A bad feeling started in Harvey's stomach. Who was going to come up with this brilliant simulation?

"No." Mike cushioned it with a smile.

"No? Just like that?" Jill's eyes widened. "Why not?"

"I can't take my guys off duty to solve fake crimes for P.R."

"You don't think they'd volunteer their personal time for this? It's a challenge, Mike. The city's honor is at stake."

She was smiling and calling the police chief by his first name, Harvey noted. Yes, Mayor Weymouth wanted this badly.

"Bad idea," Mike said. "It sounds like a lot of hoopla to me, a lot of money and man-hours invested, and it could fall flat."

"It could also unite people behind the city administration and make us look pretty good."

"Happy Days Are Here Again, and all that?" Mike shook his head.

"Oh, come on. This isn't an election year for me."

"But you'd make it an annual event, right?"

"Maybe, if it went well. Bangor is certainly looking at it that way. Maybe next year they'll challenge another town, though. And if we pout and say we don't want to play, they'll invite somebody else this year. You don't want to read in the paper about how Lewiston showed them up and won the police department trophy, do you?"

"What kind of things would the P.D. have to do?"

Mike was wavering, and Harvey's nerves kicked up.

"I really ought to get back downstairs." He pushed toward the edge of his chair.

"No, stay, Captain." Jill was commanding, rather than coaxing now. She must think she had Mike on her side. "The mayor of Bangor had a few suggestions. A bipartisan team could set up a quasi crime scene, and our competitors could be timed on finding the clues. They're thinking about planting fingerprints of Maine celebrities, for instance, and seeing how long it takes each team to find and identify them all. And they could set up a crime scene similar to the ones you fellows make for the Citizens' Police Academy."

"Hm," said Mike.

Harvey wriggled a little in his chair, wishing he were elsewhere. He enjoyed playing games and using his wits, but not on city time. The only thing that seemed a bigger waste was talking about it on city time.

12

Jill leaned toward him confidentially. "I'm thinking the Priority Unit would be our city's team."

Harvey blinked. "Not a representative committee, composed of one patrolman, one dispatcher, one detective, and one administrator? Including one female and one minority, of course."

She smiled. "You're a cynic."

"I could think of better ways to employ our best detectives."

"I promise, you won't have to do anything for the preparation," she said. "Just have your men ready to go into action Labor Day week."

Harvey grimaced. The guys would love this, giving up their Monday holiday. On the other hand, maybe he ought to get involved. At least he could put the kibosh on anything too outrageous. He glanced at Mike.

"It might work," Mike said. "It's good to have the constituents cheering for the city employees now and then."

So Jill had won.

"Make it the holiday weekend, not all week," Harvey said. "Send our people to Bangor on Saturday and have them come here on Monday. I'm not pulling my squad on a weekday." He stood up.

Mike eyed him with surprise. "All right, Harv. Don't get all hot under the collar. Jill and I will suggest that to Bangor."

The mayor nodded. "Yes, your point is well taken, Captain. If things go well and they want to extend the festivities next year, they can."

Harvey took the stairs down one level to his office. He still didn't like it, but Mike had committed himself, and there was nothing he could do about it.

Jennifer hurried to the breezeway door when Harvey drove into the garage. He walked over and pulled her into his arms.

"I am so glad to be home." He lowered his head to kiss her.

"Lousy day?" Jennifer murmured near his ear.

"You have no idea." He kissed her and held her close.

"Tell me about it," she said.

"No, you'll feel better if I don't."

She smiled. "Tough case, or stubborn people?"

"Both. Eddie's stuck with not enough evidence in a very messy homicide, and I've been helping him all afternoon. And Mayor Weymouth has a kooky idea that's going to tie up our whole unit Labor Day weekend. Mike actually went for it." He sighed.

"Do you want a shower before we leave?" Jennifer asked.

She could tell immediately that he had forgotten and was looking forward to a quiet evening at home.

"What day is it?" he asked. "It's not our anniversary yet, is it?"

"No, sweetheart. Four more days. Abby and Peter invited us to supper tonight."

"Oh, that's right. Sorry." He sighed. "I guess I'll get a shower and change. How long do I have?"

"Not long, but take what you need. I'll get Connor ready."

"Where is the little guy?" Harvey pulled off his necktie as they walked through the kitchen and sunroom. In the master bedroom, he paused beside the playpen and stooped to heft his son. "Hey, fella! Daddy's home."

Connor gurgled and laughed, clutching at Harvey's hair. Jennifer put her arms around her husband again and laid her head against his arm. Harvey looked down at her, his blue eyes contented, though the crow's feet at the corners were deep.

"I'm sorry we have to go out," she whispered. "You're tired."

"It's okay. I love your sisters. I was just thinking, *Jenny, Connor, and a comfortable bed.*"

The sound of a vehicle turning into their driveway came muffled to her. "Speaking of sisters, here's Leeanne." She reached for the baby.

"Is she going with us?"

"No, I think she's seeing Eddie tonight. Go take your shower."

Harvey walked to his dresser and unloaded his pockets. Jennifer carried Connor out to the kitchen as Leeanne came in.

"Hi! How was work?" Leeanne was living with the Larsons while she completed a summer internship that summer at the *Portland Press Herald*.

"Great. Really exciting today." Leeanne's eyes lit with pleasure. "They've offered to send me to a week of special training in investigative reporting. The speakers are all big-name award winners. And it's in Hawaii, Jenn!"

Jennifer stared at her. "Wow. When?"

Leeanne frowned. "That's the bad part. It's August seventh to thirteenth."

Jennifer's jaw dropped. "But, honey, you can't. The wedding is the twelfth."

"I know," Leeanne said unhappily, "but this is a really big deal. If I turn it down, I'll never have another chance like this."

"Oh, sweetie." Jennifer shook her head. "You promised Eddie, and he's waited so long. Do you really feel you can ask him to change the date now? It's less than a month away. You've got the invitations already."

Leeanne's face contorted. "He's not going to like it, you're right about that."

"You said you won't get another chance like this, but will you get another chance to make Eddie as happy as he is this minute?"

"I don't want to upset him," Leeanne conceded.

"But, Jenn, I think they're grooming me for something big. I don't want to lose out on this."

Jennifer saw that her sister was close to tears. "Come in the other room. I need to change Connor. Are you going out with Eddie tonight?"

"That's the plan. You guys are going to Abby's, aren't you?"

"Yes. I'm sorry. I wish we'd be here to talk this over with you and Eddie."

"I thought maybe we'd go next door."

"Good idea," said Jennifer. "Why don't you call Beth? Jeff is at the fire station tonight, and she'd probably be glad to have you there, even if you need some private time to talk."

"Now for the real reason we asked you over here tonight," Peter Hobart said, pushing his dessert plate away and folding his napkin.

"I thought you just wanted our company," his brother-in-law replied. Harvey was holding Connor and letting the baby pull his hair while he carefully sipped his coffee.

"Actually, there's a bit of news in the family, and I wanted your advice," Peter said.

Abby refilled the coffee cups around the table.

"Dad, can we go outside now?" asked ten-year-old Gary.

"May we," Peter corrected. "Sure."

Gary and his younger brother Andy bolted toward the back door.

"Dishes!" Abby called after them. The boys veered back to the table, seized their plates, forks, and milk glasses, and rushed toward the kitchen with them.

"Slow down, or you'll be sweeping up the pieces," Peter admonished.

When the back door had slammed, a deep quiet descended on the house. Peter looked at Harvey and Jennifer. "See what you have to look forward to when Connor's older? Once you have a boy, things are never calm again."

Harvey smiled and bounced the baby against his shoulder. "This guy makes his share of noise. I love it."

Abby sat down beside her sister.

"Do you miss work?" Jennifer asked her.

"Are you kidding? These three guys keep me busy."

It was only a month since Abby had married the widower, leaving her job as a nurse, and she was still settling into her role as mother and wife.

"So, what's the big news?" Harvey asked.

"Well, it involves a piece of property." Peter stood and walked to the china closet, opened one door, and came back to the table with an envelope in his hand.

"You knew Peter's uncle died a couple of weeks ago?" Abby asked.

"Yes. I'm so sorry, Peter," Jennifer said.

"I'll miss him, for sure," Peter told them.

Harvey nodded.

"Uncle Austin was actually my great-uncle, my grandfather's brother." Peter opened the envelope and took out three color photographs. "He was a great guy. He was eighty-six, but he stayed alone and took care of himself right up until the last of it."

"Was he sick at the end?" Harvey asked.

"Nope. Went down cellar to stack some wood, and his heart gave out. I went over to check on him. I'd tried to call him, and he didn't answer the phone. The doctor said he'd been dead a few hours. I was sorry he was alone when it happened, but that's the way he wanted it."

"He was a very private person," Abby said.

"I tried to get him to come live with me and the boys a couple of years ago, but he wouldn't," Peter said. "My mother tried to persuade him, too, but he was just too independent."

"So independent he never got married," Abby added.

"Yes, that's right. He doesn't have any children. Janelle and I and Uncle Jack and my cousins are it." Peter held the pictures out to Harvey. "Uncle Austin left me this property."

"What is it?" Harvey asked. The photographs showed a weathered three-story building that had seen more years than either he or Peter had, but had never seen a can of paint.

"It's an old lumber camp, up on Churchill Lake.

19

Uncle Austin bought it way back when and used it as a base for his fishing trips. He did a little renovating fifteen years or so ago, but he never tried to do the whole building. Abigail and I want to go up and look it over and see what condition it's in."

Harvey eyed him narrowly. "Frontage on a pristine lake like that. How many acres?"

"Fifty, plus or minus."

"Sounds like quite an inheritance to me." Harvey scrutinized the second photo. Waterfront, sagging dock with a canoe tied up, and a small aluminum boat with a forty horse-power Johnson outboard.

"I'll probably sell it," Peter said with a shrug. "I was up there a few times as a kid. The last time was about five years ago. It's getting pretty run down, but there is electricity and running water on the first floor of the old boardinghouse."

Harvey nodded and flipped to the third picture.

"That was the cook house," Peter told him.

"Isn't this all on paper company land?" Harvey handed the stack of pictures to Jennifer.

"Well, no, there's a little settlement at Churchill Dam, and a few families live there permanently. My uncle bought the old boardinghouse and cook shack before the big paper company deals went through, but he never tried to keep it all updated. He fixed the roof once, to keep it watertight. He always went up there to fish in the summer and hunt in the fall, and he took me a few times. It's a big building." Peter frowned at the photo of the bunkhouse.

"You think it might be worth fixing up?"

"I don't know," Peter said. "If it's not, I guess I should have it torn down for safety."

"You know," Jennifer said cautiously, "Mike Browning's been looking for something like this."

"Really?" Peter asked.

Harvey nodded. "He's been wanting to retire in the north woods and open a hunting camp."

"You mean, a guest camp?" Peter asked.

"He's been talking about it for a long time," Harvey said. "He and Sharon are crazy about the idea, but they haven't found the right property yet. Mike was planning to retire this year, but when they made him chief last summer, he told the mayor he'd stay on two years."

"So he's planning to retire next year?"

Harvey shrugged. "That's his plan, but whether or not he'll actually be able to take off his badge, I don't know."

Peter paused in thought. "Abby and I were wondering if you and Jennifer could go up there with us for a few days next week and look it over. We were thinking of going up Monday, if that's not too soon."

Harvey looked to Jennifer, and she shrugged. "We probably could."

Peter nodded. "If I decided to sell it, do you think Mike would want to take a look?"

"I wouldn't be surprised." Harvey took the photos back and studied them.

"Why don't you take those to work with you tomorrow and let Mike see them?" Abby suggested. "If he's eager to see it, have him call Peter. Maybe he and Sharon could join our expedition."

"Are you sure?" Harvey asked. "Or do you want to look it over first?"

Peter sipped his coffee. "I'd just as soon have them go if they're interested. It would save me another trip later to show them the property. I know I don't have the time or the capital to deal with it now. Abigail and I have discussed it for several days and prayed about it, and it's not really what we want to do."

"It would be a huge project," Harvey agreed.

"Yes, you'd really have to live up there to make a success of it commercially," Jennifer said.

Peter nodded. "And if we didn't use it commercially, it would just drain our finances for taxes and maintenance. We've agreed that, unless we go up there and find some compelling reason to keep the place, it's going on the market."

Eddie's truck was parked in Jeff and Beth's driveway when Harvey pulled in at his own house. As soon as they were inside, a knock came at the patio door in the sunroom.

"That's got to be Eddie." Eddie never rang the doorbell. He always knocked. Harvey handed the fussing baby to Jennifer.

"Oh, it's probably about that Hawaii thing," Jennifer whispered.

"Oh, boy." Harvey went to the sunroom, flipping on lights, disarmed the burglar alarm, and opened the patio door. "Hey, Eddie. Where's Leeanne?"

"Over at Beth's. Harv, I've gotta talk to you."

"Okay, come on in."

Jennifer stood in the kitchen doorway. "I guess I'll run over and see Beth for a few minutes."

"Leave Connor here if you want," Harvey offered.

"No, he's hungry. I'll take him." Her face was anxious, and Harvey went over and kissed her.

"Don't fret, gorgeous. Go out the back door, and I'll watch until you're in over there."

It was only a few steps from their backyard into Jeff and Beth's, under the arch where Penny, the once-a-week gardener, was training rose bushes to cover the framework, but after dark Jennifer was forbidden to walk the short distance alone. Even in their idyllic neighborhood, the Larsons and the Wainthrops had dealt with frightening experiences, and Harvey took no chances with his precious family anymore.

"You want coffee?" Harvey asked Eddie, as he saw her open Beth's kitchen door and enter the little stone cottage.

"No, I want to hit something."

Harvey sighed. "Come sit down and spill it."

Eddie followed him into the living room but refused to sit. He paced back and forth angrily, while Harvey sank into his favorite armchair.

"Come on, Ed. Talk to me."

"You knew, didn't you? You always know."

"The Hawaii thing?"

"Aha!" Eddie turned on him accusingly.

Harvey held up one hand in protest. "I didn't know. Jenny told me tonight on the way to Abby's house. It was the first I heard about it, I swear." It hurt him to see his best friend so agitated. He'd been through a lot with Eddie, and they had pulled each other out of depression and rescued each other from danger more than once, but Harvey wasn't sure he could help this time.

Eddie took another turn around the living room, circling the sofa and the rocking chair. "So, they want to send her for special training as an investigative reporter. I think that means she's looking at a long-term commitment. What do you think?"

"I think she's a very talented writer, or they wouldn't offer to send her for special training," Harvey said cautiously. "I get the impression this is something that only the best reporters get, and Leeanne is only an intern. It's unusual, I'd say."

"It's unheard of," Eddie snapped. "That's what she told me. Unheard of, for John Russell to skip over his three top reporters and pick an intern—

she's not even technically an employee, Harv! They're bribing her. Russell is bribing her to stay and work for them full time when she finishes her degree."

"Eddie, Eddie, calm down."

Eddie paced determinedly, but after two circuits stopped and faced his friend. "Harvey, what am I going to do?"

"Did she ask you to postpone the wedding?"

Eddie snorted. "Oh, yeah. The wedding is off."

"Off?" Harvey shifted uneasily. "Off, as in totally canceled?"

"What do you think? *Postponed indefinitely.* What does that mean to you?"

Harvey exhaled slowly. "Well, it could mean a lot of things. And tomorrow it could mean something totally different from what it means tonight."

"Oh, yeah, yeah," Eddie said impatiently. "Tell me she's too young. I really need to hear that. She's too young to make a lifetime commitment. Brother, I really didn't expect you to throw that one at me, Harv. That's her father's line, remember?"

"Come on, Eddie, just settle down. I know you're upset, but there's got to be a solution to this. Did you ask her to set a new date?"

"I want the old date. The one you went to bat for with her father."

"What did she say, exactly?"

"She wants to go to the seminar."

"Any chance you could go, too?"

"What, and spend our honeymoon with her going to class all day? Ha! Anyway, she has to stay in a hotel room with another woman. That's the way they have it set up."

"So, I'll pay for the extra room, and she can just tell them she'll be staying with her husband," Harvey offered.

"But she's got to leave before the wedding, Harv."

"So move the wedding up a week, to the fifth."

"Oh, yeah, like she'll go for that."

"A week isn't a huge thing, Eddie."

"To Leeanne it is. I asked, okay? She wouldn't consider getting married before the seminar. And, anyway, I really don't want to have to spend all day alone on Waikiki Beach during our honey-moon."

"How much do you hate the idea?"

"I will not go to Hawaii."

"Do you mean that?"

"Yes. She said she wouldn't move the wedding up, anyway, so what point is there in discussing it?"

Harvey took a deep breath. "Okay, time to regroup. How about moving the wedding back a week? You get married the nineteenth."

Eddie shook his head. "Any sane person would think that was reasonable, wouldn't he?"

"Well, sure."

"Not your sister-in-law! She is no longer rational, Harv. I'm telling you, I've had it. I've really had it."

"She wouldn't agree to the nineteenth?"

"Not the nineteenth, not the twenty-sixth, not any of the thirty-one days of August. She is now contemplating a spring wedding, with no date designated."

Harvey sat back and let that sink in. "Well, I think you're right about one thing, Russell wants her to stay with the paper. He wants her badly."

"He can smell Pulitzer material." Eddie's lip curled. "Oh, Harv, why couldn't she be the domestic type, like Jenny? If she'd give up this reporting thing and learn to crochet or something, I'd be so happy!"

Harvey winced. "You didn't say that to her, did you, buddy?"

Eddie stared up at the ceiling. "I might have."

"Bad move."

"I know. It just sort of slipped out."

"And her reaction was . . . ?"

"Best if I don't tell you."

"Okay." Harvey rested his chin on his hand. "Well, I'd say you'd better let things cool off for a few days, or at least overnight."

"If we don't settle this, she'll be calling all over town canceling the wedding arrangements tomorrow."

27

"Maybe that's best," Harvey said.

"Best? *Best?* Don't turn on me, Harv. You know I love her. I'd do anything—"

"Anything? Except wait?"

Eddie brought his fist down hard on the back of the couch. "*Wait* doesn't mean *wait* in the Wainthrop Woman Language. You ought to know that."

Harvey raised his eyebrows. "It doesn't? What does it mean, then?"

"It means *never,* that's what it means."

"I resent that," Harvey said mildly. "You're casting aspersions on my wife. Jenny tells me all the time to wait for things, and she always follows through. Good things are worth waiting for, Eddie."

"Sure, you can talk. You got married six weeks to the day after you got engaged. I've heard the story many times."

"Even so, she did postpone things. I wanted to get married the next weekend, and she wouldn't. She made me wait six whole weeks." Harvey realized that sounded a bit cruel, when Eddie was talking about several months, perhaps a year of waiting.

"I'm going home. I'll see you in the morning."

Harvey jumped up. "Wait a second, Ed!"

Eddie stood stock still. "Don't use that word, Harvey. If you say *wait* one more time, I'll—"

"Sorry. Don't you think you ought to talk to her

again? I'll go get her and Jenny, and the four of us can sit down and discuss it. You wait here—"

Eddie threw him a bitter look and turned on his heel.

"Oops," said Harvey. He hurried after Eddie and reset the burglar alarm as his friend crossed the strip of lawn to Jeff's driveway and climbed into his black pickup. Harvey sighed and walked slowly over to the little stone house to see if Jennifer and Leeanne were ready to come home.

Chapter 2

"Take a look at this, Mike." Harvey tossed the three photographs on the chief's desk. "I'm thinking this may be your retirement spot."

Mike picked up the pictures and studied them critically, chewing his wad of gum.

"Where is it?"

"It's an old lumber camp, up on Churchill Lake. You and Sharon could fix it up and run a hunting lodge up there in the fall."

"Lake frontage?"

"Six hundred feet. And it comes with fifty acres of trees."

Mike frowned thoughtfully. "It's for sale?"

"Yup. And you get an all-expenses-paid trip to go look it over, starting Monday. Jenny and I are going, too."

Mike looked up in surprise. "What's the deal? Are you investing?"

"That's not a bad idea," Harvey said. "Actually, we're just tagging along as guests of the current owner."

"Who is . . . ?"

"My brother-in-law."

"Jeff Wainthrop?"

"No, Peter Hobart."

Mike nodded, scrutinizing the picture of the boardinghouse. "Is this building structurally sound?"

"We're not sure. Peter just inherited it from his great-uncle. He hasn't been up there in five years."

"Hmm."

"You think you and Sharon could run a place like that?" Harvey asked.

"Don't see why not. Sharon's cousin Ranetta and her husband have a bed and breakfast in Alna. They've told us what we'd need for permits and all. I figure we'd start out just being open during the hunting season. We'd be right out straight for a couple of months, then hibernate for the winter."

"Just run it a couple of months out of the year?"

Mike ran his hand through his hair. "Well, if we found a place this summer, I'm thinking we'd try it next fall. Not this year. There'd be too much to get done. But next year I'd take my vacation all in a lump in the summer to work on it, then retire the first of September. We could advertise in all the shooting magazines and open up for the bear season August thirtieth, then the moose and deer seasons, and archery and muzzle loading, too. Muzzle loading season ends December eleventh next year."

"You've been doing your research. Sounds like an awful lot of work, though."

Mike looked at the picture again. "How many rooms do you figure the main building would make?"

"Peter thought maybe twenty guest rooms, and a dining room and lounge, if you did the whole thing. That's if you have a bathroom for every two guest rooms. If you want a private bath for every room, then twenty units. That's not counting your own suite on the ground floor."

Mike popped his gum. "If we decided to do it, we could renovate the first and second stories next year, and leave the third floor for later, if things were going well."

Harvey considered that. "You could do it, I guess. You'd have to hire a contractor and run up there every weekend this fall and next spring."

"Yes, but Sharon is really eager to find a place and get started. We didn't want to have to start from scratch. These buildings may be just what we need. It would make a nice retreat for us."

"For you and forty guests," Harvey said.

Mike shrugged. "Well, sure, that's how we'd be able to afford to live there."

"I suppose if the building's not sound, you could tear it down and build cottages. Start with a few, then add on as you can afford it. Would you guide people?"

"Thinking about it," Mike said. "I'd like to get Arnie, though."

"Arnie Fowler?"

"Yeah, he's getting his guide's license."

A widower, Arnie had retired from the police department's Priority Unit the year before and was sometimes at loose ends. He and Mike were old fishing and hunting buddies, and Harvey knew Arnie had a lot of experience in the north Maine woods.

"Arnie'd be good," he said. "So, will you come up with us?"

"I'll ask Sharon."

"We're planning to go up Monday and stay two nights. I know it's short notice to rearrange your schedule and everything—"

"I don't think that would be a problem," Mike said.

Harvey smiled. Mike's main vacation problem was always making himself take it. He hadn't taken any vacation since he'd been made chief the year before. Sharon would probably be thrilled.

Harvey had four weeks coming, but hated to leave his unit unsupervised. Two of the four men had been on board less than a year. "I guess Eddie can handle things for me for three days."

"Well, Jack could cover for me," Mike said. Jack Stewart was the deputy police chief, and Harvey suspected he was targeted to take over as chief when Mike retired.

"Great. I'll talk to Jennifer and see if Eddie thinks he can hold the fort without me." Eddie was his best detective, but with the strain of his relationship with Leeanne, Harvey wasn't sure it was the best time to go off and leave him in charge of the unit. That and the stress of the current case Eddie was trying to close. One way to find out.

Jennifer had her hands full that day. Instead of coming to their house to meet Harvey to run their usual Friday route, Eddie had called at six a.m. and asked him to jog down the street and meet him at the bungalow he had purchased for himself and Leeanne farther down the block. Jennifer was sure he was trying to avoid Leeanne. Sure enough, Leeanne had announced the postponement of her wedding at breakfast, then gone poutily off to work when Jennifer suggested that she was making a hasty decision. Connor fussed all morning, and Jennifer was afraid he was sick.

At two o'clock, her mother arrived unannounced. Jennifer felt a great weight lift from her shoulders, but then she realized what had probably precipitated the visit.

"Mom! Hi. It's great to see you." She kissed her mother's cheek cautiously.

"How could she do this?" Marilyn asked without prelude. "She begged us to let her marry that boy, and now she's thrown him over four weeks before the wedding."

"She hasn't broken up with him, Mom." Jennifer strove for a soothing tone.

"Ha! Your father hit the ceiling. How could you and Harvey let her do this?"

Jennifer sighed. "It's this newspaper thing, Mom. It's a great chance for her to advance her career. The wedding can be changed. The seminar can't."

"You're standing up for her!" Marilyn's incredulity made Jennifer realize she hadn't fully made up her mind yet about Leeanne's actions.

"Just calm down, Mom. She and Eddie are both confused right now. They need some time to talk things out and decide what they want to do about the wedding."

Connor's wails came from the bedroom. Immediately, Marilyn reverted to baby talk. "Oh, my widdle grandson is crying!" She rushed toward the master bedroom, and Jennifer let her go. Her mother emerged a few seconds later, holding the whimpering baby against her shoulder. "There, there, Connor. Wha'sa matter, sweetheart?"

"He's been kind of fussy today," Jennifer offered.

"Is he cutting teeth?"

"I don't think so. It's kind of early."

"He must be hungry."

"No, Mom, I stuffed him."

"Well, something's bothering my widdle pot-pie." Marilyn felt the baby's diaper. "Nice and dry."

"I think he doesn't feel good." Jennifer sank onto the stool in the corner of the kitchen.

"You look tired." Marilyn looked hard at her daughter for the first time. "They say the cure for a fussy baby is more rest for the mother. Why don't you go take a nap, and Grammy will take care of Connor."

"Oh, I don't know, Mom, I've got laundry going, and I need to plan supper. I don't know how many people I'll be feeding. You're staying, aren't you?"

"Well, I brought an overnight bag," Marilyn admitted, "but don't worry about cooking, dear. I'll help you with supper."

"We're going away Monday, and I need to pack for that. I'm working on a computer program, too, and I should finish it this weekend."

"Where are you going?"

"Upcountry with Abby and Peter."

"Are you taking the baby? I could keep him for you."

"No, Mom, I'm nursing him. He has to go."

"Of course." Marilyn looked disappointed. "Well, I still think you should go have a nap, dear. I can pull Harvey's shirts out of the dryer before they wrinkle."

Jennifer smiled. "I'm all right. Just don't blow

up at Leeanne the minute she gets home from work, okay? Be patient. I'm hoping she'll give up the trip to Hawaii when she realizes how hurt Eddie is."

"But she called me this morning to tell me to cancel everything," Marilyn said. "She didn't want to waste any more of your father's money than was unavoidable, she said. I was stunned. And your father was livid. You'd think he hand-picked Eddie for her and arranged the marriage."

Jennifer smiled. "We all love Eddie."

"We couldn't wait to have him in the family."

Her parents were forgetting their initial objections, Jennifer realized, but she held her peace.

"The invitations will be wasted," Marilyn went on. "A hundred and fifty dollars there. I suppose the girls will wear their dresses when and if this wedding ever does come off. Leeanne said she would cancel the church, the tuxedoes, and the food."

"She said all that?"

"Yes, she called me as soon as she got to her office."

"She did leave a few minutes early this morning." Jennifer's heart ached. "Poor Daddy. I think he really likes Eddie now."

"Of course he does! We've been thinking of him as our son."

Jennifer sighed.

"Have you seen him?" Marilyn asked.

"Not today. He wouldn't come for breakfast today. But last night he was pretty upset."

When the day of the trip arrived, Harvey was uneasy about leaving Portland. He rose early and ran with Eddie, as usual, then insisted that Eddie have breakfast with him so they could go over last-minute details. At least Eddie and Tony had come up with the evidence they needed in the homicide case and handed it to the district attorney's office.

"Harv, if I have to sit across the table from Leeanne, I won't be any good at work all day," Eddie protested.

"She probably won't show her face until you're gone." Harvey poured coffee for himself and Eddie. "You two are driving me nuts. You wouldn't go to the singles class with her in Sunday school yesterday."

"Correction, she wouldn't go with me. She didn't wait, and when I got there she was already in the class."

"So you stayed out with us. But then you left right after church, so she didn't have a chance to talk to you."

"I was upset, okay? And last night I got to church, and she was parked between Jeff and Beth, so I could tell I wasn't wanted. What am I supposed to do?"

"Hi, Eddie," Jennifer said cheerfully. She

entered the kitchen in jeans and a blue plaid shirt, carrying Connor. "Scrambled eggs this morning?"

"Uh, I guess so. Want me to hold the little guy?"

"Sure." She passed Eddie the baby and the burp cloth and went to the refrigerator.

"Where's Leeanne?" asked Harvey.

"She left early." Jennifer placed a carton of eggs and the milk jug on the counter.

"This early? It's barely seven o'clock."

"She was going to get breakfast on the way."

Eddie watched them with his huge Labrador retriever eyes while he patted Connor's back. Harvey was afraid his friend would cry if he didn't find a distraction soon. Even Connor wasn't performing the job.

"I'll have my cell phone." Harvey placed Eddie's coffee mug far enough away so the baby couldn't reach it. "If anything dicey comes up, you call me."

Eddie turned Connor around on his lap, so that he faced his father. "So, Connor's going with you."

"He has to, but I wouldn't go off and leave him, anyway." Harvey smiled across at the baby. "Hey, big guy. You like Uncle Eddie, don't you?"

Connor squealed and waved his fist, arching his back.

Eddie laughed, then sobered. "Is Leeanne staying here alone while you're gone?"

"I told her to stay with Beth," Jennifer said. "Jeff's on duty both nights we'll be gone, and Beth was anxious to have her stay over there."

Eddie nodded. "Good. No sense both of them being alone."

Harvey eyed him cautiously. "Eddie, have you talked to her at all since Thursday night?"

"It's not a matter of me talking to her. She won't talk to me."

"So, the wedding's really off," Harvey said bleakly.

"Oh, yeah."

"I'm sorry, Ed."

Eddie shrugged, but his lips twitched.

"If there's anything I can do," Harvey began.

"I don't think so."

"Don't give up on her," Jennifer said softly. "I'll try to speak to her as soon as we get home if you haven't made any headway. She's not being fair to you, Eddie."

Eddie sniffed. "Thanks." He looked at Harvey. "I've called her about a gazillion times, and I texted her. All I got back was a message that said, *When I know what I should do, I'll let you know.*"

"That's it?" Harvey asked.

Eddie nodded. "She didn't write whole words, just abbreviations."

Harvey shook his head. "She ought to be spanked."

"Watch it," Jennifer said.

"Yeah, yeah."

"Wish I was going with you and Mike and Peter and Arnie," Eddie said glumly.

"I wish you were, too," Harvey admitted, "but our unit would fall apart if we were both gone. You call me if anything goes haywire."

"Right."

Arnie Fowler, Mike's old partner, joined the party for the trip north and rode with Mike and Sharon. Harvey took Jennifer and Connor in his Explorer. Connor seemed to have recovered from whatever had made him fussy a few days earlier and slept a good part of the way. Peter and Abby and their two boys took a two-year-old SUV Peter had selected from his car lot.

The drive took nearly five hours, but Jennifer felt it was worth it when she saw Churchill Lake. The placid water was surrounded by evergreen forests, and from Peter's waterfront they could see almost no other buildings, just one near where she knew there was a dam. There were a few campgrounds down that way, too, but from where she stood on the dock, the wooded hills and a family of loons swimming a few yards out were the most prominent features.

As soon as they arrived, Gary and Andy ran

41

whooping around the grassy area between the old bunkhouse and the water. Gary located the outhouse on the edge of the woods near the old cook shack.

"I thought there was running water," Sharon said tentatively.

"There's one bathroom inside," Peter assured her. "Last time I was here, it was working."

"Let's hope." Sharon looked at Jennifer and made a tight face.

"Plumbing would be the first thing on my list if we bought the place," Mike assured her.

"Can we swim, Dad, can we swim?" Gary asked, bouncing up and down.

"After we unpack." Peter calmly loaded the boys down with bedding to carry inside.

Mike and Sharon walked slowly toward the building, evaluating every aspect.

"Doesn't look in too bad shape," Mike said.

"I'll show you through inside," Peter offered. "It actually looks a little better than I anticipated."

Abby pulled a carton out of the back of their SUV. "Let's get the food and stuff in."

Peter walked over and put a large Tupperware container on top of the box. "Where do you want this?"

Abby poked him. "In the kitchen," she hissed.

"What is that?" Jennifer laughed, eyeing the plastic box.

"A surprise."

"What kind of surprise?"

Abby scowled. "If I tell you, it won't be a surprise."

Harvey grinned. "It wouldn't have anything to do with our anniversary, would it?"

Abby's incredulity made Jennifer burst out laughing.

"I thought men always forgot the anniversary," Abby wailed. "I was going to surprise you two tonight and make Harvey feel guilty that he'd forgotten."

"Sorry," Harvey said meekly as they walked inside. "Where do you want the brooms and mops?"

"He really remembered?"

Jennifer smiled. "I gave him his present this morning. A new sleeping bag."

"What did he give you?" Abby asked.

Jennifer slipped one finger inside her collar and lifted a chain out. A sapphire pendant glittered in the light from the kitchen window.

Abby gasped. "Tell me that's not real."

"What do you think?"

Harvey had set down his load of cleaning supplies. "Makes her eyes look bluer, don't you think?" He winked at Jennifer.

Sharon leaned in to look closely. "Beautiful."

"Does Mike remember your anniversary?" Abby asked.

"Every year."

"Daddy always forgets his and Mom's." Abby looked to Jennifer for corroboration.

"That's just Dad. I don't think policemen are allowed to forget things like that."

Mike laughed. "Now we have a reputation to live up to."

Sharon grinned and looked around. The large kitchen looked neglected and dusty. "Where do we start cleaning?"

"Here, I guess," Abby said. "I like to have a clean kitchen to cook in. We didn't really know what to expect, so I brought lots of rags."

Peter put down his boxes and tested the water faucet at the square steel sink. Water burped and then gushed out.

"Yay," Abby cried. "I was afraid we might have to haul water from the lake."

They all set to work, and in half an hour the bare kitchen passed Abby's inspection and her supplies for their stay were in the cupboards.

"You want to take a look upstairs, Mike?" Peter asked. "As far as I know, the floors are safe. The third story is pretty much empty. I did some sketching, and I think you could put ten guest rooms up there. Ten on the second floor, too, although you'd have to knock out a wall or two and restructure it. Four down here, plus the kitchen, dining area and lounge. You might want to use the first-floor rooms for your personal quarters."

Mike nodded. "That sounds good. We'd need a lift or something, though, for handicapped people and elderly."

"Hmm," Peter mused. "Knock out one unit on each floor, then. An elevator takes as much space as a bathroom. Still, I suppose you've got to have it."

"Show him your drawings," Abby urged.

"Later." Peter ambled toward the stairs with Mike.

"Coming, sweetheart?" Mike called over his shoulder to Sharon.

"Let's get supper started," Jennifer suggested to Abby. "These guys are going to be hungry."

"Dad! Dad!" Andy burst through the front door.

Peter paused on the stairway.

"What is it?"

"A squirrel! Where's my bow?"

"In the car."

Andy darted out the door.

Harvey chuckled. "Those boys are regular Indians."

"Why don't you and Arnie tag along with Peter?" Abby suggested.

"You trying to get rid of us?" Harvey asked.

"Yes. Take the broom, and you can start cleaning up a place for everybody to sleep."

Harvey laughed but accepted the broom.

Jennifer smiled at him. "You'll want to be in on this with Mike. Go ahead. We're going to be domestic here. Chili and cornbread for supper."

"Romantic canoe ride later?" He bent to kiss her.

"What do you think?"

It was difficult to sleep in the creaking old building. Jennifer and Harvey had pulled mattresses off two bunks and laid them on the floor, and she kept Connor between them, her arm protectively encircling him. Harvey began to breathe softly and evenly soon after the light was out, but Jennifer lay listening to the snaps and groans of the old lumber and the muffled snores of at least three people in other rooms.

Andy and Gary were up at dawn, chasing red squirrels with their bows and arrows. When Connor was fed, Harvey offered to take him out for a walk.

"You rest, gorgeous." He stooped to kiss Jennifer. She drooped gratefully back on the mattress and closed her eyes.

"Missed him!"

"Hush, Gary," Abby said sternly in the hallway, but it was too late. Jennifer rolled over and reached for her clothes.

When she reached the kitchen, she found Sharon stirring a large pot of oatmeal on the woodstove.

She yawned. "What's all the excitement this morning?"

"Gary shot at a red squirrel, but he missed it,"

Sharon said. "Are you okay? Harvey said you were exhausted."

"I'm fine."

"He took Connor down to the dock. Have you seen the drawings Peter made of this place? He should have been an architect."

"I think he would have, if his father hadn't owned a car lot. He's very intelligent."

"Does he like selling cars?"

"I'm not sure. He left college to take over the business when his father died. He's doing pretty well. It's security for them and his mother, I think."

"I hope he likes it," Sharon said. "I hate to scc someone doing something they hate. Look at Mike. His parents wanted him to farm."

"I never knew that."

"Oh, yes. His dad was furious when Mike wouldn't stay and take over. Being a cop was a step down, as far as the Brownings were concerned."

"Wow. Are they still alive?"

"His mother's living."

"He's chief of police in the biggest city in Maine now. I'd think they'd be proud of him."

"I think she *is* proud," Sharon said. "But she still talks about the farm."

"How far did you follow the tracks?" Harvey asked Arnie.

"Not too far. I showed the boys where a buck made a scrape on a tree. Then I told them they can never, ever go off in the woods alone, even if they see a porcupine riding on a deer."

Harvey chuckled and patted Connor's back. They stood together on the small beach while Gary roved over the front of the property, looking for more evidence of wildlife.

"Peter and Abby took Andy out in the canoe," Harvey said. "Gary will have the next turn."

"I guess they don't get much chance to run wild like this, living in the city," Arnie said.

"So, Mike says you're getting your Maine guide's license."

Arnie glanced over at him. "Yeah, I passed the test last week."

"Great."

"I hope Mike buys this place, but it might be a little too rustic for Sharon."

"Mike knows he'd have to put a lot of work into it before they could open for guests. He was talking last night as though he was seriously thinking about it. And Sharon sounded as if she'd like it, being so far away from Portland. How about you? Think you'd like spending months at a time up here in the woods?"

"I'd love it." Arnie huffed out a big breath.

Harvey stooped, holding Connor carefully, and picked up the flattest rock he could find. He skimmed it out over the water and watched it skip four times on the surface before it sank. "See, Connor? See it splash?"

"How come you're so calm now?" Arnie asked.

Harvey puzzled over that. "What do you mean?"

"You never get mad anymore," Arnie said. "Not even when Abby spilled that coffee on you this morning."

Harvey shrugged. A light breeze came off the lake, ruffling his hair, and he pulled the flannel blanket up over Connor's head. "It's not worth getting mad."

"At first, I thought it was marriage that calmed you down," Arnie said, "but I've been watching you, and I decided it's more than that."

"The Lord took my temper away, Arnie. Not all at once, but gradually. I noticed I wasn't swearing anymore, and then I realized one day I didn't even want to swear."

"You used to swear a blue streak at Eddie," Arnie said.

Harvey chuckled. "Well, Eddie was a trial. But I didn't know the Lord then. Now, Tony Winfield is a challenge. I tell you, Arnie, that boy's smart, but sometimes—well, sometimes, he's Eddie, The Sequel."

Arnie laughed. "Still, I recall the night Chris was shot. You remember?"

"I'll never forget it."

"I thought you were going to tear that bird's head off. What was his name? Hanson?"

49

"Hanscomb," Harvey said.

"Right." Arnie sat down on a big rock and folded his arms.

Harvey looked out over the calm surface of the lake. Peter and Abby had gone out early and were paddling toward them in the canoe, a hundred yards out from shore. Andy sat between them, his orange life jacket bright against the green beyond. Peter looked right at home, stroking confidently. He had on a canvas vest with a lot of pockets—L.L. Bean issue. Harvey figured Peter was a guy who actually had stuff in the pockets. Abby flipped some water at him with her paddle, and his laugh carried across the quiet water. Harvey was very glad, in that moment, for Abby and Peter, but his heart ached for Eddie. He was finding it more difficult every day not to take sides.

"Awful hard when your partner gets killed." Arnie tossed a pebble in the air and caught it. "When we got there, you looked like death yourself. Like you wanted to kill Hanscomb."

"I did want to."

Gary spotted his parents in the canoe and ran toward the dock. "Dad! I saw two grays!"

"Why didn't you just shoot him?" Arnie asked softly.

Harvey didn't really want to think about his partner's death. The clouds were puffy and full, the trees all around the lake were brilliant green, and the water was very blue. It was hard to think about Chris, even after all these years. "The grace of God," he said at last. "He held me back."

"You could have. They would have cleared you."

"No, Arnie, I couldn't do that. Anyway, I wanted him to go through the system. I wanted Marcia to know we'd done everything right, and we got justice."

"Justice," Arnie said. "Is there ever justice for murder?"

"Maybe not," Harvey conceded. "I was in shock that night, but I went by the book." He flicked a glance at Arnie.

The older man was watching him intently. "That's a good thing, I guess."

Harvey nodded. "I wasn't the one who took him in, you know. I . . . I stayed with Chris until the ambulance got there. Now, the next day. That's when I was really mad. Wished I'd beat that guy to a pulp."

"Still, you're in control now."

"By the grace of God."

Arnie nodded slowly. "I wondered, when they promoted you. But you've proved yourself this year. Even when your house got robbed."

"Now, I was angry that day," Harvey admitted.

"You didn't pound that guy, though."

"No. Training, Arnie. That's what keeps me from acting out what I feel in a situation like that.

But lately, the feelings have changed. I've quit taking it personally."

Arnie stood up beside him. "There were times when I was really tempted. That one guy, Buzzell, that beat the old lady to death on Brighton Avenue, remember?"

Harvey nodded.

"Mike and I chased him down. It was him and me in an alley. I could have dropped him right there."

Harvey eyed him, wondering where Arnie was going with this. "You didn't."

"Nope, I didn't. Course, Mike came along right about then. I've thought about it lots of times since. That guy was preying on the elderly, and he killed that woman. I don't think my conscience would have bothered me a bit. And then the jury let him off. It was senseless. At least Hanscomb is going to stay put for the rest of his life."

Harvey didn't know what to say.

Peter was tying up the canoe, and Abby climbed onto the dock, holding her hand out to steady Andy.

Sharon appeared at the boardinghouse doorway. "Breakfast is ready!"

Harvey walked slowly up from the shore, happy to be there with Jennifer and Connor and other people he cared about. He glanced at Arnie. "I think Mike needed this."

"Sure. A couple of days away from the office. I told Mike, once he makes the break, he'll wonder how he stayed cooped up so long." Arnie nodded in satisfaction. "He and Sharon are going to love it here."

"I need to talk to Leeanne," Jennifer said that evening. She sat beside Harvey on the dock, her bare toes skimming the water.

"What about?" Harvey asked.

"If she's not talking to Eddie yet, I'm going to give her what for."

"I don't know if that's the best approach."

Harvey, Peter, and Mike had repaired the dock that morning, fixed a loose step, and made a list of broken windows and other items to be taken care of before winter. Jennifer, Abby, and Sharon had done a little more cleaning, but spent most of the day outside, enjoying being away from the city in the July sun, canoeing and watching a family of beavers.

"You have a better idea?" She looked anxiously at Harvey.

He shook his head. "I've been praying about it. We tried reason, and your mother tried shaming her. Eddie's done everything but grovel."

"I'm glad he won't beg," Jennifer said staunchly.

"Call her at Beth's."

"My phone's inside."

Harvey shifted Connor to his other arm and

reached in his pocket. He handed her his phone, and Jennifer pushed in the code. Leeanne didn't answer, so she called Beth.

"Leeanne's not home yet," Beth said a moment later, her voice holding a touch of concern.

"She's not home from work? It's six-thirty."

"I know."

"Has she called?"

"No. I figured she went shopping or something."

Jennifer pushed the mute button. "Harvey, she hasn't come home yet."

Harvey reached for the phone.

"Beth? Hi. Listen, will you give me a call if she's not there in thirty minutes?"

"Sure," Beth agreed readily. "I was getting a little worried."

"I'll give her office a call," Harvey said. "Just get back to me immediately if she shows up."

Jennifer shivered. "You don't think something's happened to her?"

"Not really, but that girl should be more responsible. This past week she hasn't been acting like a Wainthrop, I'll say that." Harvey passed Connor to her and punched a few buttons. A minute later he lowered the receiver and gazed at Jennifer. "She left at five."

He hit star-three on the keypad.

"Eddie? It's me. Have you talked to Leeanne today?"

Jennifer listened, rubbing her bottom lip lightly against Connor's fuzzy hair.

"Are you at home?" Harvey asked. "Let's not get alarmed, but she hasn't showed up at Beth's tonight. You want to go over and check my house? Sure. Can you think of anyplace else she would be? I hate to call George."

Jennifer stiffened. She would hate to get her parents upset, too, if Leeanne had decided to stop at the mall. But perhaps her younger sister had headed up the interstate for home, on a whim.

"All right, keep me posted." Harvey closed the connection. "She's got to quit yanking his chain like this."

"You think she did this to upset Eddie?"

"No, not that. He left a message at her office today, and she never got back to him."

Jennifer sighed. "Someone needs to sit her down and talk turkey."

"Yup. About time."

"You want to go home tonight?" Jennifer asked timidly.

"Let's see what Eddie finds out." He looked at his watch. "We could be there by midnight. Still . . ."

They sat silently watching the moon rise above the treetops, very full and orange.

"It's so peaceful here," Jennifer murmured.

Harvey slipped his arm around her, and she leaned against him, cuddling the baby close.

"Mike's open to a silent partner," Harvey said.

"He needs capital?"

"He's got enough to buy it, and Peter's not being greedy. But this place will need massive renovation."

"It's up to you." Jennifer raised her face to look at him. "You're the financial wizard in this family. If you think it's a good investment, let's do it."

Harvey kissed her forehead. "Moonlight looks great on you, kiddo. It's Mike I trust, more than the property."

"You think he could go bust with it?"

Harvey shrugged. "It's pretty far from civilization. But with the right advertising and careful supervision of the renovators, I think he can make it profitable. He talked to the forester over at the dam today, and it sounds as though the hunting's great."

"Let's invest in Mike, then."

"In Mike's retirement."

"Hmm," Jennifer said.

"Yeah."

"You hate to see him leave the P.D., don't you?" she asked. Connor stretched and gave a huge yawn.

"I'll really miss him," Harvey admitted. "Mike's been there my whole career. Twenty years we've worked together. It won't be the same."

"Still, he and Arnie will be working together again," Jennifer reflected. "Now that Mike's saved, he might have a great influence on Arnie."

"That's true. I got the feeling earlier that Arnie's softening up a little. And some days, I think I'll almost be glad when Mike retires. Like when he gets talking about that Labor Day Challenge he and Mayor Weymouth are so wound up about."

Jennifer smiled. "Have fun with it. Your team will win. You know that."

"Do I?"

The phone in Harvey's hand beeped, and he quickly raised it to his ear.

"Eddie?"

"No, it's me, Leeanne. Beth said I should call, because you were worried."

"Leeanne!"

Jennifer reached for the phone. "Please," she whispered. Harvey gave it to her and took the baby tenderly.

"Leeanne, where have you been?" Jennifer tried to put her mother's outrage into her voice.

"Relax, Jennifer, I gave one of the photographers a ride home, and we decided to stop at Burger King."

"Tell me this photographer was a girl."

"She was. Is."

Jennifer was somewhat mollified. "Well, you ought to have called Beth. She was very worried, and so were we. And now Harvey's got Eddie looking for you. We didn't know what to think."

"Eddie's looking for me?"

"Of course! What did you expect? The people who love you want to know you haven't been in a wreck or something."

"You're overreacting."

"No, I'm not. You have no right to treat people this way. You've been wiping your feet on Eddie for nearly a week, and—" Jennifer stopped and stared at the cell phone. "She hung up on me. I don't believe it."

Harvey sighed. "You were pretty harsh. For you, I mean. But I think I would have given her a few choice words myself."

"Maybe I should have just told her how scared we were, and that we're so happy she's all right." Jennifer's voice quavered.

"It's okay, babe. Call Eddie, though."

Jennifer held the phone out in the dusk and pushed star-three.

"Eddie? It's Jennifer. Leeanne's home."

"Where, at Beth's?"

"Yes. She's okay."

There was a pause. "Thanks."

"Are you going to call her?" Jennifer asked.

"I don't think so. I don't want to be told that she doesn't want to talk to me again. Goodnight, Jennifer."

She sighed and leaned against Harvey's shoulder. "Why is she doing this?"

Abby and Peter came from the boardinghouse with a tray of dishes.

"Apple crisp," Abby announced. "Sharon and I made it in the woodstove."

"I'm impressed," Harvey said.

Jennifer gave him the telephone.

"Who were you talking to?" Abby asked.

"Beth, Eddie, Leeanne, and Eddie, in that order." Harvey took a bowl from the tray.

"Everything all right?" Peter asked, lowering himself to the edge of the dock beside Harvey.

"Oh, the usual." Jennifer didn't even try to keep the bitterness from her voice.

Abby set the tray down and sat cross-legged on the planks. "Don't be so rough on her, Jenn. If she's having second thoughts, isn't it better that she has them now, instead of later?"

Jennifer sighed. "I suppose you're right."

"Where are the boys?" Harvey set his bowl on the dock and juggled Connor to the other arm.

"Here, give him to me." Abby reached for her nephew.

"Arnie's got them roasting marshmallows in the fireplace," Peter said. "You want some?"

"No, thanks." Harvey laughed. "I'll stick with the apple crisp. It's great, by the way."

"Thanks."

"Almost as good as the anniversary cake you

served last night." Jennifer squeezed Abby's shoulder.

"You know," Abby said, managing a spoonful while she held the baby, "I haven't been a Christian very long, but I know there are things in the Bible about being a good wife. I studied it out some before Peter and I were married."

"And you're living up to them all." Peter slid closer to her.

"Thanks, but I was just thinking maybe Leeanne hasn't studied that yet."

"That's a good point." Peter reached out and tweaked Abby's braid. "I think sometimes people are ready to learn things at different stages."

"Well, she's not married to him yet," Harvey said.

"True." Abby frowned. "I'm not saying she should be a good little housewife. I believe in independence for women. But if you're going to commit to a man for life, you need to consider his feelings, too."

"Nowadays, people are raised to think women are equal in everything," Harvey said.

"Aren't they?" Abby smiled at him in the moonlight.

"Most things," Peter said.

"Our mother's not a feminist," Jennifer protested. "We weren't raised that way."

"No," Peter replied, "but think about Leeanne's environment, beyond the home."

Abby nodded. "Public school, state university, and now she's working in the newspaper office. Journalists are notoriously liberal. She may be getting an earful from the other women in the office, and we have no idea."

"I'll bet she is," Peter said. "If she's told anyone there about her situation with Eddie, they're probably encouraging her to dump the chauvinistic lout and enjoy her freedom."

Alarmed, Jennifer looked at Harvey. "What can we do?"

"Keep praying. I'm not a Bible expert. I don't suppose she would talk to Pastor Rowland."

"If they'd only gone for their premarital counseling," Jennifer mourned. "Their first session was scheduled for Friday, but she canceled it."

Chapter 3

Harvey glanced up from his computer screen, toward Eddie's desk. Several times in the last hour his eyes had been drawn that way. Eddie had sat unmoving for a very long time. More than two weeks had passed since his rift with Leeanne. Harvey got up and walked across the room to stand beside his friend.

"You okay, Ed?"

Eddie nodded mechanically.

"I thought things would be settled before this," Harvey said. "I'm really sorry."

Eddie sighed and picked up a folder from his desktop. "I'm down to reports, Harv. I need a new case. Something very demanding."

"You did a good job closing this one out. It's up to the D.A. now." Harvey glanced across the office. "Why don't you see if Nate needs any help for the next few hours? I'm working on the schedule for that Labor Day weekend thing, but I'll get you something new for tomorrow."

"Will she call from Hawaii?" Eddie asked.

"I think so. Jenny read her the riot act about that. She has to let us know she's okay."

Eddie nodded.

"If it helps," Harvey said quietly, "she was still wearing the ring when she got on the plane."

"If she wants to wear the ring, why won't she talk to me?"

"I don't know, buddy. Jenny said she almost slapped her this morning."

"I can relate to that." Eddie stared at his screen saver.

Harvey started to turn away, but Eddie said suddenly, "How long?"

"Huh?"

"How long would you wait?"

"For Leeanne? Or for Jennifer?"

Eddie sighed and clicked his mouse. "She was so innocent and sweet a few months ago. Did I do this to her?"

"No, Eddie."

"I just don't get it. I mean, she is a Christian, right?"

Harvey winced. "Yes. I believe she is."

"Then how can she—" Eddie broke off, shaking his head.

"Jenn, you left me a message earlier?" Leeanne sounded very young and eager.

Jennifer sighed with relief. "Yes, honey, where've you been? It's nearly midnight."

"Not in Honolulu. It's only six. Our last session

just ended. Oh, Jenn, this week has been very rewarding. I've learned so much!"

"We've been praying for you." Jennifer's throat tightened.

"Thanks. I'll be home Sunday. Are you meeting me?"

Jennifer hesitated. "Sure, unless there's someone you'd rather see first thing when you step off the plane."

"Like who?"

"Oh, Leeanne," Jennifer wailed, "I don't understand how you can do this to him! He loves you so much. Honey, tonight should have been your wedding rehearsal. Tomorrow is your wedding day. Do you have any idea how depressed Eddie is? Baby, come home! You are driving him insane."

There was a silence.

"Leeanne?"

"Eddie and I talked about this," she said stiffly. "We agreed to postpone the wedding."

"No. No, I do not believe that. Eddie never agreed to anything. You made a decree, not a covenant."

There was another pause, then Leeanne said, "Do you hate me?"

Jennifer swallowed hard. "No! Of course not. I love you so much it hurts. It hurts awfully, Leeanne! Call him. Please, honey, just call him."

"A group of us are going out to dinner."

Harvey came from the sunroom with Connor drowsing on his shoulder and stood watching Jennifer intently.

"Leeanne, honey, where is your heart?" Jennifer moaned.

Harvey lowered the baby carefully into his crib.

"Did you ever once in all this stop to consider how *I* feel?" Leeanne gasped. "You guys just assume I'm cruel and heartless. Did you ever think I might be hurting, too?"

"No, I guess not," Jennifer admitted. "See, you're the one who's hopping around the globe enjoying herself. And Eddie—remember Eddie? He's the good-looking detective who can barely keep from crying when anyone mentions your name. You told him last spring that nothing would stop you from becoming Madame Thibodeau on August twelfth, Leeanne. Those were your exact words. Well, tomorrow's the twelfth, and no, I don't hear the pain in your voice."

Connor was crying. Harvey sat at his computer in the study, checking his stocks, but the baby's wail became louder, and he got up and went out to the sunroom.

"Jenny?"

He glanced out the patio door. Jennifer sat listlessly on the chair swing, staring off toward Jeff and Beth's house. He went to the bedroom and took the baby from his crib.

"Hey, Connor. You're awake. You want Daddy to change you?" He took him to the changing table for a fresh diaper, then carried him out to the swing.

"The little guy's awake. He wants Mommy."

Jennifer held out her arms. "We ought to do something for Eddie. He shouldn't be alone today."

Harvey sank onto the seat beside her and glanced at his watch. "Maybe I'll walk down to his house."

"I think that would be good. I worry about him."

"We got any Pepsi?" Harvey asked.

"Check the utility room."

"Well, well, well. Harvey Larson on my doorstep with a six pack," Eddie said ten minutes later.

Harvey grinned. "Just like old times."

"Not quite. Come on in." Eddie led the way to the compact kitchen. "Want a glass?"

"This stuff is warm. We need ice." Harvey set the cluster of Pepsi bottles on the table.

"I suppose Jennifer sent you over."

"Well, she mentioned it, but I felt like I needed to be here, anyway."

Eddie dropped ice cubes into two glasses and handed one to Harvey. "I thought about leaving town today. My mother's been on the phone, and Monique and even Leeanne's mother."

"I'm sorry, Eddie. I didn't think she'd drag it out this long. I don't understand it, and I feel sort of responsible."

"How could it be your fault?"

Harvey shrugged. "She was staying with us for a while. I thought everything was good. She seemed sure about you and earnest about her spiritual life. I just can't figure out what happened."

"Russell waved a brilliant future under her nose."

"Do you think that's it? She's tempted by fame and fortune?"

"The idea of having a name as a writer, being respected for her work. It's very attractive to her."

Harvey nodded. "Since she's moved over to Jeff and Beth's, we hardly see her. She comes to church and leaves right after. She hasn't eaten two meals at our house in the last month."

"It's not your fault, Harv," Eddie said dully. He poured Pepsi slowly into his glass.

Harvey sipped his drink. "At least we've learned to handle stress better than we used to."

Eddie nodded, then looked sharply at Harvey. "You didn't expect to come over here and find me passed out on the sofa, did you?"

"No, nothing like that. And I'm proud of you. We ought to call Jeff and Peter and see if they want to come over and shoot some hoops or something."

"Is Jeff off today?"

"He got off for the wedding," Harvey said apologetically.

"Oh, right." Eddie took a deep swallow of Pepsi. "Sure, let's do it. Give him a call."

As Harvey hung up from his second call, he told Eddie, "Peter and Jeff will be at my house in twenty minutes."

"Great. I'll go change."

He headed for the bedroom, and Harvey wandered slowly around the dining room and living room. The house looked a lot different since Mrs. Harder and her niece had moved out. Eddie wasn't too sloppy, as bachelors went, but the place needed a feminine influence.

The doorbell chimed.

"Can you get that?" Eddie called.

Harvey went briskly into the entry and opened the door. Tony Winfield, Jimmy Cook, and Nate Miller stood on the steps. Jimmy was holding two square pizza boxes.

"Hey, Harvey," Nate said. "Is Eddie okay?"

"Yeah, come on in, guys." Harvey stepped aside, and they filed into the living room.

"Nice place," Jimmy said, looking around.

"Eddie's getting changed. We were going to play basketball. You guys feel like it?"

"Sure," said Nate, "but we brought pizza."

Tony grimaced. "We weren't sure if Eddie would want to celebrate his narrow escape or

68

hold a wake for his relationship, but we sort of felt like his groomsmen oughta be with him this afternoon."

"Well, bring the pizza over to my house. My brothers-in-law are coming. We'll have a good game."

"I've got beer in the car, but Nate said Eddie wouldn't want it, so I didn't bring it in," Tony confided.

"I told you, he's on the wagon." Nate's exasperation showed.

"Who, me?" Eddie asked, emerging from the bedroom in cutoffs and a worn Montreal T-shirt. "Nate's right."

"Well, how was I to know you didn't fall off it?" Tony asked. "You start getting tied up with women and you lose your equilibrium."

"It's okay, Eddie," said Jimmy. "I don't drink anymore, either. Shelly's really happy about it, too."

"Well, I'm just plain not getting married," Tony said. "In fact, I'm not even getting engaged. As far as I can see, it's not worth it."

Eddie looked hard at Tony. "You're wrong. It was worth it."

"Hey, fellas," Harvey said with a smile, "Leeanne and Eddie are still engaged. We'll all get to wear the tuxedoes one of these days. Let's move this party up the street. What do you say?"

• • •

Jennifer went to where Harvey stood at the patio door, looking out over the back lawn in the moonlight.

"You've got to quit brooding, sweetheart."

He turned to face her and pulled her close. "I'm just wondering if Eddie will sleep tonight."

"Don't call him," she advised. "The guys gave him a good workout, and he's probably tuckered out. If he is sleeping, you'll wake him up, and then he'll start thinking about it again."

Harvey sighed. "I should have done more. Before she left, I mean. Can she really have changed that much?"

Jennifer slid her hands up to his neck. "She loves us, and she respects you, I know that. I don't know why she won't take your advice on this. If she really loves him—"

"Exactly. I'm thinking there's a stronger influence. I almost thought she was coming around last week. It's John Russell, I think. He has her mesmerized with a vision of her illustrious future."

"Maybe."

Harvey stroked her hair. "I encouraged her in this. I recommended her to John. Then I bought her the computer and set her up with a home office upstairs."

Jennifer nodded. "I know, and we gave her

room and board, and you fed her material for a couple of very impressive exclusives."

"I shouldn't have done it. She should have had to struggle more."

"We tried to help her every way we could."

"I don't know. I wish I knew if she's reading her Bible."

Jennifer pulled back and looked into his eyes. "Harvey, listen to me. I have two things to say."

He met her gaze, his blue eyes somber. "What is it, gorgeous?"

"Number one, this is not your fault."

He shrugged a little. "I can't help it."

"I know. It's your nature. You want to help everyone, and when you can't, you blame yourself. Second—"

"What?"

She hesitated. No sense raking up the past, but his eyes were so full of sorrow. She pulled his head down and kissed his cheek, then whispered, "I will never leave you."

He exhaled slowly. "I wasn't thinking about that."

"Weren't you, just a little?"

"Maybe. But it's been ages since I thought that way. I trust you implicitly, Jenny."

She clung to him and rubbed his back gently, wishing she could take away all the pain for him and for Eddie. And for Leeanne. She must be hurting, too.

"She's a sweet girl," she choked.

"She's always been the sweetest," Harvey agreed.

"She hasn't even asked to take the computer," Jennifer noted.

"I thought maybe she felt guilty."

"I hope so."

He squeezed her. "Eddie wants to meet her at the airport tomorrow night."

"Do you think that's wise?"

"I don't know."

"Harvey, what if God doesn't want them together? Are we wrong to try so hard to fix this?"

Confusion seemed to hit him. "They were so sure."

"I know, but—remember Abraham? He tried to come up with his own plan, and it wasn't God's way. Maybe we should back off and pray harder, and see what happens."

Eddie caught his breath when he saw her. She was more beautiful than ever, more mature somehow, more sophisticated. She looked independent, walking across the tarmac pulling her carry-on. That was it. She was self-sufficient now.

Her eyes met his, and she checked for a moment, then came on toward him.

"Hi." She stopped four feet from him. "I thought Jennifer was coming."

"I asked her to let me."

"You didn't need to."

"I wanted to." He tried to see something, anything positive, in her eyes. "Look, can we talk?"

She hesitated. "Can you listen?"

"What do you mean?"

"Everybody wants to talk to me lately. Nobody wants to listen. You, Jennifer, Harvey, Jeff, Abby, my mother, even meek little Beth. Nobody wants to hear how Leeanne feels. Everyone just wants to dump on me about how bad *you* feel."

Eddie took a deep, slow breath. "I would listen. I would do anything just to sit down with you for a few minutes."

Her eyes narrowed. "Well, I guess you're stuck with me for the ride home, anyway. I can't see getting a cab."

Eddie's stomach lurched. She might do that, even now. "Please, Leeanne. Give me a chance here."

She nodded. "I need to get my luggage."

They stood in silence, waiting for the baggage carousel to begin moving. Other travelers hovered in a circle around it, chatting with relatives. Eddie couldn't think of anything he wanted to say to her in public.

Leeanne didn't look at him. He tried not to stare, but kept sneaking glances her way. She was tanned. It took real effort to tan in Maine, but a week in Hawaii had done the trick, even during a seminar. He didn't recognize the outfit she was wearing, a moss green cotton skirt and a bright, flowered blouse. Maybe she had done some shopping in Honolulu. He ached to reach for her hand, but he was afraid she would pull away.

At last her suitcase came up, and he pulled it across to the parking garage. He unlocked the passenger door of his truck for her, then slung the bags into the back.

He sat with the key ring in his hand, not wanting to start the engine.

"Hey, *cheri*, it's late, and I have jet lag," she said softly.

He felt the tears spring into his eyes. He hated that. This was not the time to show weakness. "Talk to me," he whispered. "I'm listening."

She sat still for a moment, then turned sideways on the seat. "My feelings for you haven't changed. But a lot of other things have. I'm sorry about that in a way, but in another way, I'm not. I'm excited about it."

Eddie took a deep, slow breath. "I can't make sense out of that. Last month you couldn't wait to see me every day. Now you go out of your way to avoid me. How can you say you feel the same?"

"I do," she insisted. "I didn't intend to hurt you, Eddie. I just—need more time. I need to see where my career is headed, and when I know

74

that—" She broke off as Eddie shifted in his seat. "I know, you can't see why I need a career. I'm sorry, I just—do. That's all."

Eddie shook his head. "Would you do one thing for me?"

"What?" Leeanne cocked her head to one side.

She doesn't know how enslaved I am to her, he thought. I would do anything, anything to have things back the way they were.

He pulled in a deep breath. "Go see Pastor Rowland with me."

She frowned. "What for?"

"Are we still engaged, or aren't we?" He tried to keep the edge out of his voice.

"Well—yes, aren't we?"

"I hoped so."

"Well, we are, then."

"Good." Eddie reached slowly toward her. She didn't move when his fingers touched her hand. "Go to the counseling with me. We were supposed to start a month ago. Let's start now. Please."

Her hand stirred, and her fingers clasped his lightly. "All right. I guess we can do that."

Eddie sighed. "Thank you. I'll set it up."

He sat looking at her, wondering if he dared to kiss her.

"We really ought to get going. I have to be up in six hours." Leeanne opened her purse and shoved her baggage claims inside.

Eddie started the engine.

What if she doesn't show up?

Eddie glanced nervously across the desk. Pastor Rowland sat patiently, cleaning his glasses. Eddie stood and walked to the window.

Dear Lord, please make her come. He looked at his watch. She was only a minute late. *Lord, let me restate that. Please make her want to come.*

Leeanne's car turned into the parking lot outside, and he was shocked by the intensity of his relief.

"She's here," he said softly.

"Great." The pastor sounded jovial, as if everything was perfect now.

"I—I guess I'll go meet her." Eddie walked irresolutely toward the door, then quickened his steps down the hallway to the front door of the church.

"Hi! Am I late?" she asked. "Sorry."

"I—no. No, it's okay." He wanted to say so much, but he couldn't. He leaned forward and touched her shoulder lightly. She didn't move away, and he bent down and brushed her cheek with the softest of kisses.

"Is the pastor waiting?" she asked.

"Yes, in his study."

They walked down the carpeted hallway, and he realized his pulse was as fast as it was when he and Harvey finished their morning run.

They sat side by side, facing the pastor.

76

"Leeanne, glad you could be here."

"Thank you," she smiled.

"I understand you two have had a bit of a dis-agreement over your plans," the pastor said tentatively.

Eddie looked down at his hands. He wanted to crack his knuckles or something, but she might find that annoying.

She spoke up. "Well, we still want to get married, Pastor. We're just not sure when. I've had this new offer from the *Press Herald*, and I wanted to wait until I knew what they expect of me after I graduate in December."

Mr. Rowland nodded. "Eddie?"

He looked up. "What?"

"The wedding was to have been last Saturday. How do you feel about the postponement?"

"I hate it." Immediately he sensed that he'd said the wrong thing. Leeanne stiffened and stared at the bookshelves on the other side of the room.

"If it were up to you, what would happen now?" Pastor Rowland asked.

Eddie hesitated. "If you want the truth, if it were up to me, we'd be on our honeymoon now. I didn't want to change the date. Leeanne knows that. I didn't want her to go to Hawaii last week, and I didn't want her to quit speaking to me for a month."

He jumped up and paced to the window and back.

"Sorry, Pastor." He sat down again, careful not to look at Leeanne.

Mr. Rowland cleared his throat. "Leeanne, it's too late to adhere to the original schedule, but are you willing to talk about this, perhaps settle on a mutually agreeable alternative?"

"I—I'd need to talk to my boss before I make any decisions," she faltered.

"You're not marrying your editor," Eddie snapped.

Leeanne winced, and he wished he'd kept his lips closed.

"Sorry," he said humbly.

The pastor leaned back in his chair and studied them. "This isn't the way premarital counseling usually starts," he said at last. "To be frank, this reminds me more of a marriage counseling session. Are you two certain you want to be married?"

Leeanne turned her head slowly and looked at Eddie.

Say yes, he pleaded silently.

"We've always disagreed on my working," she ventured. She turned toward the pastor. "Eddie didn't want me to finish school."

"I never said that. I just—well, I wasn't sure you needed a degree. But you transferred down here, and I agreed you would finish up this fall. I promised your father you would finish after we got married. I know it's important to your folks."

"You're so defensive." A tear trickled down Leeanne's cheek, and she swiped it away with the back of her hand. "You know you wanted me to quit school. And you hated it when they came to interview me after the Carleton Fuller case."

Eddie shrugged helplessly. "Yes, I admit it, I hated sharing you with all of America. I want a wife of my own, not some public figure. I happen to think being a housewife is a big deal, not a dirty word. I don't want to marry a woman who's going to end up a news anchor in some New York studio and only comes home every other weekend."

Leeanne's hurt was plain on her face. "You know I don't plan to go into broadcast journalism."

"Well, now, let's talk about the role of the wife," Pastor Rowland said soothingly. "Leeanne, have you considered the biblical model?"

"I—I'm not sure what you mean."

"What does the Bible say about the role of a wife?"

"Well, I guess—" She stopped and glanced at Eddie, then the pastor. "I would love him and—and try to make a nice home for him. And we'd want to have children eventually."

The pastor nodded. "Let's look at some Scripture together." He reached for his Bible.

Leeanne shot Eddie a glance. "It's just that I

have new possibilities in my life now. Things I never dreamed I'd be able to do."

"Have you asked the Lord to show you His will as far as your work goes?" the pastor asked.

"Well, yes, when I first started my internship—"

"What about now? Today?"

She looked away.

Eddie felt impatience surging up in him. "I still can't believe you went to Hawaii the week of our wedding."

She stared at him. "We settled that."

"No, we did not."

Pastor Rowland said smoothly, "Perhaps we can—"

"We did," Leeanne insisted.

"No, you told me you were going, just like that, and when I tried to talk you out of it, you wouldn't speak to me." Things weren't going the way they were supposed to. Eddie's feelings bubbled out of control. He wanted to be sure the pastor understood how deeply she had hurt him.

Leeanne blinked, and he caught the gleam on moisture on her lashes. "Eddie, you have to understand how huge that seminar was. If I told my boss no, I would never, ever have another opportunity like that. It's like—well, imagine they suddenly called you and offered to make you head of the Secret Service for the President."

"I wouldn't go."

Leeanne frowned. "Maybe that wasn't the best analogy. It's like this: I've always dreamed of being a writer, but I never really thought I could do it. Now I'm finding out I can, and I'm good at it. People who know these things are telling me I have talent. I—I can't just walk away from that."

"So, this is a lifelong career you're looking at, not just a summer internship."

"That's not fair. I don't know what I want to do with the rest of my life, but so what if I want to work? It's not a sin for women to work, is it?" Leeanne turned toward the pastor.

"There are situations where women have to work," Rowland said carefully. "There are also women who choose to work, although it's not necessary."

"But it's not a sin, is it?"

The pastor spread his hands. "Well, Leeanne, if we can just take time to go through this together, I think you'll find that, when it comes right down to it, the wife should ultimately do what her husband feels is best, whether it's her first choice or not."

Leeanne stared at him, her mouth open slightly.

Eddie hardly dared to breathe. He'd felt that way, but he hadn't been certain God was on his side of the argument.

Leeanne raised her chin a fraction of an inch. "But Eddie's not my husband."

He stood up quickly. She was playing the trump card, after all, and he couldn't sit still and hear her reason her way out of the engagement.

"I'm sorry, Pastor, I can't do this anymore." He looked fleetingly at Leeanne, then looked away. "You can keep the ring." He turned on his heel and walked out.

Chapter 4

"Eddie! How did it go?" Harvey met him at the door expectantly, answering his imperative knock.

"Not good." Eddie pushed past him into the kitchen.

Harvey was baffled. "Come on, you spent an hour and a half with the pastor."

Eddie shook his head. "No, I didn't. I spent ten minutes with the pastor. I've been driving around for an hour and beating up my truck."

Jennifer was closing the dishwasher. She straightened, turning wide gray eyes on him.

"I'm sorry, Jennifer," Eddie said, tears in his eyes. "I let you guys down."

She shook her head. "Oh, Eddie, it's not me and Harvey who have been hurt here." She stepped toward him, her arms open, and he gave her a squeeze then turned away, wiping his eyes on his sleeve.

"It was partly my fault," he choked. "This time, anyway. I really blew it."

"Sit down and have some coffee," Harvey said gently.

"Did she tell you about the book offer?" Jennifer asked.

"What book offer?"

Jennifer and Harvey exchanged a glance.

"She called me from work today," Jennifer said. "A big book publisher approached John Russell while she was in Hawaii. They want her to write a true crime book about the Fuller case."

Eddie's mouth twisted. "Great. No, she didn't get around to that little tidbit."

Jennifer took three mugs from the cupboard. "She told them she didn't think she could handle school and work and write a book this fall, so John told her she could ease up on work, if she'd promise to sign on with the *Press Herald* after she graduates. He thinks the book is important, and she thinks—"

"She thinks she owes him," Eddie said.

Harvey nodded. "John's given her a real boost, and she doesn't want to let him down. And he doesn't want to lose her. He wants a two-year contract, Eddie."

"Two years?" Eddie laughed. "She never said a word."

"So, what did you do that was so awful?" Harvey took his coffee mug from Jennifer.

Eddie swallowed hard. "She started going on about her career and her opportunities that don't include me, and I—I basically told her it's over and left."

They were silent for several seconds.

"*Is* it over?" Jennifer whispered.

Ten days later, Eddie went to Harvey's house after supper. Leeanne's car wasn't in Beth's driveway, but it might be in the garage.

Jennifer opened the door with a smile.

"Come on in, Eddie."

"Leeanne's not here, is she?"

"I don't think so. Beth is coming over after a bit, but I think Leeanne is working on a project."

"Is she writing that book?"

"I don't know."

"Hello, Eddie!"

He swung around. Beth was crossing the driveway from her front yard.

"Hi, Beth. Jeff working tonight?"

"As usual."

Eddie extended his hand to help her up the steps. "When's B-day again?"

Beth laughed. "Baby day? Thanksgiving, if you can believe that. Of course, my mother insists he's going to be early. Rick and I were both early."

"Come on in and have some dessert." Jennifer stepped out of the doorway.

"Leeanne home tonight?" Eddie asked Beth. He bit his lip, wishing he hadn't asked, but wanting to know all the same.

"Yeah, she's working on some big story," Beth

said. "School starts next week. I don't know how she's going to juggle school and this job. It'll be part time, I guess, but still . . ."

"Has she said anything about taking her computer over there?" Jennifer asked.

"Her computer from here? No. She's using Jeff's. E-mails her stories to herself at the office."

"Is she going to write the book?" Eddie asked.

"I don't think she's made a decision yet."

"Hey, Eddie. Beth." Harvey came in from the sunroom with Connor in the crook of his arm.

"Harv, can I see you for a sec?" Eddie asked.

Jennifer and Beth went on into the living room, and Eddie said quietly, "I think it's official now."

"What?"

"She sent the ring back."

"Oh man, I'm sorry. I thought you told her to keep it."

"I did. It was a gift. Guess she didn't want to keep any reminders of me."

"She actually mailed it?"

"Yeah. She couldn't walk half a block down the street and hand it to me." Eddie pulled out his handkerchief. "I told myself I wasn't going to do this."

"What did you do with it?"

Eddie sniffed and wiped his eyes.

"You didn't pitch it off the bridge or anything, did you?" Harvey asked in alarm.

Eddie smiled wryly. "No, I just—" He broke off with a bitter chuckle.

"What?"

"I stuck it in the freezer."

"You're nuts."

Eddie shrugged. "I didn't know what else to do with it."

"Burglars always look in the freezer. That's where everyone keeps their money and cocaine."

"It cost her a dollar-eighty-three to mail it. Can you believe that?"

"Well, help yourself to coffee and dessert. I think Jennifer said something about ice cream. We need to do some strategizing on this Labor Day thing. It's creeping up on us."

Harvey parked his car across the street from the *Press Herald* building and took the elevator up to the managing editor's office.

"Captain! Good morning." John Russell rose and shook his hand. "Is this an official visit?"

"No, I just thought I'd see if my sister-in-law was free for lunch. She's been so busy, my wife and I haven't seen much of her lately."

John winked. "I've been keeping her hard at work. Got to get all we can out of her before classes start."

Harvey took the chair he indicated and said, "Actually, there is something that's been bothering me, John."

"Something I can help with?" Russell sat in his swivel chair and tipped it back.

"Well, I don't want to presume on our acquaintance, but you know I put in a word or two in Leeanne's favor last spring, when she wanted this internship."

"Glad you did. She's the brightest reporter I've seen since Martin Blake. Not that she has his style yet, but she's got a real flair for it." He nodded in satisfaction. "Yes, she's got real potential."

"Still, this job has put a strain on her personal life."

"That so?"

"You know she broke her engagement recently?"

"Don't know a thing about it."

Harvey sighed. "She was going to marry my best friend, a really nice young man."

Russell nodded. "So?"

"John, you're not pressuring her into a contract, are you?"

"Pressure? No way. I offered her pretty good terms for after she graduates. She doesn't have to accept. Of course, I hope she will."

"You've invested in her."

"Well, sure. I've encouraged her, and I've tried to teach her what real-life journalism is all about. Classroom lectures aren't enough."

"Sure." Harvey locked his fingers on the edge of John's desk. "So, she hasn't actually signed the contract?"

"She's making me a little nervous," John admitted.

"Now, why is that?"

"I shouldn't tip my hand to you, Captain."

"Would it be because she can bypass you completely, take the book contract and go on to a career as an author, leaving you high and dry?"

"Well, as you said, I have an investment."

"At intern's pay. That's nothing."

"We sent her to a high-powered seminar in Honolulu," John objected.

Harvey considered that. "Why did the publisher come to you about the book, anyway?"

"Her stories about the Fuller case came to his attention after we submitted them for a press club award. His firm publishes these true crime stories, you know? It can be very lucrative. And Leeanne was an insider on the case, a hostage, and a lucid writer. He approached me as a contact, and I decided it might be good for Leeanne, so I set up a meeting for them as a favor."

"But you'd hate to cut her loose."

John smiled. "She's a conscientious young lady. Doesn't want her grades to slip, and doesn't want to give me the short end of the stick on her work here. So I told her, take three months off, write the book and finish the degree, then come back here."

"For two years."

"She told you that."

"Yes. Do you think that's fair?"

"Absolutely, if she wants a three-month leave of absence and a guaranteed reporter's job after. And I'll pay her what our most experienced reporters get."

"How can you do that? Won't the union get on your case?"

He shrugged. "I have latitude for attracting talent. And she's good. I need the contract, you understand that. *The New York Times* would come courting if I didn't have her signed when the book launched."

Harvey stood up. "Well, I guess I'd better get down to the newsroom if I want a lunch date."

"You're not going to steer her away from me, are you, Captain? We've established a rapport, you and I."

"It's her decision, but I mean that, *her* decision. Not yours. Not mine."

John nodded. "Fair enough."

Harvey stopped next to Leeanne's desk and waited for her to look up, wondering if she would be glad to see him.

"Harvey! Hey. Whatcha doing here?"

She leaped up and kissed him, and he gave her a squeeze.

"Just wanted to take my little sister to lunch. Got time?"

"Well, sure, I guess so." She looked around the

office and leaned toward him, whispering, "Do me a favor?"

He quirked his eyebrows.

"Pin your badge on your jacket. I want everyone to know I'm going to lunch with a bigshot."

He laughed and opened his sport jacket to retrieve the badge and clipped it on his breast pocket. "Better?"

"Perfect."

At the restaurant, she sat smiling across at him as they waited for their entrees.

"So, I popped in on your boss for a minute to get some details on this contract deal," Harvey said.

"Oh?" Leeanne asked warily.

"Yeah, it sounds pretty tempting. You haven't signed yet, though."

"I've got to make a decision before Labor Day."

"It's coming right up."

"I know." She frowned, then looked up at him eagerly. "What would you do, Harvey?"

"Oh, I'm not the person to ask. I'm not a writer."

"It's a business deal. You're shrewd when it comes to business."

"Is that a compliment?"

She sobered. "I'd really appreciate it if you'd give me your opinion."

The waitress came and set their plates before

them. When she had left, Harvey looked Leeanne straight in the eye. "All right, you asked for it; here it is. If you're going to do the book, don't tie it to your newspaper contract. John has no right to pressure you into a long-term commitment. You don't owe him anything."

"But he gave me the internship and—"

"At minimum wage. Trust me, honey, he more than got his money's worth out of you this summer."

"But the seminar," she said weakly.

"Bait. He wants you on board, and he's afraid someone else is going to lure you away. That's why he's offering you a big salary after you graduate. He wants to make sure he's got your loyalty."

"So, you think I should quit the *Press Herald* and make my own deal with the book publisher?"

Harvey sat back and considered. "No, I think you should get an agent to make an independent book deal for you—that's if you really want to write the book—and keep your business with the paper separate. No strings."

"I can do that? Get an agent just like that?"

Harvey laughed. "With a publisher waving a hefty contract under your nose? Nothing could be simpler."

"If I do the book . . ." Her eyes darkened.

"What?"

"Eddie was the investigating officer."

"True. You'd have to interview him, not to mention me and Beth and Jeff and Nate, and everyone else involved. And you'd have to spend hours and hours hanging around the police station, going over records and looking at evidence. If you don't want to spend time with the people involved in the Fuller case, don't do the book. It should be fun, not torture."

"I've really missed you guys," she admitted, cutting into her chicken.

"We've missed you, too. Your room is still there, you know."

"Thanks. I think Beth really needs me now. Jeff is gone so many nights, and she gets scared sometimes, even with the burglar alarm. I think I ought to stay there, at least until the baby is born."

He nodded. "Okay, kiddo. I just didn't want you to think, since Eddie frequents my house, that you have to stay away. Just don't be such a stranger, okay?"

She nodded. "Thanks. It's been really lonely. I—I guess I've been afraid you and Jennifer didn't want to see me."

His heart clenched. "No, honey. We love you."

"I know how much Eddie means to you."

"We can love you both."

"Even if we're not together?"

"Of course." He ate silently for a few minutes, thinking about all that had changed. "Leeanne, do you feel this whole thing was a mistake? Your engagement, I mean."

She looked very vulnerable as she raised her eyes to his. "No, I never thought that. I just—I didn't handle it very well, I guess."

"You sent the ring back."

"I couldn't keep it after he said it was over." She ducked her head. "Eddie's mother thinks I'm terrible anyway. If I kept his grandmother's diamond, she'd never let him hear the end of it." She picked up her napkin and dabbed at her eyelashes. "You know, it's funny, I was sure I'd be able to get along with Marie, as a daughter-in-law. She was beginning to accept me. She was going to teach me to make tortières."

Harvey smiled. "They loved you."

"Not at first. And Lisa. I thought we could be real friends. She called me last week and yelled at me over the phone."

"I'm sorry."

Leeanne gave him a half smile. "She said I was too English for Eddie, and they knew it wouldn't last. Then she chewed me out for dumping her brother."

"Funny, that's the story going around the police station, too. That you broke up with Eddie, I mean, not the other way around."

The tears rolled down her cheeks, and she didn't try to stop them. "You and I both know he was the one who broke it off in the end. I don't know why he doesn't just tell everyone. I was stubborn and mean, and so he called it quits."

"Eddie's got class. He's very close-lipped about this. I think he wanted to give you the chance to put out whatever story you wanted the public to hear."

She sniffed. "You know, he was really mad that night at the pastor's."

Harvey nodded. "He told me. If it means anything, he regretted it deeply."

"He hasn't said so."

"Do you want him to apologize?"

She swallowed hard. "I don't know what I want these days." She picked up half a roll and buttered it, then set it down again. "I was furious at the time, but I've gotten to the point now where I can't really blame him. After he left that night, Pastor Rowland called his wife, and she came over. We talked for a long time."

Harvey felt a flicker of hope, but said nothing. He fought the urge to look at his watch. This was more important than anything waiting on his desk.

"She showed me some things in the Bible that night, things I never knew were there. She wasn't judgmental, but . . . ." She picked up her water glass and took a sip.

"So, do you think the Lord was showing you something?"

"Definitely. I've gone over to their house a

couple of times since, after work. Harvey, there's so much I need to learn."

He closed his eyes for an instant in thankfulness, then looked hard at her. "Whether you marry Eddie or not, straighten things out with the Lord, honey. That's the most important thing in your life."

"I've made such a mess of things."

"I can't deny that, but speaking as a guy who's made a few royal messes himself, those things will fall into place if you're right spiritually."

She nodded gravely. "I don't know if Eddie would consider giving me the time of day again. To be truthful, I'm not sure now if he's the one God would choose for me to marry. I thought so before. I just knew it. But now . . . There are some things we'd have to work out, I know that. And I don't know as he wants to anymore."

Harvey's heart ached for her. "Such as?"

"Well, this work thing. I don't think Eddie wants a working wife at all, do you?"

"He might agree to it for a while, but I know he wants children, and he doesn't want them raised in daycare."

Leeanne dropped her gaze. "I can't imagine Jennifer leaving Connor with a babysitter so she could go write software."

"Neither one of us would stand for that. We'd miss so much!"

"Well, Eddie's always admitted he was jealous

of your marriage. He wants a wife who will be there when he comes home at night. And, you know, I think I want that, too. I just couldn't stand being told I didn't have a choice." She took a bite and chewed thoughtfully. "Eddie's not . . . seeing someone else, is he?"

Harvey fought back a smile. "You think he could forget you that fast?"

Leeanne blushed a little, and Harvey pressed the advantage. "How about you? Dating up a storm?"

"No." She looked at him, rolling her eyes a little. "There was this guy from Hartford on the Hawaii trip. He was trying to flirt with me. Kept asking me to go to dinner with him. It scared me to death."

Harvey chuckled. "Well, you take your time and sort things out. You and Eddie can be friends, if it comes down to that. But you can't avoid him for the rest of your life. The two of you are going to stay major players in my life and Jennifer's, so you'll just have to make peace somehow."

"I'll try."

"Good girl. And one more thing. There's a computer gathering dust at our house. Would you be upset if I set it up over at Jeff's for you?"

"Oh, Harvey, I can't—"

"Yes, you can. That was a present."

"Like the ring?"

"Sort of." He smiled. At least he didn't put

the computer on ice. "I really think you need it, especially if you're going to write a book."

Leeanne's blue eyes were clear now, and her mind was zooming ahead, he could tell. "What you said about an agent . . ."

"Yeah?"

"How would I find one?"

Harvey reached for his wallet. "I might know someone."

She grinned. "You know everyone."

"Not everyone."

"But you know a literary agent?"

"I met one last summer. Remember the Martin Blake case?"

"Martin Blake's agent? But he was . . . colossal. Someone like that would consider a greenhorn like me?"

"I don't know, but if this book deal isn't up his alley, he'll know someone else. It's called networking."

She nodded, clearly impressed.

"Want me to give Bob Hoffsted a call?" He took out his credit card.

"Wow! How can you just pull a name out like that, a year later?"

Harvey smiled. "I could tell you I have an eidetic memory, but I don't. I've been thinking about this book deal ever since you told us about it, and I admit I pulled the file on the Blake murder to refresh my memory. I can call him and refresh *his* memory as to who I am, and see if he's interested in reviewing your contract."

"That would be super. Thanks so much, Harvey."

"You're welcome."

He wasn't sure if he'd helped Eddie's cause or not, but at least he'd made progress on the personal front. Leeanne knew they didn't want her to stop being part of the family. It was a start.

Chapter 5

The buildup for the Labor Day challenge grew to a frenzy. Jeff qualified for the city's firemen's muster team, and the whole Wainthrop family decided to cheer him on in Bangor on Saturday. George and Marilyn insisted that all the children and grandchildren stay at the farmhouse in Skowhegan.

"We'll put up a tent for the boys," George told Peter. Gary and Andy's excitement kept them bouncing. They would start school on the Wednesday after the holiday weekend, and the visit to their new mom's family farm was an adventure.

"They're all wound up about going to Grammy and Grandpa's," Abby told Jennifer.

"Are they excited about starting school?" Harvey asked.

"Well, yes, but Andy's going into first grade, and he's a little nervous."

"He'll be fine," Harvey said. Peter and Abby had discussed home schooling, but Abby had decided not to do that, at least not this year. She wanted time to sort out her new life, and this way she left open the option of working part time if she wanted.

"How about Gary?" Jennifer asked.

"He's cool with it. He looks forward to seeing all his friends again."

The farmhouse was full, even with the Hobart boys and Travis and Randy Wainthrop camping in the backyard. Jeff and Beth took Jeff's old room, and Abby and Peter had the boys' room. Leeanne slept on the sofa so Harvey and Jennifer could have her room. She evaded questions from her mother, when it came to her love life.

"This isn't a good time, Mom," Jennifer confided when Leeanne was out of earshot. "Just leave her alone for a while."

"Do you think she still loves him?" her mother asked anxiously.

"I'm not sure that matters right now. She's wrestling with some very big issues."

"What's bigger than love?" Marilyn asked, but Jennifer didn't really have an answer.

Eddie had stayed in Portland, on call for the police department. Harvey gave him strict orders to call him if anything serious came up, but Saturday's events went uninterrupted. Bangor won the playground building competition, but Jeff and his team made a valiant effort, edging out the Bangor firemen on the rescue drill and midnight call at the muster. The stage was set for a close finish in the Public Works and Police Department finals on Monday.

Jeff took Beth around to visit some of his old friends from the Skowhegan Fire Department that evening, and the rest of the family barbecued at the farmhouse. George and Marilyn saw the weekend as an opportunity to get to know their new grandchildren better, taking Gary and Andy to the Children's Museum after the firemen's muster ended.

"Don't spoil them, Mom," Abby cautioned when Marilyn handed out Popsicles after supper. Randy and Travis joined their "nephews" in taking the snack out to their campsite.

"A treat won't hurt them," Marilyn said complacently.

"They've been eating junk food all day," Abby replied mildly.

"Doesn't Peter's mother give them sweets?"

"Well, yes." Abby gave her mother a squeeze. "I'm not upset. I really appreciate you treating them the way you do."

"We got a bonanza in grandchildren this spring," George laughed. "Connor first, then your boys."

"Well, Connor was our first grandchild, even if he's younger," Marilyn said, "but pretty soon we're going to have a whole pack of them."

"I intend to enjoy every minute of being a grandfather." George reached for a Popsicle. "This house is too quiet with only Randy left home."

"Travis is settled in Orono?" Abby asked.

"Yes, he drove up alone for registration on Tuesday and didn't come back until last night," Marilyn said fretfully. "I'm not sure I like him living in the dorm."

"We all did it," Abby said.

"You hated it," her mother replied. "Your second year at Husson, you got an apartment with that Linda girl. She was nice, but I missed having you at home."

"Living on campus has its drawbacks," Abby said. "But we all lived through it."

"Lived through what?" Leeanne asked as she entered the kitchen.

"Dorm life." Marilyn held out the box of Popsicles. "Jennifer?"

"No, thanks," said Jennifer.

Leeanne poked into the box. "Hey, no orange left?"

"Here." George held his out to her. "Give me purple."

"Thanks, Dad. Living with Jeff and Jennifer is a whole lot better than the dorm. Cheaper, too."

"Just who are you living with?" George asked in confusion. "Jeff or Jennifer?"

Leeanne laughed. "Lately I've been staying at Jeff and Beth's. It's great."

"The dormitories are co-ed now," Marilyn said uneasily.

"Yeah, it can get pretty crazy," Leeanne agreed.

"How did you like it, Jennifer?" her father asked. "You've got a few years distance now. What was it like?"

She said cautiously, "It wasn't the best place for me, but I survived."

"I hear they have some wild parties at UMO," Abby said.

"They have rules," George said.

Jennifer shrugged. "Well, sure, but kids can always find ways to circumvent the rules."

"Not you. But I worry about Travis," Marilyn admitted. "He's a good boy, but he's impressionable."

Eddie pounded on the door at six o'clock Monday morning, and Harvey staggered to the kitchen.

"Are we running?" Harvey asked, rubbing his eyes. "I thought it was a holiday."

"Come on, Harv," Eddie chided. "It's game day. Get dressed. We've got to get to the office by eight."

"How come I have to go to the office on a holiday?" Harvey was feeling irritable. Connor was at last cutting a tooth, and he'd fussed off and on all night.

"The committee is setting up this morning. We'll do our stuff right after lunch."

"Okay, okay." Harvey yawned and headed for the bedroom. "Who's setting up for our side?"

"Emily Rood, Joey Bolduc, two guys from the Bangor P.D., and two volunteers from Brunswick. The committee will plant the actual clues at the last minute, so nobody from either side knows what they are."

The Portland team was sequestered in the Priority Unit office for the morning, and the Bangor team was given the use of the detective squad's breakroom on the second floor. At ten o'clock, festival committee members arrived and subjected both teams to a pop quiz on Maine law.

Joey Bolduc called Harvey shortly before noon.

"Hey, we're all set up at City Hall. You guys should send out for some lunch, and they'll bring you over here at one o'clock."

"Thanks, Joey. Do both teams go at the same time?"

"Yeah, we're putting you in the comptroller's office on the second floor, and the Bangor team in the city clerk's office on the first floor. I don't think I'm allowed to tell you anything else. They'll give you the particulars when you get over here."

"Eddie, call out for some sandwiches," Harvey said as he hung up.

"This is so boring," Tony complained. "Why can't we just start now? I don't see why we have to wait."

"Relax, Winfield. We're going to be in the

comptroller's office. Have you ever been in there?"

"No."

"I don't even know what that is," Jimmy Cook said.

"It's a financial officer," Nate told them.

"That's right. Now, relax for a few more minutes." Harvey used the time to check all his stocks on the Internet. Mike and Peter were nearly ready to sign the papers on the Churchill Lake property, and Harvey scribbled notes in his pocket notebook on which stocks to liquidate for his investment.

Nate paced between his desk and Eddie's. "I didn't expect to kill the whole day here. Jackie was hoping we could take the kids to the park together."

"Sorry, guys," Harvey said absently. "I tried to get out of this."

The sandwiches arrived, and they proved a good distraction for the team. Mike breezed in from the stairway at 12:40.

"You guys are up. You ready for this?"

"Sure," said Eddie. "Bring on the crime."

"The mayor's downstairs. Wants to give you a little pep talk before you go. Now, you'll be driven over to City Hall in two squad cars, with the lights and sirens."

"Hello, headache," said Harvey.

"Our own little parade," Tony chortled.

"Oh, and there are three very eager wives in front of City Hall, with assorted other fans."

The entire Wainthrop family, except for Leeanne and Jeff, crowded around Harvey and Eddie when they left the squad car.

"You're going to do great." Jennifer held Connor up so he could burble at his father for a moment.

"Where's Leeanne?" Harvey asked.

"Calling her editor with the first half of her story," his father-in-law said proudly.

"I should have known. Okay, guys, let's move." Harvey stooped and kissed Connor, then Jennifer. He glimpsed Eddie's mother and sisters, hugging him on the steps.

"Looks like everyone turned out today but your uncle Bill," Jimmy said to Tony.

"Oh, he's coming."

"Really? The governor's coming?" Nate squeaked.

"He's here somewhere," Tony said carelessly. "Probably picnicked in the park with Mayor Weymouth."

The five team members for Portland were seated in a conference room with the Bangor contingent, and Harvey studied his opponents. After a few minutes Myron Stickle, a Lewiston city councilman, entered to give them specific instructions for the game.

"Each team has free run of the office it is

assigned to, but please respect the property. You will have to find the fingerprints of six Maine celebrities and identify them using the portable computers set up in each office. As soon as you think you have all six sets of fingerprints, call downstairs, and the judges will come up."

"Who's judging?" Tony asked.

"The four judges represent towns other than Portland and Bangor, to insure an unbiased outcome. You can solve the fingerprint and homicide challenges simultaneously if you wish, deploying your detectives as you see fit, but time will be kept for each portion. Just beware as you're looking for fingerprints that you may disturb clues relevant to the homicide investigation. Detectives will examine the 'body' for clues to the mock homicide. When you are ready to name your prime suspect in the homicide, you will again call for the judges. Any questions?"

"Hey, it's a real body," Eddie said as they entered the room. "Male Caucasian, age thirty, five-foot-ten, a hundred and seventy-five pounds."

The "victim" lay face down on the blue and brown oriental rug in front of the comptroller's desk.

"Cool," Tony said, heading for the desk. "I thought they were going to use a dummy."

"All right, spread out, and be extra careful, guys," Harvey said, after a cursory glance at the "body." "Eddie, you deal with the corpse. The rest of you check everything for prints. They may have brought in objects from outside, like those books in the shelves. Be quick, and try not to get in each other's way."

Eddie walked over to the "corpse" and looked down. The man was wearing a gray pinstriped suit, and blood oozed from beneath his chest, soaking the rug and pooling on the oak floor beside it.

"That fake blood is pretty convincing. Someone's going to have to clean the rug." He bent over the man. "Hey, Joey."

Harvey glanced sharply toward him. "It's Joey Bolduc?"

"Yeah, I guess they got a dummy after all," Eddie deadpanned.

Jimmy Cook snickered, opening his fingerprint kit by the window.

Harvey spotted a spanking new copy of Stephen King's latest novel on the top shelf and reached for it with his clean handkerchief.

"Hey, Joey, how'd you pull this detail?" Tony called.

Bolduc lay still.

"Well, he's not breaking character," Nate said. "Gotta give him credit for that."

Eddie's expression changed as he studied Bolduc's body. He reached down suddenly and touched the man's neck, above the collar.

"Harvey." His voice rose, and Harvey froze, his hand in midair as he stretched for the book.

He glanced toward Eddie, then went quickly across the room and knelt beside Joey Bolduc.

"Harvey, he's not breathing," Eddie said.

Nate, Jimmy, and Tony, swung toward them.

"You're kidding," said Jimmy.

"They used a real body, a real *dead* body?" Tony stared at the dead man.

"No pulse," Harvey confirmed.

Nate swore.

"*Ne jure pas*," Eddie said gently.

"I was talking to him this morning. He was helping them set up," Tony protested.

"They killed him? This doesn't make sense." Jimmy's eyes were round and his breathing shallow.

"Idiot," said Harvey. "They didn't kill him for the game."

Jimmy ducked his head, flushing. "I didn't mean that."

Harvey stood up, rubbing the back of his neck. "Sorry, Jim. This is a shock. Call the M.E., Eddie. And don't touch anything, guys. This is for real." He took out his cell phone and punched two buttons. Eddie pulled his phone from his jacket pocket and went into the hallway.

"Mike?" Harvey said into his phone. The other three men stood listening. "Our unit's in the comptroller's office for the game, you know?

Yeah, but, Mike, it isn't a game. Joey Bolduc's been murdered. Can you get over here?"

"All right, you know what to do," Harvey told his men as he pocketed the cell phone. "Let's secure the scene and get to work."

Eddie came back from the hallway. "Dr. McIntyre's on the way, and Hogan's coming down from Augusta."

"The chief M.E.?" Harvey was surprised.

"He wants to make sure everything is by the book, I guess. McIntyre sounded quite irritated."

"He always sounds that way," said Harvey. "Call for a photographer."

"Got it."

Harvey stood for several moments staring at Bolduc's body, taking in every visible detail. A gunshot wound to the chest? Surely someone in the building would have heard the report. Although the city offices were closed for the holiday, dozens of people had helped organize the challenge.

Two members of the judging team appeared in the doorway just as Nate Miller stretched the yellow "police line" tape across it.

"You fellows are taking this seriously," said Myron Stickle.

"Can't come in here, sir." Nate fastened the tape across the doorway in front of him.

"We have to verify your discoveries, or you

111

don't get points," said Bert Fontaine, South Portland's fire chief.

Harvey went to the doorway. "The game's over, Bert. We have a real crime to solve. We'll forfeit to Bangor on the game, I guess."

"What are you talking about?" Startled, Fontaine peered past him into the office.

"That's not the dummy." Stickle strained forward, stretching the yellow tape.

"A real body was lying on the rug when we got here," Harvey said. "I've sent for Chief Browning and the medical examiner."

"Why, I—" Stickle took a handkerchief from his pocket and patted his forehead with it. "This is highly irregular."

"Who is it?" Fontaine asked.

Harvey hesitated. "We'll have to notify the next of kin first, sir, but it's a city employee."

Mike stepped off the elevator and walked quickly down the hall.

"Excuse me, gentlemen," he said when he reached the judges. "We'll brief the mayor as soon as possible. You might want to wait down in her office."

Harvey unfastened the yellow tape and lifted it for Mike. As he reached to put it back in place, he stopped with his hand on the doorjamb.

"Eddie, here's a bullet hole. Looks like it hit the doorjamb edgewise."

Mike stepped back into the hallway and

112

examined the woodwork from the other side. "Must be still in there."

Eddie came to look.

"Mark that. We'll have to cut it out," Harvey said.

"Okay."

Harvey locked eyes with him. "This is your party. I'll be here every step of the way. If you need someone to run errands or get coffee, I'm your man."

Eddie snorted. "I can think of better ways to put you to use."

"Well, just a suggestion: I think you'd better interview the setup crew ASAP. Find out if Joey ate lunch with anyone. He called us at the office about 11:45. That was the last we heard from him. Someone must have seen him after that."

"Emily Rood was working with him." Eddie carefully examined the hole in the woodwork. "Too bad we'll have to remove a piece of this."

"Yeah. Talk to Emily first if you can."

The photographer arrived, and Harvey stood back for a moment to watch. Eddie went into action, snapping orders at his men and the photographer.

Mike nodded at Harvey. "He does all right, doesn't he? Too bad you can't read his hand-writing. I'll go run interference with the mayor." When he passed Eddie, he said, "I'll hold the press off for a while, but plan to give them something within a couple of hours."

Ron Legere, the detective sergeant, arrived at the doorway. "Hey, Harvey, you want my crew to come help you?"

"It's not that big a room, Ron," Harvey said. "We've got more people in here already than I like to have, but we can use your men to do background work."

Legere nodded. "Festival committee, family, active cases, collars recently released."

"You got it," Harvey said. "And Detective Thibodeau would like an immediate interview with Detective Rood."

"I'll send her over." Legere peered over Harvey's shoulder. "Can I see him? You understand, Harvey. I'm his supervisor."

"Of course. Come on in."

Ron strode across the room and crouched beside the body. He let out a deep sigh. "Man. This is just wrong." He stood up.

"Can you locate Joey's family and break the news to them?" Harvey asked. "The M.E. will be here any second, and I'm afraid the ID is going to leak out before we can tell his family. Joey was married, wasn't he?"

"The operative word being *was*," Legere replied. "Divorced last spring. His parents live in Deering. They may be here today, but I didn't hear him say so. There's a brother, too."

"Where's his ex?"

"Not sure. I'll find out. What about the girl-friend?"

Harvey raised his eyebrows.

"You know," Legere insisted. "Patrol officer Higgins."

"Sarah Benoit's new partner?"

"Yeah."

"Were she and Joey close?"

"She's been seeing him for a couple of months, I think. She's on traffic duty today."

"Best call her in and break the news. You don't want her hearing it elsewhere. There are probably rumors already."

"Sure. Report to you, Harvey?" Legere asked.

"No, this is Eddie's case. He discovered the body."

Legere nodded. "I'll put every man on it."

The medical examiner arrived, and Harvey knelt beside him, watching closely as Dr. McIntyre made his initial examination.

"Gunshot wound to the heart at close range," McIntyre muttered. "Bullet passed through, and out to the left of the spine."

"It's in the woodwork over there." Harvey pointed toward the doorway, and McIntyre squinted at the splintered wood. "I figure the shooter was standing behind the desk."

"Pretty straightforward, but we won't take him until Dr. Hogan gets here. Help me turn him over?" McIntyre continued his examination. He lifted Bolduc's right hand and scrutinized it, then let it fall. "Temperature . . . let's see . . ." He scrawled notes on a clipboard. "I suppose you want the clothes and effects sent to you."

"Yes, sir," said Harvey. "Can you estimate time of death?"

"You in charge, Captain?"

"Actually, Detective Thibodeau is. Direct reports to him." Eddie was closing his cell phone. Harvey called him over.

"Well, it can't have been much more than an hour," Dr. McIntyre said. "Two at the most."

Harvey left Eddie with the doctor while he checked with the other men on their progress.

"There are a million fingerprints in this room," Nate complained. He was still dusting wood-work, while Jimmy searched for matches on the laptop that was set up for them to use in the game.

"Whose, so far?" Harvey asked.

"The comptroller's, his secretary's, the mayor's. We've got a list of the people on the setup committee, but we'll have to get their prints for comparison."

"Jimmy, you handle that," Harvey directed.

"Then there's Governor Johnson's prints, and Joan Benoit Samuelson's," Nate went on. "She's the runner, right?"

"Yeah, won the first Olympic marathon for

116

women. That's got to be for the game," Harvey said. "I suspect you'll find Stephen King's, too, on one of those books up there."

"I got it," Jimmy Cook called from across the room, looking up from the computer. "I think we've got Steve's and Tabitha's both. And have you ever heard of Noel Stookey? He showed up in the computer."

"Famous singer," Harvey said. "Before your time. He's the 'Paul' of Peter, Paul and Mary. I'd rule him out as a suspect. That one's for the game, too."

"There's a slew of unidentified prints," Nate concluded.

"We need a list of employees, janitors, anyone who was in here regularly, in addition to the outsiders who came in for the game." Harvey ticked them off on his fingers. "Did any of the Bangor team come up here?"

"No, they're all down in the city clerk's office. They were kept sequestered before that, just like us."

"Anybody tell them about this?" Harvey asked.

"They're probably still down there feeling a dummy's pulse," Jimmy said.

Nate stood up. "This is going to take a lot of time, Harvey."

He nodded. "I've put Eddie in charge, but I'll be right here with you. If you need someone to help run prints, I'm available."

"Does Martha Stewart live in Maine?" Jimmy called.

"She's got a summer home in Bar Harbor," Tony said. He was on his knees near the body, picking up hairs from the rug with tweezers. "Uncle Bill and Aunt Laura went to brunch with her. I hear she's death on trespassers. Should we put out a warrant?"

"Ha, ha," Harvey said without humor. "I'd say you've found all the celebrity prints. Let's get on with it."

"Say, Captain." Tony stood up.

"What, Winfield?" Tony's brain worked in odd but wonderful ways, and Harvey always listened when he had an inspiration.

"Well, I was just wondering . . ." Tony looked at the body thoughtfully.

"You were wondering," Harvey prompted.

Tony looked at him then, a grin spreading over his boyish freckled face. "Where's the real dummy?"

Chapter 6

Eddie and Dr. McIntyre looked up, and everyone in the room was quiet, pondering Tony's question.

Harvey said, "It's your call, Eddie."

Eddie returned his gaze and stood up slowly. "Okay, Jimmy, you and Nate stay on the fingerprints. Tony, I want you to get a couple of patrolmen and start a search for the dummy. I'll be surprised if it's not in the building." He turned to Harvey. "Could you help me, Harv? Just go over the body with me and make sure I don't miss anything?"

"Sure."

Dr. McIntyre got stiffly to his feet. "Well, gentlemen, I'm stepping downstairs. I'll be back up when Dr. Hogan arrives." He ambled toward the doorway, raised the yellow tape, and ducked under it.

Eddie swallowed. "This one's getting to me, Harv."

"It's because you know him."

Eddie nodded. There were beads of sweat on his forehead, although it wasn't hot in the room.

"You okay?" Harvey asked.

"I think so."

"Take your jacket off."

Eddie peeled off his sport coat. "Have they dusted this chair yet?"

"Here, lay it on my briefcase."

Eddie draped his jacket over the briefcase. "As far as I can tell, Joey was just carrying his usual gear. His gun is in his holster. He didn't draw it. So, he didn't realize he was in danger, right? I mean, he'd have reached for his weapon if he knew he was going to be shot at."

Harvey nodded. "He didn't stand a chance."

Eddie tugged at the knot on his tie. "The way he fell—splat on his face. His arms weren't spread out."

They crouched beside Joey's body and pondered every nuance for several minutes. At last Harvey stood. "I think you've analyzed everything."

"Captain?" Tony was at the door.

Harvey smiled. "Tell Detective Thibodeau."

"Oh, right. Sorry, Eddie."

" 'S'okay," Eddie said.

"We've got the dummy. He's sitting on a toilet in one of the stalls in the men's room down the hall."

"That's creative." Eddie reached for his jacket. "Did you dust for prints?"

"Not yet. We probably won't get any prints, except for the setup crew."

"Don't assume that." Eddie followed Tony into the hallway. A knot of people filled the end of the hall, kept back by a uniformed officer.

"Your public awaits you." Tony nodded toward the group, and Eddie glanced at them.

"I guess they want a press conference."

"You wanna see the real dummy first?"

Eddie sighed. "Tony, it's a dummy. You don't have to say *real* dummy. I mean, it's not like Joey is a *fake* dummy."

"But why did they bother to move him?" Tony asked, leading the way into the men's room. Harvey followed but stopped at the doorway to the men's room while Tony and Eddie entered.

"If they left him in the office, anyone looking in there would see two bodies," Eddie said. "This way, they just saw Joey and assumed it was the dummy. It bought them time."

Tony shrugged. "Sounds plausible, Shake-speare. They stashed him in here and locked the stall door."

Eddie nodded. "So anyone using the men's room would figure it was a person in there, if they saw the shoes. They had to crawl out underneath, though?"

"I'd say so."

"That means the person who did it wasn't a very big guy."

"Right."

"Could you do it?"

Tony frowned. "I suppose. You don't want me to demonstrate, do you?"

"Well, I don't think it was a kid, but still, there's not that much room between the dividers and the floor."

"You're saying someone as paunchy as the comptroller couldn't do it?"

"Something like that. Could have been a woman."

"Naw," Tony protested. "A woman carrying a male dummy into the men's room? Now, that would be noticeable."

Eddie stared glumly at the dummy. "We're sure this is our dummy? Bangor has a different one downstairs?"

"I think so."

"Let's make sure. Get Stickle or somebody else from the committee to identify this one as ours."

"Oh, brother. We're down to getting a positive ID on a dummy."

Eddie came to the doorway, and Harvey walked with him back to the comptroller's office.

"Should I do the press conference now?" Eddie asked.

"You know what you want to say?"

"Not really."

Harvey nodded. "Decide what you need to give them, and what you need to hold back."

"Did they find Joey's mother yet?"

"Yeah, Ron called me a couple minutes ago. They've told Mrs. Bolduc, that is, Joey's mother, and also his ex-wife. His mother called his brother and sisters. I think it's safe to release his name now."

"What about Debbie Higgins?" Eddie asked.

"I don't know."

"Too bad about her."

"Yeah," Harvey said. "I wish she wasn't mixed up in this."

"Joey was a fun guy." Eddie felt somehow that he needed to defend the dead detective.

"I know, and he was a good cop. He did really well on the computer training last fall. Made a few bloopers in his day, but don't we all?"

Eddie nodded.

Harvey put a hand on his shoulder. "You want me to back you up for the press conference?"

"Would you?"

"Sure." Harvey nodded toward Jimmy Cook, who was lifting fingerprints from the comptroller's desk.

"Jim, the boss and I are going down and talk to the press," Eddie said. "You okay?"

"Yeah, I'm all set."

Eddie nodded and looked over at Nate, who was examining the rug next to the body. "You and Nate, don't let anyone else in here except the M.E. Well, and Tony."

"Copy that," Nate said without looking up.

"Come on." Harvey went with Eddie to the elevator.

On the way down, Eddie quickly outlined the points he thought he should make to the reporters.

"Sounds good," Harvey said.

Eddie drew a deep breath and opened the front door. He positioned himself on the steps of City Hall. Jill Weymouth and Mike Browning came out of the crowd.

"You got this, Eddie?" Mike said.

"Yeah."

"Good. Mayor Weymouth and I will be right here if you need us." They stood behind him, near Harvey.

Eddie looked out over the crowd and swallowed. Hundreds of people jammed the sidewalk and the street beyond, where half a dozen patrolmen directed traffic, keeping it moving at a crawl. The grass no one was supposed to stand on, between the sidewalk and the building, was taking a beating.

Eddie glimpsed faces he knew. Harvey had sent most of his family home, but Jennifer and her father had stayed. Eddie's younger sister, Lisa, gave him a low thumbs-up from the curb. His mother stood beside her. Of all the onlookers, their expressions were the least distressed. *They're just proud of me for being on top of things. They never met Joey.*

Clustered on the steps below him, reporters and cameramen from every television station and newspaper in the southern half of the state vied for the best spots.

"Spell your name for them," Harvey whispered in his ear, and Eddie smiled grimly. He looked at the reporters and picked out Leeanne. When her eyes met his, she smiled sorrowfully. Eddie approached the clutch of microphones that the TV crews had set up.

"I'm very sorry to have to tell you that we have lost one of our own today," Eddie began. "Detective Joseph Bolduc was a credit to the Portland Police Department, and he was a personal friend of mine."

He took a deep breath and went on, slowly enumerating the basic facts of the case. When he was finished, he turned to go back inside, and Harvey walked beside him.

"Not bad." Harvey's eyes told Eddie it was a deliberate understatement.

"Thanks. Jennifer going home now?"

"Yeah, I told her and George to head out, and not to wait supper for us."

"How late do you want to work tonight?"

"Oh, I don't know. Not too late. You get diminishing returns after a certain point. Seven, maybe, then go home and unwind. Get a good sleep and come in early." Harvey punched the *up* button by the elevator door.

"Eddie—"

They both turned. Leeanne walked briskly toward them.

Eddie caught a quick breath. "Hey, Leeanne. I can't give you anything special."

"I wouldn't ask you to. I just wanted to . . . talk to you."

The elevator doors opened.

"I'll go up and see how the guys are doing," Harvey said. "Come over to the house later, Leeanne."

"Thanks. I may be working late on this."

When the door had closed, she looked up at Eddie. She opened her mouth, then closed it and shrugged slightly.

Eddie looked down the hall as Mayor Weymouth and several other people approached. "Look, there's an empty room upstairs where we've been interviewing people." He led her past the elevator to the stairway and through the door.

"I can't stay long," she warned, climbing the steps beside him.

"When's your deadline?"

"Nine. You looked good at the press conference. Is someone going to tape the news for you?"

"Probably my mother. I don't know."

They emerged into the upper hallway, and he took her to the door of the conference room, scanned the room quickly, then drew her inside.

"What did you want to say?" Eddie asked.

"Just that . . . I'm sorry."

"What for?"

"A lot of things. I've been really rotten to you. I've been talking to Jennifer and Harvey more lately, and to Mary Rowland. They've all kind of helped me . . . to see some things." She looked up timidly. Eddie's pulse began to pound. Her blue eyes rimmed with dark lashes had always affected him that way. He remembered when she'd been frightened of him, and he'd moved ever so slowly to gain her confidence. She looked that way now, like a doe on the alert, ready to bolt.

"What kind of things?" he asked softly.

"I've been very selfish, for one."

He thought about that. It was true, but it didn't anger him anymore. He looked up at the ceiling. "I guess I was pretty selfish, too."

She smiled, but it skewed a little. "I was thinking more about what I wanted than what you needed, or what God would want me to do. I think . . . I wanted to hurt you, but when I knew I had, it felt terrible."

He swallowed hard. "I couldn't tell."

"I was good at hiding it, wasn't I?"

He nodded.

"I didn't want you to know I felt guilty and . . . lonely."

"You didn't need to send the ring back. It was a gift."

"I—I couldn't look at it. And Marie—" Leeanne's pleading eyes filled with tears.

"What's my mother got to do with it?" he asked.

"She got after you about it, didn't she?"

"How did you know?"

Leeanne's top lip twitched. "I knew, is all."

"Well, she's French."

Leeanne laughed, just a sliver of a laugh, but Eddie couldn't help smiling.

"*Tu me manques,*" he whispered.

She caught her breath. He could barely hear her when she replied, "I miss you, too."

His left hand twitched, and he longed to reach out and touch her face. He remembered how her warm, smooth cheek felt against his.

"Call my cell phone at eight o'clock." His voice was rough. "I might have something for you then."

"I didn't come here to get information."

"I know. If you had, I wouldn't have offered."

"Don't treat me special if you're not supposed to."

He shrugged. "Sometimes a tenacious reporter keeps calling until the last minute, and sometimes it pays off."

She smiled then. "Thanks."

"I've got to get back to work now."

They stepped out into the hallway, and Leeanne started to turn to the right.

"This way, *ma belle*." He took her hand and led her to the stairway door, his heart racing. She looked up at him again in the doorway, her lashes lowered, as though she didn't dare look him full in the face. He released her hand reluctantly. "Call me. Don't forget."

"I won't."

Harvey said nothing when Eddie entered the comptroller's office, and they worked side by side for another three hours, carefully filling out their charts and grids, noting what tests the crime lab should perform on each piece of evidence.

At six o'clock, Harvey stuck his mechanical pencil in his pocket and rubbed his eyes. "I think we're about done here."

"Me, too. The CSIs will package everything up." Eddie looked around at the detectives still bent over their assignments. "Pack it up, guys. We'll start at 8 a.m., in the office." He looked at Harvey. "You going back there now?"

"There are a few things I'd like to check on."

Eddie nodded. "I want to go over the interviews and see the reports Ron's men made tonight. Then I'll do some planning for tomorrow."

"Good thinking. You'll want to schedule more interviews. Make a list, and Paula can do some calling when she comes in. Put me wherever you want me. Just use me like you would any other detective."

"Why are you doing this, Harv?"

"Because I'm the captain, and I don't want to do all the paperwork."

Eddie laughed. "Sure. As if you're lazy."

"Just letting you stretch your wings."

"You're not planning to retire or anything?"

"Rest easy, buddy. I foresee a long working partnership for us." Harvey took out his phone and called the dispatcher for an unmarked car to take them back to the police station, while Eddie checked in with the patrolman detailed to watch the crime scene on the evening shift.

"Hey, Captain, you won the challenge," Charlie Doran, the dispatcher told Harvey over the phone.

"How's that?"

"You won."

Harvey laughed. "Eddie, we won the stupid game. We came into it even with Bangor this morning, and our Public Works guys won their contest. It seems Jimmy slipped the list of celebrity fingerprints to Myron Stickle while we were talking to the M.E. Bangor didn't get all theirs until ten minutes later, so even though we forfeited on the murder, Portland won the challenge."

"Joey would love this." Eddie pulled on his jacket.

"Yeah. You'd better see the ex tomorrow."

"Roxanne," Eddie said.

"You know her?"

"I met her a few times. Before the divorce, you know?"

Harvey nodded. "Why did they get divorced?"

"I don't know, but I could guess."

"Joey was unfaithful?"

"I don't think so. He was sociable, but he loved her. It's the hours, you know? The wives get tired of waiting. First they get mad, then they get bored."

Harvey sighed deeply. Eddie knew he'd dealt with the syndrome firsthand in his youth.

"Sorry, Harv."

"It's okay. I just . . . empathize too much with these guys. No matter what anyone says, quality time is no substitute for quantity time. What's she like?"

"A little hard. Slightly disillusioned. A bit of a nag, I thought."

"Pretty?"

Eddie shrugged. "Not my type. Flashy." They went into the hallway and boarded the elevator.

"You and Leeanne are speaking," Harvey observed.

"Just a few words."

"Was that enough?"

"Maybe." Eddie smiled faintly. "What can I give her at eight o'clock that will endear me to her forever?"

"That's too easy, Ed."

"I mean for her story."

"Oh. So, we're not talking about defrosting the ring yet."

"Not yet, *mon ami*."

Chapter 7

Beth and Leeanne piled into Jennifer's minivan with the Larsons for the ride to Bible study Wednesday night.

"How you feeling, Beth?" Jennifer asked.

"Tired."

"She's been doing too much." Leeanne snapped her seatbelt in place and leaned over to goggle at Connor, who sat in his car seat, solemnly staring at her. "Hey, nephew. How you doing, pot pie?"

At the church they sat together, and Harvey held the baby.

"Let me hold him," Leeanne pleaded, leaning past Jennifer toward him.

"Later. I've been working all day, and I want to hold my boy."

"That's as grouchy as I've ever heard Harvey," Leeanne said.

"Not me," Beth told her. "He used to crab at me all the time."

Harvey smiled. "That's before I was married and mellow."

"I was afraid you'd all be working late again," Jennifer said.

133

"Well, I'm the boss, so I can knock off whenever I want." Harvey held Connor up so he could examine the baby's tooth. "I don't know where Eddie is. I told him to give himself time to get over here."

"How's it going for you?" Jennifer asked Leeanne.

"The last three days have been really rough. My editor wanted front page stories every day."

"Which have been very lucid," Harvey said.

"Thanks to what you and Eddie have fed me."

He shrugged. "Some writers would take the same facts you've had and make hash of them."

"Well, thanks. I turned my copy in early tonight and told them I am absolutely not working tomorrow. I have three classes tomorrow, and I already have a ton of homework, even if it's the first week of school."

"Who'll cover the murder story?" Beth asked.

"I don't care. Ryan Toothaker's my guess, though. He hates it how they keep assigning me the crime stories."

"He's had the police beat for quite a while," Harvey reasoned.

"I know, and I've tried to tell him it's not my fault. He figures it's because I have connections, like I'm part of the Mafia or something."

"You mean, if you weren't related to me, you'd be writing obituaries?" Harvey asked.

"Something like that."

"Forget it. I talked to John Russell. You're a good writer, and he knows I won't leak sensitive stuff to you, any more than I would to Ryan."

"Well, Eddie's been great, I have to admit. We've definitely had the most complete coverage of this case."

"I'm glad you and Eddie can at least work together." Jennifer squeezed Leeanne's hand.

"Me, too."

Pastor Rowland began the service, and they all turned their attention on him. As they stood for the first hymn, Eddie came in and slipped into a pew across the aisle with Beth's brother, Rick Bradley, and his wife. Leeanne glanced toward him, then away. She refused to let herself look at him again, but she couldn't help wondering if he had deliberately come late to church to avoid talking to her. She hoped he wouldn't stop coming to church because of her. Her parents had started going regularly in Skowhegan now, with her youngest brother, Randy. Maybe she would go home for the weekend and go to church with them on Sunday. Then Eddie wouldn't have to see her.

Jeff had Thursday off, and Jennifer invited him and Beth to dinner, along with Carl and Margaret Turner and Eddie. When Leeanne arrived home from work and learned that Eddie was coming, she almost made an excuse to go out again, but something inside her told her that would be unspeakably rude to Jennifer and Harvey and the Turners, let alone Eddie.

She went to her room to change, and when Jennifer called her down, she chose a seat between Margaret and her nine-year-old daughter, Julia, and tried not to look at Eddie. She knew that if she did, her emotions would run riot. From the first time she'd laid eyes on Eddie Thibodeau, he had always evoked a strong reaction in her, and right now, catching a glance from him might drive her to tears.

"I'm so glad you invited us over," Margaret said after Harvey asked the blessing. "It seems like we're all so busy, we don't get to see much of each other outside of church and doctor appointments." She and Carl were both doctors, and busy was an understatement in reference to their lifestyle.

"Nice to see you all," Carl agreed.

"You come over anytime you want," Jennifer said with a big smile for Margaret. "Have you moved into your new office yet?"

"Not yet, but soon," Margaret said. The Turners were having an addition built on their house, so that she could move her obstetrics and gynecology office close to home. She and Carl wanted to expand their family, but Margaret didn't want to give up her medical practice.

Eddie sat quietly between Carl and Jeff. He

answered an occasional question, and his eyes strayed often to Leeanne.

When Jennifer got up to serve coffee and dessert, Leeanne went to help her. As she distributed plates of blueberry pie, she was surprised to hear Carl bring up the topic of Sunday morning's sermon.

"I get the feeling Margaret and I totally missed the boat on some things when it comes to marriage," he said.

Margaret smiled ruefully. "Well, not completely, but yeah. Mr. Rowland talked about some things I never even thought of before—or if I did, I would think it was off the wall. But, you know, it kind of made sense."

"You all heard her say that." Carl looked around at them expectantly, waving his fork. "My wife said that Pastor Rowland's remarks on the Christian home made sense."

Harvey laughed. "I know how Margaret feels. When I first started hearing all this stuff, I wondered how people could really believe something so outmoded and pedestrian."

"But the man is supposed to be the head of the house." Carl's eyes held a challenge.

"Well, yeah," Harvey said, "but not the dictator. As I understand it now, the home is a model of the church. Christ is the head of the church, and the husband—if there is one—is head of the home. But that doesn't make the wife a lackey."

"Does he treat you like a minion?" Margaret asked Jennifer.

Jennifer's eyes widened. "Are you kidding? Harvey treats me like a princess."

"Is that what it means when they say a man's home is his castle?" Julia asked.

"Something like that," Jeff told her.

Harvey grinned. "I'd be happy to serve as a kitchen slave in Jennifer's castle."

"Aw," Beth said, and everyone laughed.

As the discussion went on, Leeanne allowed herself to look at Eddie once, then again. He was paying attention to the banter, but he seemed a little distracted. Was he thinking about what they were saying, and what the pastor had talked about on Sunday? She'd been thinking all week, off and on, about how her actions may have demoralized Eddie over the past couple of months. But his behavior hadn't been stellar, either.

We should have learned all this months ago, in our counseling. Leeanne had wondered as she sat in the pew if the pastor was purposely targeting them with the topic, but now she saw that others were deeply affected by it as well.

"It makes so much sense," Beth said.

Margaret nodded. "If we'd known God had a plan for families, our home would have been a lot different over the past fifteen years."

Carl, who was a general practitioner, smiled ruefully. "There are a lot of things I wish I'd known fifteen years ago, but I was probably too hard-headed to learn them then."

"That's the way God is," Harvey said. "He brings us along at our own pace. When we're pliable, He's always ready to teach us something deeper."

Beth shifted in her chair, and Jeff smiled at her, reaching for her hand.

"I thought I knew a lot about being a wife," Beth said. "My mom and my sister-in-law have been good examples. But since I got married, I've discovered there's a whole lot I don't know."

"But you're willing to learn," Harvey said. "And Jeff is, too. It's not all up to the wife to keep the home harmonious. In fact, I think the main burden is on the husband."

I was always so tractable, Leeanne thought. *Abby was the rebel of the family. But I had to have my own miserable rebellion at last, and it's cost me dear.* She glanced toward Eddie again. *Lord, help me to be willing to just be his friend, if that's what's best.* But her heart ached for more than that. He turned his luminous brown eyes on her again, and slowly a smile began on his face, sending a bittersweet hope shooting through her.

The Turners lingered after the meal, and Harvey suggested they all move into the living room.

"I'm taking Beth home," Jeff said in Leeanne's ear. "She's tired. You get Harvey or—somebody—to walk you home when you're ready."

She nodded with a shiver of anticipation. Would she dare to ask Eddie? She shot him a quick look. He was sitting still, listening to Carl and Harvey's animated discussion on the upcoming election. Jennifer helped Julia hold Connor, while she listened to Margaret talk about why the builders were behind schedule on her new home office.

When at last the Turners were out the door, Harvey looked at Leeanne in pretended shock. "Are you still here? You want to sleep here tonight?"

"I hadn't thought about it, but I could," Leeanne said. "Jeff's got tonight and tomorrow night off."

"Stay," Jennifer said eagerly. "Just call and tell Beth. I've missed you so much. I'll lend you pajamas."

Leeanne smiled. "You talked me into it. I wanted to talk something over with you guys, anyway." She went to the kitchen to use the phone, regretting slightly the imagined walk across the yards with Eddie. *There's time. If it's right, and if it's in God's plan, there's time.*

"All set?" Harvey asked when she reentered the living room.

"Yeah, as a matter of fact, I think they're glad to be rid of me."

Jennifer laughed. "Well, they haven't been married *that* long."

"That's right," said Harvey. "With Jeff's schedule, they need privacy when he's home."

Leeanne shook her head. "How come nobody clues me in on these things?"

Eddie stood up. "Guess I'd better get going."

"Hey, no," Jennifer cried. "You're not leaving, are you?"

He looked at Harvey, fidgeting a little with his shoulder holster. He had worked late again and come straight from the office. "Well, I, uh, thought it was a family conference thing."

"You're family," Jennifer protested.

He stood uncertainly, looking from her to Harvey, avoiding Leeanne's eyes.

"Sit down, Ed," said Harvey, and Eddie sat.

"So, what are we talking about?" Jennifer asked Leeanne brightly.

"Well, if you guys don't mind, I'd like to show you the book offer Bob Hoffsted got for me. It's pretty good for an unpublished author, I think. He says it's a good advance for someone new."

"You've decided you want to do the book?" Harvey asked.

"I think so." Leeanne sat down on the edge of the hearth and faced Harvey earnestly. "See, this is what I thought: the advance would pay off my student loans. I'd give that to Mom and Dad. They're having a rough time, with Travis in UMO this fall. They said they'd help all of us kids through, but with Abby and me in college together for a couple years, they had to get these loans. I really want to pay that back. Then later, if there are any royalties, I'll have that. And I'll have a published book as a credit."

"That will look good on your résumé," Harvey agreed.

"Well, if I ever need it," she countered. "I think . . . " She studied the wool braided rug at her feet, then met Harvey's look. "I think I want to do it."

"And what about the job?"

She shook her head. "I know I can't do both at once. Not with school, too."

"You can't give up school," Jennifer said firmly.

"No, I won't. I'm too close to finishing." Leeanne frowned down at the rug. "It's been a really tough decision, and I've been putting it off, praying about it and trying to figure out what's best. But Mr. Hoffsted said if I don't get the book contract signed really soon, the publisher might withdraw the offer. The case is getting older." She looked squarely at Harvey. "I want to quit the paper." She didn't dare look toward Eddie, but he was sitting very still.

"Quit, as in resign forever?" Jennifer asked.

"I—well, I don't know. They want a two-year contract, but I don't want to box myself in like that."

"Very wise," Harvey said.

"Really?" She was suddenly unsure. "I mean, job security is worth something, isn't it?" She twisted the edge of her cardigan in both hands.

Harvey leaned forward and covered her hands with his. "If you feel you need to support yourself for the rest of your life, then job security is probably a good thing. It's kind of like investing in municipal bonds."

Leeanne stared at him blankly, and Harvey chuckled.

"With a municipal bond, you know exactly what you're getting. The rate is steady and sure. You're not taking any risks. No unexpected losses, no surprise dividends."

She nodded slowly. "Do you invest in bonds?"

Harvey scowled at her. "What do I look like?"

"Don't you know what his latest investment is?" Jennifer asked, smiling.

"I guess not."

"He's putting fifty thousand dollars into Mike and Sharon's hunting camp."

Leeanne stared at her. "Wow." She turned to Harvey. He smiled complacently. "What if Mike blows it?"

"Then I'll buy him out and sell the property to some millionaire."

Leeanne laughed in delight.

"But Mike won't lose on this," Harvey said. "I've made him do his homework to make sure the enterprise will succeed. He and Sharon are going up this weekend with an architect. They'll use Peter's drawings as a starting point and take it from there. Mike's already researching where he wants to place his ads in January."

"They'll start advertising in January?"

"Yup, and taking reservations for next fall," Harvey said. "They plan to open August thirtieth."

"I wish I was that confident."

"Well, Mike's got thirty-five years of experience that you don't have. He knows what's realistic and what's not."

"Do you think my plan is realistic?"

"Go get the contract, little girl. Let me see it."

Leeanne hopped up and retrieved her purse from the floor beside the sofa.

"I'm going to put Connor down," Jennifer said. The baby was asleep in her arms, and she got up carefully to take him to his crib.

Leeanne handed the folded papers to Harvey. "I told Mr. Hoffsted I'd bring him this tomorrow."

Harvey studied the text thoughtfully. "There are two different issues here, and as I told you before, I think you should keep them separate. If you want to write the book, well, I'm not an expert, but Bob Hoffsted is. I'd take his word on this. It seems fair, even generous, for a beginner. Of course, it will be a massive project. Things like that always take longer than you expect. And your agent will take his cut."

Leeanne nodded soberly.

"The second issue is the newspaper. Do you think if you turn down the two-year contract, they won't want you to work for them anymore?"

She blinked, thinking about it. "When Mr. Russell talked to me about it, it seemed like an all-or-nothing deal."

"He knows you're young and inexperienced," Harvey reminded her. "He's told me how highly he rates your work. I'll bet if you said no, he'd still try to get you to come back to the paper after Christmas, on any terms."

"Really?"

Harvey shrugged. "How important is it?"

"I'm not sure. I mean . . . maybe I'd just write books." She looked at him questioningly.

"Write up the Joey Bolduc murder next spring?" Harvey asked.

"I wasn't really thinking of that."

He smiled. "Leeanne, honey, listen to me. You can write anything you want. John Russell can't tell you what to write or who to write for. If you want to write crime books, do it. If you want to write news stories, do it. If you want to write science fiction, or romance novels, or children's picture books, do it. Need I go on?"

"I guess not . . ."

Harvey looked at his watch. "Listen, I need to make a phone call. Would you excuse me for just a couple of minutes?"

He went into the study, and she glanced across at Eddie. He was sitting still in his chair, watching her pensively.

"Eddie, what do you think about all this?"

He stirred. "I'm probably not the one to ask."

Of course you're the one to ask, her heart screamed. *You're the only one who really counts anymore.* She took a deep breath and tried to keep her voice calm. "I'd really appreciate your opinion."

He leaned forward, clasping his hands on his knees. "I think Harvey's right."

Leeanne tossed her head, sending her dark hair shimmering. "Well, natch. He's always right."

"No, no, I think he'd be the first to dispute that. But . . . he's never wrong."

She laughed.

"Seriously, I think what he said about your writing is true. If God has put it in your heart to write, then you should do it. But don't let other people tell you what to write."

"I think I can do a good job on this book. I've already made some notes and an outline, and I've got the news stories I wrote when it happened. I want to try it."

"Then do it. Let Hoffsted handle the business end for you. Did Harvey tell you we did a background check on him?"

"No."

"He's clean as a whistle. We couldn't find any dissatisfied clients. I went and talked to Thelma Blake, too. She says he was always straight with her and Martin. She figures she'd be several million poorer if it weren't for him."

"You guys went to all that trouble for me?"

He turned his huge brown eyes on her, and she held her breath. If only he would give her some indication that he still loved her. She knew he cared, but he cared about her sisters, too. She didn't want to be Eddie's little sister. And she had hurt him badly, there was no denying it. He might not want to lay himself open to that again.

"If you do the book, you'll have to rehash the whole hostage thing," he said quietly. "Beth was badly traumatized—you were, too. Can you handle it?"

She made herself look away from those eyes that made her want to sing and cry at the same time. "I think maybe writing about it would help me put it in perspective."

"I had to see the department's shrink after," Eddie said.

"Because you shot Marcus Rutledge?"

"Yeah. But you never got any counseling."

"You think that's still affecting me?"

"I didn't say that. It's just—well, sometimes you think a thing is over, but months later you're still dreaming about it."

"I had a lot of support then." His eyes darkened, and she said hastily, "Not that I don't now, I didn't mean that. I just meant—well, I don't think talking to a psychologist is a magic pill that makes everything better."

"No, you're right. Since I got saved, I can see that spiritual healing is more critical. Emotions and mental images can be controlled if your spiritual life is right."

She sat very still, thinking about what he had said and very aware of his presence. What would he do if she walked over and put her hand out to touch him?

Eddie broke the eye contact first, and looked off toward the Murillo print on the side wall, where the Christ child stood with his hand on the back of a woolly lamb. "I'm glad we're talking again."

"Me, too," she breathed. "Harvey's right about another thing. We need to be friends. I'm sorry . . . " She couldn't list all the things she was sorry about, so she let it hang there.

Eddie stood up slowly and walked to the large window that fronted on Van Cleeve Lane. He shoved his hands into his pockets and stood with his back to her, looking out across the street, toward the light in the kitchen of Bud and Janice Parker's ranch house. The strap of his holster was dark against his blue shirt. Leeanne watched him, wondering if somehow she had set them back a notch or two. She shivered and pulled her cardigan close around her.

Eddie came to the house early to run the next morning, and Jeff joined them. Harvey watched Eddie carefully as they stretched in the driveway.

"How you coming on the Bolduc case?" Jeff asked, bouncing a little to touch his toes.

"It's a slow process," said Harvey.

"We've ruled out the immediately family," Eddie said. "That narrows it down to about a million suspects."

"Are you still negotiating for better hours?" Harvey asked.

"I think we'll take the four days on-three off schedule," Jeff said, "but we're not giving up the idea of twelve-hour shifts."

"Beth will need you more than ever when the baby's born."

"Yeah, I know. I'm hoping Leeanne will stay for a while." Jeff glanced at Eddie. "Sorry, Ed, I didn't mean—"

"One man's loss, another's gain," Eddie shrugged. "Come on." He set off, jogging onto the sidewalk.

Jeff looked at Harvey contritely. "Did I—?"

"Don't worry about it," Harvey said, starting off after Eddie. "But Jenny and I will help out all we can. We're used to the 2 a.m. drill."

149

After the three-mile run, they ended up in the Wainthrops' yard. Jeff walked slowly across the back lawn, panting, and sat down on the back steps. "Eddie, I didn't mean anything before. I'm not glad you broke up. We're friends, right?"

Eddie laughed. "Oh, yeah, I'm friends with everybody. Even Leeanne."

Enlightenment dawned on Jeff's face. "She gave you the *friends* spiel?"

"Yup. I'm *persona non grata* now."

Jeff shook his head. "I used to think she was tenderhearted. All those baby goats and everything. How wrong can you be?"

"Hey, *friends* isn't so bad." Harvey thought he could see hope there, but Jeff and Eddie's expressions said otherwise.

Eddie kicked at a tuft of grass beside the steps. "It's like she demoted me in July, from general to private, and now she's promoted me to private first class. Sorry, but I don't think I can stand trying to work my way up through the ranks again."

"It beats the alternative," Harvey said.

"What, mustering out? Do I get an honorable discharge?"

"I think you deserve a Purple Heart," Jeff said. "Wounded in combat."

"Or a Black and Blue Heart," Eddie muttered.

"Well, if you re-enlist, sometimes you get a signing bonus." Harvey felt the metaphor was wearing a little thin. "Look, you want my advice? I know you didn't ask for it—"

"You're right, I didn't," Eddie said. "You're the one who told her we should be friends."

Harvey sighed in exasperation. "I didn't mean it that way. I basically said you and Leeanne need to make peace, because you'll be seeing each other for the rest of your lives. Church, family gatherings, whatever, and it affects everyone around you. You can't fight forever."

Eddie sat down on the grass. "We're not fighting now. We're *friends*."

"All right, forget it." Harvey turned toward the gate between Jeff's yard and his.

"Harvey, come back," Jeff said lazily.

"Yeah, let's hear it," said Eddie. "Tell us what you'd do if Jennifer suddenly told you she wanted to be friends."

"How did this come about, anyway?" Jeff asked.

"Oh, Harvey left us alone for two minutes last night, and she laid the speech on me."

"I had to make a phone call," Harvey protested.

"Yeah, yeah, an urgent phone call." Eddie flopped back on the grass.

"Can I help it? I thought you two were ready to talk."

"Who did you call?" Jeff asked.

Harvey stooped and worked at his shoelace. "The weather," he growled.

"You had this urgent need to call the weather?" Jeff said.

"I knew I should have left when Jeff did," Eddie moaned.

Harvey eyed them both testily. "You guys are trying to push me over the edge, aren't you?"

"Not far to go," Eddie said.

Jeff laughed. "The trouble with you is, you never had brothers. You need to be picked on once in a while, Captain."

"That's right," Eddie agreed.

Harvey stared at him, then slowly walked closer. "You don't have to listen to me, Eddie. At the office, you're pretty good at taking orders, but out here, you don't have to. I'm your friend, that's all."

Eddie sat up straight. "Harv, you know I respect you more than—" He broke off. "Look, I'm sorry. This whole thing has thrown me off balance. I guess I've let my pride get in the way. Again."

Harvey looked back toward his house. Jennifer and Connor were safe inside. How could life be so sweet for him, and so hard for Eddie? In his mind he could see Jennifer, fixing him with her solemn gray eyes and saying, *This is not your fault.*

"Come on, Harvey." Jeff stood up. "Let's get breakfast, and you can tell us what your strategy would be."

"Isn't Leeanne in there?" Eddie asked looking toward Jeff's back door.

"Yeah, she came over this morning," Jeff said.

"If she's around, we can't discuss this over pancakes."

"Maybe we should eat at my house," Harvey suggested.

"No, it's my turn," Jeff insisted. "Beth was getting up when I left. Come on. We eat, we pray, we plan a campaign of reconquest."

"Well, let's eat *somewhere,* or we'll be late for work." Eddie brushed off his shorts, and they went up the steps.

"Hey, fellas." Beth was placing coffee mugs on the table. "Sit right down."

Leeanne set a carton of orange juice on the counter. "I've got to get to class. I'm out of here." She kissed Harvey on the cheek, then Jeff. "Ooh. Sweaty brothers. When you pray, remember me. I've got a test in interviewing today." She went briskly into the living room. "I'm going to Skowhegan right after school, so I'll see you all Sunday night. 'Bye, Beth. 'Bye, guys."

The front door closed, and the three men stood looking at each other.

"Sit down," Beth repeated.

"That girl is cracked," Jeff said. "She just ignored Eddie."

"It's okay when you're *friends,*" Eddie said pointedly. "What I don't get is why she needs a

153

class in interviewing. She does it every day for a living. She could probably teach that professor a thing or two."

"She needs the piece of paper," Beth reminded him.

Jeff pulled her close and kissed her temple. "Eddie's right. It would be like you taking a class in being a good wife."

Beth smiled and pushed him toward his chair. "Or you taking Flattery 101."

Jeff asked the blessing, and she poured coffee for them all, and a glass of milk for herself.

"Jeff gets three days off next week," she confided to Harvey as she sat down.

"Terrific. You want Leeanne to move back in with us?"

"No."

"Sounds good to me," said Jeff.

Beth swatted his shoulder. "She's sweet, and she's been a big help to me. I'm very thankful she's been here nights while you're gone."

Jeff shrugged. "Yeah, but she's been a brat lately."

"I think she's past that," Beth countered. "She's been very open the past couple of weeks. I think she's really trying to get things right with the Lord."

"What about with Eddie?" Jeff asked.

Beth smiled sadly at Eddie. "One thing at a time."

"Well, this is a tactical session," Jeff said. "If you don't want to hear our plans, you'd better not listen."

"Plans for what?"

"Look, fellas, maybe this isn't such a great idea." Harvey was a little embarrassed. "I wasn't saying it's a surefire cure. I was just going to tell you what I would do in this situation, that's all."

"Let me guess," said Beth. "You'd pray a lot first."

"Well, of course."

"And if you felt you should proceed?" Jeff asked.

"He'd think about how he won her the first time," Beth answered for him. "I seem to recall him hanging around night after night when Jennifer and I were roommates. Flowers, fireworks, and maybe a little poetry thrown in for good measure."

Harvey weighed that, remembering the rush he had given Jennifer. "Well, maybe. I don't remember the poetry. But Leeanne and Jennifer are two different women."

"Ha!" Jeff cried. "You can say that again. Anyone want more bacon?"

"I'm just saying, Eddie's got to move slowly here. It took time to court her the first time. You're back at Square One, buddy, and you've got to take it easy." Harvey eyed the bacon plate regretfully and passed it to Eddie.

"I think Leeanne wants to be sure she does whatever she does for the right reasons now," Beth said.

"So, what do I do?" Eddie asked.

"Wait for her to grow up," Jeff said.

"Have you really had enough of Leeanne?" Harvey sat back in his chair and waited while Eddie took a bite of his pancake and chewed slowly.

Finally, Eddie swallowed. "My ego is telling me to say yes, but the truth is, I'd do anything for her, Harv. I guess you know that."

Harvey smiled. "Then be patient."

"Now, Sarah, just tell me a little bit about Deborah." Harvey sat across the table from patrol officer Sarah Benoit in the Priority Unit's interview room. He liked Sarah and had known her since she joined the department. She had proven herself competent and was now senior partner to Deborah Higgins.

"Debbie's doing all right," Sarah said. "I think she has good instincts."

"I've looked at her personnel record. Just tell me about her as a person. Do you get along? Do you go shopping together? Any double dates?" Harvey smiled, remembering the day Sarah had gone to the lighthouse at Portland Head with him and Jennifer and Eddie.

"No, we don't mix much outside the station."

Sarah smiled ruefully. "I miss Cheryl." Her old partner, Cheryl Yeaton, had been promoted to night patrol sergeant.

"She's doing a great job," Harvey said.

"Yeah, she'll probably have your job in a few years."

He smiled. "You never know. Probably some other town will tap her as their first female police chief."

"Wouldn't that be something? She could do it." Sarah sobered. "I'm not sure what you want to know, Captain."

"You used to call me Harvey."

"That was when we went to auctions and picnics together."

He winced. "Guess we don't mix much anymore."

She searched his face intently. "Well, anyone as tight with Eddie as you are . . ."

"I thought you two buried the hatchet," Harvey said.

"We did, long ago, but . . . you know. We don't socialize."

Harvey nodded. He didn't want to think about Eddie dating Sarah again, or anyone else, for that matter, except Leeanne. Still, he liked Sarah and hoped to see her happy.

"Look, I don't want to offend you by telling you this, but Jenny and I have had you on our prayer list for over a year now. We pray for you often. I know we don't have much contact, but we haven't forgotten you. I hope things are going okay."

"Thanks. I'm all right."

"You seeing anyone?" he asked. "I thought there was a game warden in the wings."

She shrugged. "It didn't last. He couldn't take my wearing a Kevlar vest every day." She hesitated. "Am I allowed to ask you something?"

"Of course."

"Is Eddie . . . I heard he and Leeanne broke up. First they were saying she postponed the wedding, then I heard she dumped him for no reason."

Harvey began to feel it hadn't been such a good idea to bring Sarah up to the unit for the interview. He should have had Nate or Jimmy interview her. He was aware that he had paused too long before replying, and Sarah watched him keenly.

"Sorry," she said. "I know she's Jennifer's sister. I shouldn't have put you on the spot."

"Right. Well, let's talk about Deborah." Harvey opened the file folder he'd brought with him. "She's twenty-three, never been married, and she'd been seeing Joey for two to three months."

"About that, I'd say."

"She thought a lot of him?"

"I don't know. Joey had a goofy side, you

know? I'm not sure she knew what to make of him yet."

"So, they weren't serious?"

"Well, it's hard to say. We talked some, in the car. I tried to tell her not to get too involved too soon. You know how it is. A guy gets divorced, and then the next thing you know, he's hitting on the cute rookie."

Harvey sat back and thought about that. "Well, everybody's different. I'm guessing Joey's marriage was in trouble a long time ago."

"Maybe, but still, I don't think it was very smart of Debbie to start dating him so soon."

"Let's say I agree. Still, he was a very likable guy."

"Oh, yeah. But not like—" She stopped short. "Do I sound like a broken record?"

"Some guys are likable, some are . . ."

"Lovable. Everyone loves Eddie. I guess that's been scientifically proven." She gave him a rueful smile. "When it got around that Joey Bolduc was available, the women were cautious. He'd flirt anyway, before, but now he had license, you know?"

Harvey blinked. "What's that got to do with Eddie?"

"Are you kidding? There are a dozen women in this building just dying to hear Eddie's engagement is off. He's not only great looking, he's smart, sweet, and polite. You don't find a package like that often. When he held the press conference on Labor Day—" She broke off and smiled guiltily. "Sorry, Captain. I don't usually gossip about my fellow officers."

"Go on," Harvey said with amusement. "What do they say about Winfield?"

"Tony? Oh, he's cute, but nobody quite dares to take him seriously. I mean, would you want your first date to be tea at the Blaine House?"

"He does have a boyish charm."

"Spoiled." Sarah waved her hand dismissively.

"So, Deborah and Joey. Serious or not?" Harvey asked.

Her brow creased. "I'd say, potential for seriousness. She liked him a lot. She didn't like the specter of the ex, but Roxanne moved out of town almost immediately."

"To Auburn."

"Does she have a new boyfriend?" Sarah asked.

"Who's interviewing whom?" Harvey said with a smile. "No, by all accounts there's no one special in Roxanne's life."

"Well, I wish I could help you. Debbie and I were on traffic that morning, though. There's no way she was directly involved."

"Mm." Harvey studied the papers in the folder. "Who was she seeing before Joey?"

"Well, she went out with Brad Lyons once."

Harvey's eyes whipped to hers.

"I told her it was a bad idea."

"It's worse than that, Sarah. It's against regulations for a sergeant to date his subordinates."

She looked down at her hands, picking at one fingernail. "I know, Captain. Sorry. I probably should have turned her in. But I couldn't exactly tell my sergeant, could I?"

"You could have come to me, Sarah."

"It was way back a few months, after she first came on. I—I didn't feel I could at the time. I'm sorry, I ought to have known better. But I was uncomfortable about the whole thing with Eddie, and—well, I wasn't sure how it was going to go. I considered telling Cheryl, but then I thought maybe it would backfire, and somehow Brad would—" Her eyes were wary. "I guess I'm really in trouble now."

Harvey shook his head. "No, Sarah. I wish you'd told me immediately, but you're not the one this will backfire on. You'll have to make a report, though."

"It's been what, six or eight months."

"It's still an infraction. Brad knows better."

Sarah stared at him woefully.

"Is there more?" Harvey asked quietly.

She fingered her badge and shifted in her chair, then cleared her throat. "I told Debbie if she saw Brad again I'd have to report it. I knew I should have anyway, but . . . do you remember Deidre Cleridge?"

"Cleridge," Harvey mused. "The name is familiar."

"She came on board when I did. She was on the evening shift."

"Oh, yeah. Redhead? Didn't last long."

"That's right," Sarah said significantly.

"Sarah, what are you telling me?"

"Nothing. I'm not telling you anything."

Harvey made himself sit still and hold her gaze until she looked away. "Sarah, you know I'll look into this now."

"Good," she whispered. "Can I go now?"

"Sure."

He sat in the interview room for ten minutes after she had left, going over the conversation in his mind. He wished he had run the recorder, but he hadn't expected to need it.

Chapter 8

"Eddie, something doesn't feel right here." Harvey dropped his voice so low that even Tony, at the next desk, wouldn't hear. The skin on the nape of Eddie's neck prickled.

"You interviewed Sarah?" he asked softly.

"Yes, and I'm going to see Deborah Higgins, but I think there's something else."

"Besides her dating Joey, you mean?"

"Yes. Can you step into the interview room for a minute?"

Eddie followed him, his curiosity piqued. All the men in the unit were working on the Bolduc case, and there were no secrets among them.

Harvey faced him, his eyes troubled. "I don't have anything concrete, but I wanted to keep you in the loop as investigating officer. I'll be requisitioning some old files on several officers."

"What, there's some kind of internal scandal?"

"I don't know yet."

"You think Joey was dirty? Drugs or something? I knew he liked beer, but he was always sober on duty."

"No, no. I just—Sarah gave me a bad feeling about something."

"Something official?"

Still he hesitated. "Look, Eddie, I need to explore some harassment allegations."

"Harassment? Sexual harassment? We haven't had anything like that for a while."

"Right, it's been a couple of years, I think."

Eddie stared hard at him. "Sarah's making a complaint?"

"No, but . . . she implied there's been more of this going on than we know."

Eddie sighed. "Sarah had enough problems at home. Don't tell me she was being harassed here."

"I'm not exactly sure what happened, but I think several officers are involved. I want to speak to Cheryl Yeaton when she comes in for the evening shift. I may end up interviewing all the female officers, and possibly some of the civilian personnel and former officers."

"This sounds serious."

"Well, I need to find out. If I find one speck of concrete evidence, I'll take it right to Mike."

Eddie nodded. "It's got to have something to do with Joey, or you wouldn't be telling me."

"Only indirectly, I think, but I'm just not sure. Sarah wasn't very forthcoming. She's afraid she'll get in trouble for not reporting something that happened back along."

Eddie put one hand on the back of a chair and

leaned on it. "You know her father used to beat her and her mother?"

"Anything else?"

"She never gave me the details, but I knew it wasn't good."

"That probably has nothing to do with this, and I won't bring it up unless it seems relevant."

"Thanks, Harv. I just thought it might have something to do with her being shy about reporting something irregular."

Harvey nodded. "I don't expect to discipline her for that, unless the brass says I have to."

"The brass being Mike?"

"Basically."

"Under that crusty exterior, he's compassionate."

Harvey nodded. "Well, I wanted you to know. I've got to try to sift this. It may hurt some people in this department."

Eddie nodded slowly. "Joey liked to flirt, but I don't think he'd threaten someone."

"No, I don't either. Some women might find him obnoxious, I suppose, but I think most people liked him. Do you think he honored his marriage vows?"

"I don't think he was actually dating before the divorce. You could ask Bob Marshall. He and Joey worked together a lot. I think they were pretty close."

"All right, I will. What have you got?"

"Well, I've been going through all the City Hall employees and people on the Labor Day committee. I'm not finding anything suspicious, Harv."

"Okay, just don't assume you won't. What about Joey's active cases?"

"Nothing. There was a drug dealer he busted last winter who threatened to break his neck, but he's in prison."

"He might have friends on the outside. Check it out. I'm going to call Cheryl and see if I can meet with her this afternoon. I don't want to put it off over the weekend."

"What time is the funeral?" Eddie asked.

"One o'clock tomorrow."

"Is our unit sending flowers?"

"No, Joey's family decided to start a scholarship fund for kids studying criminal justice. Mike's announcing it at the funeral."

"The Detective Joseph E. Bolduc Memorial Fund?"

"Something like that. He didn't have kids of his own, but this way it will help other kids and maybe encourage some to go into law enforcement. Paula's collecting for our unit."

They walked out into the main room of the office.

"Captain Larson," the unit's secretary called from her desk near the elevator, "can you take a call? It's a Mr. Russell."

"Sure, Paula. Just what I need," Harvey muttered.

Eddie went to his desk, bumped the screen saver off, and brought in the e-mail.

"John," he heard Harvey say. He couldn't help listening. "Well, I'm sorry, but I told you, it was her decision. She told me she wanted to write the book. Well, I can't answer for her, John. If you want her to come back to work in January, it's up to you to convince her, but I don't think she wants to tie herself down. I know . . . She's terrific. Well, I think she's spending the weekend with her parents."

Eddie checked the crime updates. He'd entered the principals in the Bolduc case in the flagging program Jennifer had designed for the police department. The only new item that came up since his last log-in was a traffic ticket for one of the city hall clerks.

Harvey was off the phone and sat frowning at his computer screen. Eddie walked up behind him.

"Russell rake you over the coals?" he asked.

"He's not happy. Leeanne apparently called him this morning and told him she's not taking his offer for January."

"Do you think I have a chance, Harv?"

"I'm not ready to commit on that one. At this point, if Leeanne comes out of this right side up, I think I'll be happy. But . . . I'm still rooting for you." Harvey nodded toward the computer screen. "I've been reviewing the statement Deborah Higgins gave on Monday. I think it's time to talk to her again."

"I've asked Bob Marshall to give me an hour of his time," Eddie said.

"Good. He and Deborah will have more insight into Joey's private life than anyone else. Do you want to sit in when I talk to Deborah?"

Eddie checked his watch. "Tape it. Time's flying."

Deborah Higgins sat straight in the chair, obviously aware of the video camera in the corner near the ceiling.

"Don't be nervous, Officer Higgins," Harvey said. "This is all routine, and I know this week has been stressful for you. I'll keep it as short as possible."

She said nothing, but bit her bottom lip.

"Would you like to have another officer present?" Harvey asked.

"I . . . no." She glanced again toward the camera. "This will be kept confidential?"

"Unless it's absolutely necessary. I assure you, it will be kept secure. No one will have access to the tape but me, Detective Thibodeau, and the detective sergeant, and in case of extreme urgency, the chief or deputy chief."

"All—all right."

"Now, Officer Higgins, on Monday afternoon you gave a statement to Detective Trudeau."

"That's right."

"You told him that you had been seeing Detective Bolduc for about two months before his death."

"Yes."

"How many times did you go out with Joey Bolduc?"

She shrugged. "Saturday nights. Maybe six or eight times. I could try to count, if you want."

"That's all right. You were comfortable with Detective Bolduc?"

"What do you mean?" Her hazel eyes were wary.

"I mean, you weren't afraid of him."

She laughed shortly. "Of Joey? No."

"When he first asked you out, how would you characterize his manner?"

"He was . . . very charming."

"Did you accept the first time he asked?"

"No, I had prior plans. I told him I couldn't, but maybe some other time."

"And he asked you again."

"Yes, a week or so later."

"You said yes."

She nodded.

"Did you tell your partner, Sarah Benoit?"

Deborah's eyes flared. "Yes, I told her he'd asked me."

"What did she say?"

"She advised me to turn him down."

"Why?"

"Because of his divorce. It had only been final for three or four months, and she thought he was on the rebound."

"What did you think?"

"I thought he seemed like a fun guy, and I decided to follow my instincts."

Harvey nodded. "Did Joey pressure you in any way to go out with him?"

She smiled regretfully. "Only in ways a man pressures a woman he admires."

"What do you mean?"

"He asked me several times. He stuck a carnation in my locker door. He sent me e-mails telling me he was very interested, and he left a chocolate bar in my mailbox. He was polite, and a little nutty. I liked him. So I said yes."

"You didn't feel obligated in any way."

"No, what for?"

Harvey nodded. "Before you began to date Detective Bolduc, were you seeing someone else?"

She hesitated. "I had a boyfriend before . . . last year. I had quit seeing him, though."

"When did you stop seeing him?"

"About February." She shook her head. "I don't remember exactly, but it was after the shooting incident at the chief's house."

Harvey nodded. He'd been on the scene, too. "What was his name?"

"Do I have to? I hate to bring him into this."

"Is he employed by the city of Portland?"

"No."

"Then I don't see a problem."

She sighed. "His name is Derek Anson. He lives in Biddeford. He's a paramedic."

Harvey jotted down the name. "Why did you and Mr. Anson stop seeing each other?"

She shrugged. "It was mutual. Our schedules made it difficult after I came to work here, and, well, I think it was going to peter out anyway."

"When was the last time you saw him?"

"Saw him? Actually saw him, or went out with him?"

"Physically saw him, with your eyes."

She stared at him, then looked down at her hands on the table. "Last night."

Harvey didn't say anything. He marshaled his thoughts and waited.

"He—he came down after I got off work last night. It was his day off." She looked at Harvey expectantly, but he said nothing. "He came to see how I was doing."

"He knew about Detective Bolduc's death?"

"Yes, he heard."

"And he knew about your relationship with Detective Bolduc?"

"Yes."

171

"How did he know that?"

"I told him a few weeks ago."

"So, you'd had contact with Derek Anson since you broke up with him."

"Y-yes. He would call me occasionally."

"Did he want to get back together?"

"I—well, maybe."

She evaded Harvey's eyes, and he felt there was more she wasn't telling him.

"Do you know if Joey Bolduc ever met Mr. Anson?"

"Not to my knowledge."

"And how would you characterize your relationship with Mr. Anson now?"

"We're—we're friends."

"But you were more than that before."

"We dated for about six months, off and on."

"But you broke up with him."

"He's . . . a little intense."

Harvey studied her face. "He was possessive?"

She sat still, giving him look for look.

"Jealous?" Harvey ventured.

"I told you, it was mutual."

"All right, let's talk about something else. Have you dated other men in Portland, since you moved down here?"

"A—a couple."

"Anyone in this department?"

She swallowed and glanced toward the camera. "I—I had one date with—with one of your men."

"One of *my* men?" Harvey was startled. Nate and Jimmy were married, and happily, so far as he could tell. That left Eddie and Tony.

"I went to a Sea Dogs game with Tony Winfield."

Harvey grinned. "Good for you. Did you have fun?"

"Sort of."

"So, it didn't bother you that he *has connections?*"

She flushed slightly. "I didn't know until after. It was the second week I was here, and nobody told me about the governor. Sarah told me a couple of days later."

"So, you didn't go out with Tony again?"

"No."

"Because of his uncle?"

"No. He just seemed immature."

Harvey nodded. Tony had a phenomenal mind, but overall Deborah's assessment agreed with his own. He was surprised Tony hadn't bragged about the date within the unit, though.

"So, anyone else in this department?"

"I . . . don't think so."

Harvey picked up his coffee mug and took a sip. "I'm going to repeat the last question, Deborah. I want you to understand that I'm not trying to entrap you here. It's important that you tell me the truth. To be frank, I've heard a rumor, and I'd like to know if there's any truth to it."

She was frightened, he could tell.

"You don't need to be nervous."

Her breathing was shallow, and her lip trembled.

"Would you like me to bring in my secretary?" Harvey asked. "She's very discreet."

"N-no."

He nodded toward her mug. "Would you like a drink?"

She shook her head.

"Officer Higgins, have you ever seen any other men from this department socially? Other than Joey Bolduc and Tony Winfield?"

She leaned toward him and whispered, "If I say yes, you'll fire me."

Harvey sat up straight. "I don't have that authority, Deborah."

"But I would be fired for breaking regulations."

Harvey knew he couldn't make promises at that point. "It's possible, but I don't think it would happen in this case."

She was quiet for ten seconds, then asked softly, "Why not?"

"If we find there was wrongdoing on the part of another officer, you would not be penalized."

"And if I say no, I didn't?"

"Then this interview is over. But if I find later that you gave me a false statement, your career in law enforcement is also over." He frowned. "I'm sorry. That's the way it is. I've reviewed your record, and you seem to be doing well in your duties. I think you're a credit to this department. I'd hate to see you throw it away because of fear. Women should be able to work here without being afraid of their fellow workers or their superiors."

She blinked twice. "I—don't know what to say."

"Let me ask you this. You started work here in January."

"That's right."

"Have you had any problems of any sort whatsoever with Chief Browning since you started working here?"

She stared at him. "The chief? Oh, no. Of course not. I've barely even seen him."

Harvey nodded. "How about the deputy chief, Jack Stewart?"

"No."

"Myself?"

"No."

"The night sergeants, Cheryl Yeaton and Dan Miles?"

"No, sir."

"Lieutenant Trask?"

"No." It was a whisper, and Harvey thought she could see where he was going.

"How about Detective Sergeant Legere?"

"No."

"And Patrol Sergeant Lyons?"

She reached for her cup then and took a deep swallow of the tepid coffee.

"Deborah, did Sergeant Lyons at any time make advances to you?"

She opened her mouth and closed it.

"Take your time," Harvey said gently.

"I—he might have said some things."

"Did he ever ask you to go out with him?"

"Do I have to answer these questions?"

"Yes."

She sighed. "He told me to meet him at a bar in the Old Port."

"When was this?"

"A long time ago. March, I think."

"It was after you stopped seeing Derek Anson?"

"I—I'm not sure."

"So, Brad Lyons asked you to meet him, and you did."

She hesitated. "He didn't ask me, exactly."

"How was it, then?"

"He told me. *Be at Raffier's at 9:30.*"

"What led up to that?"

"He—talked to me before that, several times. He would . . . compliment me, only in ways I didn't appreciate."

"Did anyone else hear that?"

"I don't think so. He might have talked about me with some of the men, but when he talked to me, it was usually when no one else was close. He would . . . tell me I looked hot in my uniform, and hint that I should be nice to him, things like that." She brushed her hair back with one hand, and her face was flushed.

"I'm sorry to put you through this. Did you know that when he said things like that, he was violating regulations?"

"Yes. They told us at the Academy."

"Did you tell anyone?"

"I was afraid to."

"But why? We have a liaison officer for these things. You knew that?"

"Yes, but I thought I could handle it at first. Later . . . well, he was my sergeant. If I told on him, he would know, and I—I thought he could make things difficult for me."

Harvey sighed. "How long did this go on?"

"A few weeks. Then he told me to meet him at the bar."

"You went."

"I was afraid not to."

"Did it seem a little bit daring? Like an adventure?"

"Maybe at first," she faltered. "But I didn't like the place, and I was afraid someone would recognize us."

"What happened?"

"He wanted to go back to my apartment. I told him I have a roommate."

Harvey looked in surprise at the folder. "Do you?"

"No. I—I lied to him."

"Were you afraid of him?"

"A little. I didn't want him to go home with me. I didn't like him, sir."

"So what happened?"

"He said, 'Okay, we'll go to my place.' I was really surprised, because I thought he was married. I found out later he's got a history."

Harvey nodded.

"Well, I told him I wouldn't. He was mad."

"Did he threaten you?"

"Not exactly. Well, he said I should cooperate with him if I wanted a good evaluation. Is that a threat?"

Harvey didn't comment. "What else did he say?"

"I told him that if he didn't leave me alone, I'd rat on him. I'd had enough. I don't know why I waited until then, but all of a sudden, I didn't care anymore. I figured if he got me fired, it was better than staying in the job and letting him blackmail me. I—I went out on the street and got a cab home."

"Did Lyons ever do anything to retaliate?"

"He said a few things to me after that, real snide things, you know? Like how I was better than some people. And he gave me some real crummy assignments. But I didn't complain. I'm a rookie, and I figured I didn't have a right to complain about that. But he never . . . he never told me to meet him again."

"Did he ever touch you?"

"N-no. Well, that one night I met him, he tried, but never at the police station."

"And he left you alone after that."

"Pretty much. I think he might have started some rumors about me with the men, but he couldn't say too much or he'd be in hot water, wouldn't he? Sarah heard something, and she confronted me about it. I didn't tell her the whole story. I was embarrassed, I guess. I let her think it was a regular date."

"Did you tell Joey Bolduc about this?"

The fear came back into her eyes. "Yes, I did. Not until I knew him pretty well. It was . . . about three weeks ago, I think."

"What was his reaction?"

"He was mad. He said a lot of bad things about Sergeant Lyons. That he was a predator, things like that. Worse things."

Harvey waited.

"He said . . . he would look into it. I told him to forget it. Once I started dating Joey, the sergeant seemed to back off, and I didn't want anyone to find out what had happened between us. I was still afraid . . . that I'd be disciplined, you know?"

"All right, Officer." Harvey closed the folder. "I think we're finished for today. Please don't discuss this interview with anyone else."

"Am I going to be disciplined?"

Harvey shook his head. "No, but you understand, this statement is official. It may be used against Sergeant Lyons, especially if I find he ever made improper advances toward other city employees."

She nodded. "Captain, I was new, I was scared. I didn't want to be tossed out a few weeks into my new job. I guess I should have gone to the liaison officer, but . . . well, the sergeant made it seem like it would hurt me more than it would help me."

He nodded. "Okay. I understand."

She stood up. "Sarah told you, didn't she?"

"I'm not at liberty to discuss how I heard. I'm sorry it happened to you."

Harvey called Cheryl Yeaton at home.

"Cheryl, I'm sorry to bother you, but I wondered if you'd meet with Detective Thibodeau and me after you come in this evening."

"Sure, Harvey. Is there a problem?"

"It concerns the Bolduc case."

"I come in at 4:30, unless you'd like me to come earlier. I'll have to do my roll call."

"Could you come to our office by five?"

"I think so."

"Thanks. And just keep this low-profile, please."

"Copy that."

Harvey drummed his fingers on his desk. He ought to tell Mike. Soon.

Detective Bob Marshall, from Sgt. Legere's squad, lounged in a chair beside Eddie's desk, and Eddie had his notebook open.

"Yeah, he started dating right after he got the papers. For a few months he was kind of on the prowl, but then he settled on Deborah. She's cute, and she seemed to like him."

Harvey stood up. "Eddie, I'm going down to Records. Oh, and we have a five o'clock appointment."

Eddie raised his eyebrows.

"It concerns that matter I mentioned to you earlier."

Eddie nodded. "I'll be here, *mon ami*."

Harvey took the stairs down to the lobby, then down one more flight, to the basement. In the records room, half a dozen women worked diligently. He stopped at the supervisor's desk.

"Marge, I need a file on a former employee."

"More than is in the system?"

"I think so. I want to see the handwritten reports, if there are any."

"Officer or civilian?"

"Officer Deidre Cleridge. She was here for a short time a couple of years ago. And, Marge, this is confidential."

Marge pushed her glasses up on her nose. "Captain, everything in this room is confidential."

He followed her down an aisle between desks

and file cabinets. She opened a drawer and flipped through folders.

"There you go. Slim file."

"She wasn't here long."

He preceded her back toward her work station and turned, lowering his voice.

"Marge, I don't mean to impugn your statement, but I mean *really* confidential. I don't want anyone but the chief to know I asked for the file."

"What file?" Marge smiled and sat down at her computer.

Chapter 9

Harvey carried the coffeemaker from the break room into the interview room and started a fresh pot. He had left a stack of file folders on the table, and Mike was thumbing through them.

"Harv? Cheryl's here." Eddie came in, followed by Sergeant Yeaton.

"Thanks for coming, Cheryl. Sit down, Eddie." Harvey sat down and laid his notebook on the table. Mike slid the file folders closer to him.

"Captain," Cheryl said with a nod. "Chief. What's up?"

"A touchy subject," Harvey replied. "Have you ever experienced any form of sexual harassment in this department?"

Cheryl's eyebrows shot up. "Is this an internal investigation? I thought we were going to discuss the Bolduc murder."

"Well, we are," Harvey conceded. "I just need to ask you about a couple of other things."

She sat back, meeting his eyes squarely. "Well, the answer is no. This profession is definitely male-oriented, but I think I've been treated fairly."

"No unwelcome advances, lewd comments, that sort of thing?"

She shrugged. "There's a certain amount of disdain for women, but I'd say, no. I never felt I was being harassed. Okay, once or twice in ten years I've told a guy to shut up, but that's as far as it went." She looked around at the three of them.

Harvey took his reading glasses from his breast pocket and put them on. "I know you've never filed a complaint. Did you ever think about it?"

"No. Harvey, what is this all about?"

"Just wanted to clear the air on that before we move on to the next level."

"Which is?"

"Want some coffee?"

Eddie sprang to his feet. "I'll get it. Cream and sugar, Cheryl?"

"No, thanks, just black."

Mike held out his empty mug to Eddie, and he took it, too.

Cheryl turned back to Harvey. "I'm waiting Captain."

"Deidre Cleridge."

"Deidre—" Cheryl's brow furrowed.

"You remember her?"

"Barely."

"She was in the Academy with Sarah. They signed on together."

"Right. She wasn't on my shift, though."

"No, she was on the evening shift."

"What do you want to know?"

"Why she quit," Harvey said.

"I have no idea, but she must have filed a resignation."

"I've got it here." Harvey tapped the top file folder.

"Then why are you asking me?"

Harvey picked up his coffee mug and took a sip. "We may need your help on this."

"Whatever *this* is. You're being very mysterious."

Mike said quietly, "Deidre Cleridge was the last woman to file a harassment complaint in this department."

"First I knew about it," Cheryl said.

"Me, too," said Harvey. "I wasn't in management then, never heard a word about it. Until today, when I started digging."

Cheryl glanced toward Mike. "It couldn't have been hushed up?"

Eddie returned and set a cup of coffee in front of Cheryl. Mike reached for his.

"Thanks, Ed. I wouldn't say it was hushed up exactly. There's a fine line between protecting privacy and covering things up. I heard about it in an administrative meeting, but I was here in Priority at the time, and it wasn't really my business. Chief Leavitt seemed to think it was a minor incident, and it was taken care of."

Harvey opened the top folder. "All I know is, she started . . . February ninth that year, filed her complaint March second, and quit March twenty-seventh."

"She must have given a cause," Cheryl said.

"Personal reasons." Harvey sat back and waited for Cheryl to think about it.

"What one woman perceives as harassment, another might see as friendly banter."

"I'm pretty sure this goes well beyond that," Harvey said.

"Who was her supervisor?"

"Now we get down to the nitty gritty."

Cheryl frowned at him. "Well, I assume that, since she was on the evening shift, she was under Brad Lyons."

"Bingo."

Eddie turned his coffee cup around on the table. "You've known Brad a long time, right, Cheryl?"

"Ever since I started. He was a patrolman when I came on."

"Did he ever try to flirt with you?" Harvey asked.

"Come on, he flirts with everyone."

"All right, did he ever ask you for a date?"

"Many times. I think it was between wives two and three."

Harvey asked gently, "Did you go out with him?"

186

"No. Look, he's an okay cop, but he's lousy husband material."

Eddie smiled, and Harvey gave a sigh.

Cheryl leaned toward him across the table. "You're telling me Deidre Cleridge filed a harassment complaint against Brad?"

Harvey handed her the file folder.

When she had perused it, he asked, "What was your reaction when Brad asked you out?"

"I told him to buzz off. After eight or ten times, he got the message. But, Harvey, according to this, she alleged he pressured her for sexual favors and used vulgarity and—it wasn't like that in my case. Honestly."

"He was never your supervisor," Mike pointed out.

"True. I was under Terry Lemieux, the day sergeant, until he left here. Terry was always a gentleman, by the way. Then, when Brad went on days, I got his job on the night desk. Our shifts overlap by an hour. I see him every day, but I make sure it stays professional."

"It takes an effort on your part?" Mike asked.

She shrugged. "He's always been that way, Chief. If you put him in his place first thing, he toes the line, to a degree. I suppose a woman who was easily intimidated would have a harder time with him."

Harvey watched her carefully. "I've spoken with another female officer who felt exactly that.

She was intimidated. She wanted to report it, but was afraid to."

"Not Sarah. Please don't tell me it's Sarah, Harvey. We're very close. She would have told me."

"No, not Sarah."

Cheryl sighed. "Well, let's see, we have six other female patrol officers, Detective Rood, and a dozen or so civilian support staff."

"Eighteen civilians," Harvey corrected her. "I've also compiled a list of female employees who have worked here since Brad was hired twelve years ago. Secretaries, dispatchers, clerks, everything. There are fifty-nine, all told. Well, one's deceased. Fifty-eight."

"That many?"

"Yes, so you see my problem? It would take Eddie and me weeks to interview them all, and we're trying to solve a murder here. You're the ranking female in this department, and you haven't experienced harassment in your tenure. You're the ideal person to help us with this."

"The women would talk to you easier than they would us," Eddie said.

Cheryl took a deep breath. "I'm flabbergasted. You think this has been a serious, ongoing thing?"

"Yes, I do." Harvey opened the second file folder. "I have an active officer—one of his subordinates—who claims Lyons ordered her to meet him off duty and propositioned her. Cheryl, if you can help us, I wish you would. Mike's asked me to investigate these allegations fully. It's going to take a while, and I don't want to rush things, but we've got three new female officers we plan to hire who are at the Academy now."

She swallowed. "Sure, just tell me what to do."

"I want all of these women to feel secure when we interview them. We'll have to tape the interviews. Some of them know me, and they might feel comfortable with me. Sarah did. But some might prefer to talk to a female officer."

"Does this mean overtime?"

"Probably. I'll try to schedule things for late afternoon or early evening, when possible."

"You can take comp time when it's over," Mike said. "I'll take care of it."

"Thanks, Chief." Cheryl nodded at him.

Harvey stacked the file folders neatly. "I'll track down Deidre Cleridge myself. Other than her, we'll start with current employees. If we see a pattern, we'll have to work our way back."

"All right. But why isn't the liaison officer doing this?"

"The liaison officer is a man."

"I know. Chuck Norton. So? You're a man, too."

"Yes, but Norton isn't in management."

Mike said, "It's a volunteer, peer-appointed position. We want this handled by management.

If an employee had come forward with a complaint, it would be different, but the way this came out makes it an administrative matter."

"Will the results be made public?" Cheryl asked.

"That's tricky. We want to protect privacy, but if the investigation leads to charges, some of it will have to come out." Mike ran his hand through his hair. "Well, now you know what we're up against."

"By the way," Harvey said, "you don't need to interview my wife. She worked in Records for twelve weeks last year. I think she'd have told me if anything happened with her, but I'll talk to her about it to make sure."

Cheryl sipped her coffee thoughtfully. "Is this investigation limited to Brad Lyons's conduct?"

"Not necessarily," Harvey replied. "Why do you ask?"

"Not that it matters now, but Candi Mullins, in Records, told me the old deputy chief grabbed her once in the elevator."

"The old deputy? You mean Neilsen?" Harvey felt betrayed.

Eddie's jaw dropped. "He was married."

Cheryl nodded. "So he was. It was years ago, and he's gone now. But you might want to ask her about it, for what it's worth."

Harvey stared at Mike.

"Don't look at me," Mike protested. "I knew

nothing about this. But you interview my secretary personally, all right, Cheryl? And listen, Harvey, you'd better tell Brad about this investigation soon."

"I'd like to get some facts in hand first."

"I know, but once you start interviewing people, word will leak out. Better he hears it from you."

Jennifer carried Connor to Beth's back door and rang the bell.

"Thanks for keeping him." She smiled as Beth reached for the baby.

"No problem," Beth said.

"I'll be back right after the funeral. Harvey will probably go to the cemetery with his men."

Harvey drove toward the funeral home with an air of detachment.

He pulled up at a red light and glanced at Jennifer. "I remember the first time Brad Lyons saw you. It was when you came to the station to put the software on my computer."

"I don't remember. I guess I was just eager to see you."

"He noticed you, all right," Harvey said. "He's got a reputation around the station, but I never thought of it as a real problem."

"I didn't see him much when I worked there. Wasn't he on nights then?"

"Yes, the evening shift. You're on our list of

females who have worked at the police station since Brad Lyons was hired. I volunteered to interview you."

"Well, I don't remember him saying anything out of line to me."

"I made sure everyone knew we were engaged right off. If it hadn't been for that, he'd probably have pounced on you."

"Careful. You can't make assumptions. Candi Mullins did tell me once to stay out of his way. I assumed he had a reputation, but I didn't think much about it."

"Well, we've got an allegation now, so we're looking into it. By the way, what did you think of Detective Bolduc?"

"He was all right. Bright, but not always wise. You were a little put out with him on one case. Lax in his surveillance, or something."

"I remember." Harvey was nearing the funeral home, and he began watching for a parking spot. "He did well on the advanced computer training, though."

"Have you interviewed this woman who filed the complaint on Brad?" Jennifer asked.

"Not yet. I found out she lives in Yarmouth now. I'll probably have to run up there. I'd kind of like to get it straight from her myself. And Eddie's going to Biddeford to see Deborah Higgins's old boyfriend to see if he resented Joey."

●　●　●

Leeanne pulled on a light jacket over her Skowhegan Indians sweatshirt. It was windy, and a few
leaves were beginning to fall from the maples in
the front yard of the farmhouse. "Travis, come
with me to see Grandpa Wainthrop."

Travis had come home for the weekend, too.
The laundry was done, and he slouched in an
armchair with a textbook open in his lap.

"All right, if you'll help me with my English
outline later."

She laughed. "You don't need help with a
paper."

"This professor is sadistic. Really. They say
she never gives A's."

Travis insisted on driving the red pickup his
parents had bought him for transportation to the
university. Leeanne picked a potato chip bag
off the passenger seat and threw it to the floor.
"What a slob," she said good-naturedly, buckling
her seatbelt.

Travis pulled out onto the county road. "So,
how are you really?"

"I'm okay," she said.

"Do you miss Eddie?"

She stared straight ahead for a moment, then
turned to face him. "More than anything."

Travis nodded. "Eddie's a great guy. You ought
to make up with him."

"I've sort of been trying, but I can't tell if he

wants to or not. Every time I talk to him, I come away feeling really sad."

"Too bad. He's cool."

"So, how are *you* really?"

"Okay."

"How's campus life?"

Travis shrugged. "It's a little wilder than I expected."

"You mean, parties and stuff?"

He grimaced. "There's a lot of drinking, even in the dorm."

"It was getting bad at Farmington when I was there," she admitted.

"My roommate, Brett—" Travis shot her a glance. "He drinks all the time."

"*All* the time?"

"Every night so far. Sometimes in the daytime. More on weekends. I escape home."

"That's rough."

"It's disgusting. His friends are always hanging out in our room. I can't leave anything there or it disappears. Half the time I can't even get to bed until the wee hours because there's half a dozen people in there. And it smells. We've only had two weeks of school, and I hate it."

"Have you asked for a new room?"

"They really look down on you if you do that. There was a kid down the hall who complained, and they picked on him so bad he dropped out already."

"You haven't tried it, have you?"

"What, drinking?"

She nodded.

"There's a lot of pressure if you don't."

"But you've got to hold out against it."

"It's easier to just . . ."

"Trav, tell me you didn't."

"Why not? Did you ever drink?"

She looked away. "Once. At Melissa Woehr's. Her folks had half a bottle of wine in the cupboard, and Melissa thought we ought to sample it."

"How much did you drink?"

"One swallow. It was awful. I decided right then I didn't want to drink, and I haven't ever since."

"Well, the guys at school think you're a wuss if you don't."

"What they think doesn't matter. Haven't you read about alcohol poisoning and drunk drivers and—"

"Yes."

"You said yourself, it's disgusting the way your pig of a roommate lives."

"I—I gotta admit, I was a little—"

"Scared?" Leeanne was incredulous. "Travis, you're six feet tall. You played football, for pete's sake. This guy intimidates you?"

"Not just Brett. Him and three or four other guys. Last week they were pretty plastered, and I

195

was afraid they wouldn't let me out of the room. Brett threw me a can of beer, and—"

"And what?" She stared at him menacingly.

"And I drank it."

Leeanne shook her head in disbelief. "All of it?"

"Yup. Then they let me go."

"And?"

"I got sick."

"Good," she said fiercely.

He turned in at their grandfather's driveway.

"You won't tell Mom and Dad?"

"Travis, you can't start drinking. You don't know what it can do to you."

"Yes, I do. I don't want to. But I want to survive my freshman year, too."

"You could live at home and commute every day."

"It's too far."

She sighed. "God must have a solution to this."

His eyes darkened. "It's not a big deal. I'll avoid the problem when possible and play along when I have to."

"No, you can't. I really think you should complain. They're not supposed to have alcohol in the dorms."

"Everyone breaks the rules."

She reached for the door handle. "Whether you like it or not, I'll be praying about this."

"I don't care, as long as you don't tell Mom and Dad."

Marilyn Wainthrop peeked hesitantly into her daughter's bedroom, tapping lightly on the door panel.

"Hi, Mom." Leeanne had her suitcase open on the bed, and was folding her clothing into it.

"Heading out soon?"

"Yeah, I'd like to get back to Jeff's before dark."

"Your father thinks we should try to get Grandpa to come stay here this winter." Marilyn sat down on the opposite side of the bed.

"I think that would be great. He seemed pretty chipper yesterday, but he feels the cold every winter."

"Yes, and we worry about him burning wood. He won't switch to oil, but it's getting to be too much for him. Your dad thinks we ought to make a serious effort to have him come to us. If he wants to go back home in the spring, that's all right."

Leeanne opened the top dresser drawer and scanned its contents briefly. "I have stuff in three houses. This is crazy." She tossed two pair of knee socks into the suitcase.

"We're really proud of you, that you're writing this book."

"Thanks. I've started my outline and writing

down my own memories of what happened, and I interviewed Jennifer about how they bought the house and everything. I think it's going well."

"Will you miss working for the paper?"

Leeanne shook her head. "It's kind of soon to tell, but mostly I feel relieved."

"Honey, how are things with Eddie?" Marilyn asked softly. "If you don't want to talk about it—"

"No, it's okay. I've kind of been wanting to, but I don't really have anything to tell. He seems to be avoiding me, and I can't say as I blame him."

Marilyn took a blouse from the suitcase and refolded it. "I've been trying to pray for you. Your father has, too, but we aren't really sure what to ask."

Tears flooded Leeanne's eyes. Her mother had told her that she was a believer now, and that her dad was going to church with her and Randy and taking what he learned seriously. They struggled, as Leeanne did, trying to understand how they should live.

"We're very fond of Eddie," her mother went on. "I thought he was the perfect son-in-law."

Leeanne smiled wryly. "No, Harvey's the perfect son-in-law." She sobered. "I thought he was perfect for me, too, but—oh, Mommy!"

She burst into tears, dismayed by the intensity of grief that engulfed her. Marilyn jumped up, stepped around the foot of the bed, and enfolded her in her arms.

"Honey, it's going to be okay. One way or another, things will work out."

"I'm sorry," Leeanne gasped.

"It's okay. Go ahead and cry."

Marilyn managed to slide the suitcase aside, and they sat on the bed together.

"I don't know why I was so mean to him," Leeanne said shakily. "He's so sweet. And he is perfect for me. I'm just—very imperfect, I'm afraid."

"You still love him, don't you?"

"Yes. This has been the worst two months of my life. He let me talk to him on Labor Day, and I thought we made some progress, but lately—I don't know. I can't read him. I came up here this weekend so he wouldn't have to see me at church. Well, I wanted to visit you, too, but it seemed like he was avoiding me, and I didn't want to make it—"

"It's all right. Here, have a tissue."

Leeanne plucked one from the box and wiped her eyes. "I don't want to drive Eddie away from the church down there. He was there first, and he shouldn't have to look at me every time he goes."

"I'm sure he doesn't want you to stay away for his sake, honey."

Leeanne sniffed. "He deserves somebody better

than me. If Jennifer or Abby did what I did, I'd hate them."

"No, you wouldn't."

"I was so foolish. I let myself get all excited about seeing my byline on the front page. And then that Hawaii trip. But all that means nothing to me, compared to losing Eddie. If I have to be lonely for the rest of my life—I miss him so much, Mom."

Marilyn smiled and squeezed Leeanne's shoulders. "At least I'll know how to pray now."

Leeanne mopped her face thoroughly, sighed, and stood up. "I guess I'll take my winter sweaters." She opened the closet door and stood staring at the long white garment bag. All weekend she had stayed away from the closet. Slowly, she reached out and pulled the zipper down. Fine organza, a circlet of pearls at the neckline.

"It's a beautiful wedding dress." Her mother stood close to her.

"I'm sorry I can't take it back, Mom. If they hadn't altered it for me . . ."

"Hush," said Marilyn. "We're not taking it back."

The men of the Priority Unit gathered in their break room at 9:30 Monday morning and sat around the table with coffee.

"It was a .357 Magnum that killed Joey," Nate

200

said, tipping his chair back against the wall. "Not one of our weapons."

"Not a current one, anyway," Eddie agreed. They'd been issued new 45-caliber weapons the previous fall.

"We'd have it in the IBIS system if it were a current service revolver." Harvey got up and poured himself another cup of coffee.

"But it could be a cop, or a former cop," Jimmy said.

"It could be anyone," Tony put in, his frustration showing in the tense lines of his face.

"You're sure it was a .357, not a nine-millimeter?" Harvey asked.

"No, the grooves from the rifling are a one-in-fourteen twist," Nate said. "And the width of the grooves matches a Smith and Wesson."

"So what's next?" Harvey asked.

Eddie consulted his notebook. "Tony, I want you to go back over to City Hall. This guy was really lucky if nobody saw him move the dummy or heard the shot."

"Silencer," Nate said.

"I don't know, that's pretty rare." Eddie frowned and looked to Harvey.

"Let's go over the timetable again." Harvey sat down and placed his mug on the table. "They set up everything for the game. They were finished before noon. Joey called us at 11:47. Right, Eddie?"

"Right. Charlie Doran logged it."

"Okay, and Joey was still at City Hall when he called. Maybe from the comptroller's office. He used his cell phone, though, not the phone on the desk."

"His phone was in his pocket when we found him," Jimmy droned. "We've been over this five thousand times."

"That's how you find clues, Jim," Harvey said patiently. "Sometimes you go over and over the facts, and suddenly you realize something doesn't add up."

"What, in this case?" Tony asked.

"Well, the M.E. said Joey had been dead at least an hour when he saw him, not more than two." Harvey gazed around at the four of them.

"That puts the time of death between 11:35 and 12:35," Eddie said, "but we know he made the phone call at 11:47."

"Right," Harvey agreed. "How many people were still in the building between 11:47 and 12:35?"

"The offices were all closed, and the setup crew went for lunch," Nate said.

"There were two guys left there to make sure no one disturbed the game setup," Tony corrected.

Nate shrugged. "Yeah, but we talked to them. They didn't hear a thing."

"And they were both in the lobby downstairs,"

said Eddie. "They vouch for each other. They could see the door to the clerk's office by looking down the hall. One of them could always see the elevators, or so they say."

"But no one checked to see if everyone had left the second floor," Harvey said slowly. "It would have been easy to move the dummy if everyone but the killer left the second floor." He took a sip of his coffee.

Eddie flipped back through his notebook. "Let's go out in the office. We've asked all the crew members who they ate lunch with. It's in the computer."

They shuffled from the break room to the office and clustered around Eddie's desk.

"As far as I can see, everyone on the setup crew is accounted for during lunch. Emily Rood said she left at 11:45 and went home for lunch with her husband. He confirms it. Joey was still in the comptroller's office when she left."

"What about the judges?" Harvey asked. "They were over there looking at the setup before, weren't they?"

"Yeah, the festival chairman gave them the tour, and Mayor Weymouth met them outside her office and went to look at the game preparations with them. But that was earlier. Between eleven and eleven-thirty."

"And they all have alibis during lunch," Nate added. "Even the mayor."

Harvey smiled. "I can't picture Jill Weymouth shooting Joey."

"Well, I made them check, anyway," Eddie said.

Harvey nodded. "You're right. You have to check everyone."

"Anybody could have walked in there," Tony insisted. "There are two other doors, and a stairway."

"I know," Harvey agreed. "If we'd been detailed to set it up, we'd have posted a man outside the comptroller's door and another at the clerk's door. Sloppy, sloppy, sloppy."

"And, as we all know," Nate said with an air of significance, "if there's one thing Captain Larson can't abide, it's sloppy work."

Harvey smiled. "Okay, we've established that anyone could walk in off the street, slip past the two guards, go up the stairway, and kill Joey. But I don't think Joey stayed there for forty-five minutes alone after he called me. Joey wasn't one to skip lunch."

"Right," Eddie agreed. "I'm thinking he was dead by noon."

Tony sighed. "And we were all chugging Pepsi and eating Subway sandwiches."

"It was a nice funeral," Jimmy said mournfully. "I can't help wondering where Joey is now, though."

"Don't get all maudlin," Tony snapped. "He was a nice guy."

"Yeah, but—" Jimmy looked at Eddie and Harvey. "Are you guys having prayer today?"

"Sure," Harvey said. "I'll call upstairs and see if the chief has time. Want to join us?"

"Thanks," Jimmy said. Nate and Tony said nothing.

Harvey went to his own desk to use the phone.

"Okay," Eddie said. "We'll take a fifteen-minute break. After that, here's what we're looking at today. I interviewed Debbie Higgins's old boyfriend first thing this morning, and I got the feeling he still likes her. He claims he never met Joey, but Debbie told him on the phone she was seeing a detective. Says she called him all tearful the night after Joey was killed, and he came down to see her Thursday night."

"Giving her a shoulder to cry on?" Tony asked cynically.

Eddie shrugged. "I've asked her sergeant to send her up here at 10:30 for another chat. Tony, you go back to City Hall and see if you can confirm that anyone else was in the building during the critical time. Nate, Jimmy, get those two guys who were supposedly guarding the game area. Lean on them a little. I know they're not cops, and it wasn't an official duty, but they ought to have taken it seriously. Meanwhile, the captain's going to Yarmouth on another case."

All eyes were on him.

"Harvey's opened another case?" Tony asked

suspiciously. "I thought we were all in this together until we got Joey's killer."

"It's indirectly related," Eddie explained. "Something that . . . came up during an interview. It needs to be checked out, but we don't think it has a direct bearing on the murder case."

The other three still stood there.

"I'm sorry, I can't tell you more than that right now."

Jennifer, Beth, and Beth's sister-in-law, Ruthann Bradley, were drinking tea in Beth's kitchen when Leeanne got home from campus that afternoon. She came in the back door, laden with textbooks.

"Hi. Are you hungry?" Beth called.

"Starved. Hi, Ruthann. Hi, Jenn. What's the occasion?"

Jennifer smiled. "Ruthann and I haven't had a chance to get together in ages, so Beth called me when she came, and Connor and I rushed right over."

Ruthann's daughter Clarissa and her year-old son Ethan were playing with plastic blocks on the floor. Connor sat up in his infant seat, watching them with huge blue eyes.

"Connor loves having other kids around," Beth observed.

"Hey, I heard you got a contract to write a book," Ruthann said. "Congratulations, lady."

"Oh, thanks. It's going to be a challenge, but I think I'll enjoy it." Leeanne plucked a cookie from the serving plate on the table, and her eye fell on a lavish floral arrangement on the sideboard. "Hey, beautiful roses! Did Jeff spring for those?"

Beth laughed. "No, someone else did." She leaned back in her chair and picked up an envelope from the counter. "Special delivery for Mademoiselle Leeanne Wainthrop."

Amazement, hope, and wariness hit Leeanne at the same time. She examined the envelope carefully, and a smile spread slowly.

"I'm so glad I picked today to visit," Ruthann said happily.

Leeanne pulled a small card from the envelope. Her smiled deepened as she read it.

"What's it say?" Jennifer asked.

"Come on, Jenn, it's personal," Beth scolded.

Leeanne walked to the sideboard and touched one of the pure white roses. *"Il est doux."*

"Très doux," Jennifer agreed. "You'd better write him a thank-you note."

Leeanne threw them all an apologetic smile. *"Excusez-moi, s'il vous plait."* She picked up her books, drew one rose from the bouquet and headed for the stairs.

Eddie's pulse quickened when he saw Leeanne's message. *Merci*, it was slugged. He clicked on it.

Les fleurs sont si belles! *Merci*! *J'espère te voir bientot*! *Leeanne.*

He smiled.

"What's so funny?" Tony asked.

Eddie jumped. "What? Nothing."

Tony came and looked over his shoulder. Eddie closed the message, but not quickly enough.

"Leeanne, huh? I'm telling you, it's not worth it."

"You don't know what you're talking about," Eddie said complacently.

"Don't I? Like I said, I'm not getting married."

"I predict you will eat those words someday."

"I thought she threw the ring in your face."

"It didn't happen like that."

"So now you're sending chummy e-mails again."

Eddie shrugged. "MYOB. If you have any B."

Tony laughed and picked up a stack of folders from his desk. "I've been minding my own business, and yours, too, Shakespeare. I talked to both of the game guardians. They're sorry they did such a lousy job, but they didn't see or hear anything."

"Just great." Eddie leaned back in his swivel chair. "There was a lot of traffic outside City Hall that day. The crowd was starting to gather by noon."

"Aw, not that early, I don't think. We didn't go over until one."

"I wonder if they'd have heard a shot while a siren was blasting outside," Eddie mused.

"He was dead by noon, you said so yourself, or at least by 12:35."

"Check with Charlie Doran. Ask him if we had any units within a block of City Hall between 11:47 and 12:35. All we need is one siren."

"Come on, you think the killer waited for a siren to muffle the sound?"

"I don't know. If it was the Fourth of July, there would have been fireworks and nobody would have blinked, but it was Labor Day. No fireworks. No parade. But there was a lot of noise that morning, right? They did the Public Works thing between 9 and 11. People were watching the crews lay pipe."

"That was all over by the time of the murder."

"So what was going on then?"

"Lunch. Everybody was eating lunch. How many witnesses do we need to tell us that?"

"All we need is one to tell us something different."

Tony scowled at him.

Chapter 10

"Deidre Cleridge?"

The slim waitress turned toward Harvey and eyed him suspiciously. "I'm Deidre Cleridge Martin."

"Sorry. I didn't know you were married now." He tried to give her the smile that got Jennifer every time.

"What do you want?"

"I'm Harvey Larson, from the Portland P.D."

"Oh, yeah, I thought you looked familiar." She measured coffee into the basket of a large coffee maker. "What brings you to Yarmouth?"

"You, actually."

Her surprise was plain, but she hid it quickly. "How can I help you?"

"It's a delicate matter. Will you be having a break soon? I'd like to speak with you privately for a few minutes."

She glanced at the clock. "Now's as good as ever, I guess. Hold on."

She disappeared through a swinging door and came back almost immediately. "Okay, my boss says we can use his office. Follow me."

Harvey went with her to the entry of the

restaurant, then into an alcove, around a corner past restrooms, and into a small, cluttered office.

"You want to sit?" she asked.

"Thanks." Harvey sensed she was uncomfortable in her employer's office, and he took the chair behind the desk. Deidre sat down on the edge of the only other chair. She was pretty, he thought. Her red hair, green eyes and pale skin combined with finely-chiseled features would make her stand out. "Mrs. Martin, you were employed by the Portland P.D. for several weeks, about a year and a half ago."

She nodded.

"Why did you leave?"

She sighed. "It was personal. I . . . decided I wasn't cut out to be a cop."

"You made it through the Academy. You still wanted the job then."

"It was tough."

"Did someone make it tough for you?"

She looked at him sharply. "You must have read my record. You know I filed a complaint against my sergeant."

"Yes. The record says that was resolved."

"Huh." She held out one hand, examining her nails.

"The deputy chief reprimanded Sergeant Lyons," Harvey said.

"So I was told."

"And?"

"Why does it matter now?" She was analyzing him, and Harvey knew she was intelligent. He waited. "You've had another complaint," she said with certainty.

"What happened after you made your harassment complaint?"

Her eyes narrowed. "Will you bust him? Or will you reprimand him again and tell the woman who complained to get with the program?"

Harvey lowered his eyes. "I'm very sorry for what you went through. I wish things had been handled differently. It's my job to make sure they're handled better this time."

She eyed him speculatively. "I would love to see that man go down."

"Was it that bad?"

"Shouldn't you be taping this?"

Harvey was startled. "You really hate him, don't you?"

"Yes. I'll give you a statement. I'll testify, if it comes to that. Two weeks after the complaint was supposedly settled, Brad Lyons cornered me in the parking garage. He said I was in for a bad time as a rookie, and I'd better watch myself."

"He insinuated—"

"Oh, he more than insinuated. He backed me up against the wall and fondled me, if you can call it that when the man is threatening you."

Harvey shook his head. "You didn't complain again?"

"Oh, yes. I went straight back to the deputy chief. He had the audacity to ask me if I had a grudge against Sergeant Lyons because he had snubbed me."

"Snubbed you?" Harvey asked, confused.

"Seems good old Brad told Neilsen I had the hots for him. He ignored me, so I made the first complaint out of spite. The woman scorned, you know. When he got away with a slap on the wrist, I had a hissy fit and decided to complain again."

"And you think the deputy chief bought this story?"

"I know he did. He told me Sergeant Lyons had an exemplary record, and if I tried to make trouble for him again, I'd be guilty of insubordination. The whole thing was so sordid. I went home and cried and decided I was a little bit afraid of the two of them. I also decided I'd had enough."

"Did you tell anyone else at the time?"

She shook her head. "My partner was a man. No sympathy there. I quit and went home to my parents' for a while. Then I met Frank Martin. I decided not all men were worthless, after all."

Harvey closed his notebook. "Just cops."

Harvey drove back to Portland, ruminating on Deidre Martin's disturbing story. He went over his notes with Eddie.

"She's agreed to come down here Wednesday morning and tape a formal statement."

"So, where does this put us in the harassment case?" Eddie asked.

"I'll see what Cheryl's turned up. This thing about Neilsen bothers me. Chief Leavitt is dead, so we can't get his input. Mike swears he was out of the loop, and I believe him." Harvey sighed. "I wish she had some witnesses. I hate this case."

"Debbie Higgins says Joey was going to look into it."

"I know. I *really* hate that part."

Eddie's brown eyes focused on something beyond the room, and Harvey knew he was working out the worst-case scenario.

"This thing with Neilsen," Eddie began.

"It's the second time his name's come up," Harvey agreed.

"Have you talked to Candi in Records yet?"

"Not yet. Tomorrow, maybe."

"Would we bring Neilsen back from Massachusetts for something like this?"

Harvey scratched his chin. "Maybe I'll ask Mike to call someone in Framingham for a progress report on their chief of police. I guess I'd better clue Brad in, too. He's going to know something's up with all the female personnel parading up here for interviews this week." For the first time, he noticed a glitter in Eddie's eyes that had been lacking for weeks. "Hey, how's Leeanne? Have you heard from her today?"

Eddie smiled. "She liked the flowers, Harv."

"Fantastic."

"Now for Phase II?" Eddie asked.

"Let it sit for a while," Harvey advised.

"You don't think I should go over there tonight?"

"We may be here all night."

"Really?"

"Well, not all night, but I need to spend some time going over the statements we have so far, and I'm afraid I've got to talk to Brad before this goes any further."

"Maybe I should go over and see my mother later," Eddie said.

"Sure. Let Leeanne enjoy her white roses and dream a little."

Harvey leaned on the corner of the sergeant's desk. "Brad, can I see you for a minute?"

"Half a minute, maybe. We're right out straight. Ron's boys busted a chop shop, and two of my patrolmen brought in a carload of kids skipping school and smoking crack. The booking room's full, and I've got four in holding."

"Well, I'll try to keep it short."

Brad tossed his pen down. "Okay, talk."

"Maybe you'd like to step upstairs?"

"I don't have time, Harvey. What is it?"

Harvey glanced around. "It's a little sensitive."

"All right, all right, let's go."

Brad stood up and Harvey went ahead of him to punch the buttons on the security keypad at the door to the lobby. They stepped across to the stairway, and he paused to punch the code for that door.

"When are we going to get a card system?" Brad asked. "I get so tired of trying to remember fifty-odd thousand different numbers."

"That would be expensive." Harvey started up the stairs, but Brad stopped at the bottom. "Look, can't you just tell me here, or do I really have to climb two flights of stairs?"

Harvey turned and looked down at him from the third step. "Sorry, I thought we could sit down and discuss this."

"I'm telling you, Harvey, I'm swamped today. What is it? You got a problem with one of my guys?"

Harvey sighed. "Look, Brad, you're being investigated."

Brad stood very still, staring up at him through narrow slits of eyes, and Harvey was glad he was above him, and not too close.

"What the—"

"Easy, now. I need to notify you that you're under investigation in a personnel matter."

"What for?"

Harvey could imagine how menacing the tall,

stern sergeant would seem to a new recruit, especially a woman, though Brad could turn on a suave charm when he chose to.

"We've had allegations of sexual harassment."

Brad swore and slumped against the wall beside the closed door.

"We'll be talking to you about it—"

"Who's we?" Brad snapped.

"Well, the chief's put me in charge, but Sergeant Yeaton is helping, and Detective Thibodeau is in on it. That's it, so far as I know. We'll try to keep it low key."

"I get to know who filed the complaint, right?"

Harvey hesitated. "Actually, we don't have a formal complaint yet."

Brad blinked. "Then why on earth are you investigating?"

"Something came up as a sort of byproduct of another investigation, and we're trying to see if there's anything to it."

"So this is a rumor thing."

"Well, it's more than that."

"How much more?"

"We've got a taped statement from one woman who doesn't want to file formally, and we expect to get another statement soon. We're questioning a lot of people, Brad. The chief thinks it's serious. If we come up with much more, there will be formal complaints."

"When?"

"I'd say, expect to hear it soon."

"You're taping statements." Brad shook his head. "What am I supposed to have done?"

"When the complaint is filed, you'll get a copy, but it looks like inappropriate language, intimidation of a subordinate, and . . . well, maybe more than that."

"I'm speechless. Intimidation? Harvey, you know as well as I do you have to keep your troops in line. I probably intimidate a lot of men, too, but do they go whining about it?"

"This is sexual," Harvey reminded him.

"Fantastic."

"And, I just wanted you to know, I randomly picked a couple of your shifts from last week and requisitioned the surveillance videos from the camera over your desk."

"What?"

"Chief Browning asked me to review the tapes for potential infractions."

"You're spying on me?"

"Relax, Brad. It's not spying, it's a public record. Those cameras run all the time, and you know it. There's one over my desk, too."

"Oh, yeah. For our *protection*. Tell me about it." Brad turned toward the door and pulled on the handle, but it wouldn't open. Angrily, he stabbed at the keypad beside it and tried again, but the door didn't give.

"It's 3-1-9-9," Harvey said quietly.

218

Marie Thibodeau opened the door and grinned. "Eddie? Come in. Shut the door—it's cold out there. What are you doing here?"

"I just came to see if I could get a decent meal."

"We ate, but I'll fix you some leftovers."

"Great. Anything you cooked is great."

Eddie kissed her and stepped into the kitchen, stopping short when he saw his sister Élise at the table, holding her four-month-old son, Marco.

"Lisa! Hey! Great to see you."

She smiled up at him. "Hello, stranger."

"How's the little guy?" Eddie stepped close and put one finger out to touch the baby's cheek. "*Ça va*, Marco?"

"He's good. How are you doing?"

Eddie shrugged. "Been better, been worse."

"You haven't solved this case yet?" Marie opened the refrigerator and took out a couple of plastic containers.

"We're working on it."

"What's taking so long?" Lisa asked.

"An investigation like this takes time, that's all."

"Is it because he was French?" Marie asked, scooping food from the containers onto a plate.

"Because he was French?" Eddie laughed. "Please, you think this was a hate crime?"

"She means, is someone slowing down the investigation because of it," Lisa explained. "She thinks it's a conspiracy."

"Maman, they put their best Frenchman in charge." Eddie spread his arms wide.

"My son, the hotshot detective." Marie smiled and slid the plate into the microwave.

"How's your love life?" Lisa asked.

"Great. How's yours?" Eddie returned.

She laughed. "Come on. Are you seeing anyone?"

"Mostly I'm seeing witnesses these days."

"You'll never find another girl like Leeanne," Lisa said.

"Oh, there are lots of girls out there!" Marie brought two cans of beer from the refrigerator and held one out to him.

"I told you I don't drink that stuff now, Maman," Eddie said.

"Hmp." She held it out toward Lisa.

"Ma, I'm nursing."

Marie took the cans back to the refrigerator, then came back to the table with one of them and a glass. The microwave timer rang as she poured the beer out.

"I'll get it." Eddie stood and went for his plate and a fork. "You got anything else to drink?"

"Water. You know where we keep it."

When he had settled at the table again, Lisa said, "So, no dates lately."

He shrugged and took a bite of spaghetti. "Really good, Maman. Thanks."

"Have you seen Leeanne?" Lisa prompted.

"I see her."

"You do?" Marie asked in surprise. "Well, now."

"Sure. I see her lots. Well, not lots, but some. I saw her Thursday night."

"You went out?" Lisa was incredulous.

"No, we didn't go out, exactly. I just saw her. You said, did I see her. I saw her."

"What, you passed her on the street?" Marie sipped her beer.

"No, I *saw* her. I went over to Harvey's, and she was there."

"Did you talk to her?" Lisa asked.

"What do you care, you cat?"

"Édouard Jean," his mother warned. "You two are just like children."

"I miss her," Lisa said plaintively.

"Oh, sure. You told me last month you were going to scratch her eyes out." Eddie kept eating without giving his sister so much as a glance.

"I was mad," Lisa admitted. "Now I'm wondering if she wasn't a smart girl to give your ring back. You're insufferable. *Tu est stupide!*"

Eddie laughed. "*Moi?*"

"Can I wear the dress?" Lisa asked.

"What dress?"

"The one for the wedding. How long am I supposed to keep it before I can wear it?"

"I don't know. You want to wear it someplace
else?"

"Ansel is taking me to the theater for our
anniversary."

"Why don't you call Leeanne and ask her if it's
okay for you to wear it?"

"You don't think that would be tacky?"

"Just wear it," her mother advised.

"Well, if there's any chance . . ." Lisa gazed
questioningly at Eddie.

He sat back and wiped his lips on his napkin.
"When's your anniversary?"

"The thirtieth."

"Wait."

"You mean—?"

"I mean nothing. You asked, I told you."

"Well, now," said Marie.

Deidre Cleridge Martin arrived at the police
station Wednesday morning, accompanied by her
husband.

"Mr. Martin," Harvey greeted him. "Thank you
for coming, Deidre."

"Is this going to lead to criminal charges?"
Martin asked anxiously. The young man was
neatly dressed, and he kept possession of Deidre's
hand as Harvey led them to the interview room.

"We're not sure yet, but your wife's statement

will help us determine that. I've asked Sergeant Cheryl Yeaton to tape this session. Then we'll have it transcribed, and you and Deidre can read it over before she signs it." He smiled at Deidre. "Ready?"

"I think so."

Cheryl came off the elevator, and Harvey left her with the couple while he went up one flight to the chief's office.

"Any word from Framingham?" he asked Mike.

"Yeah, I talked to a couple of people down there. They're cagey. Don't like anyone snooping around, asking personal questions about their chief of police."

"So, they think he's above reproach?"

"Either that, or they're already not liking him and want to be the first to take a swing. I'm trying to get hold of their mayor and explain the sensitive nature of this inquiry. I may have to get Jill Weymouth in on it, but I hate to tip her on this before we know where we're going."

When Harvey returned to the Priority Unit, he was surprised to see Jeff Wainthrop sitting on the corner of Eddie's desk. He wore his fire department uniform and was deep in conversation with Eddie and Nate.

"Hey, Jeffrey! Business or pleasure?"

Jeff stood up and extended his hand. "Harvey! Glad you're here. I seem to be a witness in your murder case."

223

Harvey turned expectantly to Eddie.

"It's like this. I had Tony check to see if we had any units near City Hall at the time of the murder, but we didn't. Well, this morning he and Nate were talking about it, and Nate had a brainstorm. There might have been a siren out there that wasn't a police car." Nate stood by modestly while Eddie detailed his part in the discovery.

Jeff said, "We had a call at 11:45 on Labor Day, Harvey. The dispatcher logged it. Mark Johnson and I were sent out with the ambulance to a store down the street. A woman had fainted in the checkout line. It turned out to be a diabetic case, and we had to transport her. I was miffed because I wanted to meet Beth and Jennifer at one, when you were starting the game. We didn't get back in time. But anyway, we went right past City Hall with the siren going at approximately 11:50."

Harvey put his hand on Jeff's shoulder. "How approximate?"

"Two minutes, either way, I figure. We got to the location in less than ten. It's all in the log at the fire station."

"So, the shooter could have taken advantage of the noise to cover the sound of the shot." Eddie spread his hands, smiling. "I don't say he planned it, but it was, what do you call it?"

"Fortuitous," said Harvey.

"Serendipity," Jeff suggested.

"Luck," Nate put in.

Eddie nodded. "*Bonne chance.*"

Harvey looked expectantly at Nate. "All right, Miller, your next step is . . . ?"

"Well, sir, I checked with Eddie, and he agreed we need to talk to those guards from the game committee again and see if they heard the ambulance go by while they were watching the elevator."

"Good."

Eddie winced. "We shoulda asked them before, when we thought of a siren, but we were so sure there wasn't one, we never asked."

"Okay, Nate, get on it." When Miller had gone through the stairway door, Harvey said to Eddie, "We know why they didn't hear the shot. It's interesting, but not really evidence."

"I know, but, Harv, there's more. The lab sent a preliminary report on the fibers and hairs we found in the comptroller's office and on the dummy's clothes."

"And?"

"Two unidentified hairs on the dummy's jacket. Blond, short. They don't belong to anyone on the setup crew, or the guy who donated the jacket."

"Don't look at me," said Jeff. "Now I'd better get back to work."

As Eddie escorted Jeff down the stairway, Paula approached Harvey.

"Captain, the front desk just called. There's a Ms. Harrington here. Apparently she's been up to the chief's office, and she's coming down the elevator to see you."

As she spoke, the elevator door rumbled open, and Harvey went to meet the woman stepping out. Her short-skirted red suit and black heels looked out of place in the police station.

"Ms. Harrington?" He held out his hand, wondering if she had something to do with the harassment case.

"Captain Larson?" Her dark eyes appraised him from behind lashes too thick to be real.

"Yes, how may I help you?"

"I'm actually here to see Detective Thibodeau, but Chief Browning insisted I get your permission first."

"Oh? Is this about a case Detective Thibodeau is working on?"

She laughed. "Heavens, no, nothing so dramatic. I'm from *Portland Life* magazine." She held out a business card, and Harvey took it, managing to avoid touching the long scarlet nails.

Regina Harrington, editorial assistant, Portland Life Magazine.

The text put Harvey on guard. "And your purpose for this visit is . . . ?"

Before she could answer, the stairway door opened and Eddie sauntered, whistling, toward his desk. He tossed a glance toward Harvey and

Ms. Harrington, and kept walking, his hands in his pockets.

"Would that be the person in question?" Regina Harrington asked softly.

"Yes, ma'am." Harvey watched her approving gaze as she evaluated Eddie from head to toe.

"Oh, yes, I think I've found my man. Isn't he the Heartbreaker Hero who was featured on *Morning Nation* last winter?"

Harvey cleared his throat. "What is this for, may I ask, ma'am?"

She turned toward him, smiling. "*Portland Life* magazine is doing a feature on eligible men in the city."

Harvey laughed outright, and Eddie glanced his way before sitting down at his computer. Farther down the room, Tony looked up. He had his phone to his ear, and he turned his chair away from them.

Ms. Harrington nodded. "Good. You find it amusing. That's our hope, that the feature will be entertaining. A little frothy, perhaps, but tons of local interest. We usually do more serious pieces, but we intend to have some fun with this one. The ten most gorgeous bachelors in the city. Every single woman in town will buy a copy."

Harvey couldn't kill the smile. "I'm sorry, Ms. Harrington. Detective Thibodeau is an extremely busy man. I don't think—"

"Why don't you let him decide? It wouldn't

take much of his time. We'll arrange an interview and a photo shoot for when he's off duty."
Her eyebrows went up as Eddie stood to remove
his sport coat. "Oh, yes, I think we want a photo
in his shirtsleeves. Maybe a T-shirt, but with the
holster and badge. And those eyes! He could be
Number One, easily."

"Now, wait a minute, ma'am," Harvey protested. "Eddie is involved in a very sensitive case
right now."

"Would that be the Labor Day Murder?" she
asked eagerly.

"Well, yes. You can see how valuable his time
is."

"All the more interesting for our readers. Off
duty," she repeated. "It won't take more than an
hour. We'll just ask him about his hobbies, how
he came to be a detective, how he likes it, that
sort of thing. He's never been married before,
has he?"

"What? No, but—uh, please, I don't—" He let
it hang there as she stepped determinedly toward
Eddie.

Okay, Lord, this is your ballgame, Harvey
breathed, sinking into his swivel chair. Eddie
looked up at Ms. Harrington and began to smile
as she launched into her plea.

"Oh, what a smile!" she cried. "Yes! We've
got to have you on our cover! I knew this was an
inspiration. What do you think, Detective?"

Eddie laughed. "Sorry, I don't think it's right for me."

"Oh, come on, it will be great. Women all over the city will want to meet you."

"That's okay, ma'am," Eddie assured her. "I have enough women in my life already." He glanced toward his captain, and Harvey winked. "See, I—I'm pretty much engaged."

"Engaged?" Ms. Harrington's disappointment was palpable. "Pretty much?"

"Well, yes, sort of."

Harvey began to smile.

"Well, are you or aren't you?"

Eddie hesitated. "Let's say I hope to be very soon, and I don't think the lady would appreciate me showing up in your magazine as an available bachelor."

Chagrined, Regina Harrington opened her purse. "All right, here's my card if you change your mind. Do you know where I can find Detective Winfield?"

"Tony Winfield?"

"Yes." She was consulting a list. Harvey suppressed a chortle.

"He's right over there, ma'am." Eddie pointed toward Tony's desk.

"He's not engaged, is he?" she asked.

"No, ma'am. He's free as a bird. And did you know he's the governor's nephew?"

Ms. Harrington straightened. "You don't say.

The chief never mentioned that. Say, that's a good angle."

Eddie shrugged. "He's a nice guy."

"Does he date much?"

"Some. He's fun. Girls like him. And he drives a Mustang convertible."

"Kind of a babyface." Ms. Harrington frowned. "Still, the governor's nephew . . ." She walked briskly toward Tony's desk.

Chapter 11

Eddie went quickly down the stairs at six o'clock. He was determined to make it to prayer meeting on time. At the bottom of the second flight, the door opened, nearly smacking him in the face.

"Sarah!"

"Eddie! Sorry."

"That's okay." They stood awkwardly, looking each other over. "How you been?" he asked at last.

"Okay. I heard there was a lady from that city magazine here looking for you."

He laughed. "Not me. They picked Tony."

"Really? They asked him over you?"

"Sure, he'll be great."

Sarah shrugged. "I guess he's cute, but he's not really handsome." She flushed a little and looked down at her feet. "They probably took him because of his uncle. Funny, Ray Oliver told me they wanted you."

"I told her I wasn't exactly eligible," Eddie confided.

Sarah's face fell. "Oh. I thought you and Leeanne broke up."

"Well, we kinda did, but . . . I haven't given up hope."

She nodded. "Then I hope it works out for you."

"Really?" He tried to see her eyes, but her lashes hid them.

"Yeah. I'd like to see you happy. Don't you think one of us should be happy?" She smiled and stepped past him toward the stairs.

"Sarah—"

She stopped with one foot on the bottom step and sniffed a little.

"You're not—" Eddie stopped, wishing he had just let her go.

She took a deep breath and looked up at him, her eyes shining with tears. "I've been wishing I could talk to you lately, but it didn't seem right somehow."

"What about?"

"Remember last year, when you tried to explain to me why you left the church?"

Eddie nodded.

"I should have listened to you."

"It's not too late."

"My mom and I have talked about it."

"How do you mean?"

"She said . . . maybe you were right. Way back then, I mean. I was just mad, and I wouldn't listen. But then I got curious. I actually bought a book off a book rack at the grocery store. You know, those religious book racks?"

"Yeah. What kind of book?"

"It was about families, and how God can heal families that have fought and hurt each other. It was really interesting, but I don't think anything could fix the Benoit family."

"God can do anything," Eddie said softly. "Sometimes it's not the way we think it will be, or as soon as we wish it would be. I'm praying for my own family, and I haven't seen much change there yet. But I believe that someday they'll listen, and God can change their hearts."

Sarah looked briefly up at him, then down again. "Harvey said he and Jennifer have prayed for me all this time. Can you imagine?"

"Yes, I can imagine that."

"They really say prayers every day for people?"

"Not saying prayers like we learned. It's different. They—we—pray for people by name, and ask God to help them with their problems."

"So, it's not like they say Hail Marys for me?"

Eddie shook his head. "Listen, you ought to talk to Jennifer. She knows a lot about prayer and stuff. I know she could explain it better than I can."

"I couldn't just call her."

"Sure, you could. She'd love to see you again."

"I don't know." Sarah looked up suddenly, a little frown wrinkling her brow. "Hey, how well do you know that EMT guy?"

"Jeff Wainthrop? He's Leeanne and Jennifer's brother."

"No, not him. The one named Mark. He was with Jeff the night—you know. The night you called them for Nicole."

Eddie remembered. "Mark Johnson? I don't know him very well. I've met him a couple of times is all."

"Oh."

"Why do you ask?"

"He asked me to have coffee with him sometime. I kind of blew him off."

"Why? He seems like a nice guy. Jeff works with him a lot. I think they get along."

Sarah shrugged. "Maybe I'll say yes next time."

"How's your sister?"

"She's better. She went back to work a couple of weeks ago."

Eddie nodded, knowing the inner wounds from Nicole's ordeal would take longer to heal.

"She still says our dad never hurt her."

"Maybe he didn't," Eddie said. "She's younger than you . . ."

"She's talking about going back to live with him again. She says my mother and I are wrong about him. But we know we're not."

"I'm sorry." Eddie didn't know what else to say. Sarah's mother had never filed charges against her husband.

Sarah swallowed hard. "So, you and Leeanne are . . ."

"Listen, Sarah, I'm pretty sure she's the right one for me. I want to marry her, and I'm doing my best to patch things up. I said some stupid things before, and she said a few, and . . . well, we both needed to grow up a little. But I'm still hoping, and I'm praying about that, too. I've asked God to forgive me and to help me be a good husband. I want to spend the rest of my life with Leeanne. You understand?"

Sarah nodded. "I'm glad for you, Eddie. Really."

"Thanks. I'll see you."

"Yeah."

When he entered the church, Leeanne was already seated in the middle of a packed pew, between Jennifer and Sharon Browning, and she held Connor on her lap. Eddie sat down behind them, wishing he'd gotten away from the station a little earlier. It seemed he was always a step or two behind these days.

The pastor was speaking on forgiveness, and Eddie couldn't help applying every point to his and Leeanne's situation. When he'd tried to talk things out with her, she'd said she wanted to be friends. Would she ever be ready for more than that? And what was his responsibility if she wanted to keep it at this level?

Nothing's going to happen if I keep on working

twelve hours a day and being late everywhere I go. She might go home again for the weekend. An emptiness washed over him. He allowed his eyes to drift to the back of her head. She had pulled the top of her hair back with a green ribbon. At the neckline of her dress, he glimpsed a fine gold chain of square links that disappeared beneath the fabric. His pulse quickened. She used to wear the little jade cross he'd given her for Christmas on that chain, he was sure. She may have mailed back the diamond, but he hadn't seen the jade cross in months.

He knew he wouldn't give up on Leeanne until she was married, to him or to someone else. Time for Phase II, he decided. During prayer time he remained silent, but his thoughts churned, and his fragmented pleas went up to God for a reconciliation.

"Carl called me and said they'll come to dinner tonight," Harvey told Jennifer at lunch on Thursday.

"Oh, good. When I spoke to Margaret, she thought this would be the best night—barring any emergencies, of course." Jennifer took his empty plate away and refilled his coffee cup. Lunch at home always had the feeling of a stolen tryst, and she tried not to let him feel rushed.

"I told Eddie I want him to come, too."

"I hope you didn't phrase it as an order."

"No, but I didn't leave him a lot of wiggle room." Harvey took a sip of his coffee.

"You know, Beth hasn't been feeling very well." Jennifer sat down beside him. "I've been running over there two or three times a day to make sure she's all right. She promised to lie down this afternoon. I hope Margaret can take a quick look at her tonight. Beth's next appointment isn't for another week."

"You think it's serious?"

"She's a little crampy."

"Not good, at seven months."

"You're right."

"Is Jeff home?"

"He was supposed to get off at midnight, but there was a big fire last night, and he didn't get home until four o'clock. He slept in this morning."

Harvey turned his head toward the door. "What was that?" He got up and walked toward the entry.

"Company?" Jennifer asked.

"Florist truck next door."

Jennifer went quickly to the entry. "Let me run over and get it. I don't want Beth to get up, and Jeff might still be sleeping."

"If it's for Leeanne, bring it over here. She'll be here tonight."

"She'd better be," Jennifer said. She had not only asked Leeanne to make a point of eating dinner at their house, but had instructed Beth to send her over if she showed up next door.

When she returned to the kitchen carrying a florist's box, Harvey was pulling the bag of trash from the overflowing kitchen wastebasket.

"I can do that, honey," she protested. "You'll get your suit dirty."

"No, I'll do it."

She set the box down and opened a drawer. "Well, here, let me get you another gold-plated trash bag."

"What, the price went up?"

"Actually, the price is the same. But I used to get twenty in a box, and now I get fifteen."

Harvey tied up the full bag and shook the new one open. "Do you need more grocery money, gorgeous?"

"No, we're doing all right."

"Okay, because I don't want to spread our resources so thin you can't keep the household running."

Jennifer laughed. "We're not wealthy, but you're so careful, I feel as though I'm the most financially secure woman in Maine. Excluding Tabitha King, of course."

Harvey smiled. "What about Barbara Bush and Martha Stewart?"

Jennifer's lip curled. "They're from away."

"Has Eddie been spending his money at the florist's again?"

"Yeah, pink roses. Do you think that's significant?"

"What?"

"White last time, pink this time."

"How should I know?" Harvey made certain the trash bag fit tightly around the lip of the wastebasket.

Jennifer watched him, smiling. "Well, they're beautiful. So, how's Mike doing on his investment?"

"Good. The septic system is turning out to be quite a headache. They need an extra big leach field for that many bathrooms."

"I would think so, since there's no city plumbing up there."

Harvey sat down again and picked up his coffee mug. "There's a big setback from the lake, and he needs to have a quarter acre or so cleared. It's expensive to hire anyone to haul big equipment way up there. And once they're there, it's eighty bucks an hour."

"Ouch. What's he going to do?"

"I told him to talk to Rick Bradley. Rick's boss knew someone in Ashland, which is a whole lot closer to Churchill Lake. Rick is going up for three days next week and oversee the building of the leach field."

"Wow, terrific."

"Yeah, Mike told him to take Ruthann and the kids. They're putting them in the apartment he's finishing for him and Sharon on the ground floor. They've got the shower hooked up now, and I think they'll be fairly comfortable. They can't do any more plumbing until the drain field's done, though."

"I'm glad Rick's going."

"Me, too. He's a pretty smart guy. He made arrangements with one of the paper companies to get gravel from a pit they have about ten miles from the site."

"That will save Mike a lot."

"Yeah. I was afraid they'd have to haul it in from a hundred miles away. He's going to need a lot of gravel. All the plumbing they're putting in will be the biggest expense, for sure. But it looks like they'll get the outside part finished before snow flies, and Mike hopes to have everything in the apartment bathroom and the kitchen hooked up soon, and even a washing machine, so he and Sharon can keep going up for weekends this winter and be comfortable."

The doorbell chimed, and Jennifer turned toward the entry. "It's the flower guy." Puzzled, she hurried to the door.

"Hi, I'm sorry, ma'am, I didn't realize before that you were my next delivery. That is, if you're Mrs. Larson."

"Yes, I'm Jennifer Larson."

"Then this is for you."

He placed a second florist's box in her arms.

Harvey was carrying dishes to the sink. "Whatcha got, gorgeous?"

"As if you didn't know." She set the box on the table and lifted the lid. "Oh, honey!" A dozen yellow roses lay couched in green tissue.

Harvey smiled and pulled her into his arms. "I was afraid the idiot had forgotten you." He kissed her tenderly. "I should buy you flowers more often."

"You didn't have to."

"Can't let Eddie show me up."

"I knew this campaign had your fingerprints on it."

He laughed. "Think it's working?"

"I hope so. Eddie, with your patience and finesse behind him. She doesn't realize how blessed she is."

"I've gotta get back to work." He held her close for another moment.

"I hear Connor," Jennifer whispered, kissing his ear. "Do you want to see him before you go?"

Harvey looked at his watch. "Yeah, but I need to hurry. Lots of interviews this afternoon. I'm already late."

The wall phone rang. "I'll get it," Jennifer said. "You go give Connor a squeeze." She grabbed the receiver on the second ring. "Hello?"

"Jennifer? This is Sarah Benoit. I hope you don't mind, but Eddie suggested I call you."

241

• • •

Harvey bent over the microscope and looked carefully into the eyepiece.

"You see what I mean?" Eddie asked.

"You're right, it's not a match." Harvey sighed.

"I'm glad, I guess, but what now?" Eddie removed the glass slide and slipped it into the protective case.

"We know it's not Brad's hair from the dummy's jacket. Now we need to compare it with Derek Anson's. You said he has light hair."

"Yeah, but he's a big guy, Harv. He's as tall as Jeff, and he probably weighs two-forty. I can't see him crawling out from under the bathroom stall door."

"You never know. Thanks, Zoe." He nodded to the lab technician.

"Anytime, guys," she said.

They left the lab and walked out toward the stairway.

"What about the security tapes from the sergeant's desk?" Eddie asked.

"I took the tapes home last night and skimmed through the first shift. Talk about boring."

"Nothing out of line?"

"Oh, there were a few comments that I wish hadn't been made, but I don't think there's anything incriminating. One patrolman made some rather vulgar remarks about the dispatcher, Annie."

"Oh, Annie," Eddie said darkly.

"What?"

"Where there's smoke, there may be fire."

"She has a reputation?" Harvey eyed him narrowly. "How come I don't hear these things?"

"Because you're a captain, and you don't hang around the patrolmen's locker room."

"Well, you're not exactly in the thick of it."

"Still, you know. I go to the diner for lunch, and the guys will say things in front of me they wouldn't say in front of you."

"So, the guys downstairs think she's fast, or what?"

"I heard she's pretty free and easy."

"Any evidence, or just hearsay?"

"Uh, well, Jared Brenner claimed firsthand knowledge."

"Huh." Harvey shook his head. "Does that make it okay to gossip about her? I mean, is it all right to say Annie's easy, but not okay to say Debbie looks hot today?"

"You got me." Eddie pushed open the door to Priority. "If the woman doesn't know what they're saying, is it harassment?"

"I don't know, but it isn't right."

"Well then, you've got some women who talk as bad as the men."

"True," Harvey conceded. "Jennifer told me when she worked in Records that some of the clerks talked pretty rough. So, if the woman isn't insulted, it's not hostile, so therefore it's not harassment, but if she's upset, then it is?"

"I guess it's a fine line," Eddie said. "But we know some of it went beyond remarks. At least, the witnesses say it did in a few cases."

Harvey headed for his desk. "See if you can get Anson to come down here for another interview."

"He won't like it."

"Then we'll have to chase him to Biddeford again."

"You want to ask for a warrant for his hair?"

Harvey frowned. "I'm not sure the judge would think we have probable cause."

"I don't suppose we could pick up a stray hair or two? Like getting his fingerprints on a glass or something?"

"I don't know. We're not arresting him."

"But if it's in plain sight? Like on his jacket? He *is* a suspect."

"We don't want to blow the evidence and make it inadmissible."

"Okay, Harv. I'll see if he'll come down here tomorrow."

Harvey sat down wearily as the secretary approached his desk.

"Captain Larson, I have some messages for you."

"Thanks, Paula."

"Coffee, sir?"

"That would be great, but I can get it myself."

"I don't mind. Not that I would get it for all the guys, but you've got a lot on your plate."

"Thanks. I guess I drink a pot or two by myself every day."

Paula clucked at him. "Better watch the caffeine, Captain."

"I know, I know."

She smiled. "Do you think you could stand decaf?"

"How about half and half?"

"Well, it's a start." She went off toward the break room, and Harvey consulted his schedule. When she returned, he took the mug from her. "Thanks, Paula. I'm not sure how cost-efficient it is for the P.D. to keep us in coffee."

"I don't know if you guys could function without it."

"Could you please call Records and tell Candi Mullins I can see her anytime?" Harvey asked. "Our appointment is for two, but if she's free now, I want to move things along."

"Sure." Paula smiled and went back to her desk.

Harvey sipped the coffee, trying to decide whether she had cut it with decaf or not, then brought in his e-mail.

"Harvey?"

He turned to find Nate standing at his elbow. "What is it?"

"Something a little odd. Probably not related to the murder, but . . ."

"Let me be the judge of that."

"Okay. I went over the list of City Hall employees, and we know a few of them were there that day."

"Sure, Mayor Weymouth was there, and I saw several city council members."

"Yes, sir, but so were a couple of custodians. They showed the setup crew where to find stuff, and they were supposed to clean up after and put everything back in place in the rooms we were using when it was over."

Harvey took another sip of coffee. "Interesting. Have we interviewed them?"

"Yes, sir, but I found something new in the computer files."

Harvey glanced up at him. Nate had excelled in computer training, and Harvey had begun to turn to him first with assignments involving a lot of computer time. "What did you find?"

"This one man, Donald Lloyd, was arrested in August."

Harvey raised his eyebrows.

"He was picked up one night for an expired registration, and they found heroin in his car."

"And?"

"Well, he bailed out real quick, for one thing."

"Standard for those charges, if it was his first offense."

"Yes, sir, but he was supposed to go to court yesterday. That's how it came to my attention. I put his name—well, all the names on our witness list—on the flagging program."

Harvey nodded. He hadn't taken the time to do it himself. He was slipping.

"Well, it came up that his hearing was canceled."

"Why?"

"Lack of evidence."

Harvey frowned. "What about the drugs?"

"I don't know. They also dismissed the registration count."

"So, Lloyd didn't even pay a fine?"

"Not a penny, as near as I can tell."

"Why not?"

"DISO—dismissed for other reasons. You want me to call the courthouse?"

"Yeah. Find out what happened to the heroin, too."

"I'll try."

Nate turned away, and Harvey sat mulling the turn of events in his mind.

"Nate," he called.

"Yes, sir?"

"Find out if that man's got a record."

The elevator opened, and Candi Mullins came in. Harvey stood up.

"Hello, Candi. Thanks for taking the time."

She smiled. "I'm always ready for a break. How's Jennifer?"

"She's fine, thanks."

"I don't suppose she misses filing records? We're shorthanded."

Harvey laughed. "You couldn't drag her away from home."

Candi chuckled. "I figured it was like that. How's the baby?"

"Fantastic. Listen, you know what this is about?"

She lowered her eyes and said demurely, "I've heard things. Questions about sexual misbehavior?"

"We're just checking to see if any of the female employees have had problems with harassment on the job. Any inappropriate conduct that should be looked into."

"Well, I can think of a couple of officers with foul mouths, if that's what you mean."

"Do you want to give specifics?"

"I don't know. Since I've been married, I haven't had to put up with so much."

"But the single girls get a lot of attention around here?"

She shrugged. "I had my share of offers before I married Dave."

"Guys wanting a date? Or something more obnoxious?"

"Well, some of them are just plain obnoxious all the time, but most of them are harmless."

Harvey watched her closely. "I heard you had a close encounter with Raymond Neilsen in the elevator once."

She laughed. "Yeah, well, it made me uncomfortable at the time, but I guess it wasn't serious."

"I heard he grabbed you. What does that mean?"

"Oh, it wasn't that bad. He just kind of put his arm around me and told me what a great job the civilian workers do for the department. Got right in my face, you know? I was new here, and it disturbed me. I was always careful not to get too close to him again."

"So, you wouldn't characterize that incident as harassment?"

She shrugged. "Some guys are touchy, you know? Patting your shoulder, squeezing your hand. There are some, like Bill Theriault, who are almost fatherly. He doesn't bother me. Then there are guys you wouldn't want to get in an elevator with alone."

"Neilsen was in that category?"

"Well, like I said, I was new, and he was the deputy chief. It startled me. I didn't know what to make of it, so I stayed out of his way after that."

Harvey nodded thoughtfully. "So, what about Bill Theriault? Do you think he should be told to keep his hands off the women?"

"I think anyone offended by it would tell him. It's not sexual with him. At least I don't think so. He's close to retirement, isn't he?"

Harvey wasn't sure that mattered, but he let it pass. "Who else?"

"Hm. I don't remember anyone else touching me in a way I felt was inappropriate. But the language!"

"You're here days. Some of Brad Lyons's men have filthy mouths?"

She sniffed. "If you're going to bring up Brad, why not start with him?"

"All right, let's."

"He's crude."

"Don't some women find him charming? I mean, three women married him, after all."

"He probably can be, but he can also be vulgar in the extreme. Especially when he's been ignored by a pretty girl."

"Would you make a statement to that effect?"

She blinked at him. "This is about Brad, isn't it? You know, I can't think of a particular thing I personally heard him say, but several of the girls in our department have complained about him."

"Okay. We'll get around to them. You're sure you don't have anything specific?"

"Not things he said to women. I've heard him say a few things to other men *about* women. Some were pretty bad."

"What did you do when he said them?"

She flushed. "Pretended I didn't hear and left the room. Do you want me to tell you what he said?"

"Unfortunately, in order for me to use it as evidence, you have to either tell me on tape, or write it out in a statement."

"I think I'd rather write it."

"Fine. Let's put you in our interview room, and I'll give you some paper and a pen."

"Look, is this going to court? I mean, will we all have to testify against him?"

"I hope not. At this point it's being kept internal."

She nodded. "All right, I'll do it."

Chapter 12

"Are you sure you want me to eat at your house tonight?" Eddie called across the room.

Harvey looked up from packing his briefcase. "I thought you could run through the rest of that videotape I screened."

"I could do it here."

"Or you could do it in my living room and have a nice meal too, and get to visit with Carl and Margaret."

"I dunno."

"Come on, Eddie. Leeanne isn't going to bite your head off."

"Are you sure about that?"

"The way things are going, I'm not even sure she'll show up for dinner."

"Okay." Eddie looked at his watch. "I'd better finish my report. I'll be there in half an hour. Hey, did the florist deliver?"

Harvey smiled. "Pink and yellow. Jenny was impressed."

"Let's hope Leeanne is." Eddie yawned.

"You'd better go home early tonight. You're running yourself ragged."

"It's these two cases, you know?"

"I know."

"Or is it one case?"

"If we knew that, my friend, things would be a sight easier."

Eddie winced. "I keep forgetting who knows what. I spilled it to Tony about the harassment thing, Harv. I didn't mean to, but the guys know we're working closely with Cheryl on something and interviewing all these women."

"I know. I think everyone in the department is aware of the investigation. Don't worry about it."

"So, can we assign our men to interviews that overlap both cases?"

"Let me think about that. Better to keep them on the murder if possible, but if the cases merge . . ." Eddie was yawning again. "Do you think I drink too much coffee?" Harvey asked.

"I don't know. Some days you have to."

Eddie was fast-forwarding the security tape from the patrol sergeant's area on Harvey's video player when Leeanne came in and sat beside him on the sofa.

"Better put that away. Abby and Peter are here with the boys."

He clicked the remote. "We sure wouldn't want them hearing some of this."

"Finding what you were looking for?"

He was surprised she had asked, and even more that she had sat down near him. "Yeah, Harvey told me about a couple of spots, and he's right. The guys go lean on Brad's desk and shoot the breeze, and you never know what's going to pop out. Some of them have an inordinate interest in the female anatomy, that's for sure."

"So, these cops are hanging around talking dirty about all the women who work there? That's disgusting. The newspaper would fire them if they did that."

"Well, it's not that simple. In the first place, there seem to be a few who are the worst. A lot of guys just make a comment now and then, or fail to object when someone else does it. But there are two or three who seem especially . . ."

"Perverted?" Leeanne asked.

"I wasn't going to use that word, but they're not very classy."

"And the sergeant allows it?"

"Oh, yeah, he allows it." Eddie grimaced. "The truth is, he's one of the worst. But I shouldn't tell you that."

"I'm not working for the paper anymore."

"I know." He smiled at her and looked deep into her eyes for the first time in weeks. His throat tightened. Why did things have to be so painful?

"*Tu es fatigué*," she said softly.

"Exhausted, but I feel like I've got to keep

254

going until we find out who killed Joey. I've never had a case that drove me like this before."

"What does the harassment issue have to do with it?"

"It's complicated, and I don't suppose I should discuss it with you," he said apologetically.

"Okay, sorry. When it's over, will you explain it to me?"

"In great detail, *ma belle*." Her tender smile made his heart pound.

The doorbell rang. Eddie ejected the videotape and stood reluctantly. He took the tape to Harvey in the kitchen.

"Where do you want this?"

"I'll put it in my briefcase for now, just for safety."

"There's more?" Eddie asked.

"Yeah, I've got another tape, but I haven't had time to look at it yet. So, how's it going with Leeanne?" Harvey asked as he locked the briefcase.

"Fine, I guess, but we haven't had a chance to really talk. I mean, you know, about us. Personal stuff."

"Mm. Well, she seems amenable tonight."

"Does that mean she likes me again?"

Harvey chuckled. "Yes, Eddie, that means she likes you. It's pretty obvious now, I think. And she made a big to-do about the roses when she came home."

"Good. She thanked me, but, you know, people were around."

"Yeah, I know."

"Harvey, we need a couple more chairs." Jennifer stood in the doorway with Connor in her arms. They had set up tables in the study because Beth and Jeff, it turned out, were coming for dinner, too.

"Sure, gorgeous," Harvey said. "Give me a hand, Ed?"

Leeanne went upstairs to freshen up. She'd missed staying here with Jennifer. She got along fine with Beth, but it wasn't the same. She and her sister had been very close before everything blew up with Eddie, and she liked Harvey a lot. He treated her with more respect than Jeff did. Jeff couldn't forget that she was his little sister. He made no secret of the fact that, in his opinion, she had treated Eddie abominably. At least Harvey acted as though she had a right to some space and time to regroup.

When she went back downstairs, Carl and Margaret Turner and Julia were just coming in.

Margaret kissed Jennifer on the cheek and handed her a grocery sack. "It's slaw from the deli."

"Perfect," Jennifer said. "Thanks."

"I thought I'd have time to make something, but . . ."

"No apologies needed."

"Well, next time you're coming to our house. We owe you."

"Who's counting?" Jennifer grinned at Julia. "How are you doing? I see you've brought back the horse book you borrowed."

They soon sat down to eat, and the conversation flowed throughout the meal. When they moved into the living room later, Leeanne removed Connor from his infant seat and took a seat on the couch with him on her lap.

"Can I sit here?"

The note of uncertainty in Eddie's voice surprised her.

I've done this to him, she thought. *I've stayed away from him, and I haven't let him sit beside me at church. He's never in his life been unsure of himself, but now he doesn't know which way to jump.*

She didn't like it.

"I was hoping you would," she said quietly, and her pulse raced as his slow smile crept out. *Why, why did I hold him off so long?*

Margaret came into the room and made a beeline for her. "May I hold the baby?"

"Of course." Leeanne handed Connor to her.

Harvey and Jennifer settled in comfortable chairs, and Harvey smiled at Margaret. "Carl tells me you need to get back in practice doing that."

"What?" Jennifer nearly screamed. She clapped

a hand to her mouth and leaned close to Margaret. "You didn't *tell* me!"

"I didn't have a chance."

Jennifer leaned over and hugged Margaret. "This is the best news! Margaret, I'm so happy for you."

Carl pulled his chair close to Margaret's and sat down. "Well, Goldilocks, you and Harvey had your part in the drama."

"Is it a boy?" Jennifer asked.

Margaret laughed. "We don't know yet. I asked Carl if he wanted me to run a blood test and find out, but he said no."

Jennifer stared at Carl. "I'm proud of you."

He shrugged. "It's not so important now."

"I understand." Harvey slid his arm around Jennifer's waist, and she leaned against him.

Leeanne sat quietly beside Eddie, feeling the contentment that permeated the room. Her arm rested against Eddie's as she sat close to him, making room for Beth and Jeff beside them on the couch, and she took comfort in his warmth.

When she glanced at Eddie, his eyelids were drooping, and his long, thick lashes lay dark against his skin. She shifted just a little and let her sleeve brush against his hand. He started and sat up, throwing her a sheepish glance.

By the end of twenty minutes of conversation, he was hovering between consciousness and sleep, but when Jennifer offered more coffee all around, he roused.

"Coffee, Eddie?" Jennifer asked.

"Absolutely. Thanks."

Jennifer chuckled. "I think you've about reached your limit on sleep deprivation. Maybe you should go home to bed."

"Oh, not yet." He'd hardly had a chance to see Leeanne.

Jennifer smiled and put a mug in his hand. "Okay."

She moved on, and Eddie sipped the coffee. It was too hot, and he sucked in air.

Leeanne and Beth both declined.

"Beth?" Margaret Turner looked over at her. "Jennifer tells me you need a consult."

"Oh, excuse me." Beth pushed awkwardly up from the sofa. "Leeanne, I'll see you later."

As they left the room, Margaret said softly, "Not feeling so good this week, honey?"

Eddie had set his coffee down on a coaster on the end table, and his eyelids drooped again. When his head nodded and his eyes closed, Leeanne let him drift off.

Half an hour later, the Turners left. Jeff and Beth soon followed them out the door. Leeanne leaned over and ruffled Eddie's hair lightly. He opened his eyes and looked at her. She smiled, and he glanced around at the empty living room.

"Oh, boy," he said, stretching. "*Je dormais.*"

"*Oui. Leves-toi.*"

"*Je le regrette.*"

"Don't be sorry. You're out on your feet. Harvey told me to wake you up and send you packing."

His disappointed frown encouraged the flickering hope in her heart.

"I was hoping we'd have a chance to talk tonight." His eyes were sincere but glazed with fatigue.

"Maybe tomorrow? If you don't sleep, you won't be any good at busting crooks tomorrow."

"Did Beth and Jeff go?"

"Ten minutes ago. They told me to let you sleep."

"You shoulda woke me up. I feel like I ought to have been more polite, you know?"

"It's okay."

"Leeanne, just sit here for a minute, please?"

She looked into his eyes. He didn't speak for a moment, and she let herself return his gaze steadily, although she felt her color rise as the realization hit her: she loved him beyond anything she'd ever felt before. More than when he'd proposed, more than when he'd carried her out of Jeff's house after she'd been bruised and terrorized by a criminal, more than the night he'd told her father, *I'll do everything I can to make sure you're not sorry.*

He reached slowly for her hand and clasped it. "I know we're both really busy right now, but . . . sometime . . . *soon* . . . we need to talk. Please."

She nodded. "I'll look forward to it."

He squeezed her hand. "*Merci.*"

Jennifer came in with a tray and began making a circuit of the room, picking up cups and napkins.

"Don't mind me. I'm just the maid."

Eddie stood up. "Time to hit the road, I guess."

"Get some sleep, Eddie," Jennifer said.

Harvey peered in from the doorway, with Connor tucked up on his shoulder. "You want to skip running tomorrow?"

"No, it wakes me up. If I skip it, I don't feel right all day."

Leeanne walked with him to the entry.

"Eddie," she said softly, as he pulled on his jacket, "did I tell you I love the flowers?"

"Yeah, you did." He gazed into her eyes. "You're beautiful."

Leeanne tried to hold her smile back, but decided she couldn't, and what was the point, anyway?

Eddie put one hand up to her cheek. "That smile. That's what I've been missing."

She thought for a second he would kiss her, and a thrill of anticipation went through her. But he just chucked her under the chin, the way he had so long ago, the first time they'd ever said goodbye.

"*Bon nuit, ma cherie.*"

Chapter 13

Harvey worked at his computer in the office Friday morning, but glanced frequently around at his men. Eddie had chosen to interview Derek Anson in the office and had him seated near his desk. He asked questions and typed Anson's replies into his computer. Harvey glanced over occasionally as he reviewed the transcripts of interviews with women employed at the police station. Cheryl was making steady progress on the list of current officers and civilian workers.

"Here you go, Captain," said Jimmy Cook, handing him a stack of file folders. "I printed everything out for you: the lab reports, the ballistics report, and Joey's autopsy report."

"Thanks, Jimmy." Harvey put the folders in his briefcase, intending to take them home with him that night so he could go over them again. He added the second security tape from the camera over the patrol sergeant's desk and locked the briefcase.

Paula took her telephone receiver from her ear and called, "Captain Larson, if you have a minute, Officer O'Heir would like to see you."

"Sure, I can see him right now. Will he come up?" Harvey tried to conceal his surprise.

Paula spoke into the phone, then hung up. "He's on his way."

Harvey refilled his coffee cup. Paula was watching him with a smile, and he raised the mug in her direction.

"This is great, Paula. Is it hi-test?"

"You really want to know?"

"Well, my heart's not pounding, so I'm guessing it's at least half decaf."

She smiled, and Harvey turned toward the stairway door. A tall, burly patrolman came in and walked directly toward Harvey.

"Aaron. How you doing?" Harvey asked. "Coffee?"

"Sure, thanks." When O'Heir had his cup of brew, they both sat down.

"Now, what can I do for you?" Harvey asked.

O'Heir glanced around. Eddie was still questioning Anson, and Jimmy was working at his computer. Paula was occupied with paperwork, and Tony Winfield hovered near Eddie's desk, behind Anson.

"Well, look," O'Heir said in a low tone, "I heard you've been asking a lot of questions about—" He looked around again, then leaned closer. "You know. Sexual harassment."

Harvey nodded. "You want to go in the interview room?"

O'Heir took a deep breath. "That would be good. I don't exactly want it broadcast that I came to you."

"Okay. Come this way."

Harvey took his mug and led O'Heir to the tiny interview room and closed the door. As O'Heir sat down opposite him at the table, Harvey nodded toward the video camera on the wall. "We're taping. Is that okay?"

"Uh, sure. I guess. Do I have a choice?"

"Well, if you're going to give me some information, I assume it's on the record, or you wouldn't be here."

O'Heir nodded. "Okay. Look, this is—I feel kind of strange, you know?"

Harvey nodded.

"Well, this is about something that happened a while back. I'm not sure it has anything to do with anything. I mean, I'm not even sure what you're looking for, but—well, this has been bothering me for a while, okay?"

"Sure, Aaron. Why don't you tell me what happened, and if it's nothing, I'll tell you, but if it's something . . ."

"Right." O'Heir sipped his coffee, then leaned back in the chair with a sigh, obviously reluctant to begin.

"Are you all right, Aaron?"

"Yeah, yeah. I just—once I open my mouth, I can't shut it again, you know?"

Again Harvey nodded. This unexpected inter-view was important—he could feel it.

"Hey, is this decaf?"

Harvey chuckled. "I don't know, to tell you the truth, but I suspect I'm being weaned."

O'Heir sobered. "Listen, I want to take the test next time there's an opening for detective, and I don't want to mess that up, you know?"

"How could this jeopardize it?"

The patrolman eyed him for perhaps ten seconds, then came to a decision. "Okay, well, here's the deal. I was on the second shift. It was about a year ago, I guess, maybe more. Chief Leavitt was still here. It was warm. Maybe June of last year. I can look it up if you think it's significant."

Harvey nodded. Brad's shift again. He said nothing, but sat waiting for another piece of the puzzle.

"We brought in this broad—I mean woman. Sorry. Tommy and me brought her in. She was drunk driving on Congress Street, about mid-night, and when we stopped her, we found out she was also OAS."

Harvey mentally totaled up the fines. A mini-mum of four hundred dollars for the OUI, and another two hundred for operating after suspension of her license.

"And?"

"We had her in holding to see what the bail was

gonna be, and Tommy was writing up the report. I ran a check and found out she had a couple of priors, so we booked her. The bail was set at five hundred. When I went down to tell her, she started screaming at me."

"What about?"

"She was yelling for a lawyer."

"On the OUI?"

O'Heir put one hand to his forehead. "She claimed she'd been molested in the cell."

Outrage and adrenaline did to Harvey what the coffee hadn't. "She was alone in the lockup?"

"Yeah."

"How long?"

He shrugged. "Maybe an hour."

"Mandatory checks every fifteen minutes, and constant video surveillance." Harvey stated it as a matter of fact.

"Yeah, well, I know Tommy went down once, but I was doing the background. Someone else went the next time."

Harvey sat thinking for a moment. He lifted his coffee cup. "You gonna give me a name?"

O'Heir sighed. "The sergeant did two checks. Visuals, you know? Only . . . I don't know, Captain. She insisted he went in the cell."

"What did you do?"

"I went and asked him. He laughed it off. He said, 'You believe that? She's loaded.' I didn't know what to think. She called someone to come bail her out—I don't know who. Some guy. Husband, boyfriend. But anyway, when he got there, the sergeant says to me, 'Go bring her out.' When I got her to the desk, he's telling the guy, two hundred for bail."

Harvey watched him closely. "Any explanation?"

"I didn't say nothing 'til they left, but Brad took the two hundred and logged it, everything by the book except he'd got the bail changed. At least, he must have." O'Heir shook his head.

"She went to court?" Harvey asked.

"Case dismissed."

"You don't say. You think Brad managed that somehow?"

The patrolman spread his hands in bewilderment. "How could he? I mean, maybe he could, but I don't know. It just seemed weird."

"Did you check the videotape?"

O'Heir lowered his eyes. "I kept thinking about it for about three days. Finally, I went to the detective sergeant and told him I needed the tape from that night on a routine check."

"So Legere got it for you?"

"Yes, but it seems the tape ran out in the middle of the shift and no one changed it until the third shift came on."

"How did that happen?"

"I don't know, Captain. It was hectic that night, and I sure didn't want to ask Brad."

Harvey nodded. "Can you pull up the file? I'll need the name, date, all the particulars."

"You want me to look into it?"

"No, I'll do it myself. Thanks, Aaron. This is between you and me."

O'Heir nodded in relief. "It's bothered me, but I couldn't see what I should do about it."

"Did Tommy comment on it?"

"He thought it was strange, too, but he just kind of took it as a matter of course."

Harvey walked with him to the stairway. Eddie came to meet him when O'Heir was out the door.

"You get anything out of Anson?" Harvey asked.

Eddie glanced quickly down the room. "He's in the locker room with Tony. Bathroom break. He's not happy about me keeping him here so long, but we don't really have anything. Tony tried to get him to take his jacket off, but he wouldn't. We're hoping he'll comb his hair in the locker room."

Harvey sighed. "You can't just confiscate hair if you're not charging him, Eddie. I tried to get you a warrant, but the judge said we didn't have probable cause. Let me talk to him."

"It's reasonable suspicion," Eddie said.

"You know that's not enough."

Anson came from the locker room, and Tony trailed him, shaking his head dolefully at Eddie as he walked.

Harvey stepped forward. "Mr. Anson, I'm Captain Larson."

"Are you Deborah's supervisor?"

"No, but I'm Detective Thibodeau's supervisor. I've applied for a search warrant for your house, sir, but you could save us a lot of time and trouble right here and now." Harvey didn't tell him that his request had been denied.

"A search warrant?" Anson's dismay was almost comical. "I didn't do anything. Why would you want to search my place?"

"Actually, all we need is a sample of your hair, sir. It would be so much simpler if you'd just let us take it now."

"My hair?" He stared at Harvey. "I don't get it."

Harvey sighed. "Won't you sit down over here, sir?"

He led Anson to his desk and indicated the extra chair.

"It's like this, Mr. Anson. I don't have to tell you, but you seem like a reasonable man. We've found some hairs that might belong to Joey Bolduc's killer. If, as you say, you never met Detective Bolduc, then we could rule you out pretty quickly by comparing a sample of your hair to the ones found at the scene of the crime. You understand, it would allow us to circumvent the red tape and the trip to Biddeford, and if it checks out okay, you wouldn't have to put up with having your home searched by officers."

Anson sat staring at him stolidly. At last he said slowly, "This is unbelievable. I feel like I'm being framed. I didn't do anything, and now you want to—no. Absolutely not. This is ridiculous. Am I a suspect in this murder? I can't believe it. I happen to know someone who knew the victim. That's all. Should I have a lawyer?"

"You're not under arrest, sir, and at this point we're not making any charges. But we do have a list of people whose hair we nccd to compare with that found at City Hall on Labor Day. You're on the list."

Anson looked wildly from him to Eddie, who stood nearby, rocking slowly from his heels to his toes and back again.

"Can I see Deborah?" Anson asked.

Harvey considered. "She's probably out on patrol, but I suppose I could send for her. If you would feel more comfortable . . ."

"I don't know what game you guys are playing," Anson said tightly. "Am I a suspect, or not?"

"Loosely speaking, yes," Harvey admitted.

Anson sighed, shaking his head. "I don't believe this. I never saw the guy."

Harvey looked up at Eddie and nodded to him. Eddie went to his desk and picked up his phone.

"Mr. Anson, would you like a cup of coffee while we wait?"

"Couldn't I just go wait for her downstairs or something? Do I have to stay here?"

"Well, it would be a good idea for you to stay. Technically, you can leave anytime. But practically, if you decide you want to leave, I might have to change that."

"Is this legal?"

"Of course." Harvey thought he was sweating a little.

"Captain?" Tony had come up behind Anson and was holding a sheet of paper out over the man's head.

Harvey scowled, but reached for it. "Thank you, Winfield."

"No problem, sir." Tony stretched, his left hand brushing Anson's shoulder. "Excuse me, sir. Sorry."

Harvey pulled the paper in and read the fine print. *If recovery is successful, officer will report to lab immediately.*

He frowned and looked at Tony, who was still standing just behind Anson's chair.

"Not proper procedure, Winfield."

"I was about to go down to the lab, sir."

"Don't do that."

Tony shrugged slightly and went to his desk.

"Officer Higgins will be here in ten minutes," Eddie reported.

"All right." Harvey stood up. "Excuse me, Mr. Anson, I need to speak to Detective Thibodeau.

Help yourself to a cup of coffee if you want."

He walked with Eddie to the other side of the room. Tony sat at his desk, clicking on his keyboard.

"I can't believe this, Eddie. Tony just lifted a hair off his jacket."

"You're sure?"

"Yes, but we don't have his consent."

"You gonna keep trying to get the warrant, even though we've got what we need?"

"I think we have to. I wish Pete Bearse was here. Can you take care of this guy? I need to consult a law book or something."

"Make Tony do it."

Harvey smiled. "The punishment fits the crime?" He turned, beckoned to Tony, and walked into the interview room. When the young detective had closed the door, Harvey stood looking him in the eye for several seconds.

"What did you do with the hair?"

"In an evidence bag, Captain."

"Get rid of it."

Tony gulped. "Yes, sir."

"First I want you to look up the statutes to make sure."

"No need, sir. You're right."

"You're positive?"

Tony nodded reluctantly. "Eddie and I thought maybe, if it was on the premises and in plain sight, we could take it. I was really hoping a hair

273

would fall in the sink or something, you know? But I got on the computerized law library just now, and it's iffy. We either arrest him, or we get a warrant."

Harvey nodded. "I've tried to get a warrant. You know that. Unless we come up with something concrete, the judge won't give it to us."

"Even though he refused to cooperate?" Tony asked.

Harvey sighed. "I can try, but my expectations are low."

Eddie and Anson were again seated at Eddie's station, and Harvey went to his computer to draft another warrant application.

"So, you were upset with Detective Bolduc, even though you'd never seen him," Eddie said.

"Maybe a little."

"Jealous?"

Anson hesitated. "Are you married, Detective?"

"Not yet." Eddie was terse, and Harvey smiled wryly as he brought the form he needed up on the screen.

"You gotta understand," Anson pleaded. "I still admire Deborah. I know we broke up, but I was . . . missing her. I hoped we might get back together at some point."

Eddie was quiet, and Harvey thought, Oh, yes, he certainly does understand your plight, buddy.

"Would I be telling you this if I killed the guy?" Anson asked in exasperation.

The stairway door opened, and Deborah Higgins strode into the office, her eyes fastening immediately on Anson.

"Derek, what are you doing here?"

"Just chatting with the detectives for the last hour," Anson said sheepishly.

Deborah looked quickly at Eddie, then swung around and threw a glance toward Harvey. "I don't understand."

"The captain has applied for a warrant, and Mr. Anson wanted to talk to you while we wait." Eddie stood up. "If you'd like some privacy, you can use our interview room. I can kill the video camera in there."

"Maybe we should go somewhere else," Anson suggested.

"No tape?" Deborah asked.

"Right." Eddie's face was open, and Deborah nodded slowly.

"Come on, Derek, tell me what this is about." She and Anson went into the interview room, and Eddie followed, returning a moment later with a tape cassette in his hand. Tony sat at his desk, watching.

"Which way is it going to blow?" Harvey asked.

"Dunno. It's her call, I'd say."

Tony got up, and he and Eddie came to Harvey's area. "Think she'll be cooperative or belligerent?" Tony asked.

"We'll see." Harvey sat gazing at the warrant application. "Eddie, you know the judge isn't going to give us a warrant."

"You're probably right." Eddie held out the videotape. "This is the footage of your last interview, I take it."

His session with Aaron O'Heir. "Thanks. I want you to screen that when you have a chance. It may have a bearing on the other case."

"Okay."

Harvey leaned back in his chair. "So, Winfield, I need a legal ace in this office. I'm thinking you're it."

"What, you sending me to law school?" Tony came closer, his blue eyes sparkling.

"No, that's not in the budget. But if I have a legal question and no time to research it, I'll ask you, and you'll do the grunt work for me."

Tony shrugged. "That's cool."

"Just make sure you never give me a wrong answer," Harvey said sternly. He glanced toward Eddie. "And no more of these Laurel and Hardy shenanigans from you two. Picking hairs off a witness while I'm questioning him."

"Sorry, Harv," Eddie said. "I wasn't sure . . ."

"Next time, get Wonder Boy, here, to check first."

The door to the interview room opened, and Deborah, trim and businesslike in her uniform, came out and approached Harvey's desk.

"Captain, Derek will give you the hair sample."

Harvey jumped up. "Really? That's great, Deborah. You understand, it will help us rule him out if he's innocent."

She nodded. "That's what I told him. I mean, he could fight this on principle, get a lawyer and all that. Some people would make you do it the hard way. But I can't see bucking this investigation. We all want it over as soon as possible. Even Derek." She smiled tremulously. "He's ready."

Harvey reached out to touch her shoulder, but drew his hand back, mindful of the harassment investigation. "Thank you, Deborah. If he wants, he can stay here while Winfield runs it down to the lab."

"You'll do it that fast?"

Harvey smiled. "This is a pretty simple test. Match or no match. If I throw my weight around, we ought to be able to have the result in minutes."

"Thanks. I'd like to stay with him, if you don't mind."

"Sure. Do you want me to call downstairs?"

"If you wouldn't mind."

Harvey thought she choked a little, and he wondered if she was still afraid of Brad.

"Deborah, did anyone say anything to you when I had you called in to the station?"

"When I came in, the sergeant was watching me," she faltered. "He called me over, and I went to his desk. He said, 'You watch yourself, girlie.

There's a hundred women would love to have your job.' I—I felt like he was—"

"What?"

"Angry."

Harvey nodded. "Well, I'm going to ask Detective Thibodeau to take the hair sample right now. You can be present, and Winfield will take it to the lab. I need to step out for about five minutes, then I'll be back. Relax, Officer." He smiled, and she nodded.

Eddie took tweezers and an evidence bag from his desk drawer, and they went into the interview room. Harvey called the lab and made it clear that he needed a quick job on the hair analysis.

"Winfield," he called.

Tony looked toward him, and Harvey beckoned.

"Captain?"

"Lose that other sample."

Tony nodded, wide-eyed.

Harvey hit the stairway and bounded down the two flights, punching in the security codes in record time. In the duty area, he approached Brad's desk, his eyes on the camera overhead. Brad Lyons was in conversation with one of his patrolmen.

"Okay, put that in the evidence locker." He swung toward Harvey and frowned. "Help you, Captain?"

"How come your camera's not running?"

Brad looked over his shoulder at the video camera. "What do you know? I didn't notice. Maybe it's broken. Better ask them in the com room."

"When did it stop?"

"You got me." Brad smiled at him.

"If you turned it off when Deborah Higgins came in, I'll know it."

"A little snappish, aren't you, Harvey? Isn't the wife taking care of you?"

Harvey glared at him. "Brad, there's no camera running. I'll say this once. Don't you ever say anything about Jennifer again."

Brad grinned. "What's the matter, Harv? You're not disappointed in her, are you? I always thought she was hot. She seemed to like me, but I kept away from her out of deference to you."

"Shut up, Brad."

"Or what?" Lyons reached up and toggled a switch. "The switch is on. There must be trouble in the com room." He spread his hands in innocence. "If you ever wanted to hit me, now's your chance."

Suddenly the red light appeared on the camera.

"Oops, there she goes," Brad grinned. "So, what were you saying, Captain?"

Harvey stood for a moment, fuming silently, then turned away and went quickly to the com room.

"I need the tape from the security camera over

the patrol sergeant's desk. This shift, the one that's running now."

The technician, Richard, went to get it, and Harvey stood drumming his fingers impatiently on the edge of the console.

"Here you go," Richard said a moment later. "That camera was down for a while, though."

Harvey nodded. "But it's up again now."

"That's right."

"How long was it down?"

"Twenty minutes or so, I guess. I just found out when I came back from my break."

"What was wrong?"

"I don't know, sir. I noticed it was off a couple minutes ago. The switch was flipped, and I turned it back on."

"So someone had turned it off?"

"Well . . . I guess so. It was probably accidental."

"No doubt. Do you guys have a tape going in here? One that would show me who's been in here in the last half hour?"

"Well, uh, sure." Richard eyed him curiously.

Tony met him halfway up the stairway.

"Captain, the lab report is negative."

"The hairs don't match?"

"Right. The hairs on the dummy don't belong to Derek Anson."

"Have you told him yet?"

"Yes. He and Deborah just left. I hope that's okay."

"Yeah, sure. I was gone longer than I expected. But now I need you and Eddie in the break room."

"What is it, Harv?" Eddie asked, following him and Tony into the break room, where the unit had a television set and video player they used to view evidence tapes.

Harvey rewound the videotape from Brad's desk.

"Skullduggery at the P.D. Take a look at this. At 3:07 Brad takes your call to bring in Deborah Higgins." He stopped the tape and let it play forward. Brad, his back to the camera, answered his phone.

"Higgins? Now? She's on patrol. It can't wait? Okay, Detective. Whatever you say."

A patrolman brought a report for Brad's signature, then the sergeant stepped away from his desk and out of camera range. Harvey held his wrist up, timing the sergeant's absence. Two minutes. Two and a half. The imprint on the tape read 15:12. Suddenly the tape went fuzzy for a few seconds, then began running again. The imprint read 15:44, and Harvey was facing the camera, in front of Brad's desk. Brad turned and looked up at it, too.

"Oops, there she goes. What were you saying, Captain?"

Harvey stopped the tape. "The camera was shut off for thirty-two minutes, which, by the way, means old Richard in Com is taking a pretty long break there." He ejected the tape and inserted another in the video player. "Now. This is from the com room. Watch closely." He rewound until the imprint read 15:07, and they watched silently as the dispatchers and technicians worked. Four dispatchers sat at their consoles, wearing headphones. At the perimeter of the camera's view, two technicians were working.

"There goes Richard for his break," Harvey said, as the technician left his desk and exited the room. "Now, just be patient for a couple more minutes."

A secretary came in and left some papers on the edge of Charlie Doran's desk. Charlie barely looked up. He and the other dispatchers were constantly speaking into their headsets, monitoring calls.

"There!"

"There he is," Eddie agreed. The back of Brad Lyons's head, with his close-cropped blond hair, was unmistakable. He went to Richard's desk at the extreme edge of the picture and seemed to stand motionless for half a minute, facing the console and security monitors. His left arm and about half his body were visible. "I give up," Eddie said. "What's he doing?"

"Nothing yet," Harvey replied. "He's figuring out which switch to play with. Doesn't want to ask anyone." The imprint time changed to 15:12. "Any second now." Sure enough, Brad leaned forward, with his upper body out of the picture, then straightened and walked quickly out of the room.

"Nobody even noticed," Tony marveled.

"Why should they?" Harvey asked. "But if he'd switched it off out front, it would have been on his own camera's tape."

"He thought you wouldn't get this one?" Eddie asked.

"I don't know. Maybe he figured he'd be out of range over there."

"What if Richard had been there?" Tony asked.

"I'd bet he'd still do it. He'd hope he could do it right under his nose without Richard noticing. He could distract him or something. If he did notice, Brad could brush it off. 'Oops, sorry about that. Clumsy of me.' "

Tony swore. "We gotta get him, Captain."

"Does the governor swear, Winfield?"

"Actually, yes."

"On the job?"

Tony ducked his head. "Sorry, sir."

Harvey frowned at him. "You're trying to shed the adolescent image, right?"

"Yes, sir. I'll work on it."

283

"What next?" Eddie asked.

"I'm taking this to Mike. When Cheryl comes in—oh, I guess she's already in. It's almost five."

"You want me to send Nate and Jimmy home?"

"Yeah. If the chief hasn't left, I'll see if he and Cheryl are up for a private premiere. Eddie, you take a look at the O'Heir interview."

"Sir?"

"What is it, Winfield?"

"Is it all right if I watch?"

"Don't you have a date or something? It's Friday night."

Tony grinned. "Not until later, sir."

Harvey shook his head. "You know about the harassment investigation."

"I'd be pretty stupid if I didn't, sir."

"Well, this person doesn't want a lot of people seeing the tape if it's not necessary, but I think it's time we brought you and the other boys in on this case. It certainly overlaps the Bolduc case, and—"

"And you're thinking it's one case?" Tony asked.

Harvey set his lips in a grim line. "Not a word outside this office. But I think the chief should see these tapes before I let you guys in on the rest of it. Go home, Winfield. I'll see you Monday, ready for some hard work." He pulled his phone from his pocket and hit Mike's number.

"Don't forget to call Jennifer," Eddie whispered. He went to his desk for the O'Heir tape.

Chapter 14

Jennifer heard the garage door go up at last. It was nearly eight o'clock. She quickly transferred a dish from the refrigerator to the microwave and rushed toward the entry.

"Hello, gorgeous." Harvey swept her into his arms, and she clung to him, eager for his kiss. "I'm sorry," he whispered in her hair.

"It's okay. You'd better eat, though. Are you all right?"

"Yeah, Eddie force-fed me a chocolate bar a couple of hours ago."

Jennifer turned toward the door. Eddie was standing unobtrusively in the entry.

"Hi, Eddie, come on in."

"Thanks, Jennifer." He followed them in, looked around, then sat down at the kitchen table.

"She's at Beth's," Jennifer said.

Eddie nodded. "Jeff at work?"

"Yes, he went on at midnight. Leeanne will be staying at Beth's until Monday."

Harvey took his briefcase into the bedroom, and Jennifer began putting food on his and Eddie's plates.

"You guys are outdoing yourselves on this case. I hope you're taking the weekend off."

"I think so. Unless something unexpected comes up, that is." Eddie sniffed the food appreciatively. "Seems like I'm never home anymore. Maybe that's good."

Because the house is empty, Jennifer thought. She hoped that soon Eddie would be going home to a hot supper and a wife yearning for his kisses.

She heard the patio door open in the sunroom and knew Leeanne was using her key.

Eddie stood up when she appeared in the doorway, his eyes brimming with his longing. Jennifer smiled and turned away from the intensity of it.

"Hi, Leeanne. How's Beth?" Jennifer poured a glass of milk for Harvey.

"She's doing a little better, I think. Margaret told her to take it easy, and she is. She's watching TV in the bedroom."

"Did you go to school today?" Eddie asked.

"Yeah, I had a quiz in statistics." She grimaced. "I don't think I did very well. You guys just got home, huh?"

"Rough day," Eddie said.

Harvey came back, carrying Connor. He'd left his briefcase, suit jacket, necktie, and holster in the bedroom, and had softened into the Daddy mode.

"Look at this boy, Eddie! He's got another

287

tooth coming through. Gonna be eating moose meat soon."

Jennifer sat down with them, and she and Leeanne smiled at each other across the table. *This is right,* Jennifer thought. *This is how it should be.* She laid her hand lightly on Harvey's sleeve. He turned to smile at her, then bent over to kiss her again.

"Mushy, mushy, mushy," Leeanne scolded. "Here, let me hold my nephew. You can't eat, kiss, and rock a baby at the same time."

Eddie's brown eyes followed her as she took Connor in her arms and sat down again. Jennifer felt tears forming.

I've got to quit watching these two, she told herself. It was so bittersweet, compared to her own days of courtship. From the day Harvey told her he loved her, she'd always been able to turn to him. They had tragedy and terror to deal with, but it was easier because they faced it together.

Her thoughts changed to a prayer as her sister turned the baby so he could smile at Uncle Eddie. *Lord, help them sort it out, please. They're so right together, and they both love you. Please give them the sweet, tender joy you've given us.*

"So, what did you think of O'Heir's statement, Ed?" Harvey asked, forking open his baked potato.

Eddie's luminous eyes turned to Harvey and

focused on him. "Strange. Are we going to have to interview all the female prisoners for the last twelve years?"

"Prisoners?" Jennifer asked, fear catching at her. "The harassment thing extends to prisoners, honey?"

Harvey reached over and squeezed her hand.

"Don't concern yourself, gorgeous. We've had one complaint brought to our attention."

"You think it will end there?"

"It's got to end somewhere. And soon."

"I thought he'd leave Deborah alone after you warned him about the investigation." Eddie's voice was edged with sadness and fatigue.

"Me, too." Harvey drank half the milk down. "I know how he killed the videotape today, but what about in the cell that time? It would be too risky, if he was intending to do more than make a quick threat, like he did with Deborah today."

Jennifer looked from her husband to Eddie, piecing together what they were saying.

"Didn't they put in a whole new system in the booking area last winter?" Eddie asked.

Harvey frowned. "I think you're right. In the duty room and the lockup, too. We need to know what the old cameras were like. He may have been able to walk in under it and just reach up and turn it off, like the one in our interview room."

Eddie nodded. "The way it's positioned, I think

you could reach it without being taped. Maybe Richard could enlighten us."

"We've been upstairs too long," Harvey said. "I feel as if I'm isolated from the patrolmen's area. I had no idea any of this was going on down there."

"I wonder if the old cameras are still around."

"And I wonder if Brad has a friend in the courthouse."

"Kind of hard to nose around there without word getting back to the station." Eddie took a bite of pot roast.

"We need a female detective who's not involved in the case."

"Emily," said Eddie.

Harvey nodded. "I'll talk to Cheryl Monday. If she thinks it's indicated, I'll ask Legere to loan us Emily Rood." He finished the food on his plate.

"Apple pie?" Jennifer asked.

"No, I don't think so."

"Eddie?"

"Okay."

"I'll get it." Leeanne passed the baby to Eddie and got up. "Do you want coffee, Harvey?"

"Well . . ." He looked sheepishly at Jennifer, his electric blue eyes subdued in the soft evening light. "I've been trying to cut down on it at work, but it's a hard habit to kick."

"How much did you drink at work today?"

"Probably too much. Paula's cutting it, I think."

Jennifer frowned. "I've been watching your sugar. Do I need to start watching your caffeine?"

"I don't know. An old guy like me needs to be careful, I guess."

"Drink decaf." Leeanne placed a steaming mug in front of him.

"You can always tell," Eddie objected.

"Can you? I can't." Leeanne brought Eddie's pie and a mug of coffee and sat down again.

"I think if you two got enough sleep, you wouldn't need it," Jennifer said. "Here, Eddie, let me take Connor so you can eat."

"No, let me," Harvey protested, and stood up to lean across the table and take his son. "We ought to do something with him tomorrow. He's not going to know what his daddy looks like."

"You want to go someplace?" Jennifer asked. It seemed like ages since they'd had an outing.

Harvey sighed. "I'd really rather stay home. Rake some leaves, maybe. We can bundle him up and take him out for a walk. Then I'd like to have a fire in the fireplace and just sit and read. With you and Connor." He smiled wistfully at her over the baby's head, and his eyes crinkled.

"Sounds good."

"It sure does," Eddie murmured. Leeanne's hand rested lightly on his sleeve, and he reached over and clasped her fingers. "How about a walk tonight?"

"In the moonlight?" she smiled.

"It's chilly," Harvey said.

Eddie shrugged. "It'll wake me up." His gaze returned to Leeanne. "I need to be awake, so I'll know later what we talked about."

She smiled. "You want to run home and change first?" She eyed his necktie and dress shirt.

He smiled ruefully. "If I go home, I'll probably collapse."

Jennifer realized that Eddie, like Harvey, had changed his habits of dress since she had known him. "Hey, how come you're always wearing a tie to work now? You used to wear a denim jacket and jeans."

Eddie shrugged. "Less undercover work, for one thing."

"Why?" She turned to Harvey. "I know what happened to you. You got promoted and felt you had to dress for the job. Which is very nice, by the way. In fact, you both look great lately. But Eddie . . . you both used to do a lot more undercover, didn't you?"

"You mean before my face got plastered all over YouTube?" Eddie grimaced.

"It's not just that," Harvey said. "Mike's style was different. We get a different kind of crime now, too. Five years ago, we were out on drug raids a lot with the detective squad. Now Ron's men handle almost all of that, and we do more homicides and investigative work. I don't know, it's a subtle shift, I guess."

"Mike liked to kick down doors," Eddie agreed. "Now I feel as if the Priority Unit has more class. We use computers a lot, and the cases we get are more . . . cerebral. Espionage, art theft, celebrity murders."

"You think the criminals are getting more sophisticated?" Jennifer asked.

"Maybe. Our cases sure are." Eddie shrugged. "I'd like to think it's partly because our captain is a genius."

Leeanne smiled. "So, who solved these cerebral cases before you guys matured into it?"

Eddie shrugged. "Maybe nobody. I don't know. Some of the things we handle seem unique. The first case like it in Maine."

"Well, this harassment thing isn't unique, unfortunately." Harvey shook his head. "I'm thinking the sooner we get Brad Lyons out of uniform, the better for the city of Portland."

"Are we taking that walk?" Leeanne spoke brightly, casually, but Jennifer thought there was nervousness in her voice.

Eddie smiled at her. *"D'accord, mon enfant.* You got a jacket over here?"

"Don't stay out late," Jennifer couldn't help saying. "Beth's alone."

"We won't," Leeanne assured her, dropping a kiss on her sister's cheek.

They went quietly out the breezeway, and Jennifer began to gather up the mugs and silverware.

"Leave the dishes," Harvey said, and she laid them in the sink.

"You're tired. You want to go to bed?"

"Let's sit for a while." He held Connor carefully against his shirt as he stood up.

Jennifer put her arm around his waist. "Where are we heading? The couch?"

He stifled a yawn. "Yeah, that's good. I feel like I ought to stay up until Eddie's truck pulls out, you know?"

"You're too good, Harvey." He sank down on the living room sofa, and she settled in beside him.

Harvey put his left arm around her and cradled Connor with his right. He leaned back and closed his eyes as Jennifer's head pillowed on his shoulder. "Don't let me sleep out here," he warned.

Almost instantly he was asleep. Jennifer lay with her cheek over his heart, feeling his strong, rhythmic breathing. His muscles relaxed almost imperceptibly, and she reached over, gently easing Connor from his grasp. She curled down against Harvey's side, holding the baby on her chest, and Harvey stretched out a little, turning toward her, his arms holding her lightly, and they all drifted into sleep.

"Harvey's beat." Eddie walked slowly down the sidewalk, holding Leeanne's hand loosely. He kept his other hand in his pocket and tried not to shiver.

"Like you're not."

He shrugged. "I need to talk to you. If I wait 'til I'm not tired, it may never happen." He looked up at the cold half moon in the cloudless sky.

"It's supposed to freeze tonight," Leeanne said.

Eddie dropped her hand and slipped his arm around her waist. He held his breath for an instant, and slowly her arm crept around him. Then he breathed.

"How's the book coming?" he asked.

"Slow but sure. I'll need to go over the police records with you sometime, but you're so busy now, I thought I'd wait until you close this case."

"*Merci*. I just couldn't do any more right now."

"I know."

He squeezed her a little. They passed the Smiths' house, with a lamppost at the end of the driveway. The next house had plastic pumpkins lit on the steps, and a scarecrow propped in the middle of the lawn.

"Halloween decorations already," Eddie murmured. He rubbed her hair with his cheek. It was cold, and his whiskers were scratchy. Was tonight the night he would kiss her again? He wished he had shaved.

"Leeanne, I've been reading what the Bible says about . . . about husbands, and fathers, and . . . families. Pastor got me going on it, you

295

know? From the Bible study a couple of weeks ago."

"Uh-huh."

He stopped and turned to face her on the sidewalk. They were nearly to his house, and there wasn't any traffic on the street.

"*Cherie*, there are women in the Bible who are in business. Not many, I guess, but a few. But . . . it seems like they tend to their families first."

Leeanne nodded solemnly, her eyes dark and glistening in the moonlight.

"I don't want to talk about this," he confessed. "I'm afraid you'll get upset again, but I don't see how we'll ever make any progress if we don't talk it out, and I want to make progress. Oh, sweet, sweet Leeanne, I want to get past this and go on."

He pulled her against him, his lips brushing her cool, smooth forehead, wondering if his tears would freeze if he cried.

"I want to, too," she whispered.

Eddie took a deep breath. "Can we sit on the steps?"

"Sure."

They walked slowly up the driveway to the house. *Our house,* Eddie told himself with a pang of loss. At the steps, they sat down close together. The stairs were like ice, and he put his arm around her again. She let her head drift slowly down onto his shoulder, and they sat in silence.

"If you wanted to work," he said at last, "I think I could stand it for a while. I mean, I would hope it wouldn't last forever, but if you really wanted that . . ."

She nodded. "I would never put my children in daycare, Eddie."

"Me either. I could wait a few years, maybe, if you wanted to. But . . . my wife . . . I would hope that when we had babies, she'd be home. I think I could support us so that you didn't *have* to work outside. But if you wanted to do something like writing . . . I mean, Jennifer is still making computer programs, but she doesn't go off to some office every day to do it."

"I understand. And I think you're right. I'm sorry I ever said you were wrong, or implied it."

Eddie shivered and pulled his suitcoat tighter.

"You're freezing," she whispered. "Go in and get your coat."

"No, I—I'm all right."

Leeanne put both arms around him and felt the leather holster strap through his jacket. "You'll get sick, baby," she said. "I'll wait here."

Eddie stirred. "Come inside."

"I can't."

He swallowed. "It's our house, Leeanne. You've been in it lots."

"I know, but—"

He thought about the hours they had spent there together, painting the dining room and moving his things in. "Just step in out of the cold. I'll get my coat."

She hesitated, then stood up slowly and waited while he unlocked the door.

In the entry she stopped. "This is where the N.C. Wyeth was."

"Yeah." He eyed her curiously, relieved at the warmth that washed over him as he closed the door, and wondering what was going through her mind as she gazed at the spot where the previous owner's art had hung.

"We ought to get a print or something to hang there." She turned toward him.

His stomach lurched. She was still thinking of it as their house, too, then. She was perhaps not the most beautiful woman in the world. Perhaps. He could debate that. But regardless of the outcome, she was the one who would always hold his heart.

"Leeanne!"

Two tears spilled over her eyelids and slid down her cheeks. She stared at him, pain and fear in her gaze. Her chin went up a fraction of an inch. "I want to live here with you," she whispered.

He pulled her toward him fiercely, holding her head tight against his chest, his breathing choppy and fast as he fought the tears. "*Je t'aimais toujours*, Leeanne. I've always loved you."

She laughed the tiniest laugh and gasped, burying her face in the front of his shirt, sobbing. He remembered the first time he'd told her, and she had laughed like that. *You love me in two languages.* He tightened his arms around her, wanting to hold her forever. Her hands came up in fists, on either side of his tie, and he thought she was going to pound on him, but her fingers relaxed and stretched out, slipping up toward his collar, until they met at the nape of his neck. He shivered again, but not from the cold, and closed his eyes. She caressed him slowly, letting his hair tumble over her fingers.

"Can you forgive me?" she choked.

He heaved a ragged sigh. "That is not a problem, my love."

He traced her jawline with one finger, and tipped her face upward. With excruciating slowness he bent toward her, his lips meeting hers in a joyful shock. The last coil of bitterness unkinked inside him. He kissed her mouth, then her cheekbone, her temple, her earlobe. "I need to get you home," he whispered.

"Get your coat," she said, but she didn't loosen her hold on him.

Eddie took two deep breaths, then straightened. A tear hung trembling on her eyelashes. He fumbled for his handkerchief. "Here, *ma petite*. Let me wipe your eyes."

"I love you, Eddie. Don't ever let me be so stubborn and mean again."

He smiled at that. "What would I do?"

She laughed and caught the tear with his handkerchief. "Hold me down and kiss me until I treat you right. I don't think I could resist."

He sighed. "I would be afraid to do that. All this time, I've been afraid to touch you again."

She sniffed. "And I was afraid you never would." Their eyes locked, and she laughed again. "Get your coat, Édouard Jean."

Eddie swallowed hard. He still felt it was a risk, but it was all or nothing tonight. He put one hand up to her cheek. "I have to ask you something."

"What?" Her lips trembled.

"Are you wearing the cross I gave you?"

The look that crossed her face almost made him laugh. Wonder, consternation, perhaps a teeny letdown.

"Always." She unzipped her jacket and reached inside the collar of her blouse, pulling the gold chain up with one finger. The little jade cross dangled from it.

He smiled at her, and she smiled back. "There's one other thing."

"What?"

"Come into the kitchen."

"The kitchen? No, Eddie, I can't."

His smile broadened. "I'll be good. I promise."

Slowly she went with him through the living

room, her eyes devouring the home she had craved for months.

He nodded toward a bare corner. "We were going to put your computer there."

"Yes."

He took her hand and drew her on into the kitchen, stopping between the range and the refrigerator. She looked up at him, bewildered, and Eddie smiled slowly.

"Let's do this right." He dropped to one knee, holding her hand in both his, looking up into her intent blue eyes. "Dearest Leeanne, I love you. Will you be my wife?"

Her other hand reached out to him, and she slid her fingers through his thick, dark hair. "Of course, my darling."

He stood up and kissed her tenderly, then again, more decisively. When he released her, she collapsed against him. He wanted to save that moment forever, but he remembered his purpose in choosing this location for his proposal.

"*Pardon, ma belle,*" he said softly, reaching out and pulling the freezer door open.

Leeanne looked around at the sound, then twisted back to face him, baffled.

"Here you go." He lifted out a small box and placed it in her hands. She stared at it. *Mr. Edouard J. Thibodeau, 187 Van Cleeve Lane, Portland, ME,* in her handwriting.

"Oh, Eddie, you froze it."

301

She was so mournful, he laughed again. "What did you think, little lamb?"

"I thought—maybe—I don't know. Maybe you gave it back to your Mémé. Or threw it out the window, or something like that."

She smiled up at him through tears and lifted the lid of the box. Inside was the square jeweler's box. Eddie lifted it out and opened it. He took the ring out and clenched it in his fist.

"It's cold," he whispered, and she nodded. He held it up to his lips. *"Encore froid*. Still cold." He hid it again in his fist, and Leeanne stood waiting, smiling.

The second time he raised it to his lips, he nodded. "Your hand, *ma cherie*."

She held it out eagerly, and he slipped the band onto her finger, then kissed her fingertips.

"Eddie!" She flung herself at him, her arms around his neck, and he lifted her off the floor, kissing her over and over. Finally she pushed him away, gasping. "Get your coat. You need to take me home to Beth's."

He placed one more kiss gently on her lips. "I think we need to tell Jennifer and Harvey, too."

Chapter 15

In the first light of dawn, Jennifer roused to Connor's crying. Harvey stirred and said faintly, "I'll get him."

"No, I'm up." She jumped out of bed and went quickly to the crib.

"Hey, fella. I think it's time you moved upstairs," she whispered as she changed his wet diaper. She had it down to a few seconds now, even in near darkness. "I really do. You keep your daddy from getting his REM sleep."

She carried him out to the sofa and settled there under the plaid afghan, putting the baby to her breast and stroking his silky hair.

"Yup, you've started eating cereal and bananas, so you're big enough to have your own bedroom. Aunt Leeanne's over to Uncle Jeff's half the time, and she's really getting married now, anyway, so she won't be up there much longer. You won't be waking her up."

Connor stared up at her solemnly, and she laughed. "Five months old. You're definitely old enough to move out of Mommy and Daddy's room. But will I be able to stand it?" She leaned

303

back and closed her eyes. Connor was so much a part of her existence, it was hard to remember what life had been like without a crib in the master bedroom. She would worry about him. What if he cried and she didn't hear him? Harvey had talked about getting a monitor, so she could hear him downstairs. It would be strange, though. How long since she had been truly alone with Harvey?

She looked down at her son. He was huge, compared to that night in April when Harvey had held him for the first time, whispering, *He's perfect.*

"Separation anxiety," she said aloud. "That's what I've got. But I think it's time, young man."

She slipped into the bedroom an hour later for her clothes, and Harvey didn't stir. She turned off the bedside phone's ringer and put his cell phone in the breast pocket of her denim shirt, then bundled Connor up and took him across the yards to Beth's for breakfast. Leeanne wasn't up, but Beth was ecstatic over the news of the reinstated engagement.

"Maybe we shouldn't hold our collective breath until they set a new date," Jennifer said drily.

"No, I'm not thinking negative thoughts. They're going through with it this time, and soon," Beth predicted. "Leeanne wants Thanksgiving Day."

"That's your due date."

Beth shrugged. "Margaret says I may go early, the way things look. Besides, hardly any babies are born on the due date."

When she went home again, Jennifer puttered around, running a load of laundry and dusting, and Harvey slept on. It was nearly ten o'clock when she heard a vehicle in the driveway.

Eddie, she thought. *He's slept it out and wants Harvey to work on the case with him.* She headed for the entry, determined to keep Eddie at bay for another hour. The bell rang just as she reached the door, which startled her. Eddie never rang.

"Travis!"

She stood staring stupidly at her little brother, and he stared back, his eyes darting past her toward the kitchen, then down at his sneakers. She glanced toward the driveway and saw his red truck.

"What are you doing here?" He had never driven to Portland alone, never visited unannounced. She eyed him carefully, looking for a clue. Should she be overjoyed to see him, or apprehensive?

"Jenn, I—is Harvey here?"

A bad feeling settled on her chest. She opened the door wide. "Come on in. He's asleep."

He followed her into the kitchen, unzipping his black jacket.

"Have you eaten?" she asked.

"No. I was going to go home, but I changed my mind."

Automatically, she began measuring coffee. "Sit down. I'll fix you some eggs." *He looks so much like Jeff,* she thought. She wasn't used to thinking of Travis as full grown. He and Randy were her two little brothers, and he had been only ten when she'd moved out of the farmhouse for college.

He was well over six feet now, and was bulking up a little. His hair held the same deep gold sheen as her own and Jeff's, but he seemed less tractable than Jeff had been. He was more at odds with his father, she knew, and had yet to come to terms with God. Her heart twisted as she wondered what had brought him here.

"Hey, Travis." Harvey stood in the sun room doorway in his boxers and T-shirt, rubbing his eyes. "What's up?"

Travis had begun to sit, but he stood up quickly and faced Harvey squarely.

"I—I need to talk to you."

Harvey nodded and glanced at Jennifer. "Real coffee, gorgeous?"

"Absolutely."

"All right, I'm going to get dressed. Be right back."

Travis watched him go, then looked at Jennifer. "I've never seen Harvey so wiped."

"He's okay. He and Eddie have a couple of really tough cases going, and they've been putting in a lot of hours, is all. He'll be fine when he gets his coffee." She watched Travis peel off his jacket. A fine stubble blurred his chin, but he had an air of defenselessness that caught at her. Connor, at eighteen?

"Let me hang that up." She reached for his jacket and took it to the closet in the entry. She wanted to ask him if something was wrong, but she thought she knew the answer to that. On a Saturday morning, he had driven three hours from Orono to talk to Harvey.

He watched her dolefully as she took eggs and milk from the refrigerator and began cracking eggs into a glass mixing bowl.

"How are the folks?" she asked after a moment, her voice catching.

"Okay, I guess."

Jennifer grabbed a whisk and beat the eggs rapidly. She had probably talked to her parents since Travis had.

Harvey returned, wearing jeans and a faded Harvard T-shirt, in his stocking feet, with Connor gurgling on his shoulder and flailing his arms.

"The boy wants brunch," he said to Jennifer as he stooped to strap the baby into his seat on the table.

"I'll get it," Jennifer said, pouring the eggs into the frying pan.

"If you want to mix it up, I'll feed him. Hey, fella, look over here. Uncle Travis is here." Harvey sat down, and Jennifer slid two English muffins in the toaster oven, then reached for the box of rice cereal.

"So, Travis, how's school going?" Harvey asked.

"Uh, okay." Travis glanced nervously at Jennifer. "Jenn said you've been really busy. I'm sorry. Maybe I shouldn't have come down."

"No, that's okay. Tough case, is all. I hope we're going to wrap it up pretty soon."

Jennifer stirred the cereal and handed Harvey the bowl, then went back to the counter for his coffee.

"Is Beth okay?" Travis asked timidly.

"She's not feeling great." Jennifer had the feeling the conversation was not going to move beyond family chitchat until she vacated the premises. She set Harvey's mug on the table.

"Thanks, gorgeous."

"Coffee, Trav?" she asked, smiling at her brother.

"Uh, sure—I can get it." He stood and walked across the room.

Harvey reached for Jennifer's hand and pulled her in close. She bent to meet his kiss. "Are you praying?" he whispered.

She froze, realizing she hadn't. She had let Travis's precipitous arrival unsettle her, but she hadn't sought God's peace. She ran her fingers over Harvey's scratchy cheek. "I am now. Thanks."

He smiled and kissed her. Travis was regaining his seat when he released her, and he winked at Jennifer, then smiled at her brother.

"Coffee and kisses. Can't face the day without 'em."

Travis blushed a little.

"Milk, Trav?" Jennifer asked.

"Uh, yeah, thanks."

She went to the refrigerator for the jug, praying silently as she went. *Dear Lord, thank you that he came to us. Give me wisdom here. Harvey's got it already, but I'm a bit short of a load. Whatever it is, show us how to help him.*

She tended the eggs and muffins, setting butter, jam, and sugar on the table.

"Sausage, honey?"

"No, no sausage," Harvey said. "Well, maybe Travis would like some."

"I'm good," he said quickly.

When she set their plates before them, she took the feeding spoon from Harvey. "Hey, Connor, almost done. What a good boy." She scraped the last of the cereal from the bowl and scooped it into his mouth. A truck drove in at Jeff's driveway, and Harvey half rose to see out the window.

"That's Eddie. Going to see Leeanne, I guess."

"The engagement is back on," Jennifer told Travis.

"Really? Super. I told her to make up with him."

"I guess she listened to you." Jennifer wiped Connor's face gently. "Maybe I'll take him over there for a few minutes and get an update. I want to know if they've called Mom and Dad yet."

"Sure," Harvey said, and she thought Travis looked relieved.

When the door closed behind Jennifer and Connor, Harvey spread his English muffin with jam, no butter. He glanced toward Travis, wondering how long it would take him to spill it. The boy stirred his coffee, his brow creased in a frown.

"I'm listening, brother." Harvey took a bite of his muffin.

"I—well—something happened last night, Harvey."

Harvey nodded and chewed silently.

"In Orono." Travis put down his spoon. "See, I have this roommate, Brett."

Harvey sipped his coffee, saying nothing.

"He took my truck last night."

Harvey was startled. It wasn't at all what he had expected.

"You loaned your roommate your truck?"

"No, that's just it. I went over to the library to

study after supper. I was going to go home, but I needed to do some research, so I thought I'd spend a couple of hours at the library, then head home around eight or nine o'clock. But when I went back to the room, I realized I'd forgotten my keys, and I was locked out."

"Brett wasn't there?"

"No. I hung out in another room across the hall for a while, hoping he'd show, but he didn't. I was going to break down and go get the monitor to let me into my room, but then this guy Brian said he'd pick the lock for me."

Harvey said carefully, "And he did?"

"In five seconds flat. It made me feel real secure, I'll tell you."

Harvey nodded.

Travis licked his lips. "Well, it was nearly nine when I got in there, and I couldn't find my keys. At all. I tore the room apart. So then I'm thinking, where was the last place I had them? I was sure I'd left them in the room, but I decided to go check the truck, just in case. And my truck was gone."

"I see."

"Yeah, well, you're quicker on the uptake than I am. I just stood there staring at the place where I'd left it, but there was another car there, and I'm thinking, *What on earth? Did I park someplace else?* Then it hit me. He took my truck."

"What did you do?"

"Went back to the room and called home. I told the folks I was really tired and I'd decided to sleep at school and go home today instead." Travis sighed and picked up his coffee mug, looked into it, then set it down.

"Do you need to call them now and tell them you're here?"

"I probably should. I don't want Mom to worry."

"I take it there's more I ought to know first?"

Travis bit his lip. "Brett didn't come in until 2 a.m. I gave up waiting up for him and went to sleep. He came in stoned. I woke up and said, 'Where's my truck?' He threw the keys at me and said, 'Don't worry, your precious heap is in the parking lot.' I was really mad, but I could see it wouldn't be the best time to have it out with him, so I decided to let him sleep it off and go into it today."

"Probably wise."

"Yeah, well." Travis shook his head. "When I got up, I was still mad, you know? I started to wake him up, but he was so out of it, I gave up and grabbed my stuff and went down to the parking lot. That's when I saw the fender was caved in."

Harvey's innate radar began to blip. "Brett had an accident with your truck and didn't tell you?"

"Right. That tore it, Harvey. I was *so* mad. I just wanted to go back and pound him."

Harvey looked him over judiciously. No bruises, and the timing wouldn't allow for much of a fracas before Travis hit the interstate. "You didn't."

"No. I decided to go home, cool off, and maybe tell Dad and get his advice."

Harvey nodded and carried his coffee mug to the counter for a refill. "Okay, that's good. But on your way to Skowhegan, you changed your mind. Because you didn't have time to go home and then come here."

Travis's smile crooked. "That's why you're a detective, I guess. On the way home, I turned on the radio."

Harvey slowly raised his head and stared at Travis. The radio becoming an actor in the drama was not good. He cocked his head to one side.

Travis turned his mug around aimlessly. "It was on the Bangor station. There was a hit and run in Orono last night, after midnight. Somebody ran down a guy outside a—a bar, I guess, and—Harvey, the guy's dead."

Harvey exhaled slowly. "Is that it? Or is there more?"

"They're looking for witnesses, and—and a dark pickup."

"Did you see any activity on the highway?"

"Some. No roadblocks or anything. Just lots of cruisers up there."

Harvey nodded. "Well, one thing at a time." He

313

gave Travis what he hoped was a reassuring smile and picked up the cell phone Jennifer had left on the table. He punched in George Wainthrop's home number, hoping he could get by without a lengthy explanation.

"Marilyn, hi, it's Harvey. Listen, Travis is down here with us."

"In Portland?" She was obviously startled. "He said he was coming home this morning."

"I know, but he decided to pop down here and visit, and we didn't want you to worry. I think I may run up there with him later."

"Well, sure. Okay. Is Jennifer coming?"

"Ah, well, I'll ask her. She took Connor over to see Beth for a few minutes, but she'll be back soon. I'll see you later, okay?"

He hung up before his mother-in-law could ask more questions.

Travis was watching him, hardly breathing. Harvey punched more buttons.

"Sergeant Miles," came a calm voice.

"Dan, this is Harvey Larson. I'm at home, but I need a quick report on a hit and run that occurred in Orono last night. Put someone on the computer, please, and get me anything and everything, ASAP."

"Orono?"

"Yes, that's right. Hit and run fatal. Could be S.P. involved. And use my cell number. I may be traveling."

314

"Sure, Harvey. You want us to contact Orono?"

"No, I'll do that, once I have the particulars. Thanks."

He closed the connection and stuck the phone in the pocket of his T-shirt.

"Are you up to driving some more?"

"I guess so." Travis seemed a bit stunned.

"All right, let me get my shoes on, and we'll go out and look at your truck. You tell me everything. *Everything.*"

"I told you, Harvey."

"Tell me again."

"So, I guess we're not raking leaves today," Jennifer said plaintively. It wasn't what she wanted to say, but she knew she couldn't change Harvey's course of action, and she didn't want to, really.

"I'm sorry, gorgeous. You know I have to do this." Harvey strapped on his shoulder holster and loaded his pockets with his gear, clipping his badge to his belt.

"What if Mom calls again?"

"As soon as we leave, you call her and tell her I'm on my way, with Travis. Don't tell her what's going on if you can help it. I'd rather explain that in person. But I think you and Connor had better stay here with Beth. If Jeffrey were off duty—"

"I know," Jennifer agreed. "It's okay."

"Good. Listen, can you put my gray suit in a

bag, and give me a clean shirt and a necktie?"

"You're staying overnight?"

"No, I hope not, but I may need to look official at some point, and I don't think these old jeans are going to do it. I don't really want to drive all the way up there in a suit, though."

Jennifer went to the walk-in closet and pulled together the outfit for him. Harvey went into the bathroom, and she heard his razor humming. She was zipping the garment bag when he emerged.

"Thanks, beautiful." He smiled, and she went unresisting into his embrace.

"At least you got a good night's sleep," she choked. "Harvey, is he going to be okay?"

"I hope so. You pray, though. I'll do everything I can. And Jenny, he's not lying. I really believe he knew nothing about it when he got in the truck this morning."

She nodded shakily. "It could be bad, though."

Harvey kissed her, then held her close. "I'll call you."

"How many times?"

He chuckled. "Fret not, gorgeous. You can call me if you want. As many times as you want." He let go of her and leaned over the bed to grab the hanger of the garment bag. "Black shoes?"

"Yes. Harvey?"

He smiled and ran his hand the length of her long braid. "What, Rapunzel?"

"I think it would be better if Travis didn't

live in the dorm. I mean, even if this roommate is expelled or whatever—it's not good for a kid like him. You know that. Some kids can stand up against it, but . . ."

"I know." He kissed her again. "I need to move on this. If I could drive him, I would, but they'll want to impound his truck, and I need my vehicle so I can get back here later. You pray. The Lord knows what's best for Travis, and if we can assist in that, we will."

They went out to the kitchen, where Travis was holding Connor upright on the table. "Look, Jenn, he's laughing!"

She smiled and put her hand on Travis's shoulder. "You listen to Harvey and do whatever he tells you." She bit her lip, wondering if she should have been silent, or if she should perhaps have said more.

Travis stood up and awkwardly handed the baby to her.

"I will. And thanks for everything."

She gave him a quick hug. "Drive carefully."

Harvey sat in a bleak interview room with Travis, across the table from the Orono chief of police.

"I've got two men going over the pickup for prints," Chief Bowden said.

"Well, I hope they find some, but we've told you, Travis may have obscured any belonging to Brett Rainer, on the truck or the key ring."

Bowden nodded. "The victim was crushed against a light pole, and the state police have recovered some paint chips. They'll have them tested to see if they match the paint on your truck, Mr. Wainthrop."

Travis nodded, and Harvey thought he looked a little nauseous.

"You'll need to keep the truck here?" Harvey asked.

"For a while. Maybe a couple of days."

"Fine. What about Brett Rainer?"

Bowden folded his hands on the table. "We'll definitely bring him in for questioning. Of course, he's a student. He may have gone home for the weekend, wherever *home* is."

"Houlton," Harvey supplied. He had grilled Travis for information on his roommate when they'd stopped in Skowhegan to explain things to the Wainthrops and allow Harvey to change his clothes.

"Hm," said Bowden. "I hope we don't have to chase him to Houlton. The state police can pick him up, I guess."

"Sir, he hasn't been home for the weekend since school started, and he was pretty groggy this morning," Travis said, his voice cracking. "He's probably still in the dorm."

"Well, we'll find out. These things take time, though."

Travis looked bleakly at Harvey.

"The boy's parents are waiting outside, sir," Harvey said. "If they're willing, I'd like to take Travis over to the campus to get his things. They've decided to take him out of the dorm, as of today."

Bowden eyed Travis speculatively. "You think Rainer was drinking at the Jolly Roger Tavern last night, near where this incident occurred?"

"I don't know where he was, sir. I just know my truck was gone, and then he came back drunk, and he had the keys. That's really all I know for sure."

Bowden scanned the report in front of him. "You have witnesses that you were at the library until 7:45, then at the dormitory . . ."

"Yes, sir, I was in room 205, with Brian and Clank for about an hour after that, then I got into my own room, and I stayed there."

"Chief, he's a good boy," Harvey said. "Never had an infraction. This Rainer, though, has a record. Travis told me this morning that his roommate didn't have a vehicle at school because his license had been suspended, so I took the liberty of asking our sergeant in Portland to check the record, and Rainer had an OUI conviction in Houlton last spring. His license was suspended thirty days, but then he was caught driving OAS, and they suspended him again. That's why he has no vehicle of his own in Orono, and that's why he *borrowed* my brother-in-law's truck."

"You sure he didn't ask you?" Bowden fixed Travis with a stare.

"No, sir, I wouldn't let him drive my truck. My dad just got it for me in August, and I promised him I wouldn't let anyone else drive it." Travis swallowed hard. "But if I did, I'd have taken the room key off the ring, sir. I was locked out of the room."

Bowen nodded, scowling down at the report.

Harvey felt his patience taking wing. He straightened his necktie.

"Look, Chief Bowden, I'd be happy to work with one of your officers on this. We could go over to the dorm and see if Rainer is there now. And we could show his picture at the Jolly Roger to see if the staff recognizes him. The longer you wait, sir . . ."

Bowden sighed unhappily. "The state police are in on this, Larson. Manslaughter, you know."

"But it's not murder, sir. Your department can—"

Bowden waved his hand. "I called Portland, too, Captain. I know you're the ace on the squad down there. But this isn't Portland."

Harvey leaned toward him earnestly. "I understand, sir. But our unit has a very high rate of solved cases, much higher than S.P., and one reason is, we don't let the paint dry. We move fast. Now, I know the evidence has been compromised by Travis driving the truck before he knew it was involved in a crime, but it's not too late to get this investigation back on track."

Bowden's eyes narrowed, and Harvey sensed he had pushed things far enough. He'd either convinced him, or not. He waited.

"Tell you what, Larson," Bowden said, rising, "You go do what you've got to do at the school, then come back here. If S.P. isn't moving on it, I'll ride with you."

Harvey took Travis to his parents in the lobby of the police station.

"We're all set, George. They need to keep his truck for tests. Listen, I'd like to take Travis over to the dorm to get his things, then you can take him home."

"He can go?" George asked, relief washing his face.

"Yes, and if you really want to take him out of the dorm, I think now's the time. If you don't mind, I'd like to go with Travis, in case his roommate is in the room."

"Thank you, Harvey," Marilyn said, grasping his hand. The strain of the afternoon showed on her face.

"You want us to drive over there?" George asked.

"Yes, but you can wait outside the dorm, if you don't mind."

Harvey followed Travis's instructions and

parked his Explorer in a visitor slot outside the main entrance at the dormitory.

"You okay?"

Travis nodded. "What do I say if he asks me questions?"

"Tell him you're moving out. You've had enough dorm life, and your brother-in-law came to help you move." Harvey unpinned his badge and slipped it into his coat pocket. "Don't say anything about last night. If he brings it up, okay, but otherwise, just act like nothing happened, you got me?"

George Wainthrop had found a parking place a few spaces down, and Harvey waved as he followed Travis up the steps, carrying a couple of empty boxes. At the door to Room 208, Travis stopped and tried the knob.

"Locked." He reached in his pocket, took out the key the police chief had removed from his key ring, and opened the door.

Harvey braced himself, but he still wasn't ready. The stale stench was overpowering. The two single beds were unmade, with the covers spilling onto the floor and clothing heaped on them. The desk, chairs and dressers were buried in books, clothes, and beer cans. Everywhere, there were empty beer cans, ninety percent Coors. They marched in rows across the window ledge, one dresser and the radiator. They lay in clusters on the floor and filled a clothes basket and a string bag that hung from the open closet door.

"He collects them," Travis said apologetically.

"Is he planning to cash them in for next semester's tuition?" Harvey asked.

Travis snorted. "Thanks for not letting Mom and Dad come up here."

"Pay me back by being quick. What do you want me to pack?"

"Well, those are my books over there." Travis nodded toward the desk, and Harvey took one box and approached it gingerly. Dried up pizza, a dirty sock, and a jumble of papers obscured the books.

"Man, Trav, I don't know about this."

"Well, here, everything in the drawers on this side is mine. You do that, and I'll sort out this other stuff."

Harvey began opening drawers and plunking the jumbled contents in the boxes.

"I guess I'm commuting now," Travis said woefully.

"You don't seriously want to stay here?"

"No, but—"

"What? The dean told your father they'll switch you to day student status, and your folks will get a big refund. Most of which you'll spend on gas, I suppose."

"Yeah, but I heard you say something to Dad about me transferring." Travis turned toward him, his eyes pleading. They were the same eyes Jennifer could sway him with so easily.

"Well, I mentioned it," he said gruffly, "but your father wasn't sure that was a good idea."

Travis nodded and went on piling cassettes, books, and pens in his box.

"He did ask the dean," Harvey said. "It's Saturday, though, you know? He wasn't real keen on it, and he said it's late in the semester to be transferring, and all that. Look, he said if you really want to pursue it, you can go to the academic office on Monday, and they'll see if you could get the same classes in Portland."

Travis asked warily, "What do you think about that? You and Jennifer, I mean?"

Harvey sighed. "We'll talk about it later, okay? Let's see how this whole mess shakes down." He knocked several beer cans off a chair with his elbow and picked up a sweater. "This yours?"

"Yeah."

"Where does he get the money?"

"Huh?"

"For the beer."

"Oh, I don't know. He always seems to have plenty. But he's not above picking up any loose change I leave lying around, either."

It was nearly half an hour before Travis was reasonably sure he had gathered all his belongings. There was no sign of Brett Rainer.

"I suppose his prints are on all these cans?" Harvey asked as they piled the boxes and Travis's duffel bag in the hallway.

"Nearly all, I suppose," Travis said. He looked up at Harvey from beneath his thick lashes. "Mine might be on one."

Harvey nodded. "One out of about three hundred. Could be worse."

"Harvey, I don't drink. I just, well—aw, man, I'm not trying to put one over on you. I tried it once. He and his friends were kind of pressuring me. But I'm not going to do it again."

Harvey hefted a box. "Tell me something, Rainer likes Coors?"

"Won't touch anything else. The others are ones his friends left here, I guess." Travis followed him, carrying a box and the duffel bag. "I don't know what the big deal is. Beer is beer, right?"

Harvey waited until he was at the bottom of the stairway, then turned to face Travis. "It's not that simple. Technically, yeah, beer is beer, but aesthetically, no. There's beer, and then there's . . . beer."

"You mean, like some people are with coffee?"

"Exactly. Look, do yourself a favor and don't ever get to the point where you care."

Travis nodded. They went outside and down the steps, and George got out of his car and unlocked the trunk.

"Sorry it took so long," Travis said. "We'll have to carry down one more load."

"Take your time," George replied, shifting the jack and the spare tire a little to make room for the boxes.

"We shouldn't be long," Harvey said. He and Travis went quickly up the stairs to 208. "I think we can get this all in one trip." He bent to pick up a suitcase.

"Hey, Wainthrop, what's happening?"

Harvey straightened and turned slowly. A young man with longish brown hair slouched in the doorway.

"Brett. Uh, I'm heading home." Travis glanced nervously at Harvey.

"Home?" Brett looked around the room. "Hey, you moving out?"

"Well, yeah."

Harvey wished he could inject a little authority into Travis.

"This your old man?" Brett asked, sizing Harvey up, from his necktie to his polished shoes.

"Uh, no, my brother-in-law."

"*Brother-in-law?*" Brett looked again, then smiled. "Cool. So, you dropping out, or what?"

"No, I'm just going to live at home. I'm not cut out for dorm life."

Brett laughed. "I coulda told you that." He sobered as he met Harvey's gaze. "Hey, Trav, you're not sore cause I used your truck last night,

326

are you? I just took a little run with a couple of guys, you know?"

Travis swallowed and looked at Harvey, then back at Brett. "Well, I wasn't real happy."

"That's not why you're moving out, is it?"

"Well, not exactly."

"Because I know you told me your old man was picky about the truck, but I didn't figure you'd care. I mean you were hitting the books last night, right?"

"Right," Travis said.

Harvey met Brett's gaze. "Travis is thinking about transferring to another school, and he's going to live at home until he decides. Come on, Trav, let's roll."

Travis bent for the last box and Brett said, "See you around, man."

Chapter 16

Harvey drove his Explorer, following Chief Bowden toward the university campus, and turning off on a side street. They parked across from the Jolly Roger Tavern. It was a plain concrete-block building with few windows and a lurid sign—a leering pirate tipping a jug on his shoulder. A placard prominently displayed on the door read *We ID*.

Bowden waited for him outside the entrance. "Okay, Larson, you want to show me your stuff? I had DMV fax me this." He handed Harvey a printout of Brett Rainer's driver's license photo.

Harvey clipped his badge to the front of his suit coat, feeling he was under inspection. "That's generous of you, sir." He pushed open the door and walked in.

He looked around quickly. Two girls in short uniform dresses were setting up for the supper shift. Three tables were occupied. Harvey approached the bar.

"Hi, I'm Captain Larson. Is the manager in?"

The bartender eyed him malevolently. "In the

back." He nodded toward a doorway. Harvey walked briskly toward it, sensing Bowden a pace behind him.

He pushed open the door the man had indicated and entered a short hallway. To the left was a small, cluttered office, and a middle-aged man was seated at the desk with a pile of receipts, punching numbers into a calculator.

He looked up as Harvey entered. "Can I help you?"

"Yes, sir. Are you the manager?"

"Owner and manager. Stephen Walker." He stood up. "Cops. I told the trooper, we were very busy last night. If the hit-and-run driver was here, I don't know it. My waitresses are coming in, and you can ask them if you want, but I don't think anybody saw anything. We didn't hear about it 'til after."

"The victim had been in here?"

"Well, yeah. One of my girls remembered serving him. We pulled the slip for the trooper. He had a couple of drinks, is all. I guess he left and got run down before he got to his car. They said he parked down the street, not in our parking lot. I don't know. You know more than I do."

"You get a lot of students in here?" Harvey asked.

"Hey, we always card."

"Do you?" Harvey took the picture of Brett

Rainer from his pocket. "Do you recognize this young man?"

"What's this?" Walker adjusted his glasses and scrutinized the photo. "Can't say as I do."

"But you were here, say between ten and midnight?"

"Oh, yes, but I'm in and out of the tavern. I spend a lot of time in here."

"Which waitresses were working last night?"

"Let's see, I've got the schedule here." Walker lifted a clipboard from a nail in the wall above his desk. "Melissa, Jackie, Miranda, Ruby, and Colleen."

"Five waitresses."

"Right. Jackie served the victim."

"And the bartender who's out there now was here?"

"Right. And a cook and a dishwasher. But they hardly ever go out front."

"And are all these waitresses working tonight?"

The manager frowned and flipped a page on the clipboard. "Not Jackie, but Pat will be here instead."

"Okay, I'll just hang around and show this picture to the employees and see if it jogs any memories."

"Suit yourself."

Harvey turned and walked past Bowden into the main room. Bowden didn't look impressed yet. He went to the bartender first.

"Excuse me, your boss says it's okay for you to talk to me. Do you recognize this young man?"

The bartender paused in setting up a row of glasses and peered at the paper, then shook his head.

"Was he in here last night?" Harvey persisted.

"Might of been."

One of the waitresses approached the bar. "Pitcher of beer, Larry." She tore a slip from her order pad and went through another doorway, which Harvey could see led to the kitchen. He leaned back against the bar and surveyed the customers she was waiting on. Bowden caught his eye, raised his eyebrows, then sat down on a barstool.

"Get you something, Chief?" the bartender asked, setting a full pitcher on the bar.

"No, thanks."

When the waitress came out of the kitchen and came to the bar for the beer, Harvey smiled and said, "Excuse me, miss, I'm Captain Larson. I'd like you to look at a picture and tell me if you've seen this young man in here, specifically last night."

"Can you wait a sec? I've got customers."

"Well, I think it may be in your interest to think about this before you serve them."

Her eyes closed to slits, between heavily mascaraed lashes.

Harvey smiled at her. "This pitcher is for that table, am I correct?"

She glanced to where he was pointing and nodded.

"Did you card your customers?"

She looked at him, then at the bartender. "We always card."

"Good, good. So, those customers are all over twenty-one."

She hesitated.

Harvey smiled again. "Could I just show you this picture now?"

She reached for it and looked hard at it. "Yeah, I think I saw him. Ask Melissa. It was her table."

She picked up the pitcher of beer and went to her waiting customers. "Hey, we got cops in here. Show me your ID."

Bowden snickered.

Harvey sat down beside him. "Not exactly humorous, Chief."

"I'm not laughing at her. I'm laughing at you, hotshot. You don't think she's going to serve minors under your nose?"

"She almost did."

The waitress came back to the bar, throwing him a grimace. "Two Diet Cokes and a root beer, Larry." She turned to Harvey. "The guy paying for the beer is twenty-two."

Harvey smiled. "Heavy drinker. You think he's going to drink that all by himself?"

"Yes, I do." She picked up the tray with three glasses and went back to the table.

Bowden stifled a laugh. "Go get 'em, Captain."

"No, you go get 'em, Chief. How many bars are there in Orono? Do your men patrol them regularly?"

Bowden scowled at him. "You see me telling you how to do your job? You're lucky I'm letting you wear your badge in here."

Harvey held up one hand in deprecation. "You're right. Sorry. But what do you bet, the minute we're out of here, those Diet Coke glasses are full of beer?"

"I'll make a note of it. I'll have my guys clamp down on this place."

A pretty waitress with her hair in a bouncy ponytail approached them, a tray under her arm. She didn't look of age herself.

"Excuse me, Colleen said I should talk to you. I'm Melissa."

Harvey smiled and stood up. "Thank you. I'm Captain Larson, and we're hoping you'll recognize this young man. He may have been in here last night, and Colleen thought you might have served him."

"Yeah, I think so. Let's see . . ." She looked out over the room, frowning. "Table three, with a bunch of other kids."

"Could I see the charge slip?"

"I'd have to ask my boss."

"And what time was he in here?"

"Oh, I don't know. They stayed an hour or two. It was pretty wild and noisy last night. Football game, you know? But . . . well, I think he was here around ten or so."

"And left what time?"

"Hm. That's a toughie. But you might be able to tell from the cash register slip. It would give the time when he cashed out."

"What was he drinking, do you remember?"

She smiled. "Coors."

Harvey nodded. "I'll ask the manager for the slip."

"Yeah, he can get it for you, I'm sure."

"So, Melissa, you're a student yourself?"

"Yes, sir."

"How old are you?"

"Twenty-one, sir."

"Mm. You know this kid." He indicated the picture.

She hesitated. "Not really, but he's been in here fairly often lately. Always with other students."

"He's a freshman," Harvey said.

"Really?" She smiled, but it slowly faded from her lips. "We always card," she said woodenly.

"So, he's twenty-one," Harvey said, smiling.

"I—apparently so."

"He's nineteen."

Melissa swore softly. "Am I in trouble?"

"I'll leave that up to Chief Bowden, here, but I strongly suggest you heed the management's slogan and card, card, card. This place could have its liquor license yanked for trafficking to minors."

She grimaced. "Does this have anything to do with the accident last night?"

"You're a smart girl." Harvey smiled at her and went back to the manager's office.

"You still here?" Walker asked, looking up.

"Yes, our suspect was here last night. Drank a lot of Coors between ten and midnight. Table three, waited on by Melissa. Can you locate the order slip?"

Walker sighed. "Hold on." He pulled open a drawer and plunked a stack of bar slips onto the desk. "See, I had a feeling I should keep these handy for a while. Man, I should make you get a warrant."

"We'll be out of here a whole lot faster if you cooperate."

"Yeah, yeah. Table three?"

"That's right."

Harvey looked around and sent up a prayer of thanksgiving. He might have ended up in a life like this.

"Maybe this one?" Walker asked, holding up a slip. "Eight Coors."

"Could be." Harvey took the slip from one of the waitresses' order pads and squinted at it. He took his glasses from his inside pocket and put them on.

"I don't see any other likely candidates," Walker said. "There's a couple of others with Coors, but just a drink or two."

"So how do you know the time he cashed out?" Harvey asked.

Walker sighed. "I'll have to go into the cash register for that. Thank goodness I got the computerized one in June. Come on."

They went out to the main room, and Walker went behind the bar and began working at the cash register. Bowden sat morosely sipping coffee at the bar.

"Find what you need?"

"I think so," Harvey replied. He scanned the room. It was filling up with young people.

Melissa came to the bar and called, "Two draft and a club soda." She smiled at Harvey. "Card, card, card."

"You got it."

"Here you go," Walker said. "He paid at 11:40." He handed Harvey a slip of paper, and Harvey squinted at it in the dimness to make sure the date and time were legible.

"Thanks. Now, a copy of the bar slip, with this stapled to it, please, and a statement from you that this is the one from the customer at table three, and one from Melissa that the customer in question was Brett Rainer." He smiled as winsomely as he could.

Walker shook his head. "I had a feeling. Anything else?"

"Nope, that's it. Then we're out of here."

"Hang on. I'll get it for you."

Bowden shook his head.

"What's the matter, Chief?" Harvey asked.

"All this documentation. Takes forever."

"This is what is going to make this case stand up in court," Harvey reminded him. "You get the paint match from the truck, and I get the waitress to swear he was here guzzling the beer, and Travis Wainthrop lines up his friends who saw him at the library and the dorm. Next, we find the kids who were with Rainer and get their statements. He wasn't alone when he hit that guy, Chief."

It was almost eleven when Harvey pulled in at the Wainthrops' farmhouse that night. George met him at the door.

"Everything all right, Harvey?"

"Yes, it's fine." He smiled. "Documentation, George. It takes forever."

"You want some coffee?"

"No, thanks, I've been drinking coffee all day. I could use something solid, though. I'm a little shaky."

"Whoopie pies?"

"Great."

They sat down at the kitchen table with a Tupperware box of whoopie pies between them, and George poured coffee for himself and milk for his son-in-law.

"Thanks for all you're doing, Harvey. I wouldn't have known where to start."

Harvey shrugged. "Glad I could help. But I'm sorry it happened in the first place."

"Yeah." George sat down opposite him and opened the box. "Marilyn and I . . . we've been trying to pray for the boy, but I'm not sure I know what I'm doing there, either."

"Just talk to God like you would me," Harvey said. "I know this is tough, but you can trust him."

"Yeah, I'm starting to believe that."

Harvey was halfway through his first whoopie pie when Travis appeared in the dining room doorway in gray sweat pants and a T-shirt.

"Hey, Travis," Harvey said. "You an insomniac?"

"Not usually."

"Sit down," George grunted.

"The cops believe me, don't they?" Travis asked, reaching for a whoopie pie.

"Oh, yeah, they believe you," Harvey said. "You'll probably get your truck back Monday or Tuesday. You called the insurance company, right?"

"I called them," George said. "As soon as the cops are done with it, we gotta get an estimate."

"Did they—" Travis swallowed.

"Yeah, they picked him up this evening."

"At the dorm?"

"No, at another bar. He bummed a ride with a friend of his."

George shook his head. "Travis, I hope this is a lesson to you."

Travis said quietly, "Dad this is a whole lot of lessons to me."

George stirred sugar into his coffee.

"He had two other guys in the truck with him when he hit the victim," Harvey said. "The crime lab guys found quite a bit of evidence, actually."

"Like what?" Travis asked.

Harvey shrugged. "Fingerprints that aren't yours on your tapes and on the passenger side surfaces, for instance. Hairs, a gum wrapper, a burnt match. They did a more thorough job than I expected."

"So, do they know who else was with him?"

"Yeah, they questioned them all. The other two bailed out, but they sent Brett to the Penobscot County jail overnight. His parents are supposed to be there in the morning."

"What are the charges?" George asked.

"Well, with Brett they can go all the way from a minor consuming liquor, auto theft and driving after suspension, to leaving the scene of an

339

accident, failing to make a report, and, last but not least, manslaughter."

"Manslaughter?" Travis croaked.

"Afraid so. They'll probably concentrate on that one."

"Not OUI?" George asked.

"Well, they didn't get him until almost twenty-four hours later. It's pretty hard to prove he was driving drunk after the fact."

"These kids." George sighed. He got up and opened the lid to the wood-burning range. "Guess I'd better get some wood." He took his old green jacket from a hook by the back door and went into the woodshed beyond.

"Harvey, thanks for everything," Travis said earnestly. "Is Jennifer going to be worried?"

"I called her and told her I'll sleep here and be home in time for church in the morning."

"Well, thanks."

"Travis, I asked her if she was serious this morning. About you coming to stay with us, I mean."

He could tell the boy was trying not to let his eagerness show.

"I'd really like that. Can you give me a chance, Harvey?"

"You know what I'd do if you drank?"

Travis dropped his gaze. "I've got an idea."

Harvey nodded. "I won't expose Connor to that. Zero tolerance. See, I know what it's like.

340

I learned to drink in college, too. It was an easy class."

Travis swallowed. "I only did it that one time, and I didn't like it."

"Yeah, but you can learn to like it. It just takes practice. You start out with half a can, and if you can keep that down, you go to a whole one, then two. You just repeat, every weekend. You get to where you can drink a six pack without losing it. And somewhere along the way, you realize you like it."

George came in from the shed with an armload of wood. "Cold tonight. Gonna be an early winter."

Travis exchanged looks with Harvey.

"How did you get through school, if it was that bad?"

Harvey grunted. "Confined my extracurricular activities to weekends, for one thing. Didn't mix it with driving. Much." He shook his head, realizing George was watching him closely. He smiled. "Think how smart I'd be if I hadn't destroyed a few billion brain cells back then."

"How'd you quit?" George asked.

Harvey shrugged. "If I hadn't had to stay sober five days a week, I probably would never have quit. But after a while, when I stopped hurting so bad inside, I sort of grew out of the need, to where it was only once in while, if I got really depressed. I was really proud of myself." He grimaced. "Then I met Jennifer. She was a shock to my system. She never drank, so I didn't either. I didn't want her to think less of me. And when we got saved, I just knew it was something I would never do again."

George nodded. "You can't drink and honor God, I can see that."

"You never drank, Dad," Travis said.

"What do you know about it, puppy?" George asked.

Harvey smiled at him. "The past isn't what matters. It's what you do now."

George nodded. "I've been thinking about this dorm business. Marilyn and I are going to make a formal complaint to the university president."

"I'll support you in that," Harvey said.

George dropped two sticks into the stove and closed the lid. "When I was talking to the dean, he said Travis could transfer to this other dorm, men only. But the boy says—"

"They'd think I was gay, Dad, if I asked for that," Travis said in alarm. "You think the gays don't drink in the dorm, or what?"

"It's supposed to be for serious students, who don't want the co-ed distractions."

"Well, that's not a problem," Travis said adamantly. "I'm not living in the men-only dorm, Dad. No way. I'll drop out first."

"Easy, Trav," Harvey said quietly. He tipped

up his milk glass and drained it. "Jenny and I are hoping you can come stay with us a while. If you can transfer your classes, that'll be great. If not, well, you commute from here until Christmas, and maybe we can do something then."

Travis looked anxiously toward his father.

"Don't know why you kids all want to leave home so fast," George said sadly.

"It's not that," Travis assured him. "It's just too far, Dad. In the winter—well, Abby used to say the same thing. It's just too far when the roads are bad."

"He's right," Harvey said. "Even for an experienced driver, there's a pretty big risk."

"You made Leeanne live in the dorm at Farmington because of it," Travis pointed out.

"Well, she's a girl. Boys don't usually mind as much. And she never complained about drinking there."

"She never complained," Travis agreed. "She knew if she told you, you'd have fits and maybe make her commute, just like you are me."

George sighed and reached for another whoopie pie. "It's really that widespread? There must be good kids out there who behave themselves."

"There are," Harvey agreed. "But it's hard when they leave home for the first time and have so much freedom. The temptation is strong at these schools. There's a very small percentage who don't fall into it to some degree."

"When I was in the Navy," George began, but he glanced at Travis, and, seeing something in his face, shifted gears. "Well, never mind. I guess if it's not too much for you and Jennifer, we can see about him coming down there after Christmas. But this watchdogging teenagers is no picnic, young man."

Harvey smiled ruefully. If things had been different, he might have teenagers of his own now. But he was glad his life was the way it was that instant.

"George, if I put in enough time with your kids, maybe I'll be good at it by the time Connor hits his teens. No complaints about our short stints with Abby and Leeanne, are there?"

"No, no. Well, I guess Leeanne's come around after all. Did I tell you she called?"

"No, sir."

"Oh, yes, she and Eddie. They want to get married Thanksgiving Day."

Harvey smiled. "That's good news."

"Well, I hope so. If she doesn't call it off again."

"I don't think she will." Harvey pulled at the knot in his necktie. "Jennifer and I usually pray together before we go to bed, sir. Could we pray together, for the family?"

"I'd like that." George threw an anxious glance at Travis.

Travis meekly closed his eyes and stayed put.

• • •

Harvey spent Sunday afternoon in front of the fireplace, poring over the paperwork he'd brought home. Rain pelted the windows. Jennifer sat quietly in the rocking chair, working on a cross stitch sampler, smiling at Harvey whenever he looked up from his reading. When Connor woke from his nap, she carried him to the sofa and settled down next to Harvey to feed the baby.

"When's the last time we had a quiet Sunday afternoon?" Harvey asked.

"I think it was before we met," she mused.

"This is nice. We're usually mobbed Sundays, and I usually love it, but today . . ."

"You've had enough excitement for one weekend," she said. "I spread a rumor at Sunday school that the Larson kitchen is closed today."

"Well, I have a feeling it won't last, but while it does . . ." He leaned toward her and kissed her.

"I missed you so much last night," she confessed. "I actually thought about taking Connor over to Beth's and pajama partying with her and Leeanne."

"Our first night apart, except for the hospital," he said. "I admit I was so tired I didn't have any trouble falling asleep." He let a folder slide gently to the floor and put his arms around her. "We need to make some major decisions about Travis and let your folks know."

"Are you willing to have him come?" Her

eyes were somber gray that day. "I love him, Harvey, and I'd do anything to protect him from temptation."

Harvey sighed. "I know. But we can't control all of it. I want what's best for him, but I'm not sure I'm the best mentor for him."

She watched him silently, and he thought she was tracing his past and comparing it with Travis's present.

"Your father is growing spiritually." He leaned back and tried to look at the situation objectively. "If Travis can get along with his parents, he probably ought to stay there. And if he can't, do we really want a rebellious eighteen-year-old living in our house during our son's formative years?"

"You said he seemed contrite last night."

"He did. But when this is over, will he still toe the line?"

"It's not like he did something horrible."

"I know. It might be easier if he had. If he could clearly see himself as a sinner."

"You think he would defy you if you set rules for him?" Jennifer asked. "I can't believe he would. He respects you."

"He also knows I used to drink, and he doesn't seem to think I'm any the worse for that. I'd hate to have him thinking he can mess around now and walk away from it later, because I was able to. He has no idea the misery I went through in between."

She shifted the baby to her shoulder and began to pat his back. "He doesn't seem to realize that it was God who changed you."

Harvey nodded. "But I can't hold out faith as a criterion for his living here. That might make him try to conform just because he knows we want him to. It's got to be genuine."

"Don't you think he has a better chance of reaching that point here?"

"I don't know. I don't want to be a drill sergeant or a baby-sitter. And I sure don't want to end up sending him back to your father because I failed."

Jennifer nodded. "I can see your point. I think he needs to live at home for the rest of the semester, at least. I suspect they'll tell him he can't transfer until then, anyway. And we *could* make his coming here contingent on good behavior between now and January."

Harvey stroked her thick hair. "I'd like to have him come, I think. But we'll need to pray about it a lot and draw up some kind of ground rules for him. He's younger than your sisters were when they came, and, well—"

"He's a boy," Jennifer said flatly.

He smiled. "I don't have any experience whatever with boys who can talk back."

"You did a pretty good job with Eddie."

"Oh, please. Eddie was older when I got him. He wasn't mature, but he wasn't exactly a boy."

There was a knock at the patio door in the sun room, and they heard a key in the lock.

"Company," Jennifer said ruefully.

"Let me hold Connor, or Leeanne will steal him." Harvey reached for the baby as Eddie entered the living room.

"Hi! Where's Leeanne?" Jennifer asked. "Still at Beth's. I was wondering if we ought to watch that other video, Harv? If you want to wait, it's okay, but we don't usually have time at the office."

"That's right, I've still got a tape from one of Brad's shifts in my briefcase," Harvey said.

Jennifer stood up. "Connor and I will go next door if you guys insist on working seven days a week."

"One hour," Harvey said. "We'll buzz the slack time. I want you back in an hour."

She smiled at him and left the room.

"What day was this tape made?" Eddie asked as Harvey slipped the cassette from its case.

"The Friday before Labor Day. I wanted a recent one, but before the murder."

They sat on wicker chairs in the sunroom, facing the small television set that was usually camouflaged in a shelf unit.

"Routine stuff," Eddie said after ten minutes of silence. "Brad's away from his desk a lot."

"Yeah, that's standard, though, especially at the beginning of the shift. Let's buzz anything when he's out of camera range."

Harvey conscientiously viewed each segment where the sergeant engaged in conversation. "His usual. Some vulgarity. Nothing offensive to a woman's face, though."

The hour was nearly up when Eddie reached out suddenly toward Harvey, hitting his forearm forcefully.

"Back up!"

Harvey clicked the remote to rewind, then play. His adrenaline surged as he focused on the officer approaching Brad's desk.

"Joey," he breathed.

"His last shift at work," Eddie agreed.

"No, he was on duty Labor Day, remember?"

Eddie shrugged. "That was volunteer stuff, for the challenge."

On the tape, Joey waited until Brad Lyons was free, then leaned toward him, both hands tense on the surface of the desk.

"Help you, Bolduc?" Brad asked.

"You can help yourself, Brad. Leave Deborah Higgins alone."

Brad's back was to the camera, but his voice rose in surprise. "Debbie? I've hardly spoken to her in days. She's been in and out of here like greased lightning every day."

"As if she's avoiding you?" Joey sneered.

"Hey, what's the matter? She tell you we had a thing once?"

"You just leave Deborah alone. If you ever lay a hand on her again, you'll be the one who's sorry."

"You're jealous."

"Of you? Right. Why would I be jealous of someone who's about to get busted for intimidating a subordinate?"

"What are you talking about, moron?"

"Deborah told me everything."

"She's a liar."

"I told her if you open your mouth around her again, I'll take it to the chief," Joey said.

"Oh, yeah?"

"Yeah. Your buddy Neilsen is gone. Who will help you this time? Browning and Stewart both respect women."

"Listen, turkey, you tell that little tramp to watch her step."

"Why should I?"

"Well, let me see." Brad clapped a hand to his forehead. "Oh, I almost forgot. Officer Higgins is due for an evaluation. Hmm, I could schedule her for Tuesday. Tell her not to wear her hair in that stupid bun if she wants a good report."

"You pervert."

"Ha! She's still in her probation year. She needs

to be very careful. If I think her performance isn't up to snuff, she could be history two weeks from now."

"Maybe you ought to apply for a job in Massachusetts, if you want to keep working in law enforcement, Lyons. There's plenty of people around here who are sick of you."

"Watch yourself, Bolduc. I can have you busted to traffic duty in five minutes flat."

"Oh, really? I wouldn't be so cocky if I were you. I would trust the chief to give this thing a hard look." Joey left the area.

Harvey clicked the tape off.

"Unbelievable," Eddie said. "How can they carry on like that in front of a camera?"

"Easy. The techs have two dozen cameras to monitor. They probably rarely listen to the audio. And how often does anyone actually go back and look at those tapes?"

"Rarely, I guess."

"Almost never. The ones in the booking room and the lockup are archived until the cases are closed, but the ones in the public areas and stairways, even the duty room, are recycled after two weeks. They're just there in case something really unusual happens. Brad and Joey both knew that. Chances were that, even if a technician was monitoring them at that moment, he wasn't listening to what they said. And two weeks later, poof. It's taped over."

"Except that you grabbed it because of the harassment allegations."

"Right. Mike told me to pick a couple of recent tapes from the sergeant's area at random, and I did."

"You picked the right one," Eddie said.

"Who knows? Maybe there are lots of incriminating things on others, too. But this one should be enough."

"What are you going to do?"

Harvey pushed REWIND. "Take it to Mike."

"Tomorrow?"

Harvey frowned. "I'd better call him now. I hate to even have Brad come in tomorrow morning. I want him off the desk, and I don't want to have to confront him and break the news at work."

He stretched toward the coffee table and picked up his phone.

"Mike? It's Harvey. Where are you?"

"Just leaving Churchill. Why? You got something?"

"Could be. Stop by my house tonight?"

"Okay, it will probably be nine o'clock."

"That's all right. I'll brief you when you get here. How's the renovation coming?"

"Great. We're all set up for Rick to come up here tomorrow. Next time you visit Browning's Lodge, you'll have a real bedroom and a private bath. That is, if you hold off a few weeks."

Harvey chuckled. "I think I'll be pretty busy for the next few weeks. Through Thanksgiving, anyway. Eddie's getting married then."

"Fantastic. Are we invited?"

Mike sat scowling at the screen after Harvey had shut off the video player. "You hate to see me enjoy a weekend, don't you, Harvey?"

"Sorry. I didn't want to bring this to you at the office tomorrow and deal with it in the middle of a shift."

Mike nodded. "It's better if I confront him in private, which means tonight."

"You'll move that fast?" Eddie asked.

"Got to," Mike said. "I can't let him carry on, with proof he threatened officers like that. I'll tell him he's suspended with pay until the investigation ends."

"You want me to go with you?" Harvey asked.

Mike scratched his chin. "I'm thinking I'll take a couple of uniforms with me, no offense. No way anyone can say management covered it up that way. And besides, I don't want you and Brad mixing it up."

Harvey took a deep breath. "Thanks, Mike, I appreciate that. I really didn't want to be the one to confront him."

Mike looked at Harvey, then Eddie. "Listen, there's something else. I didn't have a chance to

353

tell you before I left Friday, but I would have told you tomorrow morning."

Harvey's interest was piqued. He waited, aware that Mike was troubled.

"Last Friday, I was looking back in my appointment book. I'd had a conversation with Jill Weymouth, and I couldn't remember if it was before or after the murder. Judith was out on her break, so I looked in the book on her desk to see what day Jill came to my office last. I was pretty sure Judith would log it in my appointment book. She's very methodical. I looked back as far as Labor Day week, and what do you think?"

Eddie shrugged, and Harvey said, "No idea."

"*Detective Bolduc* was written on my calendar for 9 a.m. September fifth, but it was crossed out."

"Joey was killed the fourth," Eddie said immediately.

"That's right. So, of course I asked Judith about it when she came back. She said Joey had called the Friday before Labor Day, asking for an appointment with me as soon as possible. I'd left early that day, and she knew I didn't plan to be in the office Monday. For the holiday, you know? So, she gave him a morning appointment for Tuesday."

"She didn't tell you, though?" Harvey asked.

"No, when she came in Tuesday morning, she'd heard about Joey's death, so she crossed out the appointment. Very neat and precise. No need to bother the boss. And she had no inkling what he wanted to see me about."

"It had to be about this," Harvey said, retrieving the tape and putting it carefully into the case.

Mike nodded. "That seems likely."

Chapter 17

When Eddie put his hand out to knock, Leeanne grabbed his arm, stopping him.

"Are you sure I look all right?"

"Of course. You're beautiful."

"I should have worn a dress."

"No, you look great." He bent and gave her a quick kiss, then raised his arm again, but the door swung open before he could knock.

"There! I thought I heard you. Come in," Marie cried.

Eddie kissed his mother's cheek, and Lisa swooped down on Leeanne, enveloping her in a hug.

"It's about time!"

"We've been missing you," Marie said.

Leeanne smiled and kissed Lisa, then Marie. As Eddie's mother took their coats, Monique and Eddie's two brothers-in-law approached.

"Leeanne," Monique said, kissing the air near Leeanne's right ear. "We're so glad things are back to normal."

"Normal? What's normal around here?" Marie cried.

Leeanne was hugged perfunctorily by Wyatt, then Lisa leaned close.

"Leeanne, I'm so sorry I was snooty to you. Can you forgive me?"

"Of course."

"I was so upset. I knew Eddie was in love with you, and I couldn't stand to see my brother hurt like that."

"I've felt that way about my brothers, too," Leeanne admitted. "I'm sorry we put everyone through a bad time."

"Well, everything's good now, right?" Marie asked expectantly.

"Yeah, Maman, everything's good," Eddie agreed.

"Sit," she said.

Lisa's husband, Ansel, held the baby. He reached out to clasp Leeanne's hand. "Good to see you again, Leeanne." She smiled gratefully.

"When you gonna solve this murder case?" Wyatt demanded.

"I worked all day on it," Eddie said wearily, sitting down beside Leeanne on the couch.

"Yeah? You arrest anybody yet?" Wyatt asked.

"Not yet."

"Too busy asking all the ladies if the cops are getting fresh with them?"

Eddie froze. "Where did you hear that?"

Marie waved her hand toward her son-in-law. "I told you not to tell him." She turned eagerly to Eddie. "Cousin Nadine's daughter-in-law's friend works there, filing or something. Nadine said all the women are being questioned about bad language and men pinching them. I told her I didn't believe it. You got better things to do with your time."

"I spent all day on the Bolduc case," Eddie said evenly, getting to his feet. "Excuse me a minute, I'll be right back." He headed for the hallway, but Leeanne saw him stop near the coat rack and was sure he slipped his phone from the pocket of his jacket.

"Give us the details," Lisa said eagerly. "How did you get back together?"

Leeanne swallowed. "Well, we started talking about things, and . . ." She looked cautiously toward Marie. "Eddie sent me flowers . . ."

"My son did that," she said proudly. "He knows what women like."

"Not women, Maman," Lisa corrected. "One woman. Leeanne is all that counts." She smiled again. "What else?"

"Well, he—" Leeanne took a deep breath. "I never stopped loving him," she insisted.

"Ah," Marie said sagely. Lisa and Ansel smiled at each other.

"It's true," Leeanne said.

"Of course. Now, what are your plans?" Marie asked, businesslike, when Eddie returned to the room.

"Mother," Monique scolded gently. "Give them time to breathe."

Leeanne looked to Eddie, and he cleared his throat as he sat down again.

"Thanksgiving Day," he said.

"What? No." Marie waved her hands. "That's a family day."

"So, it'll be a family wedding day."

Lisa beamed at them. "I think it's great. I won't have to cook a turkey."

"You don't want to change it?" Marie was still hopeful.

"No, Maman, we don't want to change it." Eddie squeezed Leeanne's hand.

"You're going to invite the whole family, though?"

"Of course," Leeanne assured her. "You gave me the list."

"You getting new invitations?" Monique asked.

Leeanne's cheeks warmed. "Yes, we just wanted to check the time with your mother, and I'll order them tomorrow."

"I'll pay for them," Marie offered. Monique scowled at her, but her mother ignored her. "Your father paid the first time. It's my turn."

"No, Maman," Eddie said. "I got it covered."

"I'm just so happy I get my daughter-in-law after all." Marie grinned at Leeanne, and she couldn't help smiling back. "You're making my son very happy here."

"Thank you, Marie."

"So, what time? People are going to want to have their Thanksgiving dinner."

"Noon?" Eddie asked. "They can go home and eat after."

"No, you gotta have the reception," Lisa frowned at him. "Have the wedding in the evening."

"They want to head for Montreal early," Monique guessed.

"No, I think we'll hang around here for a couple of days," Eddie said.

"You couldn't get new reservations." Marie shook her head sadly.

"Well, no, but I only have a week of vacation left—"

"It doesn't matter," Monique put in. "Have the wedding when you want it. If your friends want to be there, they'll adjust their schedule for it."

"How about three o'clock?" Leeanne asked hesitantly. "People can have their dinner early."

"Yeah, and they won't eat much at the reception because they're full of turkey," Wyatt said with a laugh.

Leeanne looked anxiously at Eddie. "Maybe Thanksgiving isn't such a great idea."

"Well, hey, there's time to think about it," Marie said. "Let's break out the champagne, huh?"

"None for us," Eddie said.

Marie grimaced. "Not even champagne to toast your engagement?"

"I brought some ginger ale," said Lisa. "The kids need to drink, too."

"Where are the kids?" asked Eddie.

"Out back. I'll get them." Monique got up and headed for the kitchen, and Lisa went to help Marie pour the drinks.

"We are absolutely not changing the date again," Eddie said low, in Leeanne's ear.

She nodded and squeezed his hand.

The Pelletier and Rousseau children came puffing in from the back yard.

"Uncle Eddie! Uncle Eddie!"

Eddie laughed and scooped up five-year-old Annick.

"Are you really getting married this time, Uncle Eddie?" David, Monique's oldest, asked solemnly.

"Yes. I am most definitely getting married, and you all are going to be there."

"Can we call you Aunt Leeanne again?" Annick asked, looking soberly at Leeanne with big brown eyes as melting as Eddie's.

"Of course, honey."

"You do love Uncle Eddie, don't you?" Josette asked. "Because I'm not going to the wedding if you don't."

Leeanne felt the tears start, and Eddie said gruffly. "What kind of talk is that? Of course we love each other. We never quit. We just needed some extra time to be ready, is all."

Lisa came to the doorway. "Hey, kids, come get your soda. We're going to have a toast." She passed plastic cups to the children, then served Eddie, Leeanne and herself ginger ale in champagne glasses. Marie followed with champagne for Wyatt, Ansel, Monique, and herself.

"Well," said Wyatt, surveying the room. "To a wonderful family, and the newest member. Leeanne, welcome back."

Leeanne smiled tremulously and sipped her ginger ale.

She found herself alone with Lisa in the kitchen twenty minutes later, as they carried the glasses to the drainboard.

"I'm really happy about this," Lisa declared. "Eddie is Eddie again."

Leeanne smiled. "Thanks. You—you will still be my bridesmaid, won't you?"

"Of course! Same dress?"

"Well, yes, if you don't think it's too summery."

Lisa considered. "Nah. Burgundy is good anytime, even with the short sleeves. I love the dresses."

Eddie came to the doorway. "Hen talk?"

Leeanne smiled. "You're always welcome."

He went to her smiling, and embraced her. "Look, Maman's getting nervous again. We need to settle the time."

"Well, I—whatever you think." Leeanne shot a glance at Lisa.

"*Je suis de trop*," Lisa said.

"No, stay," Eddie said quickly. "You've been through this with the family. Help us out here. What will make them happy?"

"We're already happy."

"Yeah, well, you know . . ."

"Just pick what you want. Maman will come around." Lisa flipped up the pages of the calendar over the microwave. "November twenty-third. You *could* do it in the evening. A lot of people have the next day off."

"What about the twenty-eighth?" Leeanne asked timidly.

Eddie faced her in disbelief. "I thought we agreed, we're not postponing this thing again."

"I meant October twenty-eighth," Leeanne choked, unable to meet his eyes. He was referring to their wedding as *this thing,* and she could tell his patience was near snapping. She turned away, dashing her hand at the tears. "I'm sorry."

Eddie's arms were like steel around her. "You would do that? October twenty-eighth?"

Lisa turned to the October page and studied it critically. "Saturday. Looks good to me."

"Now you're *de trop*," Eddie said darkly.

Lisa laughed. "*Pardonez-moi.* I'll stand guard at the door."

She left the kitchen, swinging the door to

behind her, and Eddie held Leeanne tight against him.

"You're willing to knock a month off the schedule? Really?"

She nodded. "We might not be able to get tuxedoes that fast."

"I'll wear a suit. You sure you want to do this?"

"This is taking too long, Eddie. Your mother still thinks I'm going to run out on you again."

"I told them, it wasn't like that."

"I know, but they'll believe what they want to believe."

"Well, Lisa wants to believe you're the greatest woman in the world for me."

Leeanne laughed shakily. "Isn't she great?"

"Yes, and she will bring my mother into line. On the wedding day, she will be the queen mother, and everybody will know it was her who pulled this whole thing off."

"I want her to *like* me, Eddie."

"I'm not going to pretend this has been easy for her."

"I know she wanted a meek little French Catholic girl in a school uniform."

"Bilingual, with an aunt who's a nun. But she's wanted a lot of things she didn't get."

"So maybe we should ask her about the date and the time, and give her what she wants for once," Leeanne said doubtfully.

"I love you." He kissed her deliberately, and

Leeanne clung to him, burrowing her face into his neck. "As long as it's no later than Thanksgiving night, I'm willing to take my mother's advice," he whispered.

Harvey entered the Priority Unit from the stairway with Eddie and Jimmy, just down from prayer with Mike and Jack Stewart, in the deputy chief's office. Ryan Toothaker was sitting in his visitor chair, and he frowned. The reporter wasn't usually allowed upstairs.

"What's up, Ryan?" Harvey glanced toward Paula. She gave him a small shrug.

Ryan stood and extended his hand. "Captain Larson. I thought it was time I touched base with you."

"On what?"

"Several things. The Bolduc murder for starters."

"Detective Thibodeau's in charge—"

"I know, but let's face it, you're in charge of the guy who's in charge."

Harvey scowled. "I don't have time for this, Ryan. Eddie can brief you on the Bolduc case."

"Okay, what about you ordering your men to clean up their language?"

"I beg your pardon?"

Ryan smiled. "Detective Winfield tells me you ordered him to quit swearing on the job."

"I did no such thing."

"Really? Winfield's a liar?"

"No." Harvey sat staring at him. "I might have suggested he improve his vocabulary. This unit has quite a reputation to live up to, and I don't think mature men need to swear on the job. I want the public to see us as efficient, decent, and respectful."

"So that's why you're interviewing secretaries and file clerks—to see if your men are living up to their decent reputation?"

Harvey began sorting the mail and messages Paula had left for him. "I'm not free to discuss open investigations, Ryan."

"All right, then, what about Brad Lyons?"

Harvey schooled his face not to show surprise. "What about him?"

"The last couple of days, when I've come for the police log, there's been a new sergeant on the desk."

"That's right, Lyons has been out for a few days, but I'm not his supervisor."

"Is he on vacation? Because Sergeant Yeaton is very tight-lipped."

Harvey sighed and set down the sheaf of papers he was holding. "Lyons is not on vacation. The truth is, Chief Browning and I were just discussing this a few minutes ago. We think by the end of the week we'll have something for you, but we're not ready yet."

Ryan smiled. "I knew it. I could smell it."

"Yeah, well, back off and quit drooling."

"Come on, Captain, what's going on here?"

"Nothing, yet."

"No, something's going on. I can go look up Lyons."

"He might be sick," Harvey said.

"He might not."

"Ryan, please."

The reporter leaned back in his chair and studied Harvey. "I was thinking he was taking a job someplace else, you know? But I'm getting very strange vibes from you, Captain."

"What kind of vibes?"

Ryan shrugged. "The I-hate-reporters-who-aren't-related-to-me kind."

"That was low. I've always been square with you."

"You know Leeanne would have broken this story by now if she hadn't quit the paper."

"I don't think so." Harvey got up and poured himself a cup of coffee. "I used to like you. I thought you were good. Now you're being nasty. Leave."

Ryan sat for a couple of seconds, then stood up slowly and headed for the stairs.

Harvey carried his coffee mug to Eddie's desk. "Did you hear that?"

"*Oui, mon ami. Très gauche.*"

"I might just call another paper and give them an exclusive," Harvey said.

"Not yet, *s'il te plait*."

"Oh, no, not until we're good and ready."

Eddie pulled his wallet from his pocket and selected a credit card.

"Shopping?" Harvey asked.

"Red roses today, I think. For Leeanne and my mother."

"Make it snappy," Harvey said. "We've got to work fast, or we'll be reading about the harassment case in the paper before we've cracked it."

"Okay. Leeanne is going to call the formalwear shop today. Do you think we can get the tuxedoes for October twenty-eighth?"

"I don't see why not. It's not prom week, and they have all our measurements."

Nate stood up from his desk across the room and came toward them.

"Captain, I've got some word on the hair samples."

"What is it?"

"That custodian, Donald Lloyd. It's his hair."

"This is the one who had his court case dismissed?" Eddie asked.

"Right. His hair was on the dummy's clothes."

"Nate had him in here first thing this morning, while we were going over things with Cheryl," Harvey explained. "I had applied for a warrant for Lloyd's hair sample, and we got it this time."

"It was a good thing," Nate said. "He didn't want any part of it, and he came in here with his lawyer. I taped everything."

"What now?" Eddie asked. "This proves nothing. He had a right to be there."

"I know," Harvey agreed. "At least we know whose hair it is—the custodian's, not someone's from outside."

"You think he did it?" Eddie asked, frowning.

"He had his story down pat," Nate said. "He and another custodian were helping the setup crew. He ate lunch with the other guy, uh—" he pulled his notebook from his shirt pocket. "Andrew Flood."

"Did we question him?"

Nate shook his head. "One of Ron's men took his statement the day of the murder. That's it, so far as I can tell."

"Get him in here," Eddie said.

Nate nodded and went back to his desk.

Eddie cocked an eyebrow at Harvey. "This Lloyd could have done it."

"That would explain a few things, wouldn't it?" Harvey asked.

Paula called to him, "Captain, Detective Rood is on the phone. She wants to see you right away."

"Tell her to come. Is she at the courthouse?"

Paula spoke into the receiver, then replied, "She's on her way in."

"Tell her I'll be here." He turned to Eddie. "All right, you dig into this custodian thing, and I'll debrief Emily. Maybe she can shed some light on these conveniently dropped charges."

After Leeanne got home from her classes at the university, she consulted with Jennifer, Beth, and Abby, in Beth's bedroom.

"I don't think there's any way it will fit," Beth wailed. "When the wedding date was Thanksgiving, I figured I'd have had the baby and be thin again."

"We can do something," Jennifer said, spreading out the skirt of Beth's burgundy gown.

"I don't think so. There's just not enough material." Beth turned to Leeanne. "Why don't you just ask Eddie's other sister to step in for me?"

"Monique? Forget it. She's a sourpuss. She refuses to speak French, even to her grand-mother."

"But this is a family thing. It might make things easier between you for years to come."

"I want you, Beth," Leeanne insisted.

"Hold on," said Abby. "What if we could match the material?"

"Impossible," said Leeanne.

"Maybe not. Where's the phone book?"

"In the kitchen, on the microwave," Beth told her, and Abby disappeared.

"I'd rather wait until Thanksgiving than leave you out, Beth," Leeanne wheedled.

"Bite your tongue," Jennifer said. "You are not changing the date again, no matter if there's an earthquake, a hurricane, and a blizzard the same day."

"Look, I'll still be there." Beth patted Leeanne's hand. "I'll be sitting comfortably on a padded pew beside my loving husband."

"Speaking of Jeff, where is he?" Jennifer asked. "Isn't he off today?"

"Yes. He went with Mark Johnson to look at a boat."

"Jeff's buying a boat?" Jennifer asked.

"No, Mark is. At least, he's thinking about it."

Abby came to the doorway. "They've got one dress left, size four. We can have it for half price and make an extra panel for Beth's dress."

Jennifer looked to Beth. "Think we can do that?"

"Ruthann could," Beth said.

Jennifer picked up her purse and unzipped it. "Do it." She handed Abby a credit card. "I'll run over and pick it up now."

"I'll go with you," Abby offered.

"Get the boys into my minivan," said Jennifer.

"Do you want me to go?" Leeanne asked.

"No, I want you to stay here with Beth and Connor, and do your homework. You've got to have that term paper finished before the wedding."

"Jenn, there's a florist truck out front," Abby called from the living room.

"Oh, brother!" Jennifer turned and scowled at Leeanne. "Don't you dare change the date! I don't care how many roses he sent you this time." She grabbed her sweater and ran for the door.

"You've got something, Emily?" Harvey asked eagerly, as she came off the elevator.

"I think so, sir. Sorry it took so long."

"No problem. These things take time."

Emily sat down in his extra chair.

"Coffee?" Harvey asked.

"No, thank you, I'm a chamomile tea person."

"Hey, Paula," Harvey yelled, "We got any chamomile tea?"

"I'll get some."

Emily laughed and turned toward Paula. "Don't bother. I'm fine." She faced Harvey, sobering. "I think I know what happened in at least one of the cases in question."

"Brad Lyons had a friend over there."

"Actually, it was Raymond Neilsen who called the courthouse the first time."

"The first time?"

"When the female prisoner complained. Lyons reduced the bail himself, I think. Just changed it on the form before it was filed."

"Rather blatant."

She shrugged. "He acted confident, and he

372

pulled it off. Nobody said a word. O'Heir wanted to, but he didn't dare. Nobody else seemed to think it odd."

"But then her case was dismissed."

"Right. There's a clerk over at the courthouse by the name of Kim Ashford. She handled the paperwork. It took me a while to find out, and it took longer to convince her to talk to me. She was a little nervous. I had to tell her I was undercover in the end, and she talked. I hope that's okay, because she was getting quite put out with me, and I was afraid she would complain to the D.A. or somebody that I was snooping. When I explained to her that we were investigating a harassment complaint, she was okay with it. We women tend to want to see the wolves get what's coming to them."

Harvey nodded. "Let's just hope she doesn't broadcast it."

Emily opened her notebook. "She looked over the old file. It was over a year ago, you know?"

"Yes."

"Well, she said at first she didn't remember it, but after she'd looked at it, she said, Oh, yes, that was Neilsen's case."

"Neilsen's case?"

"Right. She said he called her and told her to cancel the hearing because the department was dropping charges. His explanation was that the arresting officer forgot to Miranda her, and she

373

had complained, and he was sure the case would get tossed, anyway."

"So, she just canceled it? A clerk could do that?"

"She had the deputy chief's word on it."

"Hmm."

"They hadn't processed the paperwork yet."

"When did this happen?"

"The day after the arrest."

"Ashford signed a statement to that effect?"

"She's coming over when she gets off work. Didn't want to tell her boss, which was okay with me."

"She knew Neilsen, or not?"

Emily frowned. "That's tricky. She said she'd met him once or twice, but wouldn't give details. I wondered if there was something there, but she was cagey."

He nodded. "Anything else?"

"Well, she remembered the Lloyd case, in August. They'd set the hearing, and she got a call, saying they were dropping it because the evidence had been misplaced. It was unusual, and it stuck in her mind."

"Who called her?"

"Three guesses."

"Brad Lyons."

"You're good."

Harvey smiled. "She'll swear to that, too?"

"Yes, sir."

Harvey consulted the folder on the Lloyd case, then scribbled a note. "Emily, please run downstairs and ask the detective sergeant to check the evidence locker for this item."

Her eyes widened. "You think he just left it in there, but claimed it was lost?"

"Who knows? Maybe he took it home and snorted it, but if it's in this building, I want it."

Nate was leading a gray-haired man in blue work clothes into the interrogation room.

"That the custodian?" Harvey asked Eddie.

He nodded. "Want to watch?"

Eddie connected his computer's monitor to the camera feed from the interview room. They watched Nate and his witness sit down at the table.

"Mr. Flood, could you please tell me what happened on Labor Day when you were ready to leave City Hall for lunch?"

"Lunch?" Flood seemed a little befuddled. "I ate lunch . . . let's see, the city gave us vouchers that day. I went to Burger King with Don Lloyd."

"Yes, sir," Nate said patiently, "but before that. Where were you and Mr. Lloyd working?"

"Well, we did the setup downstairs first, in the city clerk's office, then everyone went upstairs and did the comptroller's office."

"And the game officials and setup crew were there?"

"Yes. Most of them left before we did."

"Who was still there?"

"The two detectives and one of the officials. Funny name, glasses. I think he was from Lewiston."

"Myron Stickle?" Nate asked.

"That's him. He was checking the position of everything, before they taped it off. Those three were there when Don and I left, and there were a couple of fellows downstairs."

"Did you and Mr. Lloyd go down the elevator?"

"I went down the stairs. Don't know what Don did. We went out into the hall together, after everything was ready for the game, but Don said he'd left his tape measure in the office. He went back to get it."

"You didn't wait for him?"

"No, I told him I'd get my truck and meet him out front."

"Was he waiting when you got there?"

"No. I had to double park for a few minutes, and I wasn't too happy. I almost went without him. An ambulance came by, and I remember I had to get out of the way. I ended up driving around the block. When I came back, Don was just coming out the end door."

"Not the front door."

"Right."

"And then what?" Nate asked.

"I picked him up, and we went to Burger King."

"How did he seem then?"

"What does that mean? He seemed like he always does."

"Which is . . . ?"

Flood shrugged. "I dunno. Am I supposed to say something particular here?"

"No, no, sir. I just wondered if his manner was odd in any way?"

"I don't think so."

"Was he out of breath?" Nate asked.

"No. Well, maybe. I honestly don't remember. He lit a cigarette, though. I didn't like that, but he said he needed one, and he couldn't smoke in the restaurant. I thought he was quitting, but I guess he gave up trying."

"He still smokes?"

"Yes, sir."

"How long would you say elapsed between the moment you entered the stairway and the moment he got in your truck?"

"Oh, I don't know. Five minutes, anyway. Maybe more. I sat there a while, then drove around the block. Probably ten minutes."

"Did you see anyone else leave the building?"

"Yeah, the girl detective and—what's his name? Sickle?"

Harvey looked at Eddie. "Emily told me Brad fixed Donald Lloyd's case in August. He called the courthouse and told a clerk they lost the evidence. They dropped the drug charge, and the registration one, too."

"Maybe he didn't want to have to face the judge and tell him how clumsy he was at losing the evidence."

Harvey shook his head. "I don't buy it. Brad wasn't the arresting officer, and the evidence seems to have been logged properly. Lloyd has a record, though. This would be his third drug bust."

"Naughty boy," Eddie said.

"Mm-hmm. I'm thinking Brad represented to him how hard the judge would be on him. Brad's good at slanting things the way he wants them to appear." Harvey turned back to the monitor.

"So, you think he got the charges dismissed in return for a favor from Lloyd," Eddie said.

"I do. Find out if Lloyd has a gun."

"We've got to bring Brad in, Mike," Harvey argued at four o'clock. "There are too many rumors flying. Ryan Toothaker may be at his apartment interviewing him now."

Mike scratched his jaw. "I think you've got plenty, but if we arrest him tonight . . ."

"What?"

Mike shook his head. "You're right. If we wait, this could blow up in our faces. Let's do it."

"You want me to take my men?"

"Yes. I'll wait here. I think, given Brad's rank, I'd better be on scene when you book him."

Harvey nodded. "We're going with criminal charges, then."

"Obstructing justice, criminal threatening, and sexual assault."

"You think the assault will stick?"

Mike sighed. "Maybe not."

"Tampering with a victim?"

"Maybe. See, that's it, Harvey. It's still so nebulous. You've got to have everything nailed down."

"He changed the bail and canceled court hearings, Mike."

"You have no proof that he didn't have reason to do that. Now, if you could prove he exchanged favors with Lloyd, kept him from a stiff sentence in exchange for getting rid of Joey . . ."

Harvey paced to the window and looked out over the east end of the city. "We've got to have him in custody."

"I think you're right. Firing him isn't enough. I'm certain he's in the middle of the Bolduc murder, but you've got to get your ducks in a row, Harv."

Mike's phone rang, and Harvey leaned on the window frame, waiting.

"Cheryl Yeaton's coming up here with a taped statement from the female prisoner, Lorraine Dowd," Mike said. "Drink some coffee and calm down."

"I'm calm."

He got the coffee and sat staring at the Turner print on Mike's wall until Cheryl walked in.

"Chief, Captain Larson. I think you'll find this interesting." Cheryl handed Mike the videotape, and Mike inserted it in his video player.

"You're not going to arrest me again for that old OUI, are you?" Lorraine Dowd asked on the tape.

"No, ma'am," Cheryl told her. "We're only interested in the behavior of the police officers that night."

"I was drunk," Dowd admitted. "I shouldn't have been driving; I know that. I haven't done it since. But I know what happened to me. One of your officers molested me."

"Was it rape, ma'am?" Cheryl asked matter-of-factly.

"No, it didn't go that far. He started talking to me, nice like, about how I could beat the charges. Then he came in the cell and—touched me. I was a bit muddled, as you can imagine, but as soon as I realized what he was doing, I started screaming. He shoved me down on the bunk and told me to shut up. I didn't, and he slapped me."

"The other officers didn't report that you were bruised, ma'am."

"I don't care what they reported, I know what happened. I told the creep I was going to sue. He put his hands on my shoulders and said, 'I don't think you want to do that.' He was hurting me. I pulled away, and I said, 'You're the one who'd better think twice here, buddy. You enjoy roughing up your arrests? My brother's a lawyer.' Then when Jerry came to get me, the officer said the bail was only two hundred, and he let me go."

"Did you tell your brother, the lawyer?"

She laughed. "My brother's a mechanic. But I was called a few days later and told the charges had been dropped."

"Why was that?" Cheryl asked.

"I don't know. It might of been a fluke. I was glad, though. I was looking at a mandatory jail sentence and a thousand-dollar fine." She looked at Cheryl and shrugged. "I was glad I hadn't followed through and sued the guy. I figured he fixed things so I wouldn't rat on him."

"And you never told anyone what he'd done?"

"I chalked it up to experience. And, like I said, I don't drink and drive anymore. So it worked out all right for me."

"Could you identify the officer who struck you from among these photographs, ma'am?" Emily opened an album.

"That's him." She pointed without hesitation.

"You're indicating the picture of Sergeant Brad Lyons."

"If you say so."

Mike clicked the machine off. "Well."

"Did you tell her she'll have to testify?" Harvey asked anxiously.

Cheryl nodded. "As long as we don't charge her with anything, she doesn't mind."

Mike looked at Harvey. "Go get him."

Chapter 18

"We're working late, guys," Harvey said as he entered Priority.

Jimmy groaned.

"You got plans, Jim?"

"Wendy's parent-teacher conference at seven."

"We should be done by then. Everybody wears vests."

"Field work?" Tony's eyes brightened.

"We're picking up Brad Lyons. I'll make the arrest." Harvey tossed his key ring to Eddie. "Bring me my vest?"

As soon as the men headed toward the locker room, he sat down at his desk and called home.

"Jenny, I'll be a little late."

"Should I go to Bible study with Jeff and Beth?"

"If I'm not there. And tell Leeanne, will you? We're closing one case, I hope."

"The Bolduc case?" Jennifer's voice thrilled with excitement.

"No, not yet, but the other one. I don't want to say it. You know what I'm talking about."

"Sure."

"I love you, gorgeous."

"Why do I feel like you're wearing your Kevlar vest?"

He sat groping for a response that would comfort her. "I don't think he'll fight us, babe. It's just a precaution."

Jennifer was silent for a moment. "I'll be praying."

"Thanks. Tell you what, I'll call you when he's in custody."

"That would be nice, if you have time."

"I will. Take your phone with you. And kiss the little guy for me."

He hung up and stared at the cartridge display that hung on the far wall.

"Here you go, Harv." Eddie laid his vest on the edge of his desk.

"Thanks." Harvey stood and took off his suit coat. When he had the vest on and had adjusted his holster, he picked up the framed picture of Jennifer on the breakwater at Rockland.

Eddie said, "I went into the observation room while Nate had Lloyd in interview earlier."

"Yeah?"

"Nate asked him if he had a gun. He said he owns two deer rifles and a shotgun, but no handguns."

"Did you believe him?"

Eddie grimaced. "He was nervous. Wanted to smoke." He looked over Harvey's shoulder at the framed photo. "She's a knockout, Harv."

"Don't know what she sees in me." Harvey replaced the frame on the shelf of phone books and software manuals.

Eddie laughed. "That was my first impression, too, but when I'd thought about it a while and seen her with you a few times, well, I can see it."

"Yeah?"

"Yeah."

Harvey chuckled. "She's worried about me. Us. Thinks we're taking a risk here. I could tell, the way her voice went higher."

"Are we?"

"I hope not."

"Brad's got a temper."

"Mm. Listen, if anything ever happened to me . . ." He gazed uneasily into Eddie's eyes.

"Don't talk that way."

"But still—I've done everything I can to protect her financially, but emotionally—she's strong, but, well, she wasn't always."

"Okay, I hear you. The same for me and Leeanne."

Harvey nodded. "Let's pray."

"You want to go in the breakroom?"

"No. I want to do it here." He looked around at the others, as they finished their preparations. "Guys, gather around here. Let's pray before we go."

Tony's eyes were wary, but Nate and Jimmy

came without question and bowed their heads, and Tony followed. Paula was still at her desk, and she bowed her head, too, as Harvey began to pray for their safety and the resolution of the case.

As he finished, he said, "amen," and Eddie and Jimmy joined in. Harvey looked around the circle, and each man met his eyes expectantly.

"Okay, let's go."

Twilight was gathering when they approached Brad's apartment building. Wives one, two, and three had modest houses, but Brad lived in a cheap third-story flat.

"Nate, Jimmy, cover the exits. Tony, take the stairs." Harvey got on the elevator with Eddie. "I still hate this case," he said, freeing his pistol.

"Me, too. But I'll feel like the Bolduc case is half solved if we have Lyons in the lockup."

"You may be right. If we just had a weapon."

"Yeah." The elevator door opened, and Eddie peered out cautiously.

They walked side by side to the door of the apartment. Harvey motioned him to stand to one side. Down the hall, the stairway door opened, and Tony positioned himself just inside it, with his pistol drawn. Behind them, the elevator door closed.

Harvey pushed the doorbell, and they heard the chime echo inside.

"S'pose he skipped?" Eddie asked.

Harvey took a sharp breath. "We were stupid to let him loose after he was suspended."

"We weren't ready to charge him."

Harvey rang the doorbell again, knowing nobody would answer.

"We going in?" Eddie asked. "He could be in there."

The elevator door slid open, and Harvey whipped around to face it. Brad stood in the car, staring at them.

"Company, on a Wednesday night."

"Come on out here, Brad," Harvey said, watching him intently.

"Guess not." Brad reached toward the control panel within the car, and the door began to close. Eddie ran toward it, but it shut tight and the apparatus began to hum.

"Tony! Downstairs, quick!" The stairway door was closing, even as Harvey turned toward it. "Idiot!" he exclaimed.

"Sorry," said Eddie, pushing past him for the stairs.

Harvey ran behind him. "Not you, me!"

"How many floors in the building?" Eddie gasped.

"Four."

"Right. I'll take two." Eddie jerked open the door at the second-floor landing.

When Harvey emerged in the ground floor

hallway, Tony and Jimmy were standing, one on either side of the elevator car.

"You sure he went down?" Tony panted.

"Yes. Eddie took the second floor."

"If it stops there, he can go up again, can't he?" asked Jimmy.

"Where's Nate?" Harvey asked.

"Out back under the fire escape."

"This thing's too slow," Tony said through gritted teeth.

Harvey hit his shoulder mic. "Miller, you hear me? Come inside. Charlie?"

"Right here, Captain," said Charlie Doran, one of the dispatchers.

"I need backup," Harvey said.

Tony jerked his head toward the elevator. "It's coming down."

"Step aside, Winfield."

Tony flattened himself against the wall on the other side of the door.

The street door opened, and a couple came in.

"Police," Harvey yelled. "Wait outside, please. Now."

The baffled woman looked at her escort. He grabbed her hand. "Come on!" He pulled her back out through the door, just as the elevator settled and the door slid open.

Brad stood inside, holding a pistol to the ear of a teen-aged boy. He smiled at Harvey. "Unlucky kid."

"Think what you're doing, Brad," Harvey said.

"Oh, I thought about it, Captain. All the way down from upstairs. No turning back now."

Eddie burst from the stairway door and stopped as he saw the open elevator. He approached slowly, his gun leveled.

Brad's gaze flicked to Eddie and back to Harvey. "Stay back, Thibodeau, or this kid will look like Swiss cheese."

The boy let out a little squawk, and his eyes rolled. He looked about Travis's age, and Harvey's heart pounded. He couldn't lose this one.

Eddie stopped a dozen feet away, but kept his gun trained on Brad and the terrified boy. "The kid was waiting for the elevator on level two. The door opened, and Brad grabbed him. I was too late."

"Just let us take a little walk," Brad said.

"No," Harvey replied. "You know me better than that."

Brad sniffed. "Nice seeing you. Push four, kid."

The boy stood motionless, and Brad shoved the gun's muzzle into his neck. "I said, push four."

The teenager reached out a trembling hand and touched the control panel.

"Say bye-bye to the kid." Brad smiled as the door closed.

Tony swore.

"Winfield—"

"I know, sir. I'm sorry."

"Stay here, Eddie, and watch the stairs, too. Winfield, up to four."

Tony rolled his eyes but sprinted for the stairway. Nate came in at the front entrance.

"Nate, second floor, Jimmy the third. Go! And buzz me when you get there. I want to know if he gets off this elevator."

"It's still moving," Eddie said, his ear against the door.

"Go!" Harvey yelled again, but Nate and Jimmy were through the door. Harvey's mic beeped. "Larson."

"Four patrolmen on the way, Captain," Charlie said.

"Copy that."

Nate's voice came over the radio. "He went past the second floor."

"Stay there," Harvey said. He looked up at the light panel above the door. The digit 3 lit up then went off.

Eddie looked at him a moment later. "The elevator's stopped on 4."

"Winfield?" Harvey asked.

Panting, Tony said, "Boss, he beat me to four, sorry. They got out."

Harvey hit the wall with his fist. "Where to?"

"The stairs, I think," Tony said. "Up."

Harvey said into his mic, "Wait for me, Tony, and watch that roof stairway." He looked at

Eddie. "Stay here. I'm going up the hard way and meet Winfield on four. Brad's got the kid on the roof. You pray. Get the elevator down here and jam it open so it stays here. And when the backup gets here, position them and come up."

Eddie nodded.

Harvey answered another call as he walked briskly toward the stairs. "Yeah, Jimmy."

"I'm pretty sure they didn't get out on three."

"No, they're above you. Stay there 'til the backup comes. I'm going up the stairs."

He passed the second-floor landing, pushing buttons on his phone as he went.

"Mike. I need you."

"Where are you?" Mike asked.

"At the suspect's apartment house."

"I'll be there."

Harvey pushed onward, thankful he hadn't given up running with Eddie and Jeff. Even so, he was breathing hard when he came out of the stairs into the hallway on the fourth floor.

"Over here, Captain," Tony called. "The stairs to the roof go up here."

"Stay put until someone relieves you here." Harvey looked over his shoulder. "You can see both stairways and the elevator."

"Got it."

Harvey pushed open the door to the narrow roof stairway and started climbing. At the top, he breathed a prayer and pushed the door open.

"Took you long enough," Brad called.

"Nowhere for you to go, Brad."

"I see the extra units. Let me go, Harvey."

Harvey stayed behind the door, peering out at him in the dusk. Sirens wailed, increasing in volume. He could make out the white blobs of Brad's face and the boy's, near the far edge of the roof.

"We're past that, Brad. We were coming to see you on an assault charge."

Brad laughed. "Don't give me that. You wouldn't put up this show of force if it was just assault."

"Well, we have to consider kidnapping now."

"And a few other things?"

"What did you think we were here for?"

"Oh, no. I'm not playing that game. Just let me walk out."

"Where will you go?"

"Do you care?"

"Of course."

"Right. You'd be glad to see the end of me, wouldn't you, one way or another?"

"No, that's not true."

"I'm walking out of here, or this kid goes over the edge."

"Not the best plan, Brad." Harvey wished he could reassure the boy somehow. "Hey, kid, what's your name?"

"Todd Crichton."

"Your folks live around here, Todd?"

"In Naples."

"What's your father's name?"

"Matthew."

"Matthew Crichton," Harvey said soothingly, knowing Eddie would hear and pass on the information. He muted the radio, so Brad wouldn't hear anything from it.

"Cut the chatter," Brad snapped. "And you can spare me the poor grieving family speech."

Harvey heard footsteps on the stairs behind him and looked over his shoulder. Tony was creeping up the stairs.

"Backup's here, and Eddie came up the elevator with two other guys," Tony said quietly. "They're in the hall on four."

"Got a negotiator?"

"I don't think so."

"The chief is coming," Harvey whispered. "Get him up here as quick as you can. Ask for an ambulance. And call the kid's parents. Matthew Crichton, in Naples."

"Harvey!" Brad yelled.

"Yeah?"

"What's going on?"

"What do you think?"

"You putting a safety net down below to catch this kid?"

"Nope."

Brad chuckled bitterly. "Well, it won't help

for you to bring on the weeping wives to talk me down. They'd all love it if I took a dive over the side."

"Just let the boy go, Brad."

"Nope. Todd and me are buddies."

Harvey fought the impulse to say, *Todd and I, idiot.*

"You don't want to add a murder charge, Brad. You're too self-protective for that."

Brad was silent, and Harvey thought he might be wavering.

"Todd," he said clearly, "we're calling your parents, and we'll tell them you're in a bad situation here, but don't worry. This will be over soon."

"Let me walk, Harvey," Brad insisted.

"Can't do it. I could get you a good lawyer, though. You want a lawyer?"

Brad swore.

Harvey swallowed hard. "I'm making the rules, Brad, and you know I'm stubborn."

There was movement in the stairway, and Harvey threw a glance over his shoulder. Mike was climbing the stairs.

"How's it going?" Mike breathed in his ear.

"Not great."

"Ask him what he wants."

"What do you want, Brad?"

"My car, and a chance to go somewhere else and start over."

"Not going to happen."

"Say good-bye to Todd then."

Harvey stiffened and whispered to Mike, "Do you think he'll do it?"

"Is he sober?"

"I think so."

"Then he won't. Does he know you've pegged him in the Bolduc murder?"

"I think he suspects it. That's why he did this. Will you take over? I'm sweating bullets here."

"You're doing fine."

"Mike, give me a break, please."

"All right."

A late concern hit Harvey, and he eyed Mike's jacket in the dimly lit stairway. "You wearing body armor?"

"You think I could go home to Sharon tonight if I didn't? She hates it when I'm on the late news as it is."

Harvey stepped down two steps, letting Mike pass him, and leaned limp against the wall, letting his pistol point downward.

"You okay, Captain?" Tony whispered. "Yeah, thanks."

"Charlie Doran is patching Eddie through to the parents."

Mike called into the growing darkness, "Sergeant Lyons, this is Chief Browning. Let's put an end to this right now."

There was a pause, then Brad's voice came

mockingly. "What do you know? I dragged the chief out away from his desk."

Mike swung the door open, and before Harvey realized his intent, walked out onto the roof, holding his hands high.

"Mike!" he said urgently, but the chief was already ten feet away.

"Brad, I don't have a gun on you. Let's talk."

"Not unless you want to talk about letting me go."

"Let the boy go first, then we'll discuss it."

"What am I looking at here?"

Harvey inhaled sharply. Brad was willing to reason, at last.

"Well, let's see," Mike drawled. "I asked Harvey to come around and talk to you, and you took a hostage. That's not good, but things could be a lot worse. Why don't you just tell me why you thought you had to do this when you saw Harvey?"

"Harvey and his pit bulls," Brad snarled. "Winfield was going to shoot me."

Harvey glanced toward Tony in the stairway. The young detective's jaw dropped, and he shrugged in innocence. Harvey put one hand on his shoulder, and Tony stood still.

"Maybe you misread the signals," Mike said lazily.

"They were going to take me in. If Harvey

wanted to shoot the breeze, he wouldn't have brought his whole squad."

"All right, let's ask him what he was going to charge you with. Captain Larson, what are the charges here?" Mike called over his shoulder.

Harvey opened the door a few more inches. "Assault on a prisoner, criminal threatening, obstruction of justice."

Brad was silent.

"You'll probably do some time," Mike acknowledged. "You're in a position of trust, after all."

"You got proof I assaulted some drunk?"

"We have a sworn statement, and some paperwork that doesn't add up," Harvey said.

"That's not proof."

Mike shrugged. "Maybe a lawyer can get you off. Let the boy go, and we'll help you get legal counsel. There's no need to make this worse than it is."

"What about the kidnapping thing?"

Mike was quiet for a moment. "I can't promise you anything, Brad. By now, the media's got hold of this. If I promise you immunity on the kidnapping, the city will be outraged. But that's nothing compared to what will happen if you hurt that boy."

Very slowly, Brad moved the pistol from the boy's neck until it pointed straight at Mike Browning.

"Move, kid," he growled. "Go quick, before I change my mind."

Todd stumbled away from him, toward the stairway. Harvey holstered his pistol and stepped out onto the roof. "Come here, Todd."

As the boy passed him, Mike clapped him on the shoulder. "You'll be okay, son. Do whatever Captain Larson tells you."

Harvey hustled Todd into the stairway, where Tony and Eddie waited.

"Watch your step now. Are you all right?"

"Yes, I think so." Todd rubbed his neck as he stumbled down the stairs.

"Did you get hold of the parents?" Harvey asked.

"They're coming down," Eddie reported. "Should be here in half an hour."

"All right, Todd, do you live in this building?"

"I was visiting a friend of mine from school. I live on campus."

"Okay, one of these officers is going to take you downstairs and get your statement. He'll stay with you until your parents arrive."

"Come on, Todd," Tony said, and as he took the young man into the fourth-floor hallway, Harvey glimpsed several uniforms.

"How's Mike doing?" Eddie asked.

"Let's find out."

Harvey led the way back up the stairs and

slowly opened the door a few inches. Mike was sitting three feet from Brad on the low wall at the edge of the roof. Brad sat with his back to the precipice, holding his pistol loosely between his knees, muzzle downward.

"All those little things add up," Mike was saying. "I know right now this seems unbelievable. Your career, your personal life, everything's a mess right now."

Mike looked totally relaxed, but Harvey knew he was coiled to spring if Brad made a sudden move.

Brad took a deep breath. "Been a mess for a long time, Chief."

"You've been a good officer."

Brad shook his head and looked away. "These women, some of 'em, you look at 'em cross-eyed and they scream bloody murder."

"This harassment thing is serious," Mike acknowledged. "Two female officers claim you threatened them because they were women, and because they wouldn't behave toward you the way you wanted. One woman left her job because of it."

"I didn't make her quit."

"You made her feel she couldn't stay and keep her honor."

Brad laughed derisively. "Honor."

"She's waitressing now."

"That's her choice, not mine."

"Well, she felt she couldn't work for you without compromising her standards."

Brad's eyes narrowed. "Maybe her standards were just too high."

"Come on, Brad," Mike said gently. "You know it's against regs for you to date a subordinate, but you went after Deidre Cleridge. And then you had Deborah Higgins meet you down at the Old Port."

"She showed up."

"She felt intimidated. She thought you would do something to hurt her career if she didn't go."

Brad sighed. "I never did understand women."

"I think that's a fair assessment," Mike conceded. "Come on, let's go face this thing. I'll be there with you."

Brad glanced toward Harvey. "I'll lose my badge, no matter what."

"If these charges stand up," Mike agreed.

"I'm not sure I can take it, Chief."

"You never shied away from a tough duty."

"Could you stand it if your own men had to book you?"

"I'll handle it myself, if you'd rather." Mike held out his hand, and slowly Brad placed his pistol in it.

Mike stood up. "Let's go."

Brad stood and turned toward the wall. "Guess I'm famous now."

"You and Winfield."

Harvey smiled grimly, wondering if Tony's participation in the magazine layout would have an adverse effect on the department.

Brad stood irresolutely, looking down at the street far below.

"Don't even think about it, buddy," Mike said quietly. "I'd have to grab you, and Sharon hates it when I do stuff like that. She'd see it on Channel 13, you hanging off the edge and me holding on for dear life. She'd make me retire for sure."

Brad turned away from the wall. "I'd hate to cause trouble for a guy who's managed to stay married as long as you have."

They came slowly toward the door, and Harvey held it open wide.

Brad hesitated as he came near and eyed Harvey dolefully. "I know this isn't over. You'll hang everything you possibly can on me."

"This isn't personal," Harvey said.

"Everything's personal."

Brad went on down the stairs, to where Eddie waited at the bottom. Harvey followed Mike, and Eddie clipped the handcuffs on Brad and frisked him.

"You got any other weapons in your apartment, Brad?" Mike asked casually.

"Sure. A .30-06 and a bird gun."

"Another pistol?" Mike asked.

"I had a nine-millimeter, but I sold it."

".357?"

"Yeah, it's in my dresser."

"I'll have the boys bring your guns in for safe-keeping. If you want a family member to come claim them, you can. Any other valuables you want us to lock up for you?"

"No."

Mike turned to two uniformed officers who waited near the door. "You two take him to the station in the unit, and I'll meet you there for booking."

One of the officers looked at Brad hesitantly, and Mike nodded.

"Sir," the officer said to Brad, "please come with us."

Harvey pulled his cell phone from his pocket and stepped a couple of yards down the hall.

"Jenny, we're all right, but I'll be at the station awhile. You'd better plan on going with Jeff."

"Honey, you're on the news."

"Already? Is it that late?"

"Yes, and I was petrified. They didn't say your name, but I knew it was you and the boys. They said you were trying to arrest a police officer on a warrant, and he had a hostage. Tell me the hostage wasn't you."

"No, it was a civilian, but that's over. Everyone's fine, gorgeous, including the hostage. I'll fill you in when I get home."

"Sharon called me."

"Call her back and tell her Mike's okay."

Eddie hovered nearby, and Harvey turned to him as he closed the connection. "Go through his apartment. I'm not sure what you're looking for, but you'll know it if you see it. And get that .357 magnum to the lab right away."

"Copy that."

When they stepped off the elevator on the ground floor of the building, reporters surrounded them. Ryan Toothaker pushed close to Harvey. "This is that little non-story we discussed this morning, Captain?"

Mike looked over his shoulder. "You handle the press, Harvey. I'm headed for the station."

Chapter 19

Harvey stood beside Cheryl Yeaton at the sergeant's desk and gazed at Sarah Benoit and Deborah Higgins. They had just come in for their Thursday morning shift.

"I asked Sergeant Yeaton to call you two aside before you go on patrol, in case you had any questions about the Lyons matter."

"Cheryl told us during roll call," Sarah said.

Harvey nodded. "Without your testimony and that of a few other women, we couldn't have found enough evidence against him, so thank you."

"You okay, Deborah?" Cheryl asked, eyeing the rookie closely.

"Yes. Well—is he here? In the lockup, I mean?"

"No," Harvey said. "They took him to the county jail last night. No bail. He's kicking about that, but we convinced the judge he needs to stay in custody, in light of the hostage he took last night."

Deborah sighed. "I didn't really think they would arrest him. It was taking so long, you know? I thought he was going to get away with it again."

"Well, he's not," Sarah assured her.

"That's right," Cheryl said. "Sergeant Lyons is looking at serious time because of what he did to you and Deidre, and he'll never wear a uniform again."

"There were other complaints, too," Harvey said.

Cheryl touched Deborah's sleeve. "Do you think you're fit for duty today? If you need a day off . . ."

"No, I'll be fine. Thanks."

"Well, thank *you* for stepping up, and for not quitting," Cheryl said.

The two patrol officers went toward the garage, and Harvey said, "Thank you, Cheryl. Some of the other women we questioned might come to you for reassurance."

"I'll handle it, Captain."

"Thanks for your hard work." Harvey went upstairs, wishing he'd had a couple more hours of sleep. At least Connor was sleeping through the night now.

"Captain, you're gonna love this." Nate's eyes sparkled as he met Harvey inside the office door.

"What's up?"

"You will never in a million years guess whose house was broken into Saturday night."

"Okay, so tell me."

"Joey Bolduc's brother. The flag came up when I turned on the computer this morning, thanks to your wife's software. I hope she made a bundle on that."

"Joey's brother's house was robbed. Is that significant?"

"It is if you know what was stolen."

"Well, let's see, do I have to guess?"

Tony stepped up beside Nate. "Twenty questions. You're good at mind games, sir."

"All right, was it something that had to do with Joey?"

"Yes," said Nate.

"Something that belonged to Joey?"

"Yes."

"Something of value, obviously."

"Yes, that's three."

"That wasn't a question," Harvey protested.

Nate shrugged.

"Joey's brother was his executor," Tony said.

Nate scowled at him. "Quit blabbing."

Jimmy and Eddie came over and stood listening.

"Hmm. This was something he inherited from Joey."

"Yes. Four."

"I give up. Just tell me."

"No, come on, you're always telling us to be patient and look at all the clues. You can figure this out," Nate coaxed.

Harvey looked up at the ceiling and pulled in a breath. "What would Joey have that was of value? His ex-wife probably got—oh, I get it. Guns."

"Bingo!" cried Nate. "In five questions."

Jimmy shrugged. "We've got Joey's .45 in the evidence locker. The rest of his guns have no bearing on the case."

"He had quite a collection," Eddie countered.

"Any handguns?" Harvey asked quickly.

Nate smiled. "A .22 and—tada!—a .357 magnum."

"So. Lots of guys have .357's," said Eddie. "Brad had one."

"Brad's gun is not the one that killed Joey," Tony said, with the air of a disappointed child. "Believe me, I ran it on IBIS first thing, and it was one that had never been put in the system before."

"He'd have ditched it if it was the murder weapon," Harvey replied.

"But you did expect to tie him to the murder," Tony said.

Harvey shook his head. "If we don't get a confession, we may never find the weapon. Nate, that's a very interesting development, but, as the fellows say, I don't think it bears on the murder."

Nate shrugged. "I'm just telling you. Joey gets shot with a .357, and three weeks later his own .357 gets stolen."

Harvey nodded thoughtfully. "The burglar most likely had no idea whose guns they were."

"I disagree with you there," said Tony. "Did this brother have guns of his own before Joey died? And was he ever robbed before that? Sounds to me like the burglar heard about the new gun collection and went after it."

"Did they steal anything else?" Harvey asked.

"Nope, just the guns," Nate said. "Took the whole gun cabinet."

"He didn't have them in a safe?" Eddie asked.

Nate ran his hand through his hair. "I don't know. I haven't read the police report. The brother lives in Falmouth."

"Get the report stat," said Harvey. "It's odd enough that we should look into it."

Eddie stayed as the other men dispersed.

"Harv, we're really no closer to solving the murder than before we arrested Brad. The only things we've got are his fight with Joey and his tenuous connection to the custodian at City Hall."

"I've talked to Neilsen on the phone, and Mike's talked to him," Harvey said. "He helped Brad out of a few scrapes, but I think it was out of stupidity. He really thought Brad's stories were true, and he didn't have a very high opinion of working women. He said he always came down on the supervisor's side unless he had direct evidence of wrongdoing, which Brad made sure he never had."

"What about the clerk at the courthouse?"

"Neilsen claimed he didn't know her personally, and if she was the one who handled the two cases I mentioned to him, it was coincidental. And he was nervous. Wants to make good in Framingham, I think."

"If they fire him, he'll have a hard time getting another job," Eddie said.

"So where does this leave you guys?"

Eddie shoved his hands in his pockets. "Well, we've gone round and round with Don Lloyd, the custodian. He's not brilliant, but he's stuck with his story. If he did it, what did he do with the weapon?"

"He might have had it on him when he jumped in Flood's truck to go to lunch."

"Mmm. I was hoping so bad that Brad's gun would match the bullet. Stupid, I guess."

Harvey stared across the room toward the cartridge display. "Brad said he sold his nine-millimeter. I wonder if he sold any other guns?"

"We can ask him. Would you admit it if you were a killer?"

"Let's ask his wives. And who did he practice shooting with? See if the shooting range has anything on record."

"It's a long shot."

"I know. I'm trying to conjure up something for you here."

Nate came to the desk, holding out a sheet of

paper. "Captain, I printed out the police report on the burglary. It lists all the guns, with serial numbers. Philip Bolduc had made a concise list because they were part of Joey's estate and he had to get them appraised. Nice lot of guns. You think they were targeted?"

"Yes. Get back on the computer and look for other gun thefts with similarities." Harvey picked up his phone receiver and dialed a Yarmouth number.

"Mrs. Martin? This is Captain Harvey Larson, at the Portland P.D. On behalf of Chief Browning, I'm calling to ask if you have any interest in coming back to work for us, ma'am. The chief has reviewed your record, and determined that you were harassed by your supervisor during your stint here. He has authorized reinstatement as a patrol officer if you want that."

"Can you baste this, Jennifer?" Ruthann Bradley handed her two lengths of fabric held together with an army of straight pins.

"I think I can handle that." Jennifer settled in an armchair near the window. Abby and Leeanne were laying a newspaper pattern on another piece of cloth Ruthann had removed carefully from the skirt of the extra bridesmaid's gown. Lisa Rousseau sat in the rocking chair nursing Marco, and Beth held Connor on the sofa.

"Thanks so much for doing this, Ruthann,"

Beth said. "There's no way I could be in the wedding otherwise."

Ruthann looked up at her with a severe expression. "Just don't go to the hospital early on us. We don't want to have to take this dress apart again."

"I'm feeling better," Beth assured her. "Margaret thinks I'm stable."

Lisa stood up, patting Marco's back. "Is it all right if I lay Marco in Connor's crib, Jennifer?"

"Sure. Let me come with you."

She laid aside her sewing and led Lisa up the stairs.

"What a cute nursery!" Lisa looked around at the Noah's ark decorations.

"Thanks," Jennifer said. "We just moved him up here. He's been sleeping in our room all this time, but he sleeps through the night, and I figured it was time we had our domain back."

"Yeah, if you wait too long, it's harder," Lisa agreed. "Should we set up the you-know-what now?"

Jennifer checked her watch. "We'd better. When we go down, we'll sneak through the study to the kitchen. We've got half an hour, but people might start coming early. Leeanne will know, as soon as that happens, but what can we do?"

"What if they're not done with the dress?" Lisa asked.

"Ruthann said she'd take it home with her and finish it if she needs to. The fitting's done, so she can handle it." Jennifer smiled. "It wasn't really a six-woman job, but we wanted to get the bridesmaids together early and just have some time with Leeanne."

"I'm glad you invited me. Monique and my mother are coming for the shower."

"Great. My mom's coming, too. I wanted her to come down last night, but she figured Leeanne would guess if she did."

"Only five weeks 'til the wedding," Lisa said with a grin. She laid Marco down and pulled a soft blanket over him.

The doorbell chimed, and Jennifer raced down the stairs. Leeanne was rising.

"I'll get it," Jennifer said quickly.

She ducked through the sunroom to the kitchen, with Lisa right behind her.

"Hi, Mom," she whispered conspiratorially. "Come on in. This is Eddie's sister, Lisa."

Jennifer kissed her mother and looked beyond her to her younger brothers.

"Randy, Travis. What are you guys doing here? This is girls only."

"Mom didn't want to drive down alone, and Dad was busy," Randy said. "We're hoping we can hang out with the men."

"Well, Harvey's working on something, but Jeff and Eddie are next door. Jeff's off today, and he and Eddie promised to stay out of our hair during the shower."

"Can we just go over there?" Randy asked.

"Sure. Maybe they'll play basketball with you."

"Can I talk to Harvey first?" Travis asked. "I mean if he's not too busy."

Jennifer hesitated. She put one hand on Travis's shoulder and leaned in close to his ear. "This isn't another crisis, is it?"

"No. Nothing like last time. I just need to see him, is all."

Jennifer nodded. "All right, he's in the study. Just knock first."

She watched him go.

"I'll head over to Jeff's," Randy said awkwardly.

"Sure. And I'm really glad to see you, Randy. I just have a million things on my mind."

Lisa had enlisted Marilyn's help in making coffee and setting set out the refreshments for the shower. Jennifer hurried to help.

"Do we need to set up chairs or anything?" Marilyn whispered. "Where is she?"

"In the living room with Abby, Beth, and Ruthann, sewing Beth's dress. We're going to set up in the sunroom." The doorbell chimed again, and Jennifer stopped whispering. "Guess the surprise is over."

As she headed for the entry, Leeanne appeared in the doorway between the kitchen and the sun room. "Did I hear Travis's voice a second ago, Jenn? Hey, Mom. Wow! What are you doing here?"

It was late afternoon before all the guests left. Harvey and Eddie helped put the furniture back in place.

"Aren't you going to show me the shower gifts?" Eddie asked, as Leeanne stacked several boxes to carry upstairs.

"Are you kidding? This was a personal shower."

"So. I'm a person."

Harvey smiled. "It means lingerie, Eddie. Come on, grab the other end of this settee."

"Cool." Eddie was still watching Leeanne.

"Yeah, well, you don't get to see it for a few more weeks," Jennifer chided.

Leeanne left the room with her pile of boxes, and Jennifer began stuffing torn wrapping paper into a trash bag while the men moved the wicker settee back against the wall.

"Don't worry, Eddie," she said. "The church ladies are giving her a housewares shower in a couple of weeks. You can see the gifts from that one."

"Yeah, you'll probably have to cart them all to your house," Harvey said.

"Guess we can save this one." Jennifer smoothed a large sheet of wrapping paper, and Harvey reached for it.

"I can do that, gorgeous." He folded it neatly as Jennifer sorted through the rest of the wrappings, removing bows and ribbons.

"Do I dare ask what Travis wanted to see you about?" she asked.

"You'll be very happy when I tell you."

"He's clear on the hit-and-run thing?" Eddie asked.

Harvey laid the salvaged paper on the coffee table. "Oh, yeah, but this is even better. He wanted me to pray with him."

Jennifer dropped the trash bag and stood still, fighting tears. She gave up and hurled herself into Harvey's arms. He held her, rubbing her shoulders, and met Eddie's eyes over her head.

"You have to know when to hold 'em and know when to fold 'em."

Eddie laughed. *"C'est bon.* Now I expect you to take some of the prayer time you've been spending on Travis and put it on my family."

Jennifer sniffed and faced him. "Lisa's very open right now."

"Maybe. It's hard, you know? We always fight."

"Jeff and I were like that," Jennifer said. "It's different now, though."

"You and Lisa never grew up," Harvey said pointedly.

"You're bad." Jennifer stooped for the trash bag. "She told me today that she can see Eddie's happier than before he converted. I didn't really have a chance to get into it, but I invited her to visit our church."

"Ansel would never go," Eddie said.

"You never know." Harvey reached under a chair for a curl of white ribbon.

"Well, she didn't sound very promising," Jennifer admitted. "The kids, you know. It's hard when your kids are small."

Eddie shrugged. "I hope she'll come, but I doubt it. And my mother. I think she's accepted Leeanne now, but I don't want her to start getting wacky ideas."

"Are you talking about me?" Leeanne asked from the doorway. She had Connor in her arms.

"Not really, but, Leeanne, Travis is saved," Jennifer said, grinning.

"Really? Wonderful!"

"Let's sit down here and thank God together," Harvey suggested as he reached for the baby.

Eddie and Leeanne took the settee, and Harvey sat down with Connor in an armchair.

"Come here, gorgeous," he said, as Jennifer headed for one of the wicker chairs.

She smiled and pulled a footstool close to Harvey's chair. "You want me to move all the furniture again?"

"Captain," Cheryl called to Harvey as he passed through the police station lobby Monday morning.

"Cheryl, you still on days?"

"Yeah, it's between me and Dan Miles to keep this shift. I love it, but he has seniority over me."

"Have you talked to him?" Harvey asked. "Maybe he'd like evenings."

"Not yet. The deputy chief's giving the sergeant's exam Friday."

"I heard. How many are taking it so far?"

"Four. We're really short-handed."

"I know. Who covered this weekend?"

"Ron Legere was here when I came in, looking exhausted. I think Aaron O'Heir and Bob Marshall each took a shift on the desk."

"Are they taking the test?"

"Aaron is."

"He really wants detective work," Harvey said.

Cheryl shrugged. "So did I. Maybe I'll still go that direction someday. But right now there are openings for sergeants."

Harvey nodded. "Was there something else?"

"Oh, yes. Big holdup last night on Fore Street. Our guys brought in two suspects and confiscated a couple of handguns. I figured you'd want to run them."

"You're right. Any handguns that come our way go in the database. Where are they?"

"In the Evidence Room. I can get them for you."

"I'll send Eddie or Tony down, whoever gets here first. Thanks."

He climbed the stairs to the third floor, but hadn't even set his briefcase down before Paula hailed him.

"The chief wants you, Captain."

Harvey sighed and turned back toward the stairway. Eddie was just coming through the door.

"Hey, Eddie, Cheryl's got a couple of guns for us downstairs. Run them on IBIS, would you?"

He went on up to Mike's office and let himself in, waving at Judith as he passed her desk.

"Harv, good morning!" Mike grinned at him and raised his coffee mug. "Help yourself."

"You're awfully bright-eyed for Monday morning." Harvey poured himself a mugful and sat down.

"We have a comfortable apartment in Churchill, including a working washer and dryer."

"Congratulations!"

"Thanks. Sharon is ecstatic. The leach field is complete, and it's seeded for grass in the spring. We finished the sheetrock in our apartment, and we're painting it next weekend. I was thinking of offering the place to Eddie and Leeanne for their honeymoon. Secluded, romantic, snug. Wood stove, indoor plumbing. What more could you want?"

Harvey was startled. "They might like that, I guess."

"You think they'd rather have room service and all that?"

"Oh, I don't know. I was thinking of sending them to—"

"Where?" Mike asked.

"Aw, forget it."

"No, I heard Eddie had reservations for Montreal in August, but they didn't go, and he didn't have any plans last I heard. This would be absolutely free, and they can use the boat."

"Kind of chilly on the lake in late October."

"Well, sure, but that's what makes it so nice when you come home to the fireside. And they can go hunting if they want."

"Sure, why don't you ask him," Harvey said decisively.

"Where were you going to send them?"

"Oh, no place. It's nothing."

"Yes, it was someplace. Come on."

Harvey shrugged. "I thought maybe Paris."

"You hate Paris."

"Eddie and Leeanne have never been. They might like it."

Mike seemed a little disappointed. "Well, I suppose. Why don't we ask them, and let them choose? Maybe they've already lined up something else."

"The wedding's coming right up. I hope Eddie's got something up his sleeve. I'll ask him."

Mike's phone rang. "Just a second Harv." He pushed a button. "Yes, Judith?" After a moment, he pushed another button. "Put him through." Mike grinned at Harvey. "I put it on speaker. She says it's Eddie, and it's urgent."

Harvey nodded.

"Mike? I mean, Chief?"

"Yeah, Eddie?"

"Could you and Harvey come down here? Right away?"

"Sure, Eddie. What's up?"

"You gotta see this, Mike. You're not going to believe it."

Mike raised his eyebrows at Harvey. "All right, we'll be right down."

They went through the outer office to the stairway.

"I'll be in the Priority Unit," Mike told Judith. They went quickly down the stairs. Eddie met them just inside the office. He grasped Harvey's upper arms and stood staring into his eyes.

"What is it, Eddie?"

"It's impossible. I ran the test three times, then I made Winfield do it. We got the weapon."

Harvey stiffened. "The murder weapon?"

Eddie nodded. "The gun that killed Joey."

"All right!" Harvey high-fived him.

"Stellar," Mike said.

Nate, Tony, and Jimmy left Tony's desk and came grinning to join them.

"This was one of the guns the night shift confiscated in the holdup?" Harvey asked.

"Yeah," Eddie said. "Cheryl gave it to me."

Tony added, "It's definitely the gun that killed Joey."

"But there's more," Eddie said, taking a deep breath. "I checked the serial number. Harv, it's the .357 Smith & Wesson from Joey's collection."

Harvey stared at him, then at Tony.

Tony nodded. "It's the same number, Captain. No doubt."

"How can that be?" Harvey walked slowly to his desk and sat down, staring blankly toward the window. He swiveled around and looked at them again. "That gun was in the collection when it was stolen."

"Right," said Nate. "And it was there when Philip Bolduc listed the guns for the estate."

"It must have been there before Joey died," Jimmy said tentatively.

"Unless his brother added a gun to the collection," Harvey said slowly.

"No," Eddie protested. "There was a list of guns in Joey's handwriting, and his brother went over them and typed a list for the lawyer. But Joey owned this gun."

"You're positive?"

"Bob Marshall saw him shoot targets with it. I showed him the list last week, after the collection

421

was stolen. He said it was Joey's writing. And the .357 was listed third. I don't see how it could have been tacked on later."

Mike looked at Harvey. "If his own partner confirms it . . ."

"I want to see that list," Harvey said.

"I'll get it," Nate said, "but it seems certain that Joey was shot with his own gun."

Harvey shook his head. "That happens occasionally in a home invasion, but Joey wasn't killed in his house. And he wasn't carrying this gun. He had his .45 on him."

"Maybe he carried two guns that day," Jimmy suggested timidly.

"Well, gentlemen, carry on," Mike said. "As usual, you're doing exceptional work. Unfortunately, I have to go visit Mayor Weymouth. She has a hare-brained scheme for raising money for the P.D."

"Don't make us sell Christmas cards," Tony begged.

"No, she got the idea from this *Portland Life* magazine spread that you're in, Winfield. Seems some cities are making calendars with pictures of their hunky cops and firemen and—"

"If you agree to that, I'll resign," Harvey said tightly. "Please, Mike. The Labor Day Challenge, then the magazine thing. Don't do this to us."

Mike shrugged. "I don't know as we've got enough single guys, anyway. They either get married or murdered around here." He headed for the elevator and hit the keypad, waving as he entered the car.

Harvey surveyed his four men. "Come in the breakroom," he ordered, and they all followed him. When they were seated comfortably, he said, "This weapon was not in Joey's house at the moment of the murder. It was at City Hall."

They all nodded.

"But," Harvey continued, "a short time later—do we know how long?"

Eddie shook his head.

"A short time later, it was back in his house. Now, obviously, Joey didn't put it back in the gun cabinet. Someone else had to do that. If his brother was the murderer, he could have done it, assuming no one would look there for the murder weapon."

"Airtight alibi, and no motive," Eddie objected.

"Families can always come up with motives," Harvey reasoned. "But it's true, Philip Bolduc has an excellent alibi for Labor Day. If he had anything to do with it, which I personally doubt, it was by proxy."

"So, who put the gun back?" Tony asked.

"Exactly."

"And when?" Nate asked.

"You tell me. Put your brains to work, guys." Harvey waited.

Nate said slowly, "Well, I interviewed Philip

Bolduc. Tony was there, and we have a tape. The way he told it, he went to his mother's house as soon as he heard his brother was dead. They talked and cried, and the sisters and their families came."

"Right," Tony agreed. "And he was the executor, so the next day he went by Joey's house to make sure it was secure."

"And it was?" Harvey asked.

"Apparently. He went back the day before the funeral and started listing things."

"Friday, September eighth," Nate said. "That's when he looked over the guns and found Joey's list. He verified that all the guns on the list were there, and later he typed up a new list for the lawyer."

"And you've compared the two?"

"They're the same, except the brother added the ammo and accessories to the list."

Harvey nodded. "So we know the .357 was there on the eighth."

Nate nodded hesitantly. "I'd say so."

"Get me the two lists."

"Yes, sir. I filed copies of both." Nate left the room.

Eddie scratched his head. "We have no idea when the murder gun was removed from the cabinet."

"True," said Harvey. "Joey didn't report any missing guns."

Jimmy rested his chin on one hand, his elbow on the table. "It could have been stolen days or weeks earlier."

Nate returned and handed Harvey a file folder. Harvey opened it and sat silent for several seconds, poring over the lists of firearms. The men waited, not speaking.

"Here's something," he said at last.

The others shifted eagerly.

"Philip Bolduc listed the serial numbers. Joey didn't; he just described the guns. The .22 rifle and the shotgun didn't have any serial numbers, but the other rifles and all the handguns did, and Philip listed those."

The men looked around at each other blankly.

"So?" Eddie asked.

Tony sat up straighter. "I think I'm with you, Captain. We're not certain this is actually Joey's revolver."

"It has to be," Jimmy argued. "It was stolen from his house."

"Someone could have planted it there," Tony said.

"They'd have to lift the other one," Eddie said thoughtfully. "Switch Joey's revolver for the one they killed him with."

"It's brilliant," Harvey said. "The murder weapon stays safely in the family collection. Even if the brother sold it, it's unlikely it would be discovered that it was the murder weapon."

"But he didn't plan on it getting stolen by some hoodlum and used to knock over a liquor store a couple of weeks later," Eddie said triumphantly.

Paula appeared in the breakroom doorway. "Captain, Sergeant Yeaton is on the phone. She says it's important."

Harvey rose. "You guys keep thinking about this." He walked the length of the office and took the call at his desk.

"Captain, our liquor store perps have confessed to robbing Philip Bolduc's house. They've told us where the rest of the gun collection is. I sent Oliver and Needham to go get them."

"How did they know he had the guns in the first place?"

"They read about Joey's death in the paper. One of them recognized the name and picture; Joey arrested him once for breaking parole. Apparently he went around to see if anyone was staying at Joey's house a few days later, and he saw Joey's brother moving the gun cabinet out. He kept that in mind until he and his buddy needed guns, then went after them."

"He could get the brother's name and town from the obituary," Harvey said, shaking his head. "Looked up the address in the phone book or on the computer. This is too easy for crooks."

"You don't think these two are connected to the murder?" Cheryl asked.

"Not directly, but we'd like to see the interviews," Harvey said.

"I'll copy the tape for you."

"Thanks." Harvey hung up and yelled, "Eddie!"

"Right here, Harv."

Harvey jumped and turned to face him. "Who inherited Joey's estate?"

"Roxanne."

"Even after the divorce? He had a will?"

"Yes, and he didn't change it. He kept her as beneficiary of his life insurance, too. Or maybe he just hadn't gotten around to changing it. But he took her off his medical coverage last spring. I checked."

"So, his brother didn't actually inherit the guns?"

"No. I thought he did at first, but it turns out he bought them from the estate. From Roxanne, that is."

"She gets the house, too?"

"I guess so. I'm not sure if they've probated yet."

"Go see Philip Bolduc. We need to know who saw him go over the guns. He was the executor, but he wanted to keep the collection. He may have had someone with him when he made that list."

"I'm on it."

• • •

"What it comes down to is this," Harvey said to Jennifer that evening. "Who had the opportunity to switch the guns?" He lay back against a pile of pillows, holding Connor upright on his stomach. Jennifer sat on the quilt on the other side of the bed, brushing out her long hair.

"Joey's brother, for sure," she said. "Did anyone go to the house the day of the murder?"

"I asked Ron Legere. He sent a couple of men by there, just to check on things. They said everything was locked up tight that day, and they didn't go inside."

"Okay, so as far as we know, Philip Bolduc was the next person to have access."

"Yeah." Harvey sighed. "We have to make that assumption. If someone broke in, the evidence is gone. I had Eddie and Tony over there all afternoon, and they couldn't find any trace of a forced entry. Of course, there have been a million people in and out of there since Labor Day. Roxanne has decided to rent out the house, and she's been moving furniture in and out."

"And Philip Bolduc moved the gun cabinet out long ago."

"Right. He says the first time he went over, on Tuesday, the fifth, he just looked around. He didn't open the gun cabinet then. He said the only things he removed were Joey's checkbook, sixty dollars in cash from his dresser, and his wedding ring. He took them for safekeeping, and they've gone to Roxanne since."

"So, the gun cabinet wasn't opened until the Friday after the murder."

"As far as we know. Joey kept a key on his key ring. It was there when we found him. The second key to the cabinet was in his desk at the house. Philip claims he didn't know where it was until that Friday, when he and his sister went to start sorting things. He found it in the desk, and that's when he opened it. Joey's list of guns was in the desk, too."

"Hmm." Jennifer held out a lock of hair and brushed it absently, her eyes focused on the window that looked out over the rose garden. Harvey began to laugh.

"What's funny?"

"You are, gorgeous. I told you before, I ought to send you to the Academy."

"Well, if you don't want me to help, why do you tell me about these things?"

Harvey patted the pillow beside him. "Come here."

She laid the brush on the night stand and settled beside him. Connor gurgled and reached toward her, and she held out her arms. Harvey let the baby wriggle onto her lap and put his arm around her as she kissed Connor's fluffy blond hair.

"What do you think, huh, Connor? Who switched the guns?" she asked.

Harvey said, "Philip Bolduc claims his sister, Donna Torrey, was there the whole time that day. On the Friday, I mean."

"But she wouldn't be in the room with him all the time," Jennifer insisted.

"He admits that. But he seems to have been aboveboard. I mean, it would have been easy for him to pocket a few things. And he could have destroyed Joey's list of guns, but he didn't. He says he's tried to be more than fair to Roxanne, and I believe him. He doesn't like her, but he's tried to do what was right."

"So, it was just him and his sister? Does Mrs. Torrey have an alibi for the murder?"

"Yes, three kids and a husband. They had a picnic on Rangeley Lake the day of the murder, miles and miles from downtown Portland. I honestly don't think it was family."

"You don't think Roxanne arranged it? She *does* inherit."

"But they had worked things out before the divorce, and Joey's lawyer even says she wasn't bitter and demanding. She wanted to the leave the marriage, and she got to take what she wanted. She didn't go after the house. She took the car and the mutual funds and just about everything else, but her new boyfriend had a nice house, so she let Joey keep his."

"And he willed it to her."

"He made the will when the marriage was

healthy, and he didn't change it. It's not an expensive house," Harvey countered.

"Okay, if you say so. But maybe he told her he was going to change the will."

Harvey frowned. "I don't know. I just don't think she wanted it that badly. And if she wanted him dead, why bother to divorce him first? Why not just have him bumped off last winter when they were fighting, and save lawyers' fees?"

Jennifer sighed. "There's really only one person with a motive strong enough. That's what you think, isn't it?"

"Brad Lyons?" Harvey gritted his teeth. "He was scared of Joey. He talked tough the Friday before, but he was afraid Joey and Deborah would go to Mike. Deborah alone was too timid, but with Joey in her corner, she could cause him a huge headache. He knew he'd crossed the line too many times, and if Mike got onto it, or put a decent investigator onto it, he'd lose his badge."

Jennifer nodded. "That makes sense. But he was at the police station when Joey was killed."

"Right." Harvey sat up a little. "So . . . I'm thinking Brad gave his .357 magnum to Donald Lloyd, a guy who would be at City Hall Monday morning while Joey was there. This guy owed him. Brad had kept him out of jail."

"You're positive he did it?" Jennifer asked.

"No. But it's possible Brad made Lloyd think

431

he would go to jail if he didn't do what he told him."

Jennifer shook her head. "Kill someone in exchange for beating a small-time drug charge?"

"I'm telling you, Brad could lay it on thick. He might have made Lloyd think he was facing major consequences. Third strike. Major time in the state prison."

"Still, he must have done more than that for him."

"Like what?" Harvey asked.

"Paid him off. Come on, you said the drug thing was minor. Possession. That's not that big a deal, is it? There are fifteen-year-olds in this city who have that on their records, and they're not in jail."

"Okay, you're right," Harvey admitted.

"I am?"

"Sure. There has to be more to it." He leaned over to kiss her. "Thanks, Jenny. I want it to be cut and dried, but it's not. Hashing things out with you helps me see it more clearly."

"Too bad he had Joey killed for nothing." Jennifer's gray eyes were full of sorrow. "You got him on the harassment without that, and his career is ruined. He didn't have to kill Joey."

Harvey pulled her close, holding her head against his shoulder and supporting Connor with his arm. "Don't take it so hard, baby."

"Detectives can't grieve?" she asked.

"It tends to muddle their objectivity."

432

She smiled at him through tears. "Well, here's an objective assessment: Brad paid that guy off. Yes, he told him he'd fix his legal troubles, but he paid him something besides."

"Brad has no money, sweetheart. He's been divorced three times. The ex-wives took him to the cleaners."

Connor grabbed two handfuls of Jennifer's hair. She winced and gently pried his little fingers loose. "Well, if you find he had opportunity to switch the guns, I'll bet you also find he had opportunity to scrape up some money somewhere."

Harvey shook his head. "Philip Bolduc says no one else was at the house that day, except him and his sister."

"So," Jennifer countered. "Did he move the gun cabinet that day?"

Harvey caught his breath. "No, I don't think so. How could he?"

"It's heavy, right?" she asked.

He nodded slowly. "Very heavy."

"So one man can't move it easily."

Harvey leaped off the bed and grabbed the jeans he had draped over a chair.

Jennifer sat up. "Where are you going?"

"To Philip Bolduc's house."

She watched as he hastily dressed and pinned his badge on the front of his sweatshirt, then buckled his shoulder holster.

"You should take Eddie with you." Her voice caught a little.

"I'm just going to ask him a couple of questions tonight."

"Like who helped him load the gun cabinet?"

Harvey nodded. "It's pretty obvious when you think about it, isn't it?" He came to the side of the bed and reached to rumple Connor's hair. "Take care of Mommy, kiddo." He stooped and kissed Jennifer fiercely. "I'll be back, genius."

Chapter 20

Harvey gave his presentation to a rapt audience on Tuesday morning. Mike Browning, Jack Stewart, Ron Legere, Cheryl Yeaton, and the four detectives of the Priority Unit were crowded into the chief's office.

"After Joey's funeral, there was a kiss-and-cry time at Joey's parents' house in Deering," he told them. "That's when his brother Philip approached Roxanne about the gun collection. He didn't want to seem crass, but he wanted to settle it with her. The guns had sentimental value beyond their monetary value. Roxanne thought about it and told him to just take them. But Philip didn't want to do that. He's a precise person, and he didn't want anyone to have a reason to complain later."

"Smart guy." Jack took a sip of his coffee.

"Yeah. He showed Roxanne the list he'd typed up and gave her the approximate value for the guns and offered to pay her that amount. She agreed, and she told him to take the cabinet as well, as a gift from her."

"Which he did," Mike said.

Harvey nodded. "Right. Except, a full gun

cabinet isn't something you can just go pick up in your car. Now, Philip drives an Audi."

"How did he move it?" Tony asked.

"Exactly." Harvey smiled. "Five points for Winfield. I went around to see Bolduc last night, asking that very question. It seems a friend of Joey's from the police station overheard part of the conversation after the funeral, and he says to Philip, 'Hey, I've got a pickup truck. I can help you with that if you want.'"

"Brad?" Nate asked.

Harvey shook his head.

"Brad's got a decrepit Toyota Celica," Eddie said. "I'm guessing Bob Marshall. He's got a Dodge Ram, and he and Joey were close."

"Ten points for Eddie. Now, here's where it gets really interesting. Bob and Philip are nailing down the arrangements, and along comes friend number two. He says, 'You guys need a hand moving that?' He's such a nice guy, you know?"

"Brad," Cheryl guessed.

"You got it. You're tied with Eddie now." Harvey leaned on the window ledge and looked down on Franklin Street. His adrenaline was pumping, and he felt they were near to closing the case at last. He turned to face them all with a smile. "The upshot was, Bob and Brad went home and changed and met Philip at Joey's house an hour later."

Tony jumped up from his chair. "That's when

436

Brad picked up the murder weapon at his apartment. He'd been waiting for a chance to dump it where it would be safe."

Jack shook his head. "Pretty risky to hang onto it all week."

Harvey spread both hands. "He wasn't under suspicion. As long as nobody made a connection between Brad, the gunman, and Joey, he could take his time."

"Why didn't he just heave it in the bay?" Ron Legere asked.

Harvey shrugged. "Didn't have a chance?"

"Maybe he was planning to, but he saw this opportunity and thought it was too neat to pass up," Eddie said. "Brad would love the irony of it. He silenced Joey before he could blab, and the murder weapon would sit innocently in the brother's den for years, with nobody the wiser."

"That's what I'm thinking," Harvey admitted.

"So, they opened the gun cabinet before they took it to Philip Bolduc's house?" the deputy chief asked.

"Well, as I understand it, Jack, it wasn't actually opened until they unloaded it in Falmouth," Harvey said. "Brad suggested they'd better check to make sure nothing shifted."

"Brad suggested," Jimmy repeated.

"Right. So, Philip gets out the key and opens it, and the three of them start looking at the guns. Bob and Brad were both trotting out the memories. I guess Bob went deer hunting with Joey last fall, and Brad claimed he was with Joey at the shooting range when he qualified with his .45." Harvey sat down on the edge of Mike's desk. "And at some point, when Bob and Philip either left the room or turned their backs for five seconds, Brad took out his own .357 and switched it for Joey's."

"Wait a minute," Tony said. "I don't want to rain on your parade, Captain, but if he didn't make the switch until after the funeral, how did Philip Bolduc get the serial number of Brad's gun on the list he made the day before?"

Harvey smiled. "Joey's friends were very helpful that day. Philip showed them the list, and they compared it to the guns in the cabinet, exclaiming over each one. 'Yeah I remember this one. Hey, that's a nice shotgun.' And Bob, in his innocence, says, 'Hey, you really ought to have the serial numbers down, Mr. Bolduc. Just for your own protection.' Maybe that's when they left the room, to get a pen or something, I don't know, but I do know the numbers weren't on that list until after the cabinet was moved. They weren't on Joey's handwritten list. I got the copy Philip gave Roxanne. No serial numbers. I thought he'd done it earlier, but no. He claims he typed them in that night and made the official copy for the estate records after they moved the cabinet."

"And he put down the serial number of Brad's gun," Mike said with satisfaction.

"Brad was mighty lucky," Tony said. "If there'd been a record of the serial numbers before that, he'd have been caught."

Harvey shrugged. "Probably not, unless Philip compared the numbers on the guns to those on the list later. Even then, they couldn't tie it to Brad. I'm sure he wiped his prints off. And if they found a stray print or two, so what? All three of them were handling Joey's guns that night."

"You're positive Bob Marshall's not tied up in this?" Mike asked. "He did initiate moving the cabinet."

Harvey nodded. "Bob's okay. And I don't think Brad planned to plant the gun there until he heard Bob and Philip talking about moving it. It just came up, and he took advantage of the situation."

"If you can get Lyons to admit to all that, you'll be doing well," Jack said.

"I don't expect him to admit it, but there's one more thing that will help in this." Harvey turned to Detective Sergeant Legere. "Ron, how often do items go missing from the evidence lockers?"

Ron was clearly startled. "Not often. Why? Is something missing?"

"When was the last time?" Harvey asked.

"Well, there was an old case where someone was looking for a knife a few months ago. I don't think we ever found it, but it was from a case that was years old."

"How about drugs?"

"We're extremely careful, Harvey. You know that."

"Still, once in a great while, you might lose a few ounces of pot?"

Ron grimaced. "It happened a couple of months ago in a heroin case. The hearing came up, and we couldn't lay our hands on the evidence."

Harvey nodded. "Donald Lloyd. He's a custodian at City Hall. We like him for Joey's hired killer."

"You're joking."

"No, it was his heroin that disappeared."

Ron shook his head in disbelief.

"Only a few people generally have access to the evidence room," Harvey said. "I'm happy to say I don't. Occasionally, a key has been entrusted to me for short periods of time, but usually if I want something out of there, I have to go get you, Ron, or you, Jack, or . . ."

"Or me," Cheryl said.

"Yes. Or, until last week, Brad Lyons."

"What's missing?" Mike asked.

"That may be hard to prove. See, Brad was hurting financially."

"It's his own fault," said Nate. "Child support going three ways, last I heard."

"Right. But if he wanted to hire someone to do a job—a big job—"

"Say, a murder?" Mike asked.

"Well, yes, just for example. He seems to have kept a string of people indebted to him in case he needed them. My boys have uncovered four cases where perpetrators are willing to admit Brad Lyons suspended their bail or reduced their charges on the spot, after booking. Donald Lloyd is one of them. He didn't want to admit it, but he finally did, under skillful questioning by Detective Miller.

Harvey nodded to Nate, and Nate gave him a casual salute.

"Lloyd believed he was looking at a mandatory jail sentence of five to ten years," Harvey continued. "Sergeant Lyons was very sympathetic, and in the end got the charges dropped. Lloyd says Brad implied that he might ask him for a favor later."

Cheryl frowned at him. "But he's not saying that favor was to murder Detective Bolduc, is he?"

"Right. Lloyd says Brad never called in the favor, but I don't buy it." Harvey turned to Ron. "Here's what I think. Once in a great while, the person with the keys to the evidence lockers might have the opportunity to make away with a few items. Not often."

"What kind of items?" Legere asked uneasily.

"A few weeks ago, your men busted a drug ring. Brought in fifteen kilos of heroin and a pile of cash."

Ron nodded diffidently. "Yeah, that was a good bust."

"How much cash?" Harvey asked quickly.

Ron shrugged. "Thirty-eight grand, I think. We're getting some back on the state program, and we'll use it to buy equipment."

"Right," Harvey said. "Thirty-eight thousand, four hundred dollars was recorded in the report."

"So?"

"So, who counted the money the night you brought it in?"

"Oh, I don't know. Let's see, there were a bunch of guys on that case. I'd have to look at my own report."

"Joey Bolduc, Bob Marshall, Lloyd Gordon, and Paul Trudeau," Harvey said. "You had eight patrolmen for backup."

Ron blinked. "I won't question you. I'd say you've done the research."

"I have. But which one of them counted the thirty-eight grand?"

"I don't know," Ron admitted.

"That was a trick question," Harvey said with a smile. "I suggest to you that none of them counted it."

"They gathered it all up in a bag," Ron mused.

"It was all over the house, you know? We kept searching and finding stashes of bills."

"So, you took it back to the station uncounted," Harvey prompted.

"Yeah, maybe."

"And who was on the night desk?"

"Oh, no."

"Oh, yes. There's supposed to be two cops together every time confiscated money is counted. But your unit was extremely busy, unloading the dope and booking—what?—seven prisoners, if my memory serves. Might you not have handed the cash in the sack to the night sergeant and asked him to please count it and log it in Evidence?"

Ron grimaced. "I might have. I honestly don't remember, Harvey."

Harvey smiled. "See, right there is temptation for Brad Lyons. You have no idea how much money is in that bag. It's up to Brad to count it and enter the amount in the log. But for a guy who needs money—"

"You're saying he planned to kill Joey way back then?" Eddie asked.

"No, but I'm saying it's possible, just possible, he might have seen the chance to take some extra cash here and there. That bust is one example."

Mike grunted. "No proof whatsoever, and never will be."

"True," Harvey said.

Ron ran a hand through his hair. "I try to be careful with stuff like that."

"We all do," Harvey said. "That doesn't mean that once in a while you or I or Cheryl—any of us—mightn't trust the wrong person."

"Any one of the officers could have pocketed a few bills at the scene, as far as that goes," Cheryl said uneasily. "We'd all like to think it never happens, but . . ."

"But if we find that Donald Lloyd was suddenly flush at about the time of the murder . . ." Harvey let it trail off.

"Have you?" Mike asked.

"Not yet," Harvey admitted. "I thought he'd have done the hit in return for beating the jail sentence, but something convinced me that he must have been paid."

"Well, that's all very interesting, but it's only speculation," Ron said.

Harvey sighed. "Okay, but the other part—the part about switching the guns. That happened."

Mike got up and refilled his coffee mug. "Get Lloyd in again and lean on him. If he's your shooter, you need more than him coming out of City Hall at the right time and beating a drug charge."

Harvey nodded. "We'll be talking to Bob Marshall, too, to get his version of the gun cabinet story. And I thought I'd have Jimmy ask your other detectives about the drug bust, Ron. Just to see if anyone remembers counting the money that night."

"You'll get my men upset. They'll think you're trying to say we were sloppy."

"Would I say that?" Harvey smiled. He turned to look at his four detectives. "Gentlemen, let's get to work."

At noon Sarah Benoit left the locker room and hurried to catch up with her partner. "Lunch at the diner?"

"Only if we eat inside," Deborah replied. "It's too cold to sit on the sidewalk today."

They walked down the block and into the little restaurant.

"Hey, Sarah," Candi Mullins called from a booth. "Have you girls seen this yet?" She held up the new edition of *Portland Life* magazine.

"It's out already?" Deborah squealed. "Let me see!"

She and Sarah squeezed into the booth with Candi and Marge.

"You girls," Marge laughed. "Seen one man, you've seen 'em all."

"I've never seen this one before," Deborah said, staring at the cover of the magazine. A handsome, thirtysomething man in a tank top, with a whistle hanging around his neck, grinned up at them.

"Who's Bachelor Number One?" Sarah asked critically.

"The gym teacher at the elementary school on Brighton Avenue," Candi replied. "Can you believe it?"

"We didn't have gym teachers who looked like that," Deborah said.

Sarah nodded. "It was Sister Ursula where I went."

Deborah flipped the pages of the magazine.

"Page forty-five," Marge said and sipped her soft drink.

"Would you like to order?" A waitress stood at Sarah's elbow.

"Oh, sure, turkey on whole wheat and coffee. How about you, Debbie?"

"The same," Deborah said absently. "Here we go. Oh, Sarah, look at Tony. He's cute!"

Sarah shrugged. "He's always cute."

Marge laughed. "Good for you, Sarah. There's more to a man than looks."

Sarah looked over Deborah's shoulder at the picture. Tony Winfield's dimples were in top form as he cleaned his Heckler & Koch .45. He was wearing a gray T-shirt, with his detective's badge pinned to the front.

Candi rose. "Looks don't hurt. Bring that down to me in Records when you're done with it, girls." She and Marge left tips for the waitress.

"They tamed his cowlick," Sarah said, still gazing at Tony's picture.

"It's a great picture," Debbie insisted.

Sarah moved over to the other side of the booth. "So, which guy do you pick?"

Debbie smiled. "This one's not bad. He's on the county commission."

"And he's single?"

"Widowed."

Sarah frowned. "They picked a widower as one of the city's ten most eligible men?"

"He doesn't seem to mind. He's too old, though. Forty-six."

"What's wrong with an older man?"

"I want a guy with enough energy to play tennis on Saturday." Debbie turned the page. "Here you go, Sarah. Number Seven. He's a chef at that Mexican restaurant on Market Street."

Sarah took the magazine. "Not my type."

"You're too picky." Debbie reached for the magazine.

"Hey, wait a minute." Sarah's brow furrowed. "I know this guy."

"The chef?"

"No, Number Eight. He's a fire fighter. Mark Johnson."

"Let me see." Deborah pulled the magazine from her hands and scrutinized the photo. "Not bad. Not a classic dreamboat, but definitely worthy of consideration. Hmm. Twenty-nine, never married, graduated from USM. He's an EMT at the main fire station."

"I know," Sarah choked.

Debbie looked up quickly. "What, you're seeing this guy or something?"

"Not exactly. I've only met him a couple of times. I didn't expect him to show up in the beefcake layout, though."

"It's not that bad," Debbie insisted. "They all have their shirts on. Except this mechanic. Definitely a narcissist."

The waitress came with their lunch, and Sarah moved her sandwich in front of her then reached for the magazine again. It was a good picture of Mark. He was in uniform, standing at the open back door of the ambulance.

"I'd let him give *me* mouth to mouth," Debbie said with a wicked smile.

Sarah frowned and thrust the magazine into her hands. "He's really quiet. I'm surprised he did it."

"Because Eddie wouldn't?"

"Eddie's engaged."

Debbie sighed. "Now *that* would have been cover material. Better than the gym teacher, even."

"Are you seeing Derek again?" Sarah asked abruptly.

Debbie's glance was wary. "You know, I've

been thinking about it. He wants me to go out with him again, but . . . remember when they had him in a couple of weeks ago for questioning?"

"Yeah, you told me about the hair thing."

"Well, he's okay, but I started remembering why I broke up with him in the first place."

"Why did you?"

"He's just . . . how do I say this? Dull. Dull as dishwater."

Sarah smiled. "As long as you don't tell me he was the insanely jealous type."

Debbie turned her eyes upward. "I think the Priority Unit has given up on him as a suspect."

Harvey skipped lunch. He didn't do it often anymore. Jennifer would be upset if she knew, and if he put off eating too long, his hands would begin to shake, but he wasn't thinking of those things at noon. He just kept going over the evidence, pulling out file folders and consulting his computer.

At two o'clock, someone put a paper bag on the corner of his desk, and he looked up.

"Thanks, Ed."

"Find anything?"

Harvey stretched and reached for the bag. "Not yet. I haven't talked to Bob Marshall yet. He's out on assignment. You want in on the interview?"

"Yeah, sure. Paul Trudeau told me he thought

Bob and Joey counted the drug money that night in August."

"Bob and Joey?" Harvey was startled. "I was so sure they gave Brad that job."

"Maybe, maybe not. Paul thinks he remembers Bob and Joey ticking it off as they put it in the bag."

"Who logged it?"

"Brad, and according to the record, he put it in the locker for them. But if two detectives were keeping count . . ."

"And only one of them is left to ask about it." Harvey unwrapped a ham sandwich and took a bite.

"There's Brad," Eddie said tentatively.

"Yup. We need his version, for sure."

"You want me to set it up at the jail?"

"Sure. He'll want his lawyer there." Harvey pulled a half pint of milk from the bag and poured it into his coffee mug. "Did Jennifer call you or something?"

"You were supposed to go home for lunch."

"I was? Oh, man." Harvey reached for the phone, and Eddie turned toward his own desk.

"I am so sorry, gorgeous," Harvey said when Jennifer answered the phone. "I completely forgot we had a date."

"It's okay. I was a little worried about you."

"Why didn't you just call me, baby?" Harvey asked softly.

"I didn't want to make you feel guilty. But I wanted to make sure you were okay, so I asked Eddie. Did you get something to eat?"

"Yes, I'm fine. Do you want to go out tonight?"

"No." He could almost see her wistful gray eyes. "I'd like to just stay home with you."

"You've got it."

"Well, if this case keeps you going late, I'll understand."

"Not tonight. I promise."

"You're trying to hang larceny on me now?" Brad asked in disbelief.

Harvey said hastily, "I'm just trying to find out who counted the drug money that night, Brad."

He sat across from Brad and his attorney in a visiting room at the county jail. Brad looked terrible. His eyes were bloodshot, and his face was thin and haggard.

"If I could look at my log, maybe I could help you," he said wearily, "but I'll tell you this. If I counted it, it all went in the locker."

"Who brought it in? Do you remember? Ron and half his squad were on it."

Brad shook his head. "Probably the sergeant handed it to me. I don't know."

"Do you remember how much was in the bag?"

"No. I don't remember counting money that recently, Harvey. I really don't. If I did, it would just be to confirm the amount for Ron."

Harvey leaned back in the metal folding chair. "How long have you had your .357 Magnum?"

Brad looked at him blankly.

"The Smith & Wesson we took from your apartment," Harvey said.

"Oh, seven or eight years."

"Where did you get it?"

"A gun shop on Forest Avenue."

"I know the place."

"He probably has a record of the transaction," Brad said testily, "but if that gun was the murder weapon, I'd have heard about it before now."

"You're right, it's not. We have the murder weapon."

Brad's eyebrows shot up. "Then why the interest in my revolver?"

"The day you helped Philip Bolduc move Joey's gun cabinet to his house . . ."

"What about it?"

"Joey had a .357 in his collection."

"Yeah. So?"

"Was it similar to yours?"

Brad shrugged. "I suppose so. I think mine's a little older. What's the deal?"

Harvey rose. "Sorry, I can't go into it."

"You just want to drive me nuts in here, don't you, Larson? You want to pin the murder on me, but you can't, so you're coming up with all these other niggling things. You're going to say

I embezzled who-knows-how-much drug money next, aren't you?"

"I'm just trying to get at the truth, Brad."

As Harvey headed toward the door and the guard opened it for him, Brad shouted, "Well, the truth is, I'm being set up here! I'm an easy target right now, that's the truth!"

Jennifer met him at the door to the garage with Connor in her arms.

"What's for supper, gorgeous?" He kissed her, then Connor. He shifted his briefcase to his left hand and reached to take the baby.

"Warmed over lunch," Jennifer said apologetically.

"Great. I'm starved."

They went into the kitchen.

"Want to eat in the living room?" Harvey asked. "I'll make a fire in the fireplace."

Jennifer eyed him carefully. "All right, that would be nice. I'll fix our plates."

When she carried them to the other room five minutes later, the fire was blazing. Harvey came in behind her, swinging Connor high as he walked. He had changed from his suit to jeans and a Portland Fire Department T-shirt.

"Hey, Connor, turn the light off," he coached, holding his son up near the switch.

Connor laughed and threw his head back.

"No, over here, bubba," Harvey said, taking

the baby's hand and guiding it to the light switch. The overhead light went off, and Connor squealed.

"You want to sit on the floor?" Jennifer asked uncertainly, holding the plates.

"Yeah, we'll have a picnic." Harvey sat down on a quilt he had spread on the floor. He laid Connor down, and the boy beat the air with his feet and hands. "Just like a turtle on his back," Harvey laughed.

"I'll get the drinks." Jennifer set the plates on the edge of the hearth.

She was coming back with two glasses when Harvey's cell phone rang. She set the glasses on the coffee table with a sigh.

"Yeah, Eddie. Okay. Yeah, that sounds good. I'll be there."

She smiled tremulously as he closed the phone.

"What's the matter, beautiful?"

"Are you leaving?"

"Now? No way!"

"Later?"

"Come here." He reached toward her. She took his hand, and he pulled her down on the floor beside him. "I am not leaving this house for the next twelve hours. Period."

She threw her arms around his neck with a sob. Harvey rubbed her back gently.

"You're not crying, are you, sweetheart?"

She reached around his neck with her left hand

to dash at the tear that rolled down her right cheek. "Why would I cry?"

He kissed her hair and held her close. "Eddie was just telling me tomorrow's schedule. I'm staying home tonight. I don't care if Jill Weymouth calls and says her house is being robbed and there's a body hanging from the chandelier. I'm not leaving."

Jennifer took a deep, shaky breath. "I'm sorry. I'm not usually weepy and possessive, am I?"

"No, you absolutely are not. You're the greatest. I spend night after night working sometimes, and you never complain." He tipped her chin up and kissed her, then pulled back to look into her eyes. "You okay?"

"Yes. Well, maybe."

"Maybe?" Concern darkened his bright blue eyes. "What kind of maybe? Jenny, what is it?"

She turned her face away from him, but rested her cheek against his shoulder. Connor laughed and reached toward her, and she put one finger into his grasp.

"Harvey, I think I might be pregnant again."

He sat stock still for an instant, then crushed her closer against his chest. "Really?"

"I—I don't know. I just—think maybe."

He laughed. "Fantastic. You want me to go to the drugstore?"

She pulled in a ragged breath. "You're happy, aren't you?"

"Of course. Aren't you?"

She looked long into his eyes and nodded, a smile slowly curving her lips. "I thought you would be. I hoped you would be. But I wasn't positive. I mean, it's so soon."

He frowned. "You're all right, aren't you? I mean, is this a problem?"

"No, no. It's great. If you think it's great, it's great."

"Oh, I most definitely think it's great."

Her smile was bigger then. "I knew you would, really. I just—there's been so much going on lately. I wasn't going to say anything until I knew for sure, but tonight I just feel like I want you to be here when I find out."

Harvey's smile was tender as he pulled her gently toward him. His lingering kiss was interrupted by Connor's loud hoots that turned to wails when no one responded.

"We'll eat supper, then we'll go to the drugstore." Harvey leaned to pick up the baby. "We'll find out tonight."

Chapter 21

Eddie met Harvey and Jeff in Harvey's driveway Wednesday morning, and they set off toward the corner on their Wednesday route.

"Don't let me forget to call the florist first thing," Harvey said.

Eddie threw him a look over his shoulder. "What's the occasion?"

"Nothing."

"Nothing?"

"Nothing. Jenny's a little depressed, is all."

"Because you're working too hard?"

"No, it's—well, we found out last night we're not expecting again."

"Not—you mean another baby?" Eddie turned around and jogged backward.

"Yeah."

Behind Harvey, Jeff said, "This is depressing? You just had one."

"I know, but we thought maybe we were having another one, and we're not, so she's a little down."

Eddie shook his head. "Two years between. That's what my mother says. That's what she did."

"Yeah, well, she wasn't my age when she got married."

Jeff stepped off the curb and came up beside him. "Doesn't the mother need some rehab time or something?"

Harvey shrugged. "I'll ask Carl. Do you think?"

Jeff shrugged. "All I know is, Beth is going to want some time to recover after this pregnancy."

"Well, sure, she's had a rough time," Harvey conceded. He was beginning to puff a little, so he concentrated on his breathing.

When they stopped in Eddie's yard twenty minutes later, Jeff walked across the lawn, gulping air. "Did you see Mark's picture in the magazine?"

"We saw it," Eddie said. "I'm glad it wasn't me."

"The phone rang all day and all evening at the fire station yesterday," Jeff told him. "The captain got mad after a while. At least they're not using the emergency line to ask for dates."

Eddie laughed, but Harvey shook his head.

"The same thing happened in our unit. I told Paula to screen all Winfield's calls and take phone numbers. He can call these women back on his own time if he wants to, but he's not taking their calls on city time."

"Think Mark will go out with any of the ones that call him?" Eddie asked.

Jeff grinned. "I don't know. Two girls came in

at lunch time with homemade cookies for him. He took it pretty well, but he was embarrassed."

"He should have thought of that before he let them take the picture," Harvey said.

"Aw, come on, Harv, it's good P.R.," Jeff insisted.

"Waste of time," Harvey muttered.

The elevator door opened, and Arnie Fowler stepped into the Priority Unit.

"Hey, Arnie," Eddie cried.

Harvey jumped up to greet him.

"You guys need a new pass code," Arnie said. "It hasn't changed in months."

"I'll tell Jack," Harvey said. "Hey, come have a cup of coffee. What are you up to?"

"Oh, I'm going north with Mike and Sharon this weekend to paint their apartment at the lodge. They're making a lot of progress up there. You guys ought to go up in November and do some hunting."

"I'll consider that." Harvey poured a cup of coffee and held it out to Arnie.

"Thanks."

Eddie said, "I'm using all my remaining vacation for the honeymoon, I'm afraid."

"Well, you and Leeanne can skip up there for a weekend." Arnie sipped the coffee and frowned. "Is this decaf?"

"Uh—" Harvey looked guiltily toward the

459

secretary's desk. "Paula makes it for me. I have no idea."

"You can always tell," Eddie said.

"I guess I can't."

"Good," Arnie told him. "If you can't tell, it's probably better for you. Unfortunately, I can tell. You got the real thing someplace?"

"In the break room," Eddie said. "That's where I'm getting mine now. Give me the cup. I'll get it for you."

"Thanks."

"Sit down, Arnie." Harvey pulled out a chair.

"Oh, I don't want to keep you from your work. I was just up to see Mike for a minute, and I thought I'd look in here. You guys are all computerized now."

"Yeah, they've got the records all in the system for forty years back now. It's great." Harvey poured his own coffee and sat down, and Arnie relented and settled into his extra chair.

"Funny thing about Bolduc's guns getting stolen," Arnie said.

"I'll say. That's the freakiest thing about this case."

"He had some nice guns."

"You've seen them?" Harvey asked.

"Oh, sure. Joey and I went to a gun show together in South Portland a couple of years ago. He sold one of his old rifles and bought a .30-06 that day."

"That was there," Harvey said. "A Winchester model 70."

Arnie nodded. "Did he still have the old Dan Wesson I sold him?"

"The what?"

"Dan Wesson revolver. A .357."

Harvey shook his head slowly. "There was a Smith & Wesson .357 in the collection. Funny you should mention it."

"Why's that?"

Harvey bit his lip. "You sold him a .357 when?"

"Couple years ago. No, not that long. I could tell you. I kept a record."

"Do that. Can you let me know today?"

"Sure. It wasn't with his other guns, huh?"

"No, it wasn't."

Arnie reached for the coffee mug Eddie was bringing. "Thanks. It's too bad. I liked that gun, but Joey was keen on it, so I let it go. Thought he'd hang onto it. Oh, well, he probably got a better offer." He sipped his coffee.

"Eddie, bring me the folder with the lists of Joey's guns," Harvey said when Arnie had left. Eddie brought it, and he opened it and stared thoughtfully at the copy of the list in Joey's handwriting.

"You got something?" Eddie asked quietly.

Harvey's eyes were troubled. "When is a .357 Smith & Wesson not a .357 Smith & Wesson?"

461

"When it's really a nine-millimeter?"

Harvey stood up. "Arnie sold Joey a Dan Wesson a while back. He's going to call me with the date."

Eddie's eyes snapped to Harvey's. "Dan Wesson? Joey's revolver was a Smith & Wesson."

"At least, we think it was." Harvey tapped the list with his index finger. "The murder weapon certainly was."

"Is Dan Wesson the same guy as the one in Smith & Wesson?"

Harvey shook his head. "His descendant. Started his own company about fifty years ago."

"But Joey wrote it on his list."

"No." Harvey shook his head. "Joey wrote *.357 Wesson.* Not Smith & Wesson. When Philip Bolduc modified the list, that gun became a Smith & Wesson."

"Or maybe before that?"

"Maybe. I'm thinking the gun Philip was looking at when he wrote it was a Smith & Wesson." Harvey stared at Eddie. "We missed something. Go over everything we have on Philip Bolduc again."

"What am I looking for?"

"I don't know, but there's something." Harvey pounded his desk so hard coffee splashed out of his mug onto the desktop. "I've let Brad Lyons cloud my thinking on this. I was positive he did it."

"He did," Eddie insisted. "He gave the gun to the custodian, and—"

"And where's the Dan Wesson?" Harvey asked grimly.

"Joey must have sold it."

"No, no. Arnie said Joey was keen on it. Arnie wasn't trying to sell it, but Joey really wanted it." Harvey swung around. "Listen, I was going to talk to Bob Marshall this morning, but I think I'll run over to the gun shop on Forest Avenue and check Brad's story about his pistol. Can you call Bob and tell him I'll see him later?"

"Call the florist," said Eddie.

"Right. Thanks."

The stairway door opened Thursday morning, and Bob Marshall came into the Priority Unit office. Harvey went to meet him.

"Bob, thanks for coming. Will you step into the interview room here for a few minutes? I want to ask you about the day you and Brad Lyons helped Philip Bolduc move his brother's gun cabinet."

Marshall shrugged and walked with him. "Sure, Captain, but I don't know as I can tell you anything new."

"How did it come about that you and Brad went over there?"

"I was talking to Joey's brother after the funeral. You know, chitchat with the family. He mentioned the guns, and we got talking about it.

He said he wanted to move the cabinet over to his place, not leave it in Joey's empty house. You know, for security."

Harvey nodded.

"So I told him I've got a truck, and I would help him."

"And how did Brad enter into it?"

"He just happened to overhear, I guess." Bob eyed him warily. "You think he was maybe listening, trying to . . . what? Have an opportunity to get in Joey's house or something?"

"I just want to know how the arrangements were made." Harvey sat down at the table, and Bob sat across from him.

"Okay, well, Brad just kind of jumped in and asked if we needed help moving something. Bolduc said sure, so after the wake we went and changed clothes and met at Joey's house. Man, that was difficult. I'd been over there a lot, you know? Most of Joey's stuff was still there. Roxanne had mentioned to me at the funeral that I ought to have something, and his brother gave me one of his hunting knives. A Schrade. Nice blade." Bob shook his head. "I still can't believe Joey's dead."

"You and Brad saw all the guns that day," Harvey said quietly.

"Yeah, I think so. All the ones in the cabinet, anyway. Were there more?"

"Well, a friend of Joey's mentioned to me one

handgun that doesn't seem to have been in the cabinet. A Dan Wesson."

Bob's eyes widened, and he shook his head. "I don't remember that. There were two or three handguns. His service revolver wasn't there. I figured you had it."

"We do."

Bob nodded. "Well, I don't know of any others."

"Okay, just thought I'd ask. Oh, and another thing, Bob. This is a totally different thing that came up recently. Sergeant Legere and I were talking yesterday about a case your unit handled in August. Big drug bust on the twenty-fourth. You remember that night?"

"Oh, let's see, that must have been down in the Old Port. Sure. We had a lot of guys down there."

"Right. The uniforms took the prisoners away, and your unit searched the house. You and Joey collected the money as it turned up. Trudeau and Gordon were logging heroin and loading it."

"That sounds right."

"How much money did you find in the house?"

Marshall's eyes narrowed. "Can't say. A lot. Over thirty thousand, I think. Thirty-eight sticks in my mind, but I could check my reports."

"Did you personally count it?"

"I think we kept a running total as it went in the bag, but it was approximate. It was officially counted once we got back to the station."

"By whom?"

He sat still for a moment. "You know, I think Brad counted it. We passed it to him, and I told him the approximate figure, and he logged it for us."

"So, if you told him thirty-eight thousand, and it was actually less, what would have happened?"

"He would have told us immediately, I'm sure."

"And if it was more?"

Marshall's lower lip twitched. "Captain, are you telling me that money's missing? Because we're going to trial on that case pretty soon."

"No, Bob, relax. The money's still in the Evidence Room. I checked on it yesterday. I'm really concerned about the counting procedure."

"Well, like I said, it was an approximate count, and we gave it to the sergeant, and he took it from there." Bob stared at Harvey. "You think Brad—oh, man."

Harvey smiled at him. "Stop trying to second guess me, Bob. You're sure Brad did the final count?"

"Well, now I couldn't swear to it. But somebody out front did. Not me. We started questioning the prisoners."

"But you and Joey knew there was roughly thirty-eight thousand dollars there, and Brad didn't contradict that."

"No. As far as I knew until this minute, everything went perfect on that case."

"Okay. Relax. It's still perfect. You're going to get convictions."

Marshall eyed him distrustfully.

"You want some coffee?" Harvey asked.

"Well, are we done?"

"We're getting there. I have a few more questions. Why don't I get you some coffee?"

"Okay. Black."

"Great. I'll be right back."

Harvey went into the office, leaving the video camera running, and beckoned to Jimmy Cook. "Get me some black coffee for Bob." He walked to Eddie's desk.

"I'm not having any luck on Philip Bolduc," Eddie said, looking up.

Harvey put one hand on his shoulder and leaned down close. "Put Nate and Tony on their computers. You fill out a couple of warrant forms and I'll sign them, then you call Bob's bank. I want a financial profile asap and a full search of his house."

"Bob Marshall?"

Harvey nodded.

"I thought you said you were sure he was clean."

"I was an idiot. I was so sure, I never looked twice at Bob, and only once and a half at Philip Bolduc. But they had as much opportunity to swap the guns as Brad did. And Brad's revolver matches the serial number in the gun shop owner's records. He bought it legally, seven years ago. Bob ought to have known about that Dan Wesson. He shot with Joey all the time. Joey *had* to have showed it to him after he bought it from Arnie."

"You think he'd have ditched it?"

"He might have. But if he thought he was safe . . . Get the warrant apps ready."

Eddie nodded. Harvey took the mug of coffee from Jimmy and went back to the interview room.

"Here we go. Bob, I don't want to keep you away from your work; I know you're busy right now." Harvey sat down, smoothing his necktie. "Listen, this may be shocking, but you're a detective. You understand I have to check into every possibility." He stared into Marshall's uneasy brown eyes. "Do you think there is any way, any way at all, that Joey might have skimmed the drug money that night?"

Marshall swallowed. "He wouldn't do that."

"You're sure."

"Absolutely. What are you trying to do here? Joey was honest."

"Okay. I believe you. And if he had pocketed some bills, you'd have known it, wouldn't you?"

"I—I guess so."

"You were both right there, and when anyone found money, say under a mattress, or in the freezer, they'd hand it to you and you'd count it and toss it in the bag, right?"

"Right. But it was really crazy that night. A lot was going on. There were a lot of suspects, and there had been shots fired. We tore the place apart after."

Harvey nodded. "So you might not have noticed if Joey had—"

"I told you, Joey wouldn't."

"Right. And if you had the opportunity, Joey would have known."

"What are you saying?"

"Just that either of you, or both, could have skimmed a little, and no one else would know. Just you and Joey."

Marshall's breathing was shallow, and his face colored as he stared at Harvey. "I don't believe this. I told you, I can vouch for Joey."

"Yes, and he could vouch for you, if he weren't dead."

Harvey's cell phone hummed softly, and he took it out and looked at it. Eddie had texted *warrant apps ready.*

Harvey looked at Marshall. "Bob, I don't like doing this to a fellow officer, but sometimes to clear someone we have to investigate their activities. That's the only way to narrow the suspects down in some cases."

"You're investigating me? For what? Skimming the drug money? You have proof it was skimmed? I don't get it. Six weeks later and an eyewitness comes forward, or what?"

"That operation was prime for some cash going missing. It was hectic, it was messy, a lot of people were on the scene. A large amount of cash was scattered throughout the building. If someone needed some money fast, it might have been tempting to just pocket a little. And the person who made the official count was given an approximate total. There was leeway everywhere."

Marshall continued to stare at him. "Brad Lyons could have . . . Listen, Captain, you won't find any mysterious deposits in my bank account. Ask my wife. Things are tight around our house. We've got two kids in college. Carol works full time, and we squeak by."

Harvey nodded. "We just have to check everything, Bob. I'm requesting search warrants for your house. Will we find any handguns?"

"Handguns? Yes. My nine-millimeter. It's in the bedroom closet."

"Thank you."

Marshall nodded slowly. "Can I go now?"

Harvey tilted his head slightly. "I'd rather have you sit tight for a little while."

"You're detaining me. I need a lawyer."

"If you want one."

Bob sighed in exasperation. "I wanted to work in this unit, but I had no idea. You're Gestapo."

Harvey winced. "Joey was a decent guy, and I intend to find out who killed him."

"You have cause to think it was me?"

"Just . . . means and opportunity, Bob."

"What, no motive?"

"That's what we're trying to find out."

Marshall swore. "Can I talk to Ron?"

Harvey hesitated. He knew he was being rough on Marshall, but he had made the decision to put his suspicions to rest, once and for all.

"Sure." Harvey went to the doorway. "Paula, could you please get Sergeant Legere on the phone for me? And Jimmy, please come in and stay with Detective Marshall for a minute."

Jimmy went into the interview room, and Harvey crossed to Eddie's desk. Eddie had the warrant applications open. Harvey quickly added his electronic signature and went to his own desk and picked up the phone.

"Ron, Hi. Could you possibly come up here for a minute? I've been questioning Bob Marshall, and I'd like to keep him a little longer, but he's uncomfortable, and he asked for you."

"What are you up to, Larson?"

"Just checking out the gun switch and the drug money thing. Bob is feeling a little hostile at my implications, I'm afraid."

"Bob's a reasonable man."

"Well, yes, but he was also close to Joey, and,

well, I've sent for warrants for his house and his financial records."

"You *what?*"

Harvey pulled the phone away from his ear. When he put it back, Legere had hung up. Thirty seconds later he stormed in from the stairway.

"What in tarnation do you think you're doing?"

"Investigating the Bolduc murder," Harvey said calmly.

"I'm short on detectives as it is, and you're so desperate to solve this case you've decided to pin it on one of my best men?"

Harvey wavered. "I could let him go back to work, but I want to be sure he doesn't make any calls before the warrants are executed."

"You're a piece of work," Legere said bitterly. "You know what's wrong with you? They promoted you too fast, that's what. Your head swelled faster than your brain did. And Mike says you're a genius." He shook his head. "Where's Marshall?"

"This way." Harvey led him to the interview room.

"Sarge," Marshall said, standing as Legere and Harvey entered. "They're detaining me and searching my house. I can't believe this."

Legere rounded angrily on Harvey. "Larson, this ends now. Get a grip. If you can't make it stick on Brad, that's not our fault."

Harvey sighed. "I never meant to imply that it was, Ron. Please sit down and hear me out." When they were seated, he asked quietly, "Coffee?"

"No! Get to the point," Legere roared.

"All right. It's very simple. Only three men had the opportunity to do this. Brad Lyons, Philip Bolduc, and Bob Marshall."

Marshall's eyes darted from Harvey to Legere. "What do you mean? I thought there was a janitor or someone you were looking at. Brad was here during the murder, and Joey's brother, I understand, was miles away."

Legere locked eyes with Marshall. "He's talking about the guns, Bob. Whoever shot Joey, or had him shot, switched the murder weapon with one of Joey's guns after."

Marshall said nothing, but his breathing was shallow, and a bead of sweat ran down his temple toward his ear.

Harvey sat watching him, his brain in high gear as he realized that, except for the motive, Bob Marshall was a better candidate than either Bolduc or Lyons. He'd had Labor Day off and was one of the detectives Legere had called in the day of the murder, to help interview witnesses. His whereabouts before one o'clock had never been questioned.

"All right, Ron, I'll bow to you on this," Harvey said, "but I'd like to monitor Bob's movements for the next two hours. No personal phone calls."

Legere swore. "Does Mike know about this?"

"No. Shall we go up and see him?" Harvey waited.

"What do you want to do?" Legere asked at last. "Handcuff Bob to Wonder Boy or something?"

"No, I don't think that will be necessary."

"Let's go, Bob." Legere stood, and Marshall followed him through the Priority Unit office, looking a bit dazed. At the door to the stairway, Legere turned. "Don't think I won't discuss this with the chief."

Harvey nodded. "As you wish, Ron."

As soon as the door closed, he exhaled sharply. "Tony!"

"Here, Captain."

"Run, do not walk, to the com room and watch Bob Marshall every second. If he leaves this building, I want to know it."

"Yes, sir." Tony was at the stairway door in a flash.

"Nate!"

"He's down in the lab, sir," said Jimmy Cook.

"All right, then, you. I'll be upstairs. You keep me apprised of any and all developments."

"Yes, sir."

Harvey went quickly to Mike's office.

"Judith, this is urgent," he said apologetically as he strode past the secretary's desk.

"Captain, wait—"

Harvey ignored Judith and knocked briskly on the door to Mike's private office.

"Come in."

Harvey pushed the door open. Mike and Sharon sat on either side of Mike's desk with sandwiches, cookies, grapes and bottled water set out on the blotter.

"Hi, Mike. Sorry, Sharon. I should have called first, but I needed to beat Legere."

"What's going on?"

"I'm having Bob Marshall's house and bank records searched, and Ron's mad."

Mike paused with a sandwich halfway to his mouth. "Do you know what you're doing, Harv?"

"Well, hc certainly had the opportunity to kill Joey. I've been looking at Brad and no one else. I have to rule out Bob."

"It's more than that, I hope."

"The gun. Arnie told me about a gun he'd sold Joey." Harvey quickly told him the story, and described Marshall's reaction when he had questioned him about it and the drug bust money.

"He's scared of me, Mike."

"Who wouldn't be?" Sharon asked. "You always get your man."

"Poor Bob doesn't want to be caught in your crossfire," Mike said.

Harvey sank into a chair. "Am I doing it again? Have I totally lost it?"

Mike shrugged. "It's noon, Harvey. Get

something to eat. Go home and eat, that's even better. Kick back with Jennifer for half an hour."

"Oh, no, I forgot about Jenny again!" Harvey jumped up and pulled out his cell phone. "Excuse me." He went out through Judith's office and into the stairway, pushing the numbers as the door closed.

"Jenny!" He sat down on the top step. "Jenny, honey, I'm sorry. I meant to come home for lunch and I got caught up in the case again."

"That's okay," she laughed. "I wasn't expecting you. Just be sure to eat, all right?"

"I will. How are you doing?"

"I'm fine. Really. We have lots of time, Harvey."

He sighed and closed his eyes, leaning against the railing. "You're right. I'm sorry. Will you pray for me? I feel like I'm moving too fast here, before I know what I'm doing, and I'm making people mad."

"What happened?"

He took a deep breath. "Can I tell you later? I think I need to get back in control here."

"Of course. And I'll pray."

"I love you." He closed the phone and shoved it into his jacket pocket. As he pulled himself to his feet, the door on the landing below opened, and Jimmy came toward him.

"Captain, I tried to call you, but your phone was busy, and the chief's secretary said you'd left."

"Sorry, Jim, what is it?"

"Eddie got the warrants and went to the bank. Nate went to Marshall's house."

"Thank you." Harvey walked slowly down the stairs and into the office, sending up a silent prayer of thanks that the judge had allowed the warrants. Paula looked anxiously toward him as he entered and gestured toward his desk, speaking into her telephone. She pushed a button, and his desk phone rang. Harvey walked wearily to it and picked it up.

"Captain, it's Winfield. I'm watching the subject, and he's in the detectives' locker room. He put something in his locker, I think, but I couldn't see what."

"Okay, Tony, thanks."

Harvey hung up and stared at the phone, then dialed Mike's cell phone to bypass Judith.

"Mike, I want to search Bob's locker."

"Harvey, I thought you were getting a grip."

"Tony's watching him on the monitors in the com room. He went in the locker room right after I had him here and put something in his locker."

"Probably what was left of his courage after you got through with him," Mike said.

"I'm serious. I think it's relevant."

"Harv, you are fishing."

"I don't think Brad Lyons did it."

"Why not?"

"I don't say he's not capable, but that custodian

is not a rocket scientist. I don't think Brad would trust someone of his caliber with something that delicate. It would be too easy for Lloyd to mess up and finger him."

"Angry people do stupid things."

"And stupid people do stupid things. But Lloyd didn't. We found a couple of his hairs on the dummy, that's it. And he was helping move around the stuff for the game, so he had a reason for that. But a detective could do a clean job of it, and would know what not to touch and all that."

"Like I said, you're fishing."

"Please let me search the locker."

"I'll think about it."

Harvey hung up with a sigh. After a minute, he called Tony back.

"Winfield, you watching Marshall?"

"Yes, sir, he's working at his desk. Paul Trudeau came in and got five dollars from him and is bringing him some lunch."

"Okay, now listen to me. Keep watching him, but also watch the locker. If he goes near it again, tell me immediately."

Harvey sat drumming his fingers on his desk.

"Jimmy!"

"Yes, sir?" Jimmy swiveled his chair toward him.

"Have you eaten?"

"No, sir."

Harvey pulled out his wallet. "Here, go get us

both something, would you please? A sandwich is fine for me. Get whatever you want." He handed Jimmy a twenty, and the detective went out.

Harvey pulled the file folder over and stared at the lists of guns. Paula left for lunch, and Jimmy was soon back with the sandwiches. Harvey's cell phone rang as he poured coffee to go with the ham and cheese.

It was Eddie. "Harv, nothing irregular in the bank accounts, except he didn't pay his daughter's tuition last month."

"What do you mean, didn't pay it?"

"They seem to make the tuition payments once a month, with a check. It's their biggest payment, followed by rent and car loan. There was no check to the college last month."

"They have two kids in school."

"Right. The boy's at another college, and his tuition was paid by check, as usual. But it's smaller than the girl's payment. I figure the kid is working and paying on it, too, or he has a partial scholarship. I could find out."

"All right, get back here."

Harvey instructed Jimmy to call the college where Marshall's daughter was enrolled and ask the status of her account.

"They paid it on time," Jimmy reported.

Harvey frowned. "But there was no check."

"Right."

"Credit card?"

"No, sir, a money order."

Harvey swiveled to looked at him. "The kind you buy at the post office with cash?"

"Yes, sir."

"Find out which post office, and get a copy of the receipt, Jim."

Harvey called Mike again.

"Harvey, this is getting tiresome. Sharon and I are trying to have a private little lunch here, and you've interrupted us three times, and Legere twice."

"Sorry, Mike, but I've got something else pointing in the direction we were discussing."

Mike sighed. "All right, you can search the locker. I'll come down in ten minutes."

"Thanks."

Before Mike arrived, Nate called in to report finding Marshall's nine-millimeter pistol at his house, but no other handguns. Harvey called Cheryl and requested two patrolmen to be sent over to help Nate make a more thorough search.

"This better be good," Mike said testily as he opened Marshall's locker for Harvey.

"He either put something in or took something out," Harvey assured him. "We're not sure which."

"What's going on?" Ron Legere stood frowning in the doorway of the detective squad's locker room.

"Hi, Ron," Mike said cheerily. "This will only take a second."

Harvey quickly probed the pockets of the jacket and jeans hanging inside, then swept the shelf with his fingertips. "Hello." He pulled out his handkerchief and lifted down a service pistol, holding it out for Mike's inspection.

Mike scowled. He turned to Legere. "Where's Marshall?"

"In his office. Larson wouldn't let him leave the building for lunch."

"Get him in here," Mike said.

Marshall came warily, staring at Mike and beyond him, at Harvey and the open locker.

"All right, Bob, why is your .45 in your locker?" Mike asked.

Marshall swallowed. "I—uh—didn't want to carry it this afternoon. I'm just doing paper-work."

"Turn around, put your hands on your head." Mike glanced at Harvey, then stepped forward and patted Bob's pockets. He froze for an instant, then reached under the detective's jacket and pulled out a revolver. "Okay, Harvey, you win this one. Here's your Dan Wesson .357."

481

Chapter 22

The arrest of Bob Marshall was the topic of dinner conversation that night. Eddie, Leeanne, Beth, and Jeff all joined Harvey and Jennifer.

"Why did he keep Joey's gun in his locker?" Jeff asked. "Why not just dump it somewhere?"

"We might have found it," Eddie replied. "He thought we'd never look at the police station."

"And it wasn't the murder weapon," Harvey added. "He thought he'd covered all the bases by switching the murder weapon for it before Brad got a good look at the handguns in the collection. Once his own gun was in the cabinet and Joey's was in his holster, he figured no one would ever know about the switch." Harvey's eyes were sorrowful. "When I asked for a warrant to search his house, Bob figured he'd better get it out of his locker, so he put it in his holster. No one would think it was odd that he was wearing a gun, and if nobody looked closely at it, he'd be home free. He was planning to carry it out of the police station and ditch it as soon as he could get away."

"But why did he kill his friend?" Leeanne

asked. "That's what I don't understand. Weren't he and Joey best friends?"

Harvey sighed. "Bob and Joey were on a drug case together in August, and they found a lot of money. Drug money. Bob pocketed almost five thousand dollars, and Joey knew it. He kept after Bob about it, but Bob insisted he needed it for his kids' college expenses, and it wasn't hurting anyone for him to lift a little of the drug dealers' cash. But Joey couldn't live with it, and he finally told Bob he either turned himself in or he'd tell the sergeant."

"They had Labor Day off," Eddie said. "Bob knew Joey was working on the game setup, and he went over there just before lunch. He saw Emily Rood, one of our other detectives, go out, and he went in and up the stairs and found Joey."

"That's right," Harvey said. "Emily was on the game setup committee, and she left City Hall to get lunch."

"Most everybody else had left, too," Eddie said. "There were just a couple of civilians inside to keep an eye on things, and Joey was still up in the comptroller's office. Bob knew if he shot Joey with his .45, we could trace it, so he used his .357. Then he made a big mistake. He didn't get rid of the gun right away."

"I'm guessing he was nearly caught while he moved the dummy," Harvey said.

Eddie nodded. "Or when he was sneaking

out of City Hall. Anyway, Ron called all the detectives in to work on the case, so Bob came to the police station and stashed the murder weapon in his locker. It stayed there, reasonably safe, until after the funeral."

Harvey said, "After the funeral, Bob saw the chance to leave the gun in Joey's gun cabinet with nobody the wiser. He jumped at it. Instead of going home to change, he went to the police station. Most guys keep a change of clothes there. And he picked up the murder weapon."

"So, he swapped the two guns, and then he put Joey's in his locker," Leeanne said.

"Right. And he told Joey's brother to write down the serial numbers, so everyone would be sure that particular gun was one of Joey's."

"Even though it wasn't the same kind of gun?" Beth asked.

Harvey shrugged. "Same type, different manufacturer. It was close enough for Bob. Brad would have noticed, if he'd seen it up close before the switch, but Bob managed to do it early, before Brad handled the revolvers. And the sketchy description Joey had written compounded the confusion."

Jennifer shook her head. "I really steered you wrong on that payoff idea."

"It's okay, gorgeous." Harvey grinned at her. "It got me thinking about the drug money, and it made me consider other possibilities."

An hour later, Beth and Jeff went home. Jennifer went to put Connor to bed, and Eddie and Leeanne sat down together in the living room. Harvey was headed into the study when the doorbell rang. He detoured out to the entry and opened the door.

"Sarah."

"Hi." Sarah Benoit stood in the breezeway shivering in her uniform.

"Come in," Harvey said.

She stepped inside. "Captain, I'd like to speak to you for a moment, please."

"Certainly." Harvey couldn't read her expression, but he thought she would call him by his first name if this was a social call. "Is it personal, or business?"

"Business."

"Let's step into the study." Harvey led her directly into the room and closed the doors to both the entry and the living room. "Have a seat." He sat down at his desk and waved her to Jennifer's swivel chair. "How can I help you?"

"I—I need to tell you something, sir."

He nearly told her amiably she didn't need to call him *sir,* but her words stopped him cold.

"What is it, Sarah?"

She twisted her hands together and looked down at the floor. "Back when you asked me about Deborah, right after Joey was murdered, and I mentioned Deidre Cleridge to you—" She glanced up at him.

Harvey nodded. "Deborah and Deidre have both corroborated what you said."

"Yes, but there was something else I should have told you. I mean, that's what started you asking everyone about sexual harassment, wasn't it?"

"Yes."

"But you never asked me."

"Didn't we? Cheryl and I had a list—you were on it."

"But I gave you that one statement. I told you about Debbie and Deidre. But you didn't ask me about myself."

Harvey caught his breath. "Sarah, I'm sorry. I assumed Cheryl would interview you again."

She shook her head. "I didn't want to talk to her. She knows me too well. So I told her you had interviewed me at length, and she let it go."

"There was something, then?" he asked gently.

She nodded miserably. "I figured if I clued you in on the others, it would be enough. And I guess it was. You busted him. But he's not going to do all that much time, is he?"

Harvey shrugged. "Four to six years actual time, maybe, but that's purely guesswork. There are so many variables."

"And then he'll get out."

486

Harvey wasn't sure what to say. "Sarah, Brad Lyons . . . harassed you?"

She began to nod, looking at him, then moved her gaze away, toward the far wall. "That's why I came down so hard on Debbie. I knew what would happen if she let him intimidate her." Tears trickled down her cheeks. "I couldn't tell anyone, Harvey. You've got to understand, all my life it's been drilled into me, *don't tell*. And my mother, if she found out—twenty years ago, she didn't want me to testify. She'll freak out for sure this time."

"Sarah, I—" Harvey stopped, feeling sick and protective at the same time. His impulse was to put his arms around her. Instead he said, "I'm going to ask someone else to come in here. Is that okay?"

"Not Eddie. Please not Eddie. I saw his truck outside."

"No, I was thinking Jennifer. Do you mind?"

Sarah shook her head and sniffed. Harvey grabbed a box of tissues off Jennifer's desk and put them in Sarah's hand. He could hear voices in the kitchen, and went to that door. Jennifer, Leeanne, and Eddie were all out there, eating cookies and laughing.

"Jenny, can you come here a minute, please?"

She looked up in surprise. "Sure." She came to his side, her face full of concern. "What is it? I thought I heard the doorbell a few minutes ago."

Harvey realized his agitation must be showing. He whispered, "Sarah's here. She's been telling me she was harassed at work by Brad Lyons. She didn't tell us before. I need you to be here for her. She's quite upset."

"Of course."

Jennifer went into the study with him, and Harvey softly closed the door.

"Sarah!" Jennifer walked quickly to her and folded her arms around her. "It's okay, honey, it's okay."

Sarah began to sob in bitter, wracking gasps. "I'm sorry."

"No, hush, it's all right," Jennifer said soothingly.

Harvey pushed his chair over for Jennifer and sat on the corner of his desk, feeling helpless as he waited for the storm to subside.

At last Sarah raised her head and blew her nose. "I know I'll have to testify," she choked.

"Would you like to tape a statement with Cheryl?" Harvey asked.

"Maybe that would be best. She'll find out, anyway. I should have just told her when it happened, but I was so scared." She wiped fresh tears away.

"I'll call her now and set it up for morning," Harvey said. "I'm sure she'll come in early for this. Unless—" he hesitated. "Unless you'd like to do it tonight."

"I'd really like to get it over with," she admitted.

Harvey sent a silent appeal to Jennifer.

"I'll go with you," Jennifer said immediately.

"Thank you." Sarah took another tissue and wiped at her eyes. "Deidre quit. But I was determined, I was not going to let him make me quit."

Harvey stepped closer to her. "That's why he panicked when we went to pick him up, and took the hostage. He thought you had turned him in. Sarah, I'm so sorry. I thought it was because of Joey. We didn't know." He remembered Eddie barreling out of the stairway in Brad's apartment building, his pistol leveled at the sergeant. *Hostage or no hostage, Eddie would have dropped him if he'd known,* he thought. *By the grace of God, we didn't know.*

Jennifer tightened her arm about Sarah's shoulders. Sarah's dark eyes were wide as she looked at Jennifer.

"That stuff you told me, when we talked before—I've been thinking about it and what you believe. I need to know, Jennifer—Would God really forgive someone like me?"

"Absolutely," Jennifer said.

Eddie entered the diner at noon Friday and quickly scanned the tables. He walked to where Deborah and Sarah were sitting, and they looked up at him.

"Sarah, I need to talk to you."

"I'm done," Debbie said immediately.

"Wait for me in the duty room," Sarah said, watching her go.

Eddie sat down in Debbie's chair and leaned toward Sarah.

"You heard about my statement," she said dully, swirling the ice in her glass.

"I saw the tape. I'm sorry, Sarah. I'm working on the case, you know."

She nodded.

"Harvey figured I ought to know, not be surprised by it later." He pushed Deborah's dishes aside and folded his hands on the table. "I'm so sorry. About all of it. Brad, your father . . . If I'd known—"

"If you'd known, things wouldn't be any different between us now."

He considered that. "Maybe. But maybe I could have done something. You know, a year or so ago."

She shook her head. "I couldn't do this then."

"Why could you now?"

"I'm not sure. I saw all these other women coming forward and admitting what they let Brad do to them. I took your advice and called Jennifer a couple weeks ago. She told me about God's forgiveness and his holiness, and she showed me where to find it in the Bible. And somehow I felt like, if that was true, I could live through one more ordeal. So I went to their house last night, and I told Harvey."

"Sarah!" He reached for her hand, but she pulled it away.

"Don't do that. People wouldn't understand."

He winced. "I'm sorry. I didn't realize you were even there last night until you and Jennifer were getting ready to leave. Is there anything I can do now?"

She pursed her lips. "If it wasn't for you—"

"I'm sorry."

"For what?"

"Whatever you were going to say."

She smiled. "I was going to say, if it wasn't for you, I might never have believed there were decent guys in this world."

He lowered his gaze. "Well, thanks. And I mean it, if there's anything I can do, you tell me."

She sighed. "I don't suppose you want to talk to my mother?"

"Sure, I'll talk to her." He hesitated. "What about?"

"I tried to tell her last night, after I got home, but she didn't want to hear it. That I'm going public with this, I mean. She didn't want to know when I was a kid, and she doesn't want to know now."

"Are they pressing charges against your father?"

Sarah shrugged. "I don't know. Cheryl asked me what I thought, but . . . he's sick, Eddie."

"Mentally, you mean?"

"Well, that, too, but he has cancer. It's bad."

"I didn't know. When your sister was beaten—"

"Yeah, he defended her from that creep. But that doesn't make him a poster child. He did plenty to me and my mom both. I don't know about Nicole. She said when she was staying with us last spring, after she got out of the hospital, that Dad never hurt her. I just don't know. Maybe it's true, and she thought I was lying."

"When was he diagnosed with cancer?" Eddie asked.

"Not long after that. In May, I think."

"Have you seen him?"

"No. I don't want to." Sarah met his gaze. "I'll never see my father again. And I really don't see the point of prosecuting now. I'm told he doesn't have long to live."

Eddie nodded, thinking of his own troubled relationship with his father. It was looking pretty good next to Sarah's nightmare. "Look, whatever happens, Leeanne and I will support you. And I'll go around and see your mom tonight if you want."

"Thanks. If you can just explain to her why I need to testify against Brad. The thought of him being released in a few years . . . I know this is awful, but I really hoped he'd killed Joey, because then maybe he'd never get out. I never would have thought it was Bob."

"We were all shocked," Eddie said. "Mike even thought Harvey was losing it when he started looking at Bob."

"Was it just . . . the money?"

"He thought Joey didn't see him take it. When Joey told him he knew and gave him a chance to put it back, Bob wouldn't. I think it must have been awfully hard for Joey. But he couldn't let it go on. Maybe there were other times. We'll never know. But Bob's admitted they had a fight about it, and Joey gave him an ultimatum. Either Bob went to the chief, or he would. He had an appointment with Mike the next day. We thought it was to tell Mike about how Brad intimidated Deborah. Maybe he was going to tell him that, too, but now we think it was mostly about Bob and the money."

Sarah sighed. "I think I'll take some time off. I have a couple of weeks coming."

"That sounds like a good idea."

She glanced up at him, then back down at her hands. "Mark Johnson asked me to go with him to your wedding."

Eddie smiled. "You like him?"

She shrugged. "Kind of. I don't know as I'm ready, though." She met his gaze directly then. "Cheryl is setting up some sessions for me with the psychologist. The department is paying for them."

He nodded. "Good. It ought to help you see

things the way they really are, not . . . the way they seem sometimes."

"I hope so. Maybe he can help me get rid of some of the old baggage, too. But I don't know about Mark. I feel as if it wouldn't be fair to go out with a man without telling him some of this stuff. I wasn't fair to you." She shook her head. "I know God has forgiven me, but . . ."

Eddie raised his eyebrows.

"Jennifer and I talked a long time after I gave my statement." Sarah smiled and gave a little sob. "She was terrific. I'll always be thankful to her for helping me the way she did."

"You talked about God?"

"Yes, and how to know I'm forgiven. That's still hard to take in. And if I tell Mark about Brad—and my father—well, sometimes people have a hard time getting past things like that."

"That's up to you," Eddie said. "I think Mark would understand."

"I don't want him to pity me."

Eddie smiled. "Pity is not the emotion you inspire, Sarah. I admire you for having the courage to face all of this."

"I'm scared to death."

"I know. But you're going through with it. And listen, if it makes any difference, when Harvey and I ran with Jeff this morning, he told us that he and Mark have been talking a lot about God lately. Mark's going to come to our church with him and Beth on Sunday."

Sarah smiled. "Jennifer says that when you give your life over to Christ, you start with a totally clean heart."

Eddie nodded. "Whiter than snow, the Bible says."

"I felt that way last night," she admitted. "This morning, it was really hard. Trying to talk to my mom, and coming in to work and facing people. Even though most of them don't know I'm testifying, I felt like all the guys were staring at me."

"The feelings don't really matter. But remember, you're not alone now."

"Thanks. And Jennifer told me I can call her anytime."

"She means that. I know Jennifer, and you can trust her with anything."

Sarah nodded. "Would it bother you if I showed up at your church?"

He smiled. "Not a bit."

They got up and walked to the checkout. Sarah paid her bill, and they stepped out into the chilly October air.

"It's funny," she said. "I felt so alone before. Like I had to take care of myself, because nobody else would. And you—" She smiled at him regretfully. "I thought you turned into some kind of adversary last year. The one person I had started trusting betrayed me."

"That was never my intention."

"I know." They walked slowly toward the police station. "I felt like you deserted me when you started talking about God. But now I understand, and I feel like I'm in a very special place. You, Harvey, the chief, and some of the other guys, too, you're all Christians. That was threatening before. Now it's very comforting." She shot him a sideways glance and laughed. "I think I'll say yes to Mark. About the wedding, I mean."

"Great. Leeanne and I would both like to see you there, if you feel up to it."

Sarah threw him a sideways glance. "You're getting married in just a few weeks. I can't believe it."

"Me either."

She smiled. "What color are the bridesmaids wearing? I don't want to clash."

One Month Later

Harvey and Jennifer spent Saturday wallpapering the room they had decided would be Travis's. They'd had a week to recover from Eddie and Leeanne's wedding, and Jennifer was beginning to get used to the idea. Leeanne had called her three times, and Harvey had shown her the one text Eddie had sent him: *C'est bon*, *mon ami*.

Harvey's tension had evaporated since he received that and learned that the district attorney was confident they would see convictions of both Brad Lyons and Bob Marshall. He'd spent a lot of his free time planning the study corner he would set up for Travis in the refurbished guest room. They'd been to a used furniture store that morning.

"It's a really neat desk," he said, smoothing a strip of the blue-striped wallpaper. "Do you think he'd like it?"

"I think *you* would like it," Jennifer returned. "Admit it. You've always yearned for a roll-top desk with dozens of little pigeon holes and a secret drawer."

Harvey smiled sheepishly. "Too old fashioned for Travis?"

"I think he needs a computer desk and a file cabinet."

"How about the computer?"

"Oh, yes, you take care of that. Of course, if you want the roll-top desk downstairs, we could give him your computer desk," Jennifer said.

"Where would I put my computer? You can't put electronics on an antique oak desk."

Jennifer smiled. "You know what, honey? With Connor's crib upstairs, I think there's room for a roll-top desk in that huge bedroom of ours. Meanwhile, I'm thinking it's time we had a dining room."

Harvey's eyes widened as he cut the next strip of paper. "Really?"

"Yes. We do so much entertaining, and it's always a scramble for enough chairs."

"So, where will you have your desk?" Harvey asked.

Jennifer frowned in concentration as she wiped the sticky wall. "Well, with Connor and Travis up here, if we use the green room for a study, there'll still be one guest room after Leeanne moves out."

Harvey laughed. "And you thought this house was too big for us."

"I know. Isn't it strange how things change?"

"I suppose in a couple of years, you'll want

Randy to come down here and stay while he's in school."

"Unless he wants to go away," she agreed. "If he'll go to a Christian college, I won't be sorry to see him go. But he wants to study criminal justice."

"I'd like to see him go to Harvard."

She glanced at him to see if he was serious. "Do they offer criminal justice?"

"Yeah. But if he wants to work in Maine, it might be better for him to go here."

"Maybe he can apply for the Joey Bolduc Scholarship. And can you imagine a better mentor for him than you?"

Harvey chuckled. "You think too highly of me."

"Never."

He moved the step stool a couple of feet along the wall. "Almost ready for the border. Where is it?"

She held up a small roll of creamy paper with dark sailing ships chasing each other along its length. "Here. I'll soak it. Where should we start it? In the corner?"

"You think Trav will like this?"

"Do you?" Jennifer asked anxiously.

"Sure, it's fine."

"I got a round mirror that looks kind of like a porthole, and some old prints of clippers."

"That's great." He arranged his tools on the stool.

"I don't know. Maybe we should have gone with a sports theme. So, things have calmed down at the police station?" She handed him the dripping roll of border.

"Yeah, pretty much. Mike's keeping Cheryl on the day shift, and she's happy. Chuck Norton went to him and resigned as liaison officer. He said he had no clue all these women were having problems and didn't dare to tell him. Mike's decided it should be an appointed position, and he's naming Cheryl."

"Good. The women ought to feel comfortable with her now."

"I hope so. Mike's got her working out a system for having a heart-to-heart with each female officer every three months. We don't ever want a repeat of what happened with Brad."

"Mike's good when it comes to women's issues. He's tough, but he's sensitive."

Harvey climbed the step stool carefully. "I think he must have discussed all this with Sharon. There's something about his love for her that keeps him respectful of all women."

"She makes a good chief's wife." Jennifer shrugged. "She'd make a great first lady."

Harvey laughed. "Don't suggest that. She's doing her hardest to get him retired. The last thing she wants is Mike in politics."

"Do you think Jack Stewart will do a good job when Mike retires?"

"Oh, I think so. I told Mike to make sure he's aware of every wrinkle. I think Jack's capable of running things smoothly, and he's quick-witted." He smiled down at Jennifer. "You ought to hear him pray, Jenny. I don't think you'd have doubts about him if you were in the office during our morning break, when we all pray together."

"Still, it will be the end of an era when Mike goes."

"I know. He's made a lot of changes for the better during his short tenure. But I think Jack can keep on in the same direction."

"And Mike wants to be in Churchill now," Jennifer said. "His heart is there."

"He wants us all to go up next month for some hunting."

"Are we going?"

"Do you want to?" Harvey asked. "Mike Junior and his family are going up opening weekend, but Mike thought maybe the next week we could go. Eddie and Leeanne will be back from Montreal."

"Oh, they're going with us?"

"Mike wants them to. I think he was disappointed they turned it down for the honeymoon."

Jennifer smiled up at him. "They turned down your offer, too."

"That's okay. Eddie really wanted to take her to Montreal, and he was able to work it out, so I have no complaints. I told him if they want to go to Churchill with us, I'll fix it with the chief for him to take an extra week without pay. Mike won't be a problem."

"Mike's got the plumbing done, right?" she asked anxiously.

"He's got four completed guest rooms on the second floor now, with full, working baths."

"Just checking." She stood back and surveyed his handiwork. "Hey, this looks great. You ought to go into the painting and papering business."

"No, thanks." He climbed stiffly down from the stool. "As long as I only do it once in a while and have a gorgeous helper, it remains an enjoyable hobby."

He pulled her to him and kissed her, and she twined her arms around his neck.

"Listen, maybe we ought to take a little trip ourselves," he said.

"I thought we were going to Churchill."

"I meant, just you and me. Not the whole family." She pushed back a little to look at him, and he said hastily, "You know I'm crazy about your family, but Mike's talking about a big house party that week. He's asking Abby and Peter, and Jeff and Beth, everybody."

"Wow."

"Yeah, he thought it would be neat, and it would. But I was thinking, maybe after that we could get away someplace . . . you know . . . room service and maybe a night at the theater. I've got tons of vacation time stacking up. Jack's telling me to use it so the city doesn't owe me."

"You want to go away?" She was surprised. "I thought 137 Van Cleeve Lane was your favorite place on earth."

"It is." He pulled the covered elastic from the end of her braid and began unweaving her hair. "I just want to be someplace where there aren't any clocks or phones for a couple of days. Before we get Travis here, you know?"

"No privacy when college kids are living with us," she agreed.

Harvey nodded. "I hope he'll bring his friends here. If he doesn't, I'll start to worry."

"So, do you want to leave Connor with somebody?"

"Well, that could be a problem," he admitted. "He's not completely weaned yet. I guess we'd have to take him."

"You're really tired, aren't you?" She put her hands on his shoulders and looked deep into his eyes. It was the first time he had ever suggested leaving the baby overnight.

"Maybe we could just turn off the phones here and put a *no visitors* sign on the door," he said.

"And hide the clocks in the basement." Her enthusiasm was rising. "If you really want to go away, we can, but—"

"No, let's stay here. I'll take a whole week off

in December. We can take Connor out to see the Christmas lights and buy a tree."

"Dad will want us to come up there and cut one."

"All right, but let's get two or three."

"Christmas trees?" she asked.

"Sure. Let's put one in the sunroom and one in the living room—"

"And a little one in the new dining room."

"Okay, gorgeous. And you have to pick out the decorations and a dining room set. Not a heavy, gruesome one like the Baileys had in there."

"Agreed."

"I'll help you set it up," Harvey said. "We'll have a ball. And if Beth or Leeanne will babysit, I'll take you to the opera."

"You hate opera."

"Not hate, but . . . well, I'll put it this way: I'll take you anyplace you want to go."

Jennifer smiled and laid her head on his chest. "You used to say that when we were dating. Anywhere but bungie jumping."

"I mean it." He kissed the top of her head.

"This is where I want to be. But no wallpaper or anything. Just you."

"Maybe you'll want to have a little tree trimming party?" he suggested.

She shook her head, burrowing into his shoulder. "Just you and me and Connor."

"One big night out?" he coaxed.

"All right, find a musical or a Shakespeare comedy." She raised her head. "I hear Connor."

"Go get him," Harvey said. "I'll clean up here."

Jennifer eyed the tools, buckets, and wallpaper scraps that cluttered the room. "Pretty messy."

"Not for long. Go get the boy."

She smiled and turned away. "I hope the next one's a girl."

She hadn't thought he heard her, but his hand came down gently on her shoulder, and she turned.

"I hope she looks like you. And you pick the name this time."

"Phoebe," she said without hesitation.

"Really? Grandma Lewis's name."

"I know. I like it. You love her so much, and she got you started, thinking about the Lord."

He smiled and dropped a light kiss on her forehead. "Phoebe Larson, then. Soon."

Dear Reader,

Thank you for choosing *The Labor Day Challenge*. This is Book 6 in the Maine Justice Series, which features the men of the Priority Unit and their families. These characters care about justice, love, and faith, and I hope you enjoyed their adventure. Group discussion questions are just a few pages away.

This story deals with problems of sexual harassment and dishonesty in the workplace. It also finds Harvey trying to extricate Jennifer's younger brother from a mess without making things too easy for him. Harvey struggles with his role as a police officer and a brother, and his future role as a father.

This series is dear to my heart. I hope that if you enjoyed it you will tell other readers and perhaps post a review on Amazon, Barnes & Noble, Goodreads, or other venues of your choice.

I hope to continue the series, God willing. In the meanwhile, I will be re-issuing some more of my backlist books, including *The Crimson Cipher*, a historical suspense story set in 1915. A young woman is hired as a civilian cryptographer for the Navy to help decipher the enemy's messages.

For a sneak peek at *The Crimson Cipher*, flip a few pages. I hope you enjoy this excerpt.

Sincerely,
Susan Page Davis

About the Author

Susan Page Davis is the author of more than seventy published novels. She's a two-time winner of the Inspirational Readers' Choice Award and the Will Rogers Medallion, and also a winner of the Carol Award and a finalist in the WILLA Literary Awards. A Maine native, she now lives in Kentucky with her husband Jim, two of their six children, and two cats, sweet Sora and naughty Arthur. Visit her website at: www. susanpagedavis.com, where you can see all her books, sign up for her occasional newsletter, and read a short story on her romance page.

Find Susan at:
Website: www.susanpagedavis.com
Twitter: @SusanPageDavis
Facebook:
https://www.facebook.com/susanpagedavisauthor

Sign up for Susan's occasional newsletter at
https://madmimi.com/signups/118177/join

Discussion Questions

1. Leeanne causes major upheaval in the family when she decides to postpone her wedding to take an opportunity offered her by her employer. She goes on the defensive when those who love her don't seem to sympathize with her. What advice do you have for Leeanne?

2. Eddie's reaction to Leeanne's news isn't the best. The wound festers, and he displays some unbecoming behavior. Is Eddie just impatient?

3. George and Marilyn Wainthrop are new believers. Harvey steps in to help them with a difficult situation. Do you think he should stand back and let them handle it? Do you agree with Leeanne when she says that Harvey, not Eddie, is the perfect son-in-law?

4. Tony makes a procedural mistake. He should know better. If you were his supervisor, how

would you react to his antics in obtaining hair samples? Does Harvey handle this well?

5. Mike is eager to leave the city behind and live in the remote north woods. Do you think he will actually retire? Do you think he and Sharon will make good hosts?

6. Jennifer seems to have mixed feelings when she thinks she might be pregnant again. Connor is five months old. Any thoughts for Jennifer? For Harvey?

7. Sarah steers Harvey toward investigating sexual harassment within the department. Why doesn't she tell him right away that she is a victim? Should she have told Eddie when she was dating him?

8. Leeanne insists she never intended to break up, and that she never stopped loving Eddie. Yet she takes a couple of months to settle the issue. What holds her back?

9. Eddie shows maturity and leadership at work that he doesn't seem to have mastered in his personal life. Do you think he and Leeanne will ever have another big blow-up?

10. Is it time for Harvey to bring a female

detective into the Priority Unit? And do you think women will be treated better throughout the department now? Have you ever witnessed harassment of this type? If so, did you speak out against it or take other steps to stop it?

Books are
produced in the
United States
using U.S.-based
materials

Books are printed
using a revolutionary
new process called
THINKtech™ that
lowers energy usage
by 70% and increases
overall quality

Books are
durable and
flexible
because of
Smyth-sewing

Paper is
sourced using
environmentally
responsible
foresting methods
and the
paper is acid-free

Center Point Large Print
600 Brooks Road / PO Box 1
Thorndike, ME 04986-0001 USA

(207) 568-3717

US & Canada:
1 800 929-9108
www.centerpointlargeprint.com